I0822415

Shadows of Man

Sundering the Crowns
Book One

by
L. James Rice

TWELFTH

STAR

ISBN: 978-1-951068-15-8 paperback
ISBN: 978-1-951068-14-1 e-book
ISBN: 978-1-951068-16-5 hardcover

Dedicated to my Angels, Demons, and Ghosts.

Books by L. James Rice

Sundering the Gods

Eve of Snows

Trail of Pyres

Whispers of Ghosts

Sundering the Crowns

Shadows of Man

Silhouettes in Doom
12/12/2024

The Monsoon Straits Trilogy

The Contessa of Mostul Ûbar

Best Painted in Blood
Coming 2024

Prequel to Eve of Snows

The War of Seven Lies
06/01/2024

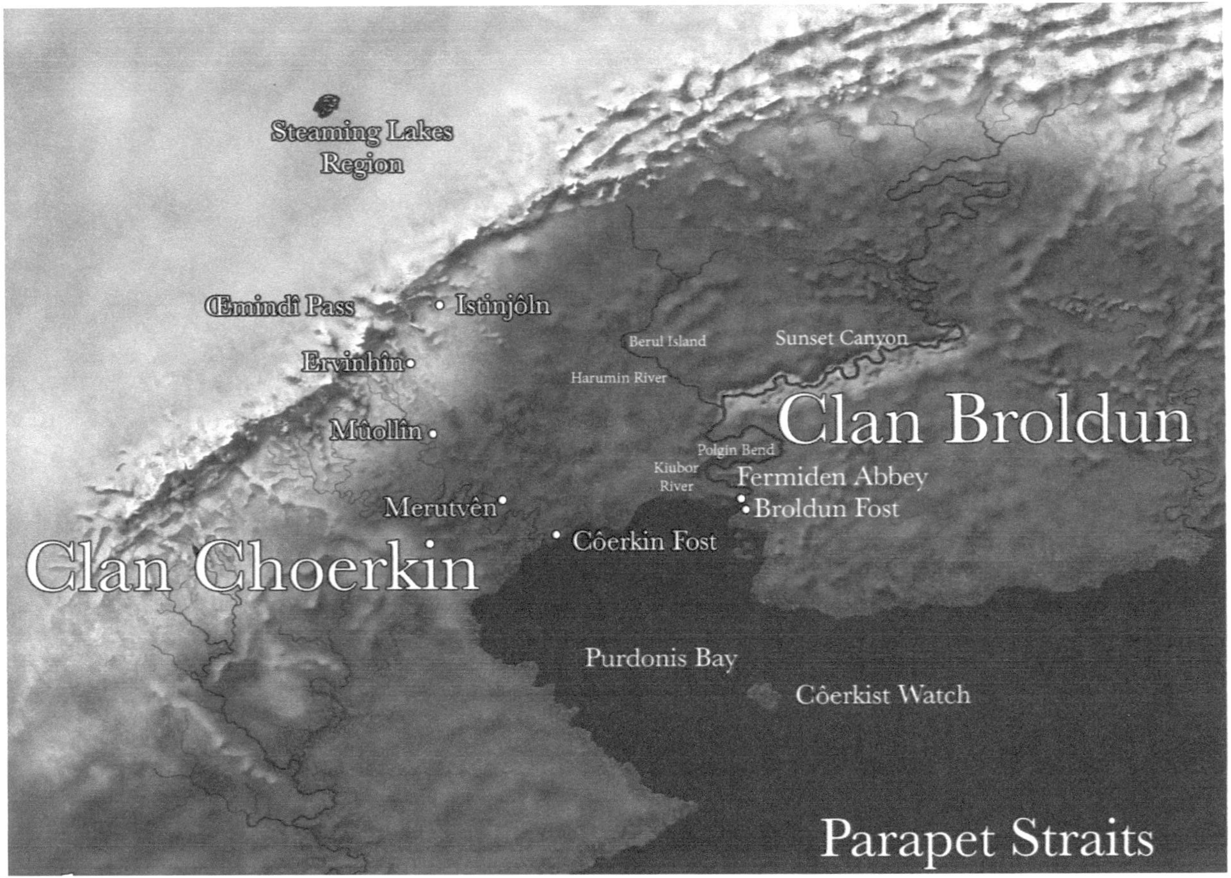

Steaming Lakes
Region
Œmindî Pass
Istinjôln
Ervinhîn
Mûollîn
Merutvên
Clan Choerkin
Berul Island
Harumin River
Sunset Canyon
Clan Broldun
Polgin Bend
Kiubor
River
Fermiden Abbey
Broldun Fost
Côerkin Fost
Purdonis Bay
Côerkist Watch
Parapet Straits

Gulf of Vôlgrâhar
Orstân Rift
The Foundations (Dragonspan Mountains)
Ferminki Bridge
Yurbol
Ôfelun
Helebôm
Ilu-Strono Plains
Turûrot
Wisdom Cliffs
Helmvelîn
Highstone (Shuntiskâ)
Faldan
Ekwumor
Shînvedorn
Molîkîn
Ômkinter
Kâmar
Ôsho
Erenfol Walking Well
Sundial of Teremhôst
Roemhien Pass
Mulshahar
Kônu Bay
Dölden
Gigan
Green Mountain
Barkûsh
Œrinklîn
Yusduiên
Klondibik
Danlok

Gulf of Elelêu
Iludetrê Highlands
River
Berubondâ
Ofrijôlu
Avelêonô
Fron Cunêô
Emenol Mountains
Triforkonô
Compubênô
Pêelesinzu
Lintêere River
Pôlertu
Geropôlêz
Molfetu
Nêindelê Bay
Ran Belekê
Lûtcêu
Troponô
Ocean's Coast
Gulf of Tomulok
Componêu
Seraru
Vitolêô
Bodânêô
Boxukolu Ocean
Scandêcê
Armêle River
Tanmeranzu
Fron Rôvijêô
Kôlekâ
Midênu
Nûmil Bay
Brexê
Mâbuhon River
Eburetcê
Teskutonô
Lemezjêu
Îxôlu Bay
Oltumênu
Emulên Isles
Ercôberêtôs
Montôltok
Emerald Shores
Fer Temôtêu
Aprelêu
Felânêâ
Exkemi Point
Îxôl-Illu Strait
Seahawk's Horn
Nodoru

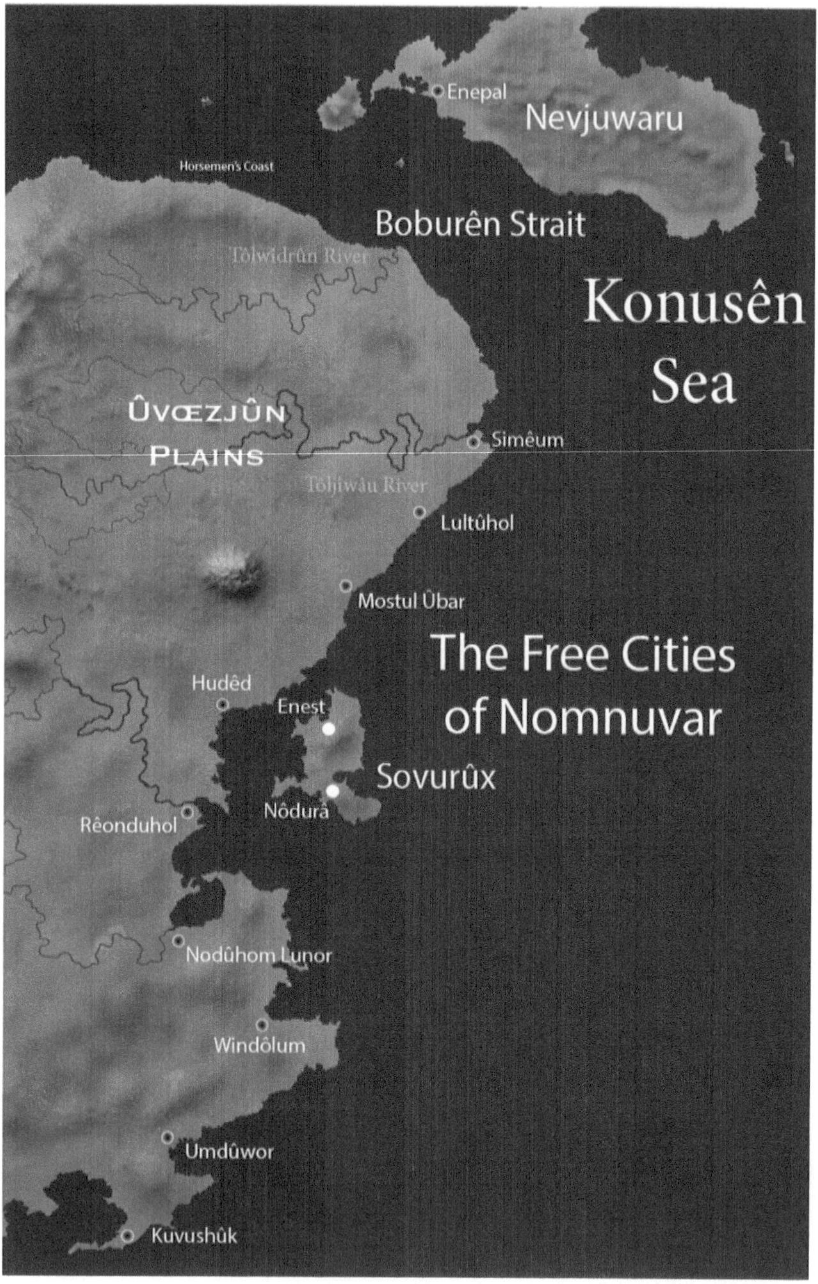

Enepal
Nevjuwaru
Horsemen's Coast
Boburên Strait
Tôlwidrûn River
Konusên Sea
Ûvœzjûn Plains
Simêum
Tôljiwâu River
Lultûhol
Mostul Ûbar
The Free Cities of Nomnuvar
Hudêd
Enest
Sovurûx
Nôdurâ
Rêonduhol
Nodûhom Lunor
Windôlum
Umdûwor
Kuvushûk

Medrisên Sea
Bêmerû
Pôn
Todyûl
Tebôhûu
Chitorâ
Zâgarn
Kelêf
Môtûu
Choru
Lîopu
Arkudân River
Elumîsênê River
Tebûul River
Mônderu River
Rôqwu
Yungilêtunu
Hîvukûqwunowu
Medrisên Strait
Amû-Bêdê
Inzefin
Hemu-Nêbrû
Merhubrêsh
Nokbrotu
Teruhedû
Anû-dodo
Imê-nurodu
Sarbodô-no
Toltûk
Embodu-kâ
Hemu-Kojôn
Nokosu-Imor

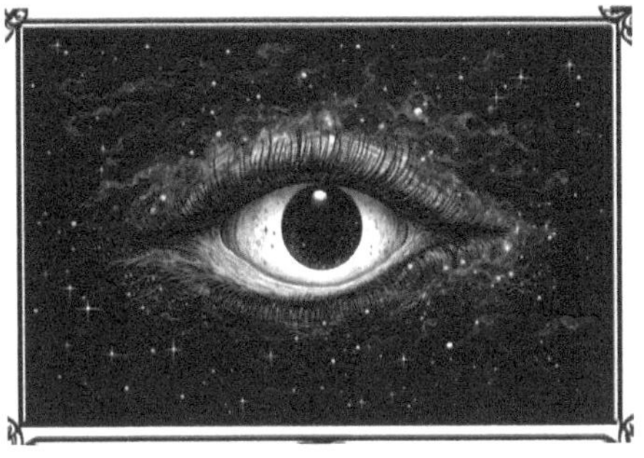

One

Starscaped Cage

What comfort the stars? A heat so distant it brings no warmth.
Poets and lovers lionize the stars and put the Lion in the Twelfth Star.
Starry-eyed dreamers,
Starry-eyed believers,
Starry-eyed leavers.
The stars are but a distraction from the
Consumptive Darkness between.

—*Tomes of the Touched*

15th of Beldrên, 507th Year of Remembered Time

Ieru's mother didn't give birth to her in the stars, but the night sky, bleak and beautiful, was her home. Silent stars in every direction, here in the infinite dome of Skywatch, and never one could she reach no matter how far she walked or ran across the invisible plane that kept her from falling into the Twelve Hells. Or so her family told her. Her elders spoke a thousand tales that might be truth or lies, but as with the surrounding sky, there was no telling reality from illusion. When she arrived at Skywatch, she believed in the binary nature of reality versus the imaginary—even if she didn't possess the words. The stars

wandered the heavens, circling her in such a way that often she felt the universe centered around her. Her auntie told her this wasn't unusual for a great many children, but Ieru sensed this was a fault in their characters rather than a rational conclusion drawn from observing the heavens; after all, she was the only child living in the sky. She'd been the only child on arrival, and she remained the only one even after living years enough she should be growing into a woman and leaving the girl behind.

Seven Heavens. Seven years old. Forever. She wondered if the floor kept her from falling into the hells or kept her from escaping them.

Her clearest memory of Skywatch was her arrival on the island of Kaludor, staring up at the white dome of Skywatch as she approached hand in hand with her mother. In a world of squared buildings, it brought a sense of awe before stepping inside to realize how mundane the bubbled exterior of this legendary holy site was. The night sky drew widening eyes to stare at the stars and moon despite the sun shining outside. A dozen priests welcomed her, including the old woman everyone called her grandmother, a sweet woman who bent to kiss her forehead. It was the first time she met her Grammu and Auntie, but by now, it seemed like she'd known her kin forever, in particular now that Grammu had been dead for years.

Her waking memories struggled to recall a time outside this night sky surrounded by countless stars she'd nonetheless tried to count. She was proud to have reached one thousand three hundred and something or another once before losing track, but what she wanted more was to gaze up and count to one. "I want to see the sun."

Niseem grinned as she always did. Auntie's teeth were as white as when they'd first met, and not a single new wrinkle creased her brow since she and Grammu had taken Ieru into the sky. Her one gray hair had grown no companions. "Someday, my sweets. Someday."

"When the Evil Queen is gone."

"Mmhmm." The woman pulled back her black hair, hair that hadn't grown since the Evil Queen's arrival, and tied it in a knot that hid the single silver strand. She dug a ripe red apple from her robes and handed it to her with a smile.

Ieru glared at the apple, as glaring at Auntie wouldn't be prudent. "Where'd you pick this?" In her dreams, she walked in the grass with bare feet and climbed trees to pluck their fruit, satiating her hunger and sweet tooth at the same time, but her memories of such things faded the same as her dreams. Not even hunger remained after the arrival of the Evil Queen. No hunger, no aging, no dying, unless the Evil Queen willed it.

"Sometimes, when you aren't looking, fruit falls from the stars. These apples were a favorite of your grandmother's. She wandered the heavens, always looking for apples."

"Grammu Meris liked apples?" Ieru took a bite, sugary juices bringing a moan and water to her mouth, but the pleasure didn't last. "You snuck from the stars again, didn't you?"

Niseem tussled Ieru's hair. "You used to believe my stories."

"I was a little girl, then."

Auntie eyed her with a softness reserved for those times when memories prodded sadness. "It's difficult to look at you and see you for who you are."

"I want to see the sun. I *want* to grow up."

"You know—"

"It's impossible, except it isn't. In the garden, plants grow, and so does hair."

Brows knitted as Auntie grew peevish. "Where did you hear such rubbish?"

Irritable or not, today was one of Ieru's stubborn days. "I heard Sotru talking last week. It's true, isn't it?"

Niseem sighed and rolled her eyes, attempting a tussle that Ieru dodged. "Plants grow, and so does hair, but that doesn't mean people age. Or if they do, it doesn't mean they age proper-like. Fruits grow too fast, misshapen, and sometimes pop. Do you want to pop, my sweets?"

The notion put a stir to her gut, but she didn't call her stubborn days stubborn without cause. "I just might."

"Ieru—"

"Never mind." She stood and stomped her feet as she strode into infinite night, and the lack of chiming footsteps made her tromp harder, demanding to make noise that never came. Grammu Meris used to let her run in the musical stars, playing a song with her footfalls, sliding into a wild cacophony that always seemed to blend into almost a song. Grammu Meris was the sweetest woman she'd ever known, sweeter even than her mother, or at least, what little Ieru remembered. Like so many other things in her past, she saw her mother most in dreams, but then, if she struggled to close her eyes and see the sun, how could she expect to paint her mother in her mind's eye?

She stopped and spun to find the omnipresent stars without a soul around to drag her home. A shooting star whooshed overhead, and instead of saying a prayer like the fool adults would suggest, she turned southeast to wait for the stars she *could* count. The first always foretold the arrival of the eighty-four. Some claimed the first star belonged to Sol, King of the Gods, and the shooting stars that followed represented the war between the Seven Heavens and Twelve Hells, seven multiplied by twelve, mystic numbers she once believed and now scoffed at. On one stubborn day, she'd asked if the heavens did battle with only half the hells, would forty-two be a mystic number?

Auntie sent her to prayers straightaway without dinner.

Not that it mattered since she never grew hungry.

Ieru didn't set out with the intent to be naughty, not like on so many other stubborn days, but when the Shower of Stars appeared in the sky above like they did every repetitive day, she ran. Hoping no one saw her. Planning not to stop even if they did. The stars rained in a glorious fire show she'd watched a thousand times, and her breaths came fast, lungs swelling and burning with fatigue until she dove, arms splayed like wings and her feet high, gliding across the invisible floor on her chest. It was an instant that slowed in time so that she relished the rub of the floor on her skin through her linen robes, every hair prickling across her body in a wave of seductive energy.

A gust of air lifted her hair.

Eyes, tiny and disembodied in the sky, stared into her eyes for the flash of a blink and disappeared. *Who are you? Where did you go?*

Fresh air. A pulse into her lungs forced her to breathe as she slid.

Silence shifted into a song of chaos, like a xylophone with a dozen children pinging a nonsensical tune, until her slide stopped, and the chaos of sounds took on a peculiar order. She rolled over, wide eyes staring back at the shooting stars as the last echoes of her entry faded. Heart racing as paranoia drowned in the freedom of breathing.

She stared.

She prayed.

No one watched her at all.

No one followed.

Whose eyes? The sight and sensation of being watched brought a creep of chills. *I should run back to Auntie Niseem.*

No, she'd been in these stars for years without feeling threatened. A smile spread, and Grammu Meris' words came back to her: *fear in the stars is a figment to be forgotten.* The memory soothed her worry. *I'm alone. No one saw me.* A part of her knew that she lied to herself; part of her

suspected that who watched her wasn't anyone she knew, but without proof, what she knew felt wrong.

She crawled to stand, and joy filled her to drive away the paranoia as the universe's invisible floor chimed at the brush of her gentle touch. She took deep breaths, then ran. Each stride brought unpredictable notes, but if there was nothing random about the placement of the stars, so too was there nothing random about the pitches of her footfalls. They blended, always, hinting at a deeper meaning, a deeper sense of order in chaos, of a deeper meaning to her meaningless life.

She leaped high and drove her feet into the floor—the boom of a bass steel drum greeted her—and she rolled to leap again, a glass xylophone followed by the drum again. She waved her arms in the air as Grammu Meris taught her, as if she conducted a choir, breaths swelling her chest, puffs stretching her smile until the music disappeared into the stars.

Then her beating heart turned to stone.

A woman appeared from nowhere, sitting with her back facing Ieru, and chills froze the joy from her veins. Slender and blond, it took only a flicker to recognize even from behind that the woman wasn't from the holy enclave of her family. Was it this woman who'd watched her? No. The eyes were her imagination getting the best of her. This woman was real.

Ieru wobbled, the unnerving shock of this stranger's impossible arrival bringing a quiver to her knees. The thrill and wonder of the musical stars turned into a trap, the slightest step giving her away. She eased her arms to her side, relaxed, and held her balance.

"I feel you." A young woman's voice, strong but unthreatening. "I've felt you before, but never so near."

Ieru knew enough of the powers of prayer not to doubt the woman's words. If this stranger could feel her, she might run, but she

wouldn't be able to hide until she entered the shooting stars. And if the woman was who she suspected, running was pointless. An exhale let her heart beat again and loosened her tongue. "You're the Evil Queen?"

The woman rose with a queen's grace, her slender frame draped in white that caught and glittered with the light of the stars. "Is that what they call me?" She spun on a toe, the floor singing like the rim of a crystal goblet.

She was beautiful. Lips curving into an elegant smile. Blue eyes twinkling. No, green eyes. No. Blue. Ieru blinked. *Blue.* "They told me you were pretty, but I always imagined you ugly."

The smile turned to a smirk licked by a flick of the tongue. "My name is Eliles."

"Ieru."

"Nice to meet you, Ieru." Her head cocked. "You don't feel as young as you look."

Ieru's brow furrowed, and she stomped a high-pitched chime. "It seems I have you to blame for that."

The Evil Queen stared, her beauty dulled by her smile dimming into solemnity. "I am sorry for that."

She shouldn't believe the Evil Queen, Ieru understood this as truth, but her words brimmed with disarming sincerity. A sigh before she shrugged. "It is what it is."

"Is it so easy to accept?"

"No. It isn't. But the stars are stuck, and so am I."

The Evil Queen squinted. "The stars aren't stuck."

Ieru stared up, thousands of beads of light above. "They are. Forever moving, but forever returning where they started."

"The Shower of Stars repeats every day where you live? I suppose that makes sense. Do you remember how you came here?"

"Grammu told me to sit and close my eyes in the stars, and she brought me here."

"Grandma?"

Ieru hesitated but reckoned no harm in naming the dead. "Grammu Meris."

The Evil Queen's head rocked back, her forehead creasing. "High Oracle Meris was your grandmother?"

Ieru crossed her arms. "Some say you killed her."

"No. No. Her death was... a tragedy."

The Evil Queen didn't lie as well as an Evil Queen should. She didn't care enough to *feel* the word she used. "How did my grammu die?"

Silence followed, stretching long enough she didn't expect an answer, and once she heard it, she would've preferred it never spoken. "She leaped from the tower of Herald's Watch. Nobody knows why. Others think someone pushed her."

"You?" But the Evil Queen was a bad liar, and her manners suggested she spoke the truth now. "Or not by you. I suppose it doesn't matter. I remember seeing the tower from our ship when we arrived. Mother pointed and told me it belonged to the Choerkin lords."

"How long were you here? Before aging stopped."

"Time in the stars is, you know... A month I think."

A hand cupped the Evil Queen's lips and chin. "Have you been outside since?"

Ieru snorted. "No. There's an evil queen out there who wants to incinerate me."

The woman laughed. "Please. Call me Eliles."

Ieru flashed a mocking smile before rolling her eyes. "Burn me up if you like. Eliles."

"Would you like to see where the stars aren't stuck? Or to go outside?"

The temptation bit at her gut, the idea of seeing the sun again teasing her. "I shouldn't. I can't trust you."

The woman grinned. "Am I a mighty Evil Queen?"

"You wouldn't be much of an evil queen if you weren't."

"So, I wouldn't need to give you a choice, but I am. I promise to return you to your people whenever you like."

Ieru sucked a bit of apple from her molars and cleared her throat. Grapes didn't fall from the sky any more than apples, but somewhere on the island, they grew. "Another time, maybe?"

"While true that we might have forever, our meeting was chance. Who is to say when chance favors us again?"

Ieru groaned with fidgeting feet, then strode toward the beautiful evil. "It seems my stubborn day is only stubborn in one direction."

Eliles giggled and squinted at her approach. "Stubborn day?"

"That's what Grammu called the days when I had a mind of my own, the one that gets me in trouble." She stopped halfway. "Why did you come here?"

A finger waggled in Ieru's direction. "A fine question. I used to come to the Shower of Stars more often, hoping to meet the adherents who hide here. Give them a chance to speak with me. Most of my time in the stars now is to see where my friends are."

"Friends?"

"People not on Herald's Watch. The stars can point me to them, even let me see the faces of those close enough."

Ieru strode with a song in her steps. "I didn't know the stars could do that. I just enjoy the music. Do you know how or why the stars make songs?"

"Whoever built this place crafted the floor from *latchu,* the word for unbreakable glass in the language of the Edan, but how or why it makes music?" She shrugged.

Ieru arrived by Eliles' side. "We sit?"

A nod. "The stars we see now are from an age past. Hundreds of years before your arrival on the island." They sat side by side with legs crossed, and Eliles said, "Elinwe, guide me to the stars of now."

Ieru opened her eyes wide, determined not to miss the journey like she had with Grammu. The stars spun with nature's rotation, blurring with such a speed that the dots turned to whirling streaks of white. Fascinating, beautiful, and disconcerting. She opened her mouth to speak, but her throat didn't make a sound until the stars jerked to a halt. "Wow."

The Evil Queen laughed without a hint of evil. "I agree. It doesn't grow old."

Ieru smirked. "Neither do I."

"None of us do. What do you want to do first, see where people are around the world, or go outside?"

Ieru's lips twisted. "Outside. Grapes. If they're ripe."

"I make sure some are always ripe."

Ieru stood, putting voice to the worry behind her decision. "Everyone I knew on Kaludor might be dead, and I'd rather not know.

"I pray not." Eliles sighed as she rose to her feet. "Welcome back to the five hundred and seventh year of Remembered Time." The stars rang to the steps of the Evil Queen's feet. "Follow close; the stairs are tricky to see."

When Eliles' body stepped down and appeared cut in half, Ieru ran to catch up. "Holy hells." Her eyes widened as she glanced about, expecting Auntie to appear and cuff her ear. "Sorry for them words."

The Evil Queen was nothing more than shoulders and a head when she replied, "No worries. Artus Choerkin's tongue has hardened my devout ears these past years." Then her head disappeared.

Ieru eased close, glancing down to see Eliles, but she couldn't spot a single step. "Is this some evil trick to get me to fall on my butt?"

"You climbed to get up there, didn't you?"

"Grammu lit the steps."

A giggle from below. "Gods, I never thought of that."

In an instant, a spiral stair appeared, glowing the pure white of Elemental Light, casting no shadows. Ieru strode the steps with confidence and a smile. "You didn't pray out loud. Did they lie about your Fire? Are you a priestess of Light?"

"No. Fire is my specialty, as you'll see. I have a knack with many Elements." The Light disappeared, and a ball of Fire appeared over the Evil Queen's head as she walked toward a black wall.

"You're just showing off, now."

She grinned at Ieru over her shoulder. "It isn't often I have someone new to impress. Are you studying for the priesthood?"

"Do you imagine I have a choice?"

A silent shake of the head as Eliles reached and pulled, natural light flooding the room with a blinding glare that forced a hand over Ieru's eyes. Her heart pounded as she stepped into the dry heat of day, blinking as her eyes adjusted from years of nocturnal existence.

Ieru's breath left her. She'd come to find the sun, but the sky blazed as if the sun had come to find her, swallowing the island whole.

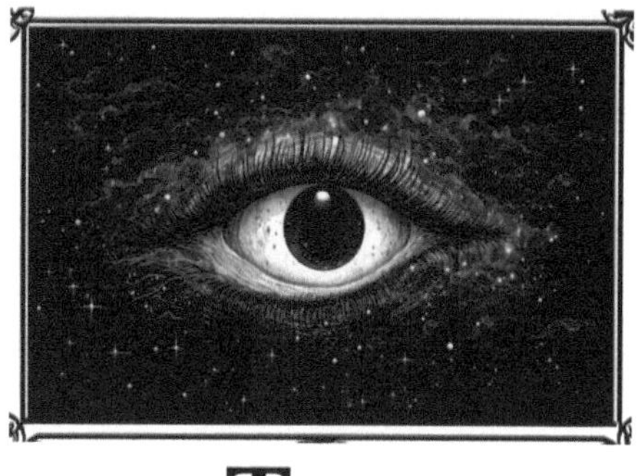

Two

Land of Eternal Sun

Every drip, every drop,
every stain, every blame,
you can't stop the bleeding
without finding the wound
in your screams or your dreams
in the artery or the vein,
in your vanity or your pride,
through truths or lies where you hide
the gape, the pulsing, the killing,
the weakening, the fading, the denying
of a wound unfounded and unbound
and leaking toward your end.

—*Tomes of the Touched*

Jeru stood frozen despite a conscious desire to turn and run back into the night. "What have you done?"

"It's safe, I swear on it."

"What? How? Has Sol returned to the world?" The return of the King of Gods was the only option that came to mind.

"No. A God Wars artifact called the Sliver of Star allowed me—"

"So much of any Element would twist or kill, let alone Fire."

"Yes, or rather it should. Some say Sol gifted me blood born of Fire, and, well, the Sliver allowed me to summon so much Fire without dusting my bones."

Ieru turned to her, staring up at the Evil Queen's head wreathed in the sky's flames. "Why? Even if you could?"

The lady's face sank. "They told you so little?"

"They told me an Evil Queen trapped us with a wall of Fire—"

"Eliles. Please."

"It's what they say. Eliles."

She giggled and nodded her head uphill. "Come on. The gardens aren't so far away." She meandered up the street with languid strides. "*Why* might be more important than *how*. Maybe. Lord Priest Ulrikt made a terrible mistake in Istinjoln. You know of Istinjoln?"

"A monastery in the north. Grammu and all the others prayed and trained there."

"Yes. Lord Priest Ulrikt failed to summon the gods back to our world. Instead of gods, demons from the Age of God Wars entered Istinjoln, demons known as Shadows of Man. They take possession of the living and kill every soul in sight. Hundreds, thousands of them."

Ieru sucked her lip, mind a chaotic blur, except for a suspicion stuck sure-footed in the tempest. "The way you say mistake?"

Eliles hesitated like the priests in the stars when they considered lying to her. "It might have been on purpose. I'd prefer to believe not, but... Anyhow, our people fled, and many of the Clan Choerkin came to this island. The Shadows, one Shadow who spoke with the voice of Ulrikt, was building a bridge of ice to reach us."

"And with this Sliver of Star, you stopped him."

"Yes. Destroyed the bridge and maybe killed the Shadow. I couldn't stop the Fires now if I wanted to."

They strode without further words, Ieru dragging her toes, her breaths shallow and rapid. How could her Grammu and all the others have kept such secrets? All her friends and all her other kin left behind, maybe Taken by demons. Evil Queens wouldn't save people; they'd feed them to demons. So much to rethink.

Eliles pointed as they crested a rise, and Ieru's eyes landed on the iron bars of a gated garden. "Are there so many thieves?" She grinned, thinking of her Aunite Niseem and all the other adherents she'd seen with fresh fruits and veggies. "Apple thieves?"

"It depends on who you ask and their definition of thief. But no, the fence predates the Fire. All who help tend the garden are welcome to eat their fill."

Ieru wanted to run as her mouth filled with saliva. "I will garden every day." Her brows wrinkled. "Or would I pop?"

"Pop?"

"Auntie told me fruit pops in the garden, so I might too."

"Who's your aunt?"

"Niseem."

Several quiet strides before Eliles opened the unlocked gate and led her inside. "Well, no *person* has popped, nor any birds I know of, but time within the garden isn't as stable as I'd like. Is that why you came? Hoping to age?"

"No, I came for the grapes."

A voice thundered from behind a wall of grapevines, "Who the godsdamned hells is that, and why'd ya promise her my grapes?" The shaggy, middle-aged face of a man appeared over the canopy.

"Ieru, this is Artus Choerkin, vintner and all-around grape hoarder."

She slipped behind Eliles' dress as the man squinted at her. "She some sorta demon or another dragon?"

"High Oracle Meris' granddaughter."

The man's scrunched face suggested he was more surprised by this answer than if she declared the girl to be a dragon. "From the stars?" He grinned. "That's worthy of a few handfuls of grapes, then. Welcome to the vineyard, young lady."

She stepped from behind hems. "I'm not as young as I look."

"Neither am I." He winked and plucked a bunch of dark purple grapes, holding them over the row for her. "Come on now, don't be shy."

Her feet could deny her tongue no longer, and she trotted to take them from his hand, popping one into her mouth with a crunch. Sweet dominated the tart on her tongue into a blissful blend, forcing her to wipe her mouth before stuffing several more past her lips. "Gods. Oh, gods. I want to live here."

"Aye, the stars are beautiful but don't taste so good. So, how'd you find this lass?"

"Chance. Serendipity. Fate, maybe?"

"You sure she ain't a Face?"

"Certain as I can be."

Ieru glanced between the two as she chewed and, after a swallow, asked, "What's a Face?

The big man grunted. "A priest who can change how they look, talk... smell even. I'm supposin' they can look like anybody."

She recalled Grammu whispering about the Face of Ulrikt years ago but hadn't a clue what she had meant before now. "Creepy." But not creepy enough to keep her from refilling her mouth.

"It is at that, little girl."

"I'm not a little girl."

"Aye, right. My apologies."

Eliles strode close, nabbing a grape from the vine and eating it. "I don't think there are more Faces on the island, but one can't be certain. "

Artus asked, "How many priests are there—" but Eliles shushed him. "Let the girl be."

He shrugged with a smile. "She's eatin' my grapes; that alone should afford me some questions."

Ieru shrugged. "I don't mind, but I don't know. Never bothered to give a count. Twenty? But the stars behind the stars is a big place. Easy to hide." She glanced around. "My turn. How many fruits and veggies have you got?"

The Choerkin laughed. "A girl after my own gut. The orchard has two sorts of apple trees: pears, peaches, mulberries, and a lonely peach tree."

"Strawberries?"

A frown. "No. I try not to think on that. A sad lack of berries."

Eliles said, "Beans, peas, cabbage, lettuce, tomatoes, potatoes, carrots, and a good many more. Plenty for the cooks to cobble together a good meal even if it always seems to include fish."

"It's funny how much I want to eat, though I never get hungry."

Eliles' head bobbed in agreement. "It is, isn't it? Some people will go weeks." She nodded toward the tower. "I doubt the Choerkin in the tower has eaten more than three times since arriving."

"Ivin Choerkin?"

"You heard of him?"

"The Evil Queen's master who returned from across the seas."

Eliles coughed. "Master?"

Ieru shrugged. "Just what I heard. They say he came back to reclaim the island... and you."

A snort from the lady but laughter from Artus. "Oh, that's a gem, it is."

"A man named Solineus brought him to me all but dead, and I healed him. He's hidden himself away in the tower most every day since."

"Too bad. I heard he's cute."

A grin. "Handsome, yes. And married. Children."

"Even more too bad, I guess."

"Some things aren't meant to be."

Artus cast Ieru a wink. "We seem to have plenty of time for that to change, don't we?"

Time was what they had plenty of, but time stood as a bitter reminder. "Are there others who, well, look my age?"

Eliles shook her head. "I'm sorry."

Her words brought a pang, but she smiled to hide it away. "Good. I'm still unique, then." She tossed a grape into her mouth and bit to douse the need for a false smile.

"My turn. Is your mother or father here on the island?"

Grinding teeth stopped, and after blinking away a faint image of her mother, she muttered, "My mother's gone; I won't talk of her. My father I never met." Her tongue cleaned her teeth of grape, and she swallowed. "My turn, then I should be heading home."

"Fair enough. What would you like to know?"

Her hands flopped to her side. "Gimme a flicker." Lips pinched, and she stared at the ground, then to the flames. A thousand questions should come to mind, or so she'd swear, but only one reached her tongue. "When can we—" Something flashed through the wall of flame, streaking the oranges and reds like a monstrous blade that trailed smoke or steam. She pointed with eyes wide. "What the hells was that?"

Both spun to follow her finger, but the thing was gone. Eliles asked, "What was what?"

"If I knew, I wouldn't be asking!"

"Aye, lass, a wing through the Fire, maybe?"

Ieru eyed the man. "Maybe."

The pair shared a look. "Gods be damned. You thinkin' she's back?"

Ieru blurted at the man, "Who's she?"

Eliles answered, "A dragon."

Ieru snorted before her lips parted for a laugh, but neither smiled. "Dragons aren't for real."

"Says the girl who lives in the stars."

"Horseshit. Excuse my tongue."

A smirk from the man. "For a little lass, she has a mouth I appreciate."

"I'm not that young!" Arms slapped her hips.

"Easy girl, just yankin' yer chain."

Her nose flared. "About the dragon too?"

Eliles rolled her shoulders, mouth stretched straight. "Not about that. In fact, she may have known your Grammu."

Ieru's mouth dropped open, a quiver through her body at the words she was about to spew, but not but air came out as a wing cut the fire again. Her tongue hung on her lip as she stared long past its disappearance, then, "I'm going back to the stars." And her feet carried her away in a daze.

Eliles' voice called from behind. "I still owe you."

She took five more strides before managing to stop and speak. "You do. The outside world."

"When can we meet again?"

"I can't always get away. One day this week."

"I'll be there."

Knees bent, and feet fell without uttering another word. An Evil Queen for a friend, a dragon in a flaming sky, and a Choerkin from an age-old prophecy holed up in the keep. She might be stuck in a seven-year-old body forever and forced to live in the eternal repetition of a

single day in the stars, but at least the island was no longer the boring rock she thought it was. Her heart quivered, and a crooked smile creased her face. "And grapes." A terrifying, but all and all, better than good day.

Eliles watched the girl's form stride away until she disappeared down the slope of the hill. Artus snorted and spat. "Hells of a coincidence."

"You don't believe that."

A chuckle. "I don't. You're sure you'd know her from a Face?"

She groaned and rolled her eyes. "If she's a Face... I don't know what to tell you. I tried everything to pierce its veil. Nothing."

"Then she's for real?"

"Best I can tell. And our winged friend returning after being gone so long? She chooses today?"

"Your winged friend, not mine."

Eliles raised her eyes to the fire, then turned a circle, half expecting a long-dead priestess to come walking her way, but the streets remained empty. "I don't think she's a threat."

"You don't think a dragon is a threat?"

She giggled at the absurdity. "I mean, she isn't our enemy. She saved Solineus. She told me enough to solve the garden's riddle."

"Forgive me if I find it hard to trust something that can eat me." He grinned, but she knew something more serious was on his mind.

"If you've got something to say."

"You should tell Ivin about the girl."

She snorted. "No. If he wanted to know what happens on Herald's Watch, he could come find out for himself."

"What happens?" He paused. "I wanted to say nothin' happens, and hells if that isn't true most times, but when something does happen, it's big. Bigger because so little else changes."

Eliles put her hands on her hips. "If you want him to know, you go tell him."

"Why the hells are you so scared of him? Puppy love?"

Her eyes flew wide, and she wanted to scream that everyone should be afraid of him. "How dare you?"

"Dare I? The watery eyes and kiss you two shared? Forget 'em."

"I have."

"Then go tell him."

"You!"

"If it comes from anyone else, he'll know yer avoidin' him."

She huffed. "And he's avoiding me. I'll tell him when I see his face outside that tower." Eliles stomped away, making sure she headed away from Choerkin Keep. She kicked at an upturned pave stone. "Foolishness."

Let the man come to her even if he never did. The notion aggravated her further. Puppy love. It had felt like more at the time, a desperate girl trapped in Istinjoln Monastery and their flight from the Shadows of Man, their fight for survival, and her letting him go with only the fantasy of his return. She never loved him. He never loved her. Their feelings were nothing more than the fancy of two people forced together and driven apart; attraction denied creating a false connection to haunt her dreams. This sense based on self-preservation built over years of hopelessness while ensnared in her flaming trap, not so different than Istinjoln's stone walls in its denial of freedom and the chance for love until *he* showed up.

He rode into Istinjoln first and now, dragged onto Herald's Watch, but the result was the same: Hope for something more. False hope both times.

She turned to glance at Choerkin Keep rising behind her.

No. He needs to come to me.

THREE

Impossible Tour

Green eyes scream of the growing inside
without heralding the way to eternity's obfuscation,
of inundation and monumental deification
of the Warlord's cause in an age of warring gods.
Wink to blink and dare reality
to show Doomed Face looped in the mortal coil.

—*Tomes of the Touched*

Ieru kneeled beside Eliles, crouching with trepidation. The woman she struggled not to think of as Evil Queen turned with a smile. "Who would you like to search for?"

It was the question she dreaded. The only people she knew were alive lived in the stars, and she didn't care much about what they might be doing. In many ways, she preferred not to know who was dead; in her mind, everyone but Grammu Meris lived somewhere, eating and laughing, watching the sun set and rise. "Nobody I know. Not this time. Not yet."

"I understand. Every time I ask..." Eliles sighed. "Let's see what we find, shall we? Elinwe, show me my friend Rinold, known as

The Squirrel." The universe blurred and in a rush the stars below and in front of them disappeared, replaced sea, then land, passing over distant cities with a speed Ieru couldn't fathom. Within flickers, they passed over a massive mountain chain, a forest greater than she ever imagined, and arrived to overlook a sweeping sea of grass.

Their travel slowed, and Ieru rediscovered her breath. "Where are we?"

"I'm not sure. We passed over the Dragonspan Mountains and a forest an old map calls Rigendôur. That means we're... I don't recall the name of these plains. Look. There."

Eliles pointed to dark specks on the horizon, a hundred or so, Ieru guessed. Flickers later, the specks turned to blobs, then shifted into men on horseback. "This is amazing."

"It is! I get closer now than I used to. On Kaludor, I can see faces and once managed to speak to a Colok."

Ieru snorted with a laugh. "What good to talk to an animal?"

The lady grinned. "They talk back. And in this case, he helped my friends." Their approach slowed but didn't stop, following the riders at their pace. "See that thin fellow up front? Riding beside that giant of a man?"

Ieru squinted. Maybe she did, maybe she didn't. "Yes."

"I think that's Rinold. On Kaludor, he was a tracker for the Wolverine. We fled the main island together."

Her eyes settled on the man she figured Eliles spoke of. "Never heard of him."

"I suppose not. Let's see... Elinwe, show me the way to Meliu."

The vision reversed, reeling backward and swinging their view to the east. In moments, they flew over a great river and arrived at a city so huge it widened Ieru's eyes more than the journey itself. Thousands milled in the streets, lines of wagons, carts, walkers, and riders lining the stone roads entering the city's several gates.

"Gods. They built a city so fast?"

A chuckle from the Evil Queen. "No. The city is called Endelêun, and from what Solineus said, the people who used to live there abandoned the city long ago. Most folks of the seven clans reside there now." She pointed. "See the massive pyramid on that mountain?"

She giggled. "Could I miss it?"

"That's Tomarok."

Elinwe's vision floated ever closer to the stepped structure and a cluster of buildings and smaller pyramids sitting around its base. All together, it could be called a small city resting above the greater one. Fires burned atop three lesser, flat-topped pyramids that sat near the base of the gigantic stepped pyramid and robed priests walked across a grassy courtyard. "A temple of some sort?"

"Very good—" The woman's breath caught, and her focus returned to the pyramid. The vision stopped in place. A woman strode from a passage at the top of the pyramid. Red hair and black robes flowed in what must be a strong wind.

"A High Priestess."

"Not just. It's Meliu. I didn't know she'd ascended to the high priesthood."

"She looks young. Maybe she'll be Lord Priestess one day."

"Maybe." A pause with short, tense breaths. "Lord Priest Ulrikt promised me the position once. What seems long, long ago."

Ieru smirked. "Jealous?"

A longer pause. "I'm jealous of many things, but that isn't one of them. I am the Evil Queen, after all. What better title could I have?"

Ieru smiled with a laugh. "Better a queen than a lord priestess. Show me someone else. This is fun."

"It can be. Elinwe, show me... get ready for a ride. Elinwe, show me Solineus Mikjehemlut."

The world before her eyes jerked backward, rushing at a pace in reverse so that her blood shifted in her head, and it forced her to lean. Blurring forests and mountains before she closed her eyes, regaining her sense of balance within flickers. She didn't reopen her eyes. Waiting.

"We've slowed and are moving forward again."

Ieru peeped through one squinting eye to see a village beside open water. Fifty buildings, most constructed of wood but a few of stone, sat beside straight dirt roads. Warriors trained on an open field, and this was where Elinwe's vision took them. To a tall, handsome man with two swords on his back as he gazed over the field of mock battle. A slight and gorgeous woman with long black hair stood beside him. The vision didn't stop until she could guess the color of his eyes. "His eyes are blue?"

"Yes. I thought he might be sailing by now, headed south, but he's just across the Parapet Straits. Not far east of them is the Eleris, the Mother Wood of the Edan, and other Woodkin."

It proved difficult to pull her eyes from the couple. "She's not Silone."

"No. I'm not sure where she's from. I don't even know her name."

"Why did moving backward feel so, so... Whatever."

"I don't know. Shorter distances are easier, and moving forward is more comfortable than back, but I've grown used to it. Spinning can topple you. Do you want to see something interesting? Maybe, at least?"

"As if this isn't?"

Eliles giggled, but her face fell solemn within the beat of her heart. "When I trained for the priesthood in Istinjoln, my master was named Dareun. Elinwe, show me Master Dareun."

Elinwe's vision rotated several degrees and streaked the world in reverse, pulsing Ieru's head into a spin, but without the force of before. They passed over what must be the Parapet Straits, her eyes catching several icebergs that earned the waters their name before returning to land

and spinning so fast she leaned. She planted palms on the cool floor and, this time, smiled. "Woohoo!" And the ride ended too soon, overlooking a stone fortress nestled at the base of mountains with a winding road leading to a wide-open gate, but it was a faint beam of light rising into the clouds from beside the tall central tower that spoke to where Dareun was. "Istinjoln Monastery? He never left? Did the demons Take him?"

"No, he never left because he died there before the demons came. Do you see him?"

"You said the stars won't show us dead people." She squinted as the vision approached closer. Istinjol's interior was a maze of buildings, inconsistent in size and shape, but her eyes settled on a small building in the middle of her sight with a single brick chimney. "His body is in that building?"

"A good guess; he's sitting on top of it, but his body, well, I'm not sure where it is."

Ieru's eyes flicked to a flash of movement in the street; her heart pounded, and a chill spread across her shoulders, though she only caught a glimpse of blackness. "Was that?"

"A Shadow of Man, yes. Sometimes, you can see Taken wandering the streets, but for the most part, they hide in the tunnels. Once, I even watched a raiding party of Colok clear the first courtyard, but the Taken and Shadows aren't so foolish to fight long, and they retreated into the buildings. Into the tunnels."

"They think?"

"More than we gave them credit, at first. But more to the point, where is Dareun?"

Ieru refocused on the building's roof despite a hint of movement in the shadows. Elinwe's vision stopped, drawing no closer. "He hides well."

"He's not hiding."

"I don't know what you expect me..." Her eyes widened; the faint form of a figure sat hunched in the middle of the building. She could see the roof through him. "That's him in the middle? Is he a ghost of some sort?"

"They Sundered his soul from the Gods after torturing him, leaving him unable to travel the Starry Road to the Seven Heavens."

Ieru grimaced. "That's horrible. And he just sits there?"

"He didn't used to. He has sensed me watching before, and sometimes, I wonder if he doesn't go places he wants me to see."

"What would be important about this building?"

Eliles giggled. "Probably nothing, it's wishful thinking."

"It's a little sad." More than a little, it was downright depressing to watch a man's untethered soul sitting and waiting to fade into nothingness. "Could you save him? With the Sliver of Star?"

"A beautiful thought, but no. You have a good heart."

Ieru smiled, but her question was less about sentiment than simple curiosity. "Can you see people in the Stars?"

"No. Worried about me spying on you?"

"Maybe a little. What about the rest of the island? Do you get close enough to count their hairs?"

Eliles laughed. "No. I give people their privacy unless I've a reason to know where they are. And that's rare."

Curiosity wouldn't be staunched on a stubborn day. "Mmm. Show me someone anyhow."

Her smile faded with a sigh. "I've been meaning to check up on someone. But only this once. Understand?"

"Yeah, yeah. Show me." She flashed a cutesy smile.

"Elinwe, show me the way to Ivin Choerkin."

The ghost of Dareun disappeared as Elinwe's vision surged backward, soaring over Choerkin Fost and Purdonis

Bay until alighting on the island with a quick spin to the east. The highest tower of Herald's Watch and its surrounding keep appeared, and for a flicker, disappointment reigned as she feared they wouldn't go inside, but in short order, her eyes pressed against the stone walls then passed through in a flutter of light and dark. Three walls later, she blinked to find herself in a dining hall. All the stars were gone.

It was almost as if she sat beside the big blond man resting in a chair with his boots kicked up on a table. Best guess, he napped. She whispered, "It's like we're there. Will he hear us?"

"No, or at least I don't think so. I would have to concentrate for our voices to carry as far as I know. It'd serve him right, considering he's ignored everybody since arriving."

Something in her words and a feeling in Ieru's gut. "You like him. Like, kissing him kind of like." Eliles glanced, and Ieru blushed. "I shoulda kept my mouth shut."

"No, it's fine. I did. Or I do. He's married with two children now."

"And yet he's trapped here with you."

"Trapped sounds like an unfair relationship, don't you think?"

Ieru's head rocked with a snort. "It's all the relationships I know. Except you."

"And I'm the one who trapped you."

"No, you freed me." She looked at the snoozing man, wondering whether the Choerkin was worthy of such a beautiful priestess, evil queen, or not. Handsome enough, no doubt.

His eyes opened, and he jerked upright in his seat; Ieru squealed and slid backward on her butt, then realized he didn't look at her. His eyes seemed to focus on the orange glow of dying fire and remnants of logs.

"It's all right. I think he awoke from a dream."

Ieru giggled at her own foolishness, but then the man waved his arms and pointed, his voice thundering. "To the hells with you! Be gone and never return." He stomped to stand in front of the hearth with his fists balled, and for all the world, Ieru would swear he was about to punch someone who wasn't there. "Show your face again, and by the gods, I swear I'll pound your skull until your brains leak from your ears."

Eliles said, "We best leave. Elinwe, show me the stars of now." The infuriated man and the dining hall faded into the night sky, and the woman stood. "I'm sorry. I need to go."

"What were we watching?"

But the evil queen ignored her, trotting to the stairs and disappearing with a song in her wake but without another word.

And without returning Ieru to the time of the Shower of Stars. She leaned back to think. Some days, she might've sat to wait, but today was a stubborn day. Who was she kidding? With a chance like this, every day was a stubborn day. And what better invitation to explore the island? Maybe Eliles had meant for her to stay.

The notion satisfied her, and she jumped to her feet with a song from the stars. Now, if she could find the stairs without falling down them.

Four

Tower of a Man

I mean to come home to you every night, but I find myself lucky to find my way to your locked door, to stand wondering why, if this is my home, I possess no key.

—*From The Ghost's Loving Lament,*
by Imorêum Grâ

Eliles climbed the broad steps leading to Choerkin Keep's main doors and stared, realizing that she'd sped her way here without a plan. If locked, would she knock it off its hinges or burn it down? Maybe leave? She raised her knuckles, but knocking felt silly. She pushed instead, and to her surprise, the door swung open, unlocked and unbarred.

She ran the moment her surprise wore off and slid around a dusty corner to find the doors to the dining hall wide open. Her mouth opened to yell the man's name, but her eyes found Ivin sitting with his feet propped on the table, dozing just as the stars had first shown him. "What the hells," she muttered too loud.

Ivin stirred, eyes blinking open to gaze at her. "Eliles? What? Is something wrong?"

"No. I don't know." She fidgeted before taking steps his way, none too eager to admit that she'd spied upon him. "How are you?"

His boots thudded to the floor, and he sat straight. "Same as any other day, only someone, left unnamed, has interrupted my nap. Not that I can't sleep all day if I want. I'll never lack for sleep on this island. A far cry from my father bellowing me awake every dawn."

"A quiet eternity does have its perks."

"Please, sit. I doubt you came here for small talk."

"I'm not sure why I'm here." He pulled a chair from beneath the edge of the table and sat within feet of him, as close as she'd been in months. Her gaze wandered to the fireplace, its hearth dark and cold. No fire, no embers, not even trails of smoke rising. Ivin's screaming at air wasn't the only change from the vision in the stars, and for the first time, she mistrusted Elinwe's visions. "I felt the need to see you, to make sure you were well."

He squinted with a raised brow, not buying her story. "Did you bring food? I'm not hungry but feel a peculiar desire to eat."

"You should come down to the inn more often. People are curious, and it wouldn't hurt you to get to know them."

"Did my uncle send you? He's always pestering me about getting out of this tower."

"No, but he's right."

He smirked. "To get more sun?"

She giggled. "I don't know about that, but talking to people can ease burdens. Have you been angry of late?"

Ivin rocked back in his seat. "Angry? No. Frustrated, no doubt about it. Far as I know, there could be three wars raging, and me stuck on this island with Kinesee and my twins... Angry isn't the right word."

The mention of his wife's name brought a pang to her heart, and the memory of their one kiss before he departed this island with no

hope of ever returning. "I know." Silly and pathetic to pine for a man she'd spent so little time with.

He rubbed his eyes and yawned, proof he didn't sleep much. Hopeless, and yet here he sat. "Better than dead, I suppose. But why did you really...." His head cocked to peer around her, eyes narrowing. "Who's the girl? Is she real?"

She turned but saw no one. "I see nobody."

His head lolled back. "Ah, shits."

She looked behind herself a second time, craning farther. "Ieru! I'm so sorry, child."

Ivin perked with a smile. "She's real then?"

Eliles laughed. "Very. I met Ieru in the stars and forgot to take her home."

The girl took timid strides to stand beside Eliles with a grin. A nervous wave. "Hello, Lord Choerkin."

"Ivin, please. Kotin Choerkin was and is the lord of this tower." His lips pursed. "The stars. You mean she *lives* in the stars with the holy?"

"I do."

"I didn't know there were children on the island."

Ieru snorted. "There aren't. There's *a* child. Me. But I'm older than I look."

Eliles said, "She arrived on the island not long before the Eve of Snows."

Ivin stared, and Eliles grew nervous for the girl. And a flicker later terrified.

"High Oracle Meris was my grammu." Meris' sins were legion in Choerkin eyes, not the least of which was being accused of the murder of Ivin's mother and newborn sister. In the past, Eliles would've trusted his holding his temper, but Elinwe's vision spooked her.

Ivin licked his lips, his gaze blinking between the two of them. "You're damned certain I'm not dreaming?"

Eliles shook her head, taking Ieru's hand. "No dream, but no way to know whether they told her the truth. The first time she met Meris was when she arrived on the island."

A cool gaze on the man's face, unreadable. "I see."

Ieru shrugged, gripping her hand. "It's what they told me. My mother was a priestess in Feledês and fell from her horse. She lay in the woods for two days, and when they found her, she needed a healer better than any they had at the tiny church. They left with my momma on a wagon and sent me to Herald's Watch."

"Did your mother live?"

"I don't know. Word never arrived, or at least they never told me if it did."

"I'm sorry for that. I know how painful it is to lose your mother." He smiled. "I'll tell you what, if you don't hold my kin against me, I won't hold yours against you. Deal?"

"Deal." The girl squeezed her hand. "What did she do?"

Eliles interrupted, "Stories for another time."

Ieru leaned into her ear. "Who was he yelling at?"

And she whispered back, "Later."

"We're keeping secrets from me already?"

She let go the girl's hand and pulled out a chair for her to sit. "Maybe a couple. Solineus is still at the Silone encampment on the Blooded Plains."

He nodded with a sigh. "Surprising. He must be plotting something with Rikis and the Wolverine."

"The Wolverine has been up and down the river and near Istinjoln a couple of times the last several months, but the monastery is quiet, best I can tell."

Ivin smiled. Good. Anything else I should know about?"

The name Meliu arrived on her tongue, but she didn't utter it, unwilling to let him know she'd spied on one of his past lovers. Plus, she wasn't doing much of anything. "Rinold rides into the plains with a hundred men or more, but it was peaceful."

Ivin chortled. "A hundred warriors don't ride because they expect cake and beer at the end of their trail. The City of Endelêun should be safe, thank the gods, but if Rinold heads south, it's with cause. He wouldn't leave Little Sister and his newborn." He sighed. "Not newborn anymore, but still a babe. One of the Histê kings might be causing problems."

Eliles turned to Ieru. "Little sister is Puxele's nickname. She's Rinold's wife and one of the finest hunters I've met. His nickname is The Squirrel, and the man in front of you is Ratsmasher. It gets confusing." She turned back to Ivin. "A hundred isn't enough for war either. Everywhere I could see remains quiet."

"Small blessings, at least. So, you came to ease my worries and introduce me to your new friend? Except her arrival was an accident as something made you forget to take her home. Why are you here?"

Eliles rolled her eyes, releasing a tight breath that flapped her lips with a sputter.

Until Ieru blurted, "You were yelling at nobody."

"I was what?"

Eliles cast the girl a grinning glare. "Thanks for that." She turned toward Ivin with what she hoped was a pleasant and innocent smile, uncertain whether his face wore a smirk or frown. "We were in the stars, and she asked to see someone on the island, so I asked the stars to show you."

"You spied on me?"

"The first time, I swear."

An awkward silence ensued, broken again by Ieru. "You were napping, then jumped awake and yelled. Threatened someone's life, but nobody was there."

A hand stroked Ivin's chin as he stared at Eliles, and she refused to break the eye contact. "She speaks the truth. That's why I ran over here. But when I arrived, you were asleep."

"So, what the hells are you two saying? I've heard of walking in your sleep."

"No, there was a smoldering fire in the hearth in the vision."

"I'm not sure what to think of your watching me, especially when it might not have been me at all."

"I won't do it again, I promise."

He eyeballed her until she dipped her gaze. "No. Watch me. Tell me what you see."

Her brow wrinkled as she raised her eyes. "What aren't you telling me?"

"We need to know how honest the stars are if we're to judge what you see."

There was no way to argue his point, even if there was nothing any of them could do about events in the wider world. "Come and see for yourself."

"No!" A deep breath exhaled between puckered lips. "I don't belong in the stars. Just tell me what you see."

Still, he hid something from her. "No secrets?"

"Everybody keeps secrets."

If she disagreed, it'd be a lie; she never told him about the crown they found in the shrine Kotin Choerkin buried after his wife and daughter's deaths. "Fair enough. To a point."

"Try not to watch when I piss."

Ieru giggled, and Eliles said, "I'll resist. I swear on it. The garderobe is off limits."

"Once we have answers, then I'd rather you stop watching, just in case I make a fool of myself."

"Of course." She smiled, but couldn't help asking, "Do you start fires here?"

"Until you start growing more trees, I assume your friend at the Salty Frog took all the cords of wood for the cookfire."

"Seden. You'd know her name if you quit playing at hermit."

"Hermits don't live in castles."

Ieru said, "He has a point. But, so does she. If I didn't leave the stars, I'd still think an evil queen ruled the island instead of a grumpy Choerkin."

"I like this girl. She reminds me of all the other feisty ladies I know. But if I rule here, it's the tiniest kingdom I ever heard of."

"Better a king of nothing than a nothing. Or a princess of the stars like me."

Eliles laughed at the girl's quip. "An evil queen, a king of nothing, and a princess of the stars. We make a formidable threesome."

Ivin stood and clapped his hands. "It's been days since I've eaten. Your combined pleas and the siren's song of stew suggests we see what Seden and the Salty Frog has to offer. Shall we feast as royals?"

Eliles turned to Ieru. "I've no idea who all will be there. Are you ready to meet more people?"

The girl grinned with a shrug. "There aren't more than two dozen people living outside of the stars; how bad could it be?"

"Well, ladies, let's eat." Ivin offered his arm to Ieru, and she jumped at the chance to hook his wrist with an elbow, but when his other elbow pointed Eliles' way, she hesitated.

She'd buried her feelings for the man—superficial, childish feelings no more than puppy love—then buried them deeper when he returned to her married. He was being polite. Playful and taking advantage of the talk of kings, queens, and princesses. An elbow meant nothing.

She curtsied. "Your lordly kingliness." Her hand slipped past his, and they joined elbows for a stroll. A mistake she recognized in an instant as she walked beside him, with every step they took and every word they shared digging like tiny shovels toward a past that was more dreamed than lived.

FIVE

Departing the New

To not believe in right and wrong is to not believe in yourself, and to not believe in yourself is failure.

—Lord Priest Somutor of Rokan

Solineus stood on a windblown hillock overlooking New Fost and the swarm of Silone, who worked every day to expand and improve on growing a village into a fortified city. Men, women, and children. So many children. A testament to the people keeping busy at more than building with lumber and stone.

Sîu leaned into him, bundled in furs and yet somehow still showing more skin than Silone women thought proper. "I'm not asking."

He chuckled and rested his arm around her shoulder. "And I appreciate it, I promise." After a month of patience, she'd pestered him every day about when they'd sail south until he begged her to stop. Now, once a week, she reminded him she wasn't asking. "Missing your family or running around naked?"

"I can run naked in our room anytime I like."

"And get no complaint from me."

Captain Meledên and the *Onyoño Fî* sailed east months ago, but not before Solineus knew another option coming their way. Other ships had come and gone, but Captain Intœño and the *Entîyu Emoñô* would be worth the wait. In fact, the wait was an advantage, a chance to keep an eye on the coming war in the north.

Sîu didn't see things the same way, and it was as if she could read bits of his thoughts, not just see his aura. "There is war coming to the south too. We should be there."

"When the *Entîyu Emoñô* arrives, we'll leave. I swear on it."

Rikis appeared from around a wall to save him, his arms bare and rippled with muscle. He pointed to the strait and humps of icebergs flowing past like predators. "A dangerous year for sailing."

Sîu's eyes widened. "Don't you dare."

A big grin from the big Choerkin. "My apologies, m'lady. I overheard your conversation and couldn't resist."

"You're a wicked man."

"Aye, and I'd love to keep you both here. We could use you when we strike Istinjoln."

The Wolverine and Rikis plotted this strike since Solineus and his swords returned, but decisions and strategies were slower to arrive. Solineus said, "Istinjoln is a war away for me. And you. Until the Edan are willing, you're wise to wait, build, and train."

"Not so far out as maybe you think. Decisions may be coming for us all."

A chill ran Solineus' spine. "Speak plain."

"Aye, well, a rider arrived this morn from the edge of the Eleris. The Crown and Stars you've been waiting for arrived in port there, and rumor is, when they arrive here, Inslok will be with them."

"Any word on why?" One glance at Sîu's smile told him how much she cared whether the Edan was on the ship or not.

"You promised. A dozen times or more."

His gut squirmed. "I did, and we will. After we hear whatever there is to hear."

Rikis said, "They could arrive any time. The rider, Morikin, was surprised they didn't beat her here."

"She didn't hear why Inslok was coming?"

"Nah. But they don't leave their woods for no small thing, aye?"

"Inslok more than any other, and you never know what the hells an Edan will think important."

Sîu said, "Their auras are so bright and clear they unnerve me."

Rikis said, "Aye, their glow is something other."

Solineus grinned but didn't enlighten the man on what she meant. "I don't think Istinjoln will be in range for some time, but I pray I'm wrong."

"I know I shouldn't get my hopes up, but my mind goes there every day, today more so than most. The other night, I dreamt we got Eliles off Herald's Watch and went to war with the Sliver of Star."

Solineus chuckled. "I reckon that would change everything." *But Eliles sits trapped for eternity in her Fire.* He'd said this a hundred times and thought it a thousand more since arriving at New Fost, to dispel the dream of her freeing Kaludor from Shadows, but the fantasy persisted.

Sîu said, "You will retake Kaludor without her. I have faith."

Rikis sighed. "Some days, I figure myself a fool. I've lost faith in the Pantheon of Sol, yet somehow, I believe mere mortals can change things."

"I've seen a dragon answer this man's call—"she gripped Solineus' arm"—to save us. If such a thing can be, then there is no limit to the miracles we can look forward to."

Solineus grinned and slapped the man's beefy shoulder. "Some would say we lost. Lost Kaludor. Lost our loved ones. People even

feel they've lost themselves in the hardships faced. Me? I lost who I was but found who I *am*. I say we won because we're still alive to fight, but that doesn't mean you or anyone else can fix the past. Choerkin Fost, Herald's Watch, nowhere will ever be as you remember again. Dragons, The Touched, the Edan, the Sliver of Star, not one or all can bring back what is behind us. We've won and will win again no matter how many losses come between."

Rikis' wan grin was of a man who wanted to agree, but it took flickers before the confident smile he wore for the people in New Fost returned. "When the Edan arrives, we'll know more of victories to come."

"I reckon so."

They stood in silence a moment studying the scene below. "Well, I should finish letting everyone know we've company a comin'. We'll miss you in the fight to come, but I know other fights need you, too."

"Every fight to come needs all of us, but that isn't what fate dealt. I'll do my best to be back when you siege Istinjoln."

"And if that news comes today?"

Solineus glanced at Sîu's frown. "We all know that's a moon dream." He borrowed the phrase from Sîu's islander language and smiled at her.

"Aye, well, I'll see you in town."

Solineus nodded and swept Sîu into a hug as the man descended the hill.

"Looks like we'll be leaving soon. I won't bother to ask whether you're ready."

"I've even got that big sword wrapped."

"Should I ask Inslok about the sword?" He'd kept the sword he found buried stashed away since arriving in New Fost. It wasn't easy to keep something so long under wraps, but if anyone spotted the

enchanted flamberge blade, there wasn't a soul who wouldn't know about it by the end of the day.

"You kept it secret from the Edan once."

"How the hell do I explain finding a sword buried where I washed ashore without a memory?"

"Lie. Tell him it was a gift from me."

Solineus chuckled. "I'm guessing that lying to an Edan is tricky. Whether he called me on it or not is another question."

"How do you explain the sword to yourself?"

He exhaled and turned back to the Parapet Strait, eyeing a peak of ice flowing east. Far to the west and years ago, an iceberg sank the ship he was on and wiped his memories clean, an iceberg not so different than those floating by. "The Lady in the Blue showed me the way." The Lady in his visions, except the visions hadn't returned since finding the sword.

"She might be harder to explain than the sword."

"Something in my gut speaks to not showing it off or asking questions."

"Then don't."

A snort-chuckle, and he turned back to her. "I'm glad I found you."

"I am easier to explain." She took his hands and eased herself to the ground, pulling him to sit beside her, and they stared out to sea. "I hope the Luxuns are good at avoiding the ice flow. Until meeting you, I didn't even know what ice was."

"Will you miss it?"

"No. Will you?"

He squinted and sighed. "I will. The cold is in my veins. I was born to it." He pressed tight to her side. "The cold makes warmth all the more pleasant."

The *Entîyu Emoñô* dropped anchor that evening, and Inslok disembarked without wearing his Edan glow or fanfare. Solineus escorted him to what people called The Great Keep even if it was incomplete and only two poles high. The interior was little more finished than the scaffolded exterior where masons and laborers had a candle earlier finished working for the day. A roaring fire burned in a massive hearth, and a table finished in the past month sat in the middle of the hall.

Rikis said, "Welcome! We've the honor of holding the first meeting here and sitting before the hearth's first fire with an esteemed friend from the Eleris."

Inslok strode to stand before Rikis and Pikarn with a quick nod, what passed for a bow for the Edan. "New Fost has progressed with impressive speed."

"Please, have a seat."

As the two took seats, Pikarn glided to Solineus' side. "Where's yer sweet young gal?"

"Aboard the *Entîyu Emoñô* waiting to depart. Yours?"

"Last I knew, still on Berus training men in swordplay. I hope to see her again soon."

Solineus chuckled before taking a seat across from Inslok, and the Wolverine sat by his side.

Rikis poured wine. "I hope your arrival brings good news our way."

"Uncertain news, but favorable." He tipped a glass of wine for a sip and kept its bowl resting in his palm. "Several scholars have read The Ôxêum Codex, and there are indeed references to Gates such as the one spawned in Istinjoln."

"That is excellent news."

"At the Battle of Fuginihimin-tûmumot, they speak of closing one such Gate, but the method and techniques aren't detailed. One thing is quite clear: the longer a gate stands open, the harder it is to close.

And in this instance, a powerful entity on the other side is assisting in keeping it open. Information suggests if not for her, it would've closed on its own with nobody on this side keeping it open."

Solineus said, "The Queen of Shadows."

"Yes."

Pikarn cleared his throat. "Last we knew, there's still a second gate, a small one, in the Chanting Caverns. Would the Queen be able to hold them both open?"

"Unless there is some natural connection, some force present in the caverns, to hold it open, the Queen or some other entity would need to hold it open as well."

Rikis said, "There could be some demon as powerful as the Queen there, too?"

"Unlikely. We suspect the Queen is a singular threat. I do not doubt she is powerful enough to hold several gates open at once. The better news is that while the Ôxêum Codex is a history, it references another tome that should offer details on closing these *Elnishestodu,* or Plane-Gates."

"I feel a big godsdamned 'but' coming."

"You are correct. The book referenced is the *Maruques inû Elnishestodu,* and not even the wisest knows if we hold a copy."

Rikis slumped in his chair with a chortle as Solineus leaned forward to question the Edan. "They haven't invented librarians in the Eleris?"

Inslok owl-blinked his way. "Librarians are esteemed colleagues and scholars, but there are thousands of unnamed books and unread books in the libraries of the Eleris. Many are damaged. Their titles were lost. Thousands more are in languages we cannot yet read."

Pikarn grumbled, "I didn't even know there were so many gods-be-damned books in the world."

Solineus said, "Tell me there is some hope?"

"Edan scholars are esteemed for a reason. If we possess the book, the scholars will find it. If not, then the hope becomes to find it ourselves."

"Find it where?"

"Ôxêum would be the obvious place to start."

Solineus scratched an itch growing behind his ear. "A beautiful idea, seeing as the city of Ôxêum disappeared with the Great Forgetting."

"And found by Ûvîn Lô."

"The dead Archangel Glimdrem spoke of?" A memory clicked in his head. "Glimdrem has been to Sutan where this Uvin found the Ôxêum Codex. He might be useful if ever we sail for Sutân."

A peculiar look passed over Inslok's face, a brief hint of emotion. "Yes. I am sad to say that the Volvrolan banished him from the Eleris. Nothing in his journals of Sutan suggests a location for Ôxêum."

Solineus squirmed as brows scrunched. "Banished."

"It is not a human concern."

"It is when he's the only person I know who has been to Sutan."

"It is not your concern. There were other Trelelunin with him, though I doubt they are eager to return."

Solineus snorted and stared. "Fine, but these journals of his would eliminate some possibilities and shrink the area to search." He rolled his eyes and slapped the arms of his chair. "As if we're sailing to Sutan to find Oxeum anyhow. How long will it take to search the libraries?"

"Unknowable."

"A guess, and assume it's the last book they look at. Gods know it would be if I were looking."

"A year? Maybe two?"

Solineus glanced at Pikarn and Rikis. "Not so bad."

Rikis perked with a smile. "Not so bad at all."

Inslok nodded, his voice grave. "There were interesting bits of history in the Codex as well. Coincidences. The Totokotwonu, followers of the Dontupûor, defeated the rulers of Oxeum... or rather, this is what some scholars believe. There are conflicting versions in the histories. But what is true is that the Dontupûor Pantheon had a hand in creating the Shadows of Man."

Solineus scowled. "Coincidence, you say?"

"The Dontupûor were powerful in the Age of God Wars, maybe on the verge of winning before the Great Forgetting broke the world if some texts are true, but we know little of them."

"Gone?"

"The Totokotwonu vanished along with their gods. If a mortal people worships them now, we have no knowledge of it."

Solineus sighed and leaned back in his chair. "The Sliver of Star, did it belong to them?"

"Nothing in the Codex or any other tome our scholars have read mentions anything like the Sliver of Star."

Pikarn shook his head. "All this speculatin' is a distraction. Ancient history that mightn't even be true. We got ourselves one to two years to prepare, maybe sooner! Whenever the hells this book is found. So the question is, how to best be ready, aye?"

Rikis sat straight. "The Wolverine is right."

Inslok said, "That's why I'm here."

Solineus stood, palms to the table. "That's my cue to join Sîu. If I stay much longer, she'll put a dart in my neck and drag me away."

Rikis eyed him. "Your input could be valuable."

"You three know what you're up against as well or better than I. You can fill me in on any plans before I leave."

Pikarn watched the man's two swords depart as much as he watched the man, wishing he had weapons like those instead of a wineskin and a squeeze to fight off the Shadows of Man. He found it hard to blame Solineus for planning his departure with a woman like Sîu, a fire-breather with eyes to melt a man's will, a bewitching beauty with slender shoulders and a gentler tongue who could still drop a moose with a poisoned dart. On the other hand, he wanted to shake her until she saw the good sense in their staying.

The door shut with a bang and jiggle. "That son of a bitch will be back when we need him most, never you doubt it."

Inslok surprised him with a reply. "He is a remarkable soul. Even if we don't need him, we will want him with us when the time comes."

Rikis downed his glass of wine and poured another. "Why are you here? I'm beginning to think the Edan don't fear leavin' the Eleris as much as legends say."

A straight face. "I am unusual in that respect. The Minister of Knowledge proposes a joint venture to Kaludor."

Pikarn let loose a whoop. "Hells, yes! Where we goin' and when?"

The Edan turned his unnerving gaze upon him. "Where you take us, and assuming we get authorization, we depart in no later than twenty days."

"Where I take you? What the hell do you mean by that?"

"The Minister wants us to visit the Gate in the Chanting Caverns. At the Shrine of Burdenis."

A quiver ran up his spine until his head twitched. "The Shrine, you say? I lost my best man down in that hole."

"From the stories I recall, you are the only member of your patrol here who knows the way."

Pikarn's mouth gaped for a flicker, the tip of his tongue drying. The only other man nearby who'd been to the shrine with him was

Ivin Choerkin, and the bastard got out of this by being trapped inside a wall of Fire. "Aye, sure. But I didn't lead the way in nor the way out! How... I've dreamed the journey so many times I don't trust my memory."

"The Edan do not possess a map of the Chanting Caverns. Even your flawed memories are better than anything we have."

"All right, aye, I get your point. If'n we find the Crack of Burdenis, it isn't so bad after that. It's gettin' there."

"Would the Colok know the way?"

"I shittin' hope so, but I doubt it. Unless we've a one-in-a-thousand priest here in New Fost, I'm the best we got. What the hells does the Minister think we'll find?"

"First, she wants to know how the Gate is held open, by the Queen of Shadow, one of her minions, or by some artifact or other connection."

"And?"

Inslok sipped first, then finished his wine with a gulp. "Whether on this first trip or later, this Gate is the one we close first. We can make the Caverns safer than Istinjoln to test theories."

"Oh aye, that makes perfect sense, except if'n we fail and piss the Queen off, she might just send a godsdamned army of Taken and Shadows with us sitting in a hole with one way out."

"Your concerns are understood, but not to undertake this mission would be foolish. I will go myself, if the Volvrolan approves, along with Limereu and Neseldun, both of whom you know already. With a contingent of Trelelunin warriors and, with luck, Colok to assist in any combat, you and whoever chooses to go will be as safe as possible."

"Oh, I see; well, being the only fool likely to die eases my spirits; it does. I swear on it."

Inslok blinked, and his nose curled. "There is no telling what demon may have been spawned in Istinjoln or the caverns that could kill us all."

Pikarn smirked at Rikis. "I'm supposed to feel better about that?"

"I believe so."

Inslok's gaze passed between the two of them. "So you won't guide us, then?"

The Wolverine snorted. "Piss poor guide I'll be, but I'll guide you straight to The Forges if that's what it takes."

"Good, though I'm uncertain why it took so long to reach the conclusion if it was foregone."

Pikarn grunted with a chortle. "If I die in that there hole without makin' my case, I'd be pissy for an eternity in whatever hell or heaven I end up in."

"I see. You are a strange man."

The Wolverine grunted with a nod before Rikis said, "I will join the party too."

His nod froze, and his grunt shifted to an awkward snort. "The shittin' hells you will."

"You're going to stop me, old man?"

Kotin's eldest boy had a point. Youth, reach, and power were all on his side. "You're still a welp I could kick into the river if I liked."

"Stiff as you are in the morning, I'm not so sure you can kick at all."

"I'll kick you in the evenin' then when I'm good and limber."

If their behavior perplexed Inslok, it didn't show on his face as he said, "Pikarn is the only human we need, though we might find our way without him in time; whoever else goes is of no consequence."

"No way I stay behind in New Fost after that jab."

The boy had his father's blood, no doubt about it. "We'll straighten that one out over arm wrestling later. What's yer plan, Edan?"

"First, I'll return to the Eleris and get the necessary permissions. Volunteers and supplies. Then we sail for your river camp to make contact with the Colok and convince them to join us."

"Kills me to say so, but the more Colok we have with us, the better I'll feel."

"They are a sturdy and violent people, and their knowledge of the area will be useful. Have you any thoughts on where we could pitch a second camp closer to the Shrine of Burdenis?"

Pikarn ripped a bite of jerky with his teeth and chewed. "Apologies. I think better when eating." He ground the meat between his teeth for half a wick. Snow's Eye stood too far away, and the best he knew, no similar towers stood closer to the Omindi Pass. "There was a cave-in, though I think now it mighta been intentional. A mine right close to the Chanting Caverns. Maybe connected before the collapse." He looked at Rikis. "Where Ivin and I found the priestess Meliu. I'd wager it might serve your purpose. The Colok might have other ideas."

"Excellent. I'll request the Luxuns deliver me to the Eleris come morning, and I'll return within the fortnight. Gather supplies, and whoever will go with you."

Rikis said, "It'll be done."

Inslok stood and departed the room without another word.

"He called me strange? That fella is one freaky son of a bitch."

Rikis grinned. "Arm wrestling?"

"I'm sure I said drinking contest."

"You said arm wrestling."

Pikarn rolled up his sleeve and plopped his elbow on the table. Twenty years ago, he figured he might've made this a contest. "Get your ass over here. I'm gonna make you get up before I take you down."

Muscular blue arms wrapped Solineus in a brief and perfunctory hug before Captain Intœño stepped back to appraise him. "It is good to see you again, my friend."

The man's friendliness struck him as peculiar. His time aboard the *Entîyu Emoñô* had been brief. "Likewise, Captain."

Captain Intœño turned to Sîu with a broad smile, the feathers on his head fluffing. "Sîu, I never imagined seeing such a beautiful equatorial flower so far north." His hug for her was less brief, and everything made a little more sense.

She backed from the man's arms with a smile. "I'll be pleased to be an equatorial flower again."

Solineus said, "You didn't mention knowing Captain Intœño."

"The Captain has traded with Pôn since I was a child."

Intœño winked at Solineus and spoke in the islander's tongue. "The poor girl has had an affection for me since being a tiny girl." She gasped and put her hands to hips in a dramatic gesture. "And further in her defense—"he cleared his throat"—there are a dozen Captain Intœños, and the last she saw me, I helmed the *Semêyu Ûñis.*"

"You've such a big family?"

Sîu said, "Luxuns don't share their true names with foreigners."

"This is so." He smiled back and forth between them. "Such a small world that brings you two together. You are together? And me! Or is this less coincidence than I thought?"

Solineus said, "We heard through the Edan that the *Entîyu Emoñô* was expected within six months and waited for you."

"With the offer of carrying an Edan to this place, I could hardly have sailed past even if I wanted not to see you. Tell me, friends, what you want of me."

"Pôn!" Sîu laughed. "Pôn and warm winds."

A sage nod from the Captain. "We Luxuns will swim in ice, but I know your human sensitivities. With the unfortunate situation on Kaludor, I plan to turn back for the Gorôtan. These trips have been less profitable since the Shadows came, but they are still worth my time. We could catch the weather across the Monsoon Straits and be back in Pôn in six months, maybe seven, without costing either of us a Moon or Crown."

Solineus said, "I have a better idea to please this lady. We sail west to Mulshahar from here, then onward to Pôn."

A smirking grin and flat feathers. "This would freeze the profits in my hull." His head cocked, and a single feather popped higher in the middle of his head. "Mulshahar? Why?"

"I'd swear you've a special sense for profits."

"I do, except where you Silone and your demons are involved."

"And if I say Mulshahar followed by Helmveline?"

A second and third feather crept upward. "I can't sail to Helmveline."

"Nobody can, not yet. The Iron Wing of Helmveline and I have a trade arrangement."

"By river somehow?"

"One of the great rivers, the Mûulbon, spills into the Monsoon Straits and runs to an ancient city called Endeleun that we Silone have claimed."

"Your people have been busy."

"Busy staying alive, mostly. The river splits at Endeleun, and there are great falls, but one narrower river moves up toward the Dragonspan Mountains and Helmveline. The jungle is dangerous as the hells and the river too, but we've already got a road down from the north. We took a ruined city at the river's mouth in the Straits, though I can't say if we still hold it."

"I know this place; we call it Ilnôvisu."

"It might have a dozen names, but one old map of Meliu's named it Zeginhôlt, but most Silone call it Mûulbon's Mouth. Someday soon, it'll be the hub of a trade wheel between Mulshahar and Helmveline."

"You're thinking big but not big enough. You could be the wealthiest man in the world."

Solineus chuckled and rubbed the back of his neck, uncomfortable with such a prospect. "I want to make sure my people thrive, and I reckon the Smiling Men will do their best to make sure I make them wealthier first."

"Every city and kingdom has its version of Smiling Men. And there are the Boboru, too. Still, one of the wealthiest men in the world."

"How about we make each other two of the wealthiest men?"

"I'm listening."

"I've one partner now, and I could use a second. Who better than you to sail the Monsoon Straits?"

A quick breath through a smile. "There are better. All Luxuns, of course."

"They aren't standing in front of me."

"To do this right will be expensive, and I have commitments in my hull."

"I have hundreds of thousands of *smeden* in a bank in Mulshahar."

His lips puckered. "Hundreds *of* thousands, not hundreds *and* thousands?" Solineus smirked as the Luxun licked blue lips. "I've one promise to keep: getting the Edan home. Then, if I convince my crew, we sail for Mulshahar and Pôn."

"Perfect." Solineus lifted the two-hander from his back, its hilt and blade wrapped so it looked more like a long-nosed diamond in shape than a sword. "I need this hidden where no one will find it."

"We are Luxuns, not smugglers." He smiled with a roll of his shoulders. "But still, I have a couple of nooks. What is it?"

"A secret. I'll show you when we're far out to sea."

The Captain stepped back to stare. "It's not alive? The last time didn't work out well."

"No. It's metal."

"And no one is coming for it? The last time, that didn't work out well either."

"Not that I know of."

"Well, in that case, I have for it the perfect spot. I assume you and the lady would like a cabin? I've a space next to cabin mine so that we can add a bed." He stopped and turned to them. "Assuming the crew agrees to this journey, of course."

Sîu said, "Personal space would be good, especially if it has a stove to warm things."

"Can I trust you two with a fire? The last time—"

"It didn't work out so well?"

"Better than the wild beast, as no one was eaten, but it charred the deck before doused."

Solineus grinned. "I'll do my best at keeping her warm without if need be."

The Captain laughed and led them toward his cabin and whispered. "Let us hide your secret before it is a secret no more. Then we'll share a bottle, yes?"

"Sounds good." Solineus sauntered behind the Captain and leaned into Sîu's ear. "He's a different man than I remember. How well did you know him?"

"He and my father got drunk every night on his visits to Pôn, so I know him well enough to say that despite outweighing him by twenty bricks, *do not* match him drink for drink."

By sundown, Solineus decided her advice was the best he'd heard for years; the slight man drank like a Broldun but held his piss better.

Six

Realities of a Man

Mortal Statue unsituated into a fall,
by rope, chain, or chisel,
the courage to topple the dead's headstone
compares not to felling the living despot's ego.
Mortal Statue, eyes open and unseeing,
Mortal Statue, mouth closed and speaking,
Mortal Statue, ear open but unhearing,
will you fall from immortal stature?

—*Tomes of the Touched*

Seden always could cook, and the Salty Frog had been a favorite of the Choerkin men long before it was the last tavern on Herald's Watch. Even without hunger, ten days without food heightened the flavors of every bite of a meal that might once have been experienced as drab into the finest feast ever. Ivin retired to the keep alone and with a swollen belly several candles later, happy he'd made the journey, happy to have seen half a dozen souls, happy at having made Eliles happy, but curious as the hells about a young girl who appeared without warning from the stars.

More curious yet as to why their spying eyes from the stars of Skywatch had deceived them. Wondered, too, if it hadn't been deception at all, but a reality somehow dragged from his dreams.

On arriving at the empty fortress of Choerkin Keep, he barred the tower's door, and while meaning to climb high to his bed, he found himself meandering to the dining hall. He patted his swollen gut, feeling like a snake who'd swallowed a goose's egg, and stared at the room lit through windows by the eternal fire outside. His father's death on this table, poisoned by a devious monk or a Lord Priest's face, felt like a lifetime in the past. Three lifetimes, maybe. Sometimes, it felt like something that hadn't happened yet—other times, like a nightmare, a false memory that should fade upon waking.

"I sleep little and therefore awake but rarely. How can I expect horrors to fade?" His voice carried a dull, lifeless echo in the room.

Why require sleep when doing nothing when awake? Why require being awake when sleeping was so damned pointless? Eating, drinking, sleeping, pissing, all as pointless as living.

Eliles' voice echoed in his mind, "Why so angry?"

With a gasp, he awoke in the dining hall with his feet propped on the table where his father died. Rapid blinks brought on by the sting of smoke drifting from a dying fire; had he forgotten to open the flue? He glanced at the glowing embers and their smoldering billows of smoke, realizing there was something wrong with there being a fire.

He closed his eyes and leaned his head back. Of course, there was something wrong with the fire; smoke billowed from its flames to fill the room, but what did he care? Peneluple would pitch a fit, but she'd been dead fifteen years. What was done was done. His thoughts drifted, and more fire appeared in his mind's eye, the candelabra hanging above alighting. Peaceful and soothing. His mother had loved the candles and the shadows they cast dancing on the walls and ceiling.

Iron grated from the hearth—someone opening the flue—wood clunked, and fire popped and hissed. "What would your dear mother have thought of you blackening her ceiling with soot?"

He recognized the voice despite not hearing it for years, and Ivin jumped to his feet with a start, eyes clear and awake. Tokodin kneeled by the fireplace's mortared stone, wearing the drab brown robes of a monk, the scars on his face glowing in the light of the burgeoning fire. On the mantle above rested the bottle of booze The Touched had gifted the monk. "You son of a bitch, what are you doing here?"

"Correcting your fire, it seems." He stood, nabbed the bottle, and popped the cork. A quick drink later, he said, "You're still angry over my poisoning your pa? Hells, man, if you'd poisoned mine, I woulda thanked you."

The monk's father had given him the scars on his face if Tokodin hadn't been just weaving a yarn for sympathy. "I don't even know if you done that, but you're still a son of a bitch."

"No argument from me, none at all." A pull from the bottle. "What you thinkin', maybe some wicked fairy tale poisoned him instead of me?"

"The Lord Priest's Face is real. I've seen one, maybe even more than one."

"Horseshit, or maybe whore's shit. There ain't no such thing as a Face. Changing their looks, their voices, slipping inside another's reality."

Ivin shook his head with a chuckle. "Inside another's reality. A dream. I'm dreaming."

The monk saluted him with his bottle. "Right, right, you only wish it was so easy to dismiss me and send me away. To have my head stuck on a stake for flies to lay eggs in my brain after the crows eat out my eyes. I'm not so easy to get rid of as all that."

Ivin spun with his gaze trained into the shadows of the ceiling above. "Are you watching, Eliles? Watching my dreams?"

Tokodin laughed, the humor turning to shriek. "That pretty bitch? No whelp of yours will she ever carry. That tainted and painted whore of some vanquished and forgotten god?"

Ivin stomped to the man in a fury and swung, but the monk dodged the blow without bothering to take the bottle from his lips.

"I expected more from a Choerkin." Ivin's fist passed through the man's jaw. "Ouch! Please, good sir, don't hit me again."

Laughter as Ivin stepped back. "To the hells with you."

"Which hell? I can't go to them all." The monk cocked his arm to throw a punch, and Ivin didn't bother to move. Pain splintered through his cheek as the man's fist landed; caught flat-footed, Ivin fell to the floor, his head fingers from hitting the table's edge. Tokodin stepped to stand above him. "What kind of idiot stands there and lets a bloke hit him?"

Ivin rubbed his face, surprised the man hit so hard. Or rather, that he could hit him at all. "The Choerkin kind, it seems."

Tokodin offered his hand, but when Ivin grasped for his palm, his fingers passed through. Tokodin clucked his tongue with a chuckle. "This gets funnier and funnier."

He turned his back as Ivin groaned his way back to standing. "I'd kill you if you weren't already dead."

Tokodin leaned against the hearth and swigged his drink. "Dead am I? Was it your people who killed me or some fairy puck who changes faces more often than his clothes?"

Whether a dream, an apparition, or a joke sent by the gods, Ivin figured he may as well ask questions. Explore possibilities he'd mulled since the loaded and magic dice were slipped into his pocket. "The dice you gambled with in the Chanting Caverns were loaded. Magic. Did you know that?"

The monk laughed, and who could blame him? "Magic? Loaded! Good gods, I woulda won more if they were."

"Loaded against you."

"By fate and the gods? Who would care to do such a thing? Pretty little Meliu? I loved her best, you know, but it was you who took her to your bed."

Ivin tensed as a hazy vision of the priestess appeared, translucent and beautiful with hair more red than ever with the fire behind her shining through. "She cared for you. It wasn't her. Who else would've done it?"

Tokodin sniggered. "Your wicked Face?"

"Who could it have been?"

"According to your tall tales, anyone. You tell me."

"Maybe there was a Face at the Crack of Burdenis, and maybe not. But no doubt there was one here when someone murdered my father."

"Not someone. Me."

Ivin ignored him. "Were you the real you, and the Face told you to poison my father? Commanded it?"

Tokodin's words eased into a slur as intoxication settled in. He pointed with a wobbly finger. "Recall, now, that I'm just a dream who knows no more than you know." He chuckled before his Adam's apple danced with four deep swallows of liquor. "But if I were a livin' man who weren't so drunk as to piss 'imself in his sleep in a candle or three, I'd insist no. I always liked you, Ivin; you know that's a lie. You're a godsdamned Choerkin, a cocky whore bitchin' son..." He wobbled and belched, a finger tapping his head with a crooked grin. "A whore-son son of a witch, takin' pokes with all them purty girls 'cause'n of yer gods be damned lordly name. And that peeurty face of yers, so liken yer mother's."

"You never met my mother."

"But you did, and I'm you, remembers." He tapped his temple. "Keep a thinkin'."

"I don't want to believe you killed him."

"Like you don't want to believe your wee shittin' sister killed yer mother?"

The blow hit harder than the monk's fist. "Watch your words."

"Or what, ya gonna hits me again?" Another smirking drink.

It was a peculiar admittance to himself that after all these years, he'd come to agree with his father that Meris murdered them both. "I should've trusted Kotin's instincts."

"I've heard tell that the trag... one of the great tragedies of dying young is to never... Ah hell, to never what? Ah yes. To never realize how wise your dumb ass parents really were. Happy for you, he died first."

Ivin's fists clenched, but he swung with words. "How'd that work out for you?"

A finger circled in the air as he drank, and then he stared at Ivin with glazed eyes. "My pa was a genius who taught me there's no love without a belt. That there's a heap of wisdom a man can take to the grave."

"Served you well in the hells has it?"

He snorted. "The gods always carry a belt. Don't you go a doubtin' my word, Choerkin."

"On that, we agree."

Tokodin plopped into a chair. "Still sweet on One Lash, ain't ya? Oh, how many cocks she teased in Istinjoln, you'll never know."

Fingers dug into Ivin's palms as his teeth ground with eyes pinned on the hardwood floor. A breath escaped with revelation, and he looked up. "I'd never say that about her."

"Ho! Ho! Ho! Whore!" With each utterance, his head jerked, and his smile grew wider, so wide that it should take hooks to

stretch his cheeks so far. He snorted and took a drink. "Wouldn't you now? Maybe you're right, but godsdamned for certain yer wrong. I'm you."

"No."

"I'm not you?"

And for the first time since declaring this a dream, he questioned his judgment. He spun a circle, searching for anything out of place, proof of it all being in his head. And his eyes landed on the fireplace without flames, no smoke. And no smell of smoke in his nose. "Eliles! If you're watching, come to me."

Tokodin held forth his bottle. "You need this more'n I do, Choerkin."

Ivin swung his napping chair to face the monk. "We'll see."

"So confident in the Vanquished, are you?"

"Confidence in her."

He took a swig, but when Ivin looked close, the bottle appeared full. A dream. He could smell the liquor on the man's breath. "Your father was a drunk."

"You never met m' father."

"No, but I'm you. Remember?"

Tokodin pointed and laughed, liquor splashing from the mouth of the bottle. "Now you're just dicin' with my brain. But that means you're just dicin' on yourself."

"Am I? I guess you would know, me being you and you being me and all."

Tokodin's scars bunched as his cheeks scrunched. Ivin blinked, and in that instant, the face he confronted changed to his own, but the voice remained the monk's. "Has yer addled Choerkin brain ever considered, if such a farce as a Face exists, that Tokodin was the Face all along?"

For a flicker, the concept tickled his suspicions, but he'd become accustomed to foolhardy notions feeling real in dreams. But was it a dream? He glanced at the fireplace; no fire, no smoke, no embers, no sign of a fire in ages. "No." But where in between had he lost sight of Tokodin? At what point... "The boy, Joslin, the Face killed and became him."

A blink and Tokodin's visage reappeared. "Then I musta poisoned Kotin, and I deserved my drunken head on a spike."

"There was more than one Face."

The man's head lulled, resting chin to chest. "Just how many gods-damned Faces are in your dreams, anyhow?"

Ivin locked his gaze on the man. "Sit with me and find out."

Tokodin took a swig from the bottle. "Ahh, you think the pretty witch is coming to save you from a dream. The mighty warlord." Another drink before offering it to Ivin with arm outstretched.

"How the hells isn't that thing empty by now?"

"Hey now! This is my dream, too, and in my dream, the alcohol never runs out." He belched with wide eyes and grabbed his mouth. "Shits, that one about came up."

"You should've never touched the stuff, you're an ass when drunk." Ivin stared as Tokodin slugged down gulps one after another, remembering the monk getting drunk at Snow's Eye. The man was always a pain in the ass, but he wasn't always belligerent. Offensive. Insulting.

A groan broke his chain of thoughts. "You look as a man thinking a thinkin' and a thought."

"The Touched gave you that bottle."

Tokodin tapped his temple with the cork. "What of it, mighty Choerkin?"

Doors slammed, and Ivin lurched in his seat, spinning with his hand at his hip despite not having a sword. The doors to the room stood closed.

"What of it, mighty Choerkin? "

Ivin turned back. "I don't know."

Hands gripped his shoulders, and he surged to his feet, startling a fading monk.

He surged to his feet a second time, chair squawking, drowning out the echo of incoherent words.

"Are you all right?"

He spun wide-eyed, hand again at his waist and this time finding a hilt. But the blue eyes staring him in the face belonged to Eliles. Through panting breaths, he spoke, "Dreaming? Was I dreaming?"

"Yes. I was watching."

"You saw him?"

"Saw who? No. You talked in your sleep and asked for me."

He fumed a flicker, then spun to pound the table, fists hammering until sweat beaded on his brow and reason told him he was acting the fool. His forehead struck the table and stayed there until he caught his breath and laughed. "Tokodin."

A gentle hand rubbed his shoulder. "What did he say?"

"He confessed to killing my father. Sort of. And he kept drinking that damned bottle of liquor he got in the Tomb of the Touched, getting drunker and drunker." He reached for fading memories of the dream. "How well did you know him?"

"Little better than you did. He took the monk's robes years before the three of us came together. Why?"

Ivin took a deep breath and hopped up to sit his ass on the table. "He changed after he started drinking the stuff, or do I imagine it looking back?"

She giggled. "Everyone changes when they get drunk."

"How's your memory of our conversation with The Touched?"

"Not perfect, but what I recall I've repeated in my mind a thousand times. I've written down what seemed important."

"What he said to Tokodin?" She shook her head, and he deflated. "Remember anything?"

She stepped back and sat in his napping chair. "I never gave much thought to what The Touched said to him."

Ivin closed his eyes, a vision of the skeletal riddle-master dim but the bottle clear as day. He snapped his fingers and pointed at her. "He warned Tokodin. Something about its age."

"About making a dragon forget its lies."

They shared a stare. "Someone who forgets their lies is bound to be caught. What if this wasn't some ordinary liquor but magiced in a way to show his true self? His anger, the real him?"

"Bitter and withdrawing from the party. If we'd listened closer, would we have caught his true feelings? Known not to trust him? Was The Touched trying to warn us?"

"Father." Eyes clenched; missing a clue that could've saved Kotin's life was unbearable. His head rocked back as his eyes opened to stare at the ceiling. "The Touched knows so much; did he give the bottle to the monk to light the fire and kill my father? What if the bottle drove him to madness on purpose?"

Eliles' brow furrowed into doubt, but in Ivin's words, not in The Touched's intentions. "He doesn't know that much. He's seen things and knows things, but the future isn't decided. And aside from that, I think he's trying to help us."

Ivin's lips sputtered in disgust. "How can we trust a man who served the gods? I don't mean served Sol like the priests do today. He served them face-to-face during the God Wars. If you're looking for a man corrupted by their power, it's him. It's... what do you mean helping us?"

The girl blushed and shied, her eyes moving to the floor, and her beauty in that moment struck him. Her next words shattered her spell. "I've spoken with him twice while you were in the south."

A slack-jawed gaze that didn't bother to find her hiding eyes landed on her knees, and it was flickers before he recovered his voice. "How the hells haven't you told me this before?"

Demure shame turned to livid fury in an instant. "Maybe if you'd come around more than here and there, I would've had a chance to tell you."

"More than enough chances! More than enough." His teeth ground with the desire to scream I am the Warlord Choerkin. You will not keep secrets, but here on this island, he claimed no title but a simple name. "Son of a bitch!" He glanced around, wanting to throw something, but if he broke one of his mother's prized chairs, her ghost would haunt him to no end.

"Quit acting like a child."

He huffed deep breaths until the rhythm pounding his chest eased. "I'm not. And don't say that's what a child would say even if it's true."

Her scowl eased. "Fair enough."

"How did you speak with him?"

"I don't know, not really, anyhow. He found me in the stars of Skywatch and changed his story about how. But both times, his words proved useful. Solineus visited him again, too."

Ivin pinched an itch on his chin and cleared his throat. "With an Edan party, yes. Helped you how? Are you sure he isn't helping us just to help him?"

"I can't prove his motivations any more than I can prove yours, but he helped me find the adherents in the stars, amongst other things."

"Godsdamnit, I want you to tell me everything he said."

"I will."

"Good."

"Fine. But not now. Suffice to say I trust him."

Ivin wanted to trust her faith in the man but couldn't, not even when gazing into her eyes like now. "We've been manipulated and toyed with, our people driven thousands of horizons by murder and lies, so excuse me if I don't trust him."

She shrugged. "I can't blame you. You could come to the stars and see if he shows up?"

"Why so eager to get me into that godsdamned building?"

"So you can godsdamned see what's going on in the world without my telling you about it. With you by my side, we could find other people. It works best with someone who knows the people, not just their names."

"And do what if I could see? I can't get off this island."

"The Touched was in the stars and the Great Kî. Solineus brought you and left again."

"And neither of us know how except Artus saying he swam here. Got any ideas on that?"

"The point is that it's possible. If we find a way, why not know or at least have an idea of what's going on? So you know which direction to go?"

The world outside Herald's Watch evolved without him and without his time moving, or that's how it often felt. "It's easier to imagine being trapped in time and place instead of just a place."

"Even things here change. You missed the tumult, but witness our new young friend from the stars."

"Skywatch isn't... But I will. In time. Give me time."

She stood with a smile. "We have all the time you need."

The woman he'd dreamed of hundreds of times strode from the room, and as her footfalls echoed into silence, he returned to his nap-

ping chair. A cricket chirped from the direction of the kitchens, and he smiled at the normality of the song. The tune of this cricket's ancestors no doubt kept Kotin awake at night, but Ivin paid the music no mind back then and took solace from it now. Even here, where nothing was normal, a small, resolute piece of nature remained unchanged.

"Do the crickets still disturb your sleep, Father?" His smile fell at the lack of an answer. "What would you think of your son being afraid of the stars as you were?"

Seven

Murderous Debate

All things to everyone is nothing to no one,
a song in the purse and gold in the eye,
the silver in the dapple-tongued lie,
a chameleon of faces,
a chameleon of words,
a chameleon of all things to everyone,
spunk and bluster,
hissing and lisping,
one-armed and limping,
show me the how, oh Leaf-Tongued Liar.

—*Tomes of the Touched*

Meliu sat beside Sedut, both women wearing their robes of the High Priestess, both with full glasses of Helelindin wine in hand, and both staring at the same passage in the *Codex of Sol* written without encryption in Canonic Silone. Holy scholars from every clan, eleven in total today, studied them, making certain any discovery or question would be relayed to their betters.

The agreement to read and study the *Codex of Sol* was struck months ago, three times a week, minimum, since finding the book

deep beneath the city of Endelêun. By now, they'd read the thing a dozen times. By now, no one bickered over the subtleties of translation. No, the words stood plain on the page; it was the interpretation that vexed folks now. A translated riddle was no less a riddle, and this was the depressing conclusion so many came to. Still, the truth was worse: Prophecies were riddles without a single inarguable answer until the event happened, and even then, its meaning spun further riddles.

That's why wine became so important.

Meliu sipped, set her glance down, and rubbed her temples before continuing. "And the City of Oxêum, once felled, will speak to the world once more before twice, and behold, the burnt bones of destiny's hands will grasp again the life taken and take a life. The Gate of Emuluhûzu will split wide the world's womb."

Edmun of Remenok said, "Where are we on the Gate of Emuluhûzu?"

"The same place we were last week and the month before. Nowhere and everywhere."

Sedut spoke in what, for her, was a soothing tone, "Can you blame the man for asking?"

"I can, and I do." Meliu stood in a huff, spinning her chair, then clutching her head to stare at the ceiling and oak beams. "Nobody knows a damned thing about Oxeum, but oh bless me, how people want to swear the Gate of Emuluhûzu is the gate in Istinjoln, but what the hells! The demon trying to get through, her name isn't Emuluhûzu. So maybe it's the gate in the Chanting Caverns, but why name such a minor gate? Is there such thing as a minor gate that lets demons into our world? If so, or if not, who or what the hells is Emuluhûzu anyhow? Your sister's cousin's bastard brother on your mother's side, perhaps? And what about bony, burning hands? Nobody knows!"

Sedut waited flickers before saying, "All better now?"

Meliu grabbed her wine and slugged the burn down her throat until her glass was empty and her eyes watered. "Now I'm better." Sedut filled her glass, and Meliu swallowed it down, though slower. "Right. Now I'm better." She straightened her chair and sat again, but her eyes were still unwilling to focus on the page. Or maybe she was getting drunk.

The Red Wanderer Prophecy refocused, and her eyes stared at the words without reading them. She knew everything that came next, and maybe that was the problem more so than anything else. "A warlord's rise and fall and rise again the portents demand, the Warrior of Sol, the Blessed Damned in the eyes of the Bone Prophet who walks the Living Stars unbidden and unknown in his knowing, the Toucher, the Touching and the Touched. A mirror in the river of time, King Priest Esreriun the First's murder unholy and his Holy Rise and Dead Once and Dead Again Warlord after communing with Sol the Lion Forever Mighty wages war, bringing the rise and fall of Once a Queen, saving destiny's twins and destroying the binding of Forgetting since Forgotten in the darkness of Shadows living in Dark."

She stopped and looked up, shocked the group let her get so far without a question. Her outburst may have done some good.

Sedut broke the silence. "We all know the tale of Esreriun killed on the battlefield in service to Sol, battling the Totokotwonu."

Edmun said, "Killed in battle, not murdered."

"Couldn't they be one and the same? An assassin could be called a murderer even if the attack took place on the field of war."

"Yes, of course, High Priestess. But if we are here to parse words and their meaning, this one stands out. And consider the reference to a mirror. I think we all agree that Ivin Choerkin is the Warlord named."

Meliu said, "We agree, but our vision may be dictated by the times in which we live."

Edmun's head bobbed. "True, but assume we're right. The Choerkin was killed, poisoned, by a Silone. Many contend at the hand of the Ravinrin who also died. Murder, even if it was a priest who attacked him. A mirror would demand that King-Priest Esreriun, too, was killed by a Silone or an ally."

Speaking of Ivin's murder always brought a sickness to her gut, but with two glasses of wine quaffed, the burn was stronger than normal. The implications staggered her mind to the point of not wanting to consider them, even if they'd been on her mind since Solineus took Ivin's body north. "You're saying that Sol will send Ivin Choerkin back to us a vessel of his power?"

"I'm not saying it *will* happen, merely pointing out what the Red Wanderer Prophecy might say."

"The Wanderer Prophecy has flaws."

"If any one prophecy didn't, we would be farther along in our estimations of their worth and meaning."

"Esreriun was King Priest, while Ivin Choerkin almost severed the souls of thousands from the pantheon." She omitted the part where he did so because she underestimated the scroll's ability to function despite being incomplete. "Most priests believe his soul will fall to The Forges."

"Only if Sol is so vengeful that he forgets the Choerkin led the people to the holy city of Endelêun."

"We don't even know if Ivin is alive or dead."

"There are several passages in various prophecies speaking to his return, so I'd say he is."

Edmun's retorts felt directed at her and came with such accuracy aimed at her heart that she questioned if this priest wasn't the Face of Ulrikt. The possibility squelched what little of her mood was inclined to debate. "Yours is a valid opinion."

"This brings us to Kinesee and her twins, where the prophecy speaks of a queen and destiny."

"Can we at least leave her children out of this conversation for a time?" The crack of her voice brought her back to a more dignified reality. "The Touched, do we have any ideas?"

Either the topic or her flash of anger brought silence across the room. She was the only priest she knew of who had heard the story of the giant skeleton who called himself The Touched, and seeing as she promised to keep that secret, she hoped it was the former.

Edmun cleared his throat. "There are rumors of Ivin Choerkin and Eliles of Istinjoln speaking with a skeleton to retrieve what turned out to be the true Sliver of Star spoken of in several prophecies."

She wanted to scream but sighed instead. "I hadn't heard that one. Please note in your journals that a rumor speaks of a skeleton that may be the Bone Prophet."

Sedut stood. "Might I suggest we adjourn early for today?"

Meliu thought, *Dear gods, please do,* knowing that Sedut's word would carry any vote. "I put an early recess to a vote."

The number of *ayes* echoing in the chamber eliminated the need to call for *nays*, and Sedut said. "I thank you all for coming today. We will gather again in three days."

Meliu sat and pinched the bridge of her nose, staring at her eyelids until the sound of feet departing came to an end. But when she opened her eyes, she knew to expect Sedut still sat beside her.

"You might as well leave as well."

The woman grinned and raised her glass. "When there's still wine left?"

Meliu snagged the bottle and poured. "Not for long."

"You're in more of a mood than this passage in the *Codex of Sol* warrants."

"Am I?" She sipped as her free hand circled before flopping to her lap. "I am. The council meeting has me flustered."

"I suspect I know how you'd vote if the vote was due."

Voting on a change in canon was still months away, but tension already burned with a fever. "Canon will likely change, but should it? Saying nay will keep the peace between the High Priests. And maybe the clans."

Sedut leaned in her seat and stared. "Do you think young Hulerê should die for being able to heal?"

Hulerê was the young girl capable of healing the blows of The Maimer's Lash without leaving a scar, a miracle of sorts. "Of course not! But I'm not sure she should be made a priestess."

"Eliles was ordained in Istinjoln. Tell me you don't see it."

"One Lash. Yeah, I see it even if others choose not to."

"And *what* don't you choose to see?"

Meliu stared back after a big swallow of wine. "What the hells are you talking about?"

The woman smirked. "There is a saying among the Priests of Light, isn't there? Something like, 'standing too close to the Light may blind you,' am I right?"

"A warning, yes."

She shook her head with a laugh. "Speaking of standing too close... One Lash. Three lashes. Eleven Lashes. Thirteen lashes. Four of the lowest counts in the history of the Church since the Great Forgetting."

Meliu looked at her, confused. "Eliles. Ulrikt. Me. You. Enlighten me to your point."

"The Lord Priest Broldun bore forty-nine scars."

Meliu scoffed. "Everyone knew his ascension was political."

"Priests hunted the Children of the Vanquished Gods for centuries, but it wasn't until Lord Priestess Sadevu that the Church paid for their capture. The result? Her successor, Lord Priest Ulrikt, with three lashes. He raises the reward again, and the result? Eliles, with one lash."

"The tinker brought her to Istinjoln. There was no payment rumor ever spoken of."

"Me with thirteen scars for lightning. You with eleven lashes praying for Light when Dark is your *strength.* As easy as Dark comes to you, how many lashes do you think you would've born if they allowed training in Elemental Dark? Three? One? None?"

"What the hells are you saying?"

Sedut raised her hands in exasperation. "Lord Priestess Sadevu paid to bring the Children to Istinjoln, and Ulrikt was one of those, but Sadevu had stopped murdering them. She read the *Codex of Sol* and saw the Light blinding you. Ulrikt was one of those. I was one of those. *You* were one of those. With Sadevu, the Church stopped murdering the Children and *trained* them! Did your father bring you to Istinjoln because he couldn't afford to feed you or because he couldn't afford to *not* bring you to Istinjoln?"

The air left Meliu's being as the words rolled from Sedut's tongue, and tingles shivered the length of her body. A numbness and silence in her brain. It took three breaths before she could speak. "No." Her father was a wicked drunk, but selling his blood to die?

"Put the pieces together, Meliu. You know it's true even if you can't prove it."

"No." If she'd used Dark, what sort of evil would her father have believed her to be? "No."

Sedut stood and took steps toward the door before turning back. "For over four hundred years, they murdered children like us. The gifted. The chosen. Chosen by our gods! Not chosen by devils and demons or The Vanquished. You know it's true. When the time comes,

you will vote for the hundreds or thousands of children like us who died instead of serving their people and their faith. You will vote for all those children like us who will be born after."

She stalked from the room with heavy steps, the door slamming behind her. Leaving Meliu alone with the chills fading from her goosebumps, alone with her thoughts tied into knots, alone with a revelation that altered her view of herself, her father, the Church, and maybe more impossible still, altering her view of Lord Priest Ulrikt.

Eight

Questions of Motive

The Queen of Totokot bore the Scepter of Disdain into the Halls of Mokumoru with a determination of the Goddess' will, but on seeing the child's eyes of victory wavered and quaked. A mother's weakness testing the mettle of faith and devotion did she overcome, striking the boiling pots with black flames, igniting a decade of anguish for an eternity in heaven and a handful of The Conqueror's touch.

—*Fragment,*
found in the pages of The Ôxêum Codex

Kinesee awoke to the screams of children as often as she did from dreams of Ivin or Solineus returning to her, so every night she awoke, she found herself soothing someone. Some nights, she thanked the gods it was the twins instead of her, others, the polar opposite. No matter what awakened her, come the dawn, she wished for a better night's sleep come sundown.

She rolled from bed the morning of a day she couldn't put a number to, but she was pretty sure the month was Beldrên, and glanced at the plush velvet chair beside the dresser. "Hello, Nanny."

The woman, who often sat in the room to watch the children, didn't answer. She didn't so much as acknowledge that Kinesee spoke. But then, if her mouth had moved, odds were good Kinesee wouldn't have heard the words anyhow. Even when chatty, the voices of ghosts tended not to make noise except under rare circumstances.

The apparition stared in her direction, but Kinesee couldn't be sure if she saw her. Not all the time, anyhow. Once in a while, the haunt's eyes would follow her, smile at the twins, or frown when Kinesee did something silly to get her attention, but most of the time, they ignored each other. Today wasn't one of those days.

Kinesee's feet slid into furry slippers, and she trod to stand right in front of Nanny. She had tried to talk to Nanny after months of studying Canonic Silone, but the most she'd gotten in return was a quizzical stare bordering on fear. A ghost being afraid felt wrong, but some folks figured that ghosts didn't always know they were dead. Or, they feared being banished by those who could see them. Or, they feared the gods dragging them back to The Forges on being found. This woman, however, didn't look like she deserved the torment of the Forges or the Twelve Hells. If anything, she appeared a sweet lady.

"Good morning."

Today was indeed a rare day. The ghost looked up at her, and her mouth moved in response, but Kinesee heard no words. Rinold had mentioned something similar at some ruins in the jungle.

Her heart jumped, excited for anything but a blank stare. "I'm sorry, I can't hear you."

The apparition gestured to the eastern window where the sun shone.

"Yes, good morning. I wish I could hear you."

The ghost stared.

Kinesee stared.

Kinesee giggled from frustration. "I'm sorry! I can't do this." She turned, strode to the door leading into the sitting room, and snuck inside. She whispered, "Good morning, real nanny."

Netebel smiled. She wasn't much younger than Kinesee at fifteen, a daughter of solid Choerkin stock whose parents now raised goats on the fields outside the city. Tinker, Kinesee's little black devil of a goat, spent much of her time eating and frolicking with their herd, so she'd gotten to know her family. They were also fisherfolk like Kinesee's real parents back on Kaludor, which endeared the girl to her even more. "The ghost is here?"

Kinesee nodded, and the girl slipped to the door to peer into the bedroom. "Where?"

"The chair."

Flickers later. "I wish I could see her."

Kinesee looked back and sighed. Nanny sat gazing their way. "She's there. Trust me."

"Oh, I do."

"How are the twins? I didn't want to wake you this morning, but they weren't going to let me sleep."

"They were bears earlier, but they sleep like angels now."

"Figures."

"Don't it, though?"

"Can you sit with them and call the wet nurse when they awake? I fear I'll be busy this morning." The idea of a wet nurse had brought terror at first, the idea of someone else feeding her children, but Kovin and Neesebelu had appetites enough to torture her breasts. She looked forward to the day of weening them and held a great deal more sympathy for Tinker's ordeals with her babies.

"I can and will, m'lady."

She gazed at the cribs and the sleeping blond heads. "I feel guilty leaving them." For the first four months, she left their sides only when nature and duty demanded, but today, she hadn't tried to weasel her way out of her duty as hard as she might have.

"They are asleep, and they will be fine. They have two nannies, after all."

"I have indeed. Thank you."

She stepped back into the bedroom to find Nanny gone from her chair, but Nileu, her handmaiden, waited for her. Within wicks, she was presentable to the world and stepped into the hall where she gained a four-man escort clad in maille who followed her to the Great Hall of Endelêun Palace.

She entered the room prepared to be the last to arrive, and her expectations didn't disappoint. "Sorry, I'm late."

Tedeu Ravinrin smiled. "You missed nothing but banter anyway, my dear."

Kistenu Broldun smirked. "I'm not sure why you're here anyhow. Clan Emudar sits on islands a thousand horizons away."

Kinesee took her seat next to Roplin Choerkin. "I can at least keep my grandfather informed of decisions made here via pigeon." The first generation of birds trained to fly from Endelêun to Molikîn took to the air a month ago, lending a bit more speed to communications reaching Mulshahar and, from there, Adinvan Mikjehemlut.

Roplin said, "And as my sister-in-law, I appreciate her input."

Kistenu said, "You are here and welcome. I was saying I understand that with twins, we'd understand you missing a meeting."

Tedeu cleared her throat. "We're all here, minus Warlord Broldun, which answers whether he has returned or not." Chuckles from around the table. "This, then, raises the question of why we're here. Wiirê scouts have, at long last, found Silonê slaves in a Histê city."

Murmurs from around the table before Locust Mulharth asked the question that had popped into her head in an instant. "And your boy, Locust?"

"My grandson, who I raised after his parents Walked the Starry Road, bless them. There's no way to know if he is among the slaves, but does it matter?"

"It does. Clan-blood —"

"Mustn't be valued more than all those others willing to give their lives. Everyone taken was a warrior who fought for our survival."

Kinesee's mouth opened before she knew what words would come out. "I hold my tongue often, but not now. Emudar will support any move to free them."

Locust eyed her. "No offense to the daughter of Mikjehemlut, but your father and grandfather are safe on the islands."

"My grandfather harasses our enemy to distract them from Endelêun, and my father... nobody knows where he is, but with his penchant to charge into trouble, how many think wherever he is makes him safe?" Chuckles around the table. If we have the chance to save our people, we must."

Locust gave her the slightest of nods. "Is there a chance? Where have they been found? Behind bars or working in fields? Fighting in the pits?"

"The city of Ghustusvarênu, though I may butcher the pronunciation." She raised a hand to halt any questions. "All I know is it's far to the west of here but not so far as the Medrisên Coast. Some of our people worked in the fields, and others fought in the arenas."

"They could be dead before we get there."

"Of course. But they might not be."

A door creaked open, and when Kinesee glanced, she caught sight of Meliu slipping into the room.

"How many horizons? Five hundred? A thousand? And when we get there, how many guards do we face?"

Tedeu kept her composure. "You know I don't have those answers. An old wive's tale says the strongest twin is born first and second, the wisest. Perhaps that's why your father gave your younger twin his name instead of you."

Kinesee grinned. The matron of the Ravinrin had the politest temper she'd ever known.

"You insult my father now?"

"Only a Mulharth wouldn't realize I insulted you. Where is your brother, Borun? We could use some wit on your side of the table."

Roplin stood and banged the table with his fist before words caught fire. "Lady Ravinrin, I understand your aggravation, but Locust's questions are not out of line."

She cast the Choerkin a cold stare. "If my grandson is alive, I will have him back."

"Nobody is saying you won't, gods willing, but we can't just go traipsing into Histê territory and take them. We'll need to coordinate with Wiirê tribes, locate our people, and get them out alive. Losing more of our people to the slavers or seeing them killed in a noble but hopeless effort is not an option."

Kinesee said, "Adinvan and the Emudar might know the city if it's closer to the coast."

Tedeu said, "The Wiirê spoke of the city as sitting beside a river that leads to the Medrisên Sea, but it will take months to send messages back and forth."

"I'm not saying it'll be easy."

Meliu's voice rose as she walked toward them. "If I might interrupt?"

Roplin said, "If your words are useful, by all means, high priestess."

"I've spoken with several of the Wiirê who brought the good word of our people found alive, but the information is second-hand. Ghustusvarênu is hundreds of horizons away but less than fifty from the coast—a big city with thirty thousand souls at least. However, from what I hear, these cities aren't as formidable as the great cities of the Tek: low walls and half a dozen gates. People come and go as they please. And why not? Who the hells could invade them?"

Kinesee said, "So, we send word to the Emudar and let them figure it out."

"Well, yes. But we can't just send a message. Best we know, none of the Emudar speak Wiirê. Without help from the local tribes, how far will they get?"

Tedêu leaned in her seat. "What are you suggesting?"

"I'm suggesting you send me and my Wiirê friends to the islands. Or Mulshahar. Wherever I can meet up with the Emudar."

Meliu was a hero to the Silone people, but everyone knew to fear her, and fear bred mistrust, in particular with anyone from the Church who betrayed its people. Despite knowing her better than anyone else in the room, Kinesee still didn't trust her motivations to be pure, so she spoke what she wagered everyone else thought. "What do you gain from this?"

Meliu's brows arched in shock, and a pang of guilt struck Kinesee's gut. "For me? I'll remind you that I tried to save them once before. I almost died in killing the Breath Stealer."

"Is the Council of High Priests sending you?"

"No."

"Which raises my question with even more sincerity. What do you gain?"

Meliu stared, and Kinesee locked eyes with the priestess. She wanted to say something, her lips twitched, but whatever it was, she didn't want to say it aloud.

Tedeu saved them both, standing with hands planted on the table. "I don't care. She is right, and right is right. If her offer is sincere, then I accept it. I don't care why. Just save my boy."

Kinesee bowed her head to stare at her toes. "Lady Ravinrin is, of course, right." She raised her eyes. "But we need to talk."

Meliu's lips twitched, and if it were anyone else, she'd say the priestess was nervous to speak with her. "Of course. I have time now."

Roplin stood, "Whoa, whoa, whoa. No one but Tedeu and Kinesee have agreed to this, this... out of the wilds notion. If a Histê army comes, we will need you. It's a grave risk and one I'm not sure the Church will approve of."

Kinesee said, "So we are sending *someone*?"

"I didn't say that."

Meliu said, "I don't plan on giving anyone a choice."

Kinesee said, "We need to talk." She stood and faced the clan lords and ladies. "I'm sure you have business to attend to where I'm unneeded. As has been pointed out."

Kinesee strode straight past the shorter priestess, the woman following close behind. Once in the hall, Meliu said, "The twins are well?"

"Their eyes aren't glowing with the Fire of Sol, nor were their first words to spout prophecy." Kinesee turned as they reached an empty alcove, and the door closed behind them. "Does your journey have anything to do with Ivin? Do you still love him so much?"

Her face surpassed the shock of earlier. "No!" The shock faded. "Sort of."

"What the hells do you mean sort of? What do you know that I don't?"

"Nothing, and that's the trouble. I need to know."

"You need to know more about my husband than I do?"

Meliu met her gaze this time. "Not how you think. You love him. He's the father of your children, so of course you need to know if he lives, but for me, I need to know... prophecies. Now that I've read the original work... You remember hearing of how Ulrikt came back to life in Istinjoln?"

"Yes, of course." Though, in truth, she'd have to admit having paid little attention back in those days.

"The Sliver of Star was prophesied as raising the next King Priest from the dead."

The priestess stared at her, eyes widening as if she should understand. And in flickers, she did. "No. Ivin, a king priest?" The notion was worthy of a laugh.

"King or king priest, the difference in Canonic Silone can be a tick on a single letter. And if he was raised from the dead by the Sliver after seeking guidance from Sol? What priest would deny him the title? He was a step and stumble from king already."

"He's trapped in the tower of Fire." The woman's face was a stark blank. "You're saying he could come back to us?"

"I don't want to give you false hope, and it might be more nightmare than dream. If he communed with Sol, he might not be the man we knew."

"The soul stone kept his spirit from the Starry Road."

"Maybe. Look, we don't even know if he's alive. Things are happening in the Church, and they point in maddening directions before coming to unpredictable ends. We don't know for certain; we suspect the *Codex of Sol* is part of a collection. The prophecies hint only at the times after our arrival here."

"More books; more prophecies?"

"Yes. And histories. But if I talked to Solineus, I could learn, maybe, how worried I should be."

"It's so scary?"

She licked her lips. "It could be. Or not."

"The Nesfereum? Rin?" It had been ages since she'd thought about the people who might still want her dead because of some prophecy.

Meliu's lips pinched. "No one has tried to kill you for a long time."

"What aren't you saying?"

The priestess checked the hall in both directions before speaking. "I'm not sure what the Nesfereum wants with you. This is gonna sound crazy as the hells." Kinesee knew it was true as the priestess broke into speech patterns from her villager life.

"Crazier than what I've seen already?"

"A white lion. I've seen a white lion several times."

"Visions?"

"Yes, and more. He's looking for someone, maybe you."

"And now you think to tell me?"

"He's not evil! He helped me. Maybe it saved Ivin's life if it was saved."

Kinesee stared, her thoughts awhirl with what she'd learned of Rin, brother and enemy of Sol, known as the Ice Lion. "If Ivin's destiny was to be a king priest for Sol, why would Rin help Ivin? Why look for me?"

"I. Don't. Know. Competing prophecies? That's why I need to know more. And I have a chance to save those men. I can't turn my back on them."

"You're hiding something."

Meliu laughed. "I'm always hiding something because, after a time, I'm talking out of my ass! Dancing Bastards, don't you get it? You won. You married him, you had his children—"

"And right now, he might be in the arms of Eliles."

The words were like a punch to the priestess' chest, knocking the air from her. "I'm so sorry." She shuffled her feet, staring at the marble tiles before making eye contact again. "Look. There will be a meeting of High Priests, and I think the result will feed a line of prophecy that runs straight to Ivin. I don't even know if Solineus is on Pôn, or in Mulshahar, or fighting godsdamned Shadows of Man on Kaludor, but if the line of prophecy continues the way I guess, I'll find him in Mulshahar, the city of Red-Gold domes. Any answers he has about Ivin might help me."

"And I can't go with you. I'm useless." Her stomach twisted, and she realized she hadn't eaten anything.

"A mother is never useless unless she isn't being a mother."

"I stink with a sword, I can't go nowhere... but I'm good on a horse. How pointless is that?"

"You, pointless? You've negotiated with kings and maybe saved your people. You led us to the original *Codex of Sol.*"

Kinesee sighed at the remembrance of heady days. "The past. All the past."

Meliu grinned and put a hand on her shoulder. "The White Lion doesn't look for you because you're unimportant."

"Maybe he doesn't anymore."

"No, he does. My bet is that Ivin isn't the only Choerkin referred to the other codices."

"Maybe his children. Go on, you get going. I'll do my best with the clan lords."

Meliu hugged her, a surprising gesture that stiffened Kinesee's spine. "I'll send word as soon as I hear anything."

All she mustered in response was, "Thank you."

Meliu released her from the awkward embrace and disappeared down the hall as Kinesee stood uncertain of what to say to the lords. *I*

could leave them; they don't expect my return, but her feet carried her back to the hall anyhow.

All eyes turned to her as she strolled back to her seat.

Roplin squinted her way. "Well?"

"She has an ulterior motive, but her heart is in the right place."

"Meaning what?"

"She feels she owes the men she tried to save once, of course, but she hopes to find Solineus in Mulshahar, something to do with Ivin and the prophecies in the *Codex of Sol.*"

Roplin snarled, "Of course it does. That cursed tome."

"We should help her the best we can."

Tedeu's voice came strong, "Clan Ravinrin will send warriors and supplies even if nobody else will."

Kinesee said, "Emudar has no men to send until she reaches the Medrisên Sea, but the Choerkin?" She cast Roplin a sidelong glance.

"Of course, she will have Choerkin support."

Locust sprawled in his seat, an unenthusiastic frown beneath his mustache. "Mulharth, too. Whatever is needed."

Within a wick, the seven clans agreed, a rarity these days. *Maybe I'm not totally useless. Just mostly.*

The lords departed the hall within wicks of the decision, and Kinesee meandered toward her bedroom with bodyguards in her wake. Toward the twins. Toward the mundane life of a mother... *Mundane? Who am I kidding?* She laughed at herself, and her strides picked up pace.

As she climbed the final stair leading to her chambers, the memory struck her, and she spoke aloud to herself. "In my dream that led to the *Codex of Sol*, there was a mural of Sol and Rin fighting, and Rin turned to look at me. Rin is looking for me." She stopped in stride as she approached her door, and her escort almost tripped over themselves behind her.

Meliu said it: Kinesee led them to the original *Codex of Sol.* If such a singular book could be found in Endelêun, why not others? Priests searched the tunnels but found nothing, but maybe they weren't the right eyes to find them. Maybe it was Kinesee's destiny.

She smiled, looking forward to seeing the twins and looking forward to a search that would drive Alu crazy. That's what little sisters were for, after all.

Nine

Picking Roads

The Tumultuous Terror makes the riddling winds,
the words spoken to carry to echo to fade to scramble,
in fame the Lame Dame, not of Fire.
Sinister slithers the soul of the Craven Raven
once innocent in the sublime...
what time? Why, hello! meaning goodbye
buried amid small talk in between where the truth rides
scrambled words to straighten thoughts.

—*Tomes of the Touched*

"I dream of mountains and snow, and you godsdamned brung me to a sweltering flatland." Rinold agreed to join the Warlord Broldun on his expedition because the notion of sitting in the saddle without buildings and suffocating walls sounded better than sitting cooped and wondering when a ghost would spring up from nowhere and disappear again. Puxele and others dismissed the spooks as harmless apparitions as if they were the trick of sun or mirrors, but a ghost in jungle ruins killing a man before his eyes had buggered his ability to shrug them off.

Polus said, "Quit yer bitchin', little man, or next time I'll leave you to yer snottin' toddler."

Rinold snorted as his horse stumbled in a hidden rut, one of thousands buried in grasses high enough to tickle the horse's belly. "That snottin' toddler snores less than you."

Trading barbs aside, the Sundumdobu Plains—as one of Meliu's old maps named them—bored him to the point he missed the jungle. Until he recalled all the mosquitoes and other biting insects. So far, at least, the plains didn't seem so eager to kill him as the jungle, though that might change if the hundred horsemen riding behind abandoned him. Prides of lions, proper lions with manes, watched them from atop stone outcroppings, and packs of wolf and dog-like critters sometimes eyed them from afar, but he reckoned these flatlands were like the jungles, where the most dangerous beasts were the ones you didn't see.

The most dangerous of all were the Histê, the people they were out here scouting for to begin with.

A rumble so powerful the vibration shook through hooves, to saddle, to his sore ass, and first, he looked to the clear blue skies for a thunderstorm from the east. Nothing, and still nothing, when he scanned the horizon in every direction.

His first instinct in the confusion was to stop and listen, but even as his balled fist raised to signal a halt, heels tapped the horse's ribs, and he rode up the next rise until cresting its crown. The view brought him and everyone behind him to a stop as soon as they topped the hill. A herd of beasts stretched far as the eye could see, blackening the valley below for horizons. Most appeared bovine, similar to the cattle raised in the Tek nations, though he wagered them twice the size, but the herd wasn't a single species. Deer bigger than he ever dreamed grazed in smaller clusters outside the main group, and monstrous tawny-haired beasts with long, curling tusks and great seven-pronged horns sprouting from their heads stood tall and imposing right in the midst of the flow, their legs like massive trees.

Polus spat. "Now there's a godsdamned stampede I don't wanna see."

"Aye. I also don't wanna see anythin' that could scare such monsters *to* stampede."

"Agreed."

Rinold watched as the mass moseyed through the valley, leaving a swath of trampled land behind them, amazed that their numbers rumbled the hills at their pace. "If a man could domesticate a few of those, he'd never go hungry."

"You sure you ain't got a little Broldun in you, always thinking with your belly? It'd take a city wall for the fence, which helps explain the walls of Fôlgumhîêr. But who the hells is gonna scoop the great piles of shit once you tame one?"

"For a Broldun, you make surprisingly accurate points."

"One thing for damned sure, them critters aren't gonna help us find the Histê we're looking for."

The herd wasn't a solid mass, with gaps as they grazed, sort of a living river with potential fords. "I doubt those giants would even see us as a threat. We might ride right on through without them givin' us a mind."

The thought sounded crazy even as he spoke it, and Polus gave him a twisted-lipped smile. "You really wanna take that chance?"

"Nope. What the hells would you even call those tusked and horned behemoths?"

"Why don't you ride on down and ask, seein' as you aren't a threat?"

"Genuine genius."

"Nah, genius is sitting here and waiting for them things to clear out of the valley before we move on."

A dozen men scythed tall grass around them, bundling for the horses to feed but more to keep some toothy monstrosity from walking

or slithering into camp unseen. If bedding for the night, they'd clear an even wider piece of ground.

Rinold sat on a tied twist of grass for an impromptu chair, staring at the river of flesh passing below when Polus strolled to his side. "It's one hells of a sight, eh Squirrel?"

"Puxele would love it."

"Not my Irose." He laughed as he stepped to snag a bundle of grass, pulling it back with him to sit. "Never much for the wilderness or animals, her, except to cook and eat 'em."

"That much they have in common. When the Wiirê had me dangling in a cage, I prayed and swore I'd never leave her side again if I ever got back to her. Yet somehow, here the hells I am in the middle of nowhere. It ain't fair to her."

"Fair's somethin' you think on when somethin' bad has happened to you or you've got too much time to think. You think my being here is fair?"

"I'd suppose she's grateful your ass is elsewhere."

He chuckled. "Maybe for a day or so. Them beasts down in that valley don't waste time on fair. I've heard tell that great men don't give the notion a second thought."

"I've never been in the head of a great man to know."

"Mmmm, sure, neither have I. You think when Solineus runs one of those latcu Twins straight through some bastard's steel armor, he thinks twice about how unfair it is he has them swords?"

"No. I suppose I never gave it a second thought m'self."

"That there's because there are bigger things than fair in life. Fair is for dice and horse racing, not life and death."

If they found a Histê patrol, they wouldn't get down from their horses to make it more fair, and for a flicker, it felt like they should. "What the hells do you think them Histê were doing out this way?"

Finding the tracks of men through the grass of these plains stood as impossible without luck, in particular after two weeks gone by. And that was if they managed to find a trail to start with.

"You know I don't know, or we wouldn't be out here."

"You're warlord now, you're supposed to know shit."

"I'm the wrong man for knowin' things, always been better at killing. Leastwise clobberin' folks."

Rinold reached into his haversack, pulled out a flask of Broldun whiskey, took a swig, and offered the big man a drink. "You like to sound like a fool, but you ain't one."

Polus raised a hand to the flask. "Save mine for the night's fire. The Wiirê didn't give us much to go on. No cities for a hundred horizons we know of and no roads they knew of."

"Old roads could be buried like they were in the jungle."

Polus pulled a strand of grass and stuck it between his teeth for a nibble. "What if that's it? Might the sons of bitches be looking for an old road?"

"Why?"

"Well—"the stem wiggled up and down as he took a moment to think"—we're in dry times now, but what're these lands like in the rainy season? Muck, I'd wager, in particular, where herds like that pass, more'n enough to slow down an army. Peoples long gone woulda had roads."

Rinold snorted. "Like I said, you ain't the fool you play. It's a guess, but a decent one."

"Good nuf we should keep an eye out ourselves. What else?"

"Ruins."

"A castle."

"So they can sit and hunker down?"

Polus chuckled. "A place to stow nuts, Squirrel, but no. The *Codex of Sol* and my dear son of a bitch father had a few words in common.

Folks tend to think of them as a place to defend, but the real point of a castle, any fortress, is to project power. Best with cavalry, but footmen will suffice."

"Spending enough time with Meliu to read so much Codex, I'm surprised the wife has left you alive."

He snorted. "She's a flame-haired beauty, but lil Meliu is scarier than my bride any day. Don't tell Irose that, mind."

"I won't." Rinold thought of castles for a flicker. "A fortress would be more important for them, seeing as we have the horses. Any ordinary camp could end up worse than Fôlgumhîêr." Memories of the battle haunted him still, women and children dying in the fever and flames of combat.

"Or the bridge. They won't go throwin' some army at us without a plan again."

"They need a place to call home, a base."

Polus' face scrunched. "If my father was sittin' in their camp handing out advice, it'd be the river."

"The river is quite a ways from where folks spotted the bastards, and floating down is easier than up." He watched as the herd thinned below, aged and sluggish beasts following up the rear, and tried to think like a warrior instead of a tracker. "They were rebuilding that city down south when we done interrupted. They shit 'emselves thinkin' of the ghosts of Endelêun, I guarantee it; they want Mûulbon's Mouth back. The southern Histê anyways."

"Now we're thinkin' alike. They want to cut the thread between. Control the river."

"Block reinforcements."

"And supplies."

Rinold puffed and whistled. "I don't recall seein' no marks down the rivers on Meliu's maps. You?"

"Nah, but rivers change. Or at least they can. Hells, if you believe in the Great Forgetting, the godsdamned world changed. The maps are a roll of the dice, assuming... not a word I like much, but assuming the world changed more than the thinking of kings, there'd be castles and cities along a big old river. And come to think on it, them who went down the river never mentioned old towers or nothin'."

"Nor bridges and roads. And a road is going to be tricky to find if we don't know where to look." He cast his gaze to the trailing members of the herd below, beasts with limps and small groups of lithe deer with straight horns. A swath of barren ground stretched back and over the hill. "We've got a road below."

Polus arched his back and stared. "Your eyes are good if you see bricks."

"No, but you made my point for me. Some of them roads in the jungle sat beneath a hand or more of dirt. Buried like that and with this grass atop? We won't find them. But if this herd crossed the road, we might."

"A mighty slim might. Slimmer seein' as we don't know it's what they're looking for."

"Been a week, and we sure haven't found them. On foot, not so much taller than the grass, who sees who first? If we're right about them and a castle, it wouldn't hurt none to be moving south and warning them at Mûulbon's Mouth."

Polus whistled. "I'm warlord now, and you got a wife with a temper; we don't wanna be gone so long."

Rinold chuckled. "Agreed. Let's follow this new road for a time, two or three days, find nothing we cut for the river, and half ride back to Endeleun, the other half ride for Mûulbon's Mouth to see if they've had any warnings."

Polus grunted with a nod. "What the hells're we waiting for? Let's ride."

Rinold grinned at the man as the Broldun leaned to stand. "We didn't have herds like this on Kaludor, but I wager predators follow the road too, looking for the old and dying."

Polus sat back down. "Whiskey then. Let's give the meat eaters a candle or two to pass."

Rinold handed him the flask. "You'll enjoy it. I filched it from some fool Broldun's private stash."

Polus saluted before taking a swig. "I'm impressed. A Broldun and his whiskey aren't so easily parted."

They sipped and stared as vultures swept from the sky to land on a pile trampled into something unrecognizable, and wicks later a pride of forty-two lions, the four males looking like they weighed as much as a horse, sauntering to the sides. Vultures scattered, but the great cats ignored the dead meat and the people sitting on the hill watching.

Rinold sat with legs twitching to jump onto his horse and flee. He'd grown used to mountain lions on Kaludor, but these things would make snacks of those cats. *They're a good quarter to half a horizon away, plenty of time to get the hells out of here.* The words soothed his rational nerves, but another part of his brain screamed like a monkey being sized up for dinner. Despite looking their way, the pride continued onward, leaving the dead untouched for the return of vultures.

They waited for another half-candle before watering their mounts and following the desolated path east. The ground clopped harder beneath hooves, the soil pounded and packed until the next rain, and he wondered about his theory of it revealing a lost road. By nightfall, their trail curved southeast, and they'd found nothing, so they made camp on an overlook for a fireless meal and what amounted to more of a nap than a night's sleep with yapping, howls, and roars interrupting their snores much of the night.

Rinold hefted weary feet into stirrups at the crack of dawn and worked out the saddle pains in his ass a half-candle later. Lunch consisted of hard biscuits and jerky, harder and jerkier with every day on the plains, and he wondered again how the Broldun talked him into this ride. Wondered how it'd been so *easy* to talk him into this ride was more like it.

But toward midday, the clunk of hooves changed, more hollow in their reverberation, though he doubted hollow was the right word. A change so subtle he almost missed it before calling a stop. He climbed from the saddle and took a knee, stabbing the ground with his dagger and prying dirt four times before hitting stone. He stood, took a shovel from the side of his saddlebags, and dug, the clunks suspicious enough to convince him he was hitting something other than a random rock about three fingers beneath the surface.

It didn't take long for him and two other men to clear a piece of cut granite big enough to be his coffin. He stepped back to admire centuries-old rock. "Don't know if it's a road or not, but sure as shit, it ain't there by accident." He pulled a compass from his pocket, a gift from Wayfinder Kurin. "The length points due north-south, so I'd wager this road runs east-west if built like those in the jungle."

Polus dropped from his saddle with a thud and pulled a pick from another man's saddle bag. He strode east and struck a blow to the ground with a clunk, proving he found stone. Rinold followed him all the way to where the grass still grew tall and was rewarded with a rocky thud as the tip penetrated the ground a few fingers deep.

Polis grinned. "Well, Squirrel, we found some nuts, but how the hells do we follow them?"

A shiver ran Rinold's spine until his scar twitched. He spun, eyes dancing over the hills until alighting on men watching them from atop a northern hill. "We got visitors."

Polus grunted and stared. "Histê? Wiirê?"

"Too far for me to guess."

"Six of 'em. We could ride them down and find out."

"Six could lead to a thousand easy enough. One Breath Stealer and we all might be dead."

Polus shifted his weight and hefted the pick over his shoulder. "Aye, we see how it works, don't we? They're scared of our horses and steel while we're scared of their magic, and peace is kept."

"For a time, but how long?"

"Until someone believes they have the advantage, or until they see no other choice but doom."

Rinold chortled as he strode back toward his horse. "You're soundin' more and more like an educated man, hanging around Meliu and them books."

"Sad that I couldn't make it all the way through my life as a drunken fool, but I made it farther'n most, mmm?"

"A point to be proud of for—" Six figures stood down the herd trail to the west. "What the hells." He spun to face north—no one there—and when he turned back to the west, they were gone. He pointed. "Did you see them bastards?"

"See who?"

"Did any of you on horseback see men to the west?"

Orinôk Tugarn, a Broldun cousin, pointed and said, "Just them on the hill."

Rinold turned to see the group still there, shifting their stances maybe but otherwise unmoved. "Hells, I think I'm goin' crazy." A chill pimpled his arms despite the heat and sweat beneath his armor as he stepped into the stirrup, rising into the seat because deep down, he knew crazy was wishful thinking.

The Broldun's horse spun with his weight as he mounted. "What's your problem, Squirrel?"

"Six men yonder, six men gone, and six men where they started." He spat and faced the horsemen, standing in his stirrups to yell. "Silone! Men of Kaludor! Eyes open! No nappin' in the saddle! We got more'n animals to worry upon."

"You're shittin' yerself over six men?"

"My eyes are better'n yours, and I know what I saw. Good news, it might mean there ain't no Breath Stealer. Bad news is it's ghosts or somethin' we haven't met afore."

"Think we can follow the buried road?"

"Nope, but east to the river and back to Endelêun is sounding better and better."

"Ride out!" Polus waved his arm and flicked his reins. "I'm thinkin' ghosts have you plum ratt— Shits."

Rinold followed his gaze to the hill, and six figures were gone. "Got me plum what?"

"Godsdamned things just faded away like a mirage."

It didn't take long for Rinold's eyes to land on the hill to the south, farther away, but two-legged dots stood watching them. "We shoulda brought us more priests."

TEN

Squatter's Paradise

A sense of reality is nothing more than the scent of sweat, blood, and decay. Joy, fortune, and hope are the delusions that survive the common and noble alike until the day's reality, the year's reality, and the lifetime's reality show its mocking and unavoidable face one last time.

—Nekark Ar-Bdêin,
Three days before his execution

Lôdumâ Ar-Bdêin rested his chin in his palms as he eyeballed the checkered board and carved-stone figures. The warrior astride his horse served to remind him of how long it'd been since sitting in the saddle to ride in anything but circles. He dreamed of the hunt, with hounds baying, the thunder of hooves, and the rush of wind on his face. A gray fox dashed into the woods, leaping a stream, but his arrow flew true and skewered the animal before it reached a thicket.

"Where the blazin' bedamned are you?"

Lôdumâ's head lolled to gaze at Gimin. Glistening black eyes stared back without a hint of whites; his eyes darkened years ago by the Silone witch, Meliu. The man's mind took months to recover from

the horrors the woman set upon him, but his eyes refused to recover even after years, and it made Lôdumâ wonder if it altered his view of the world. "I believe a bear was about to try and steal my kill. Or perhaps we were to be set upon by a sounder of boars."

In the past, the man might've laughed, but Gimin sat as an emotionless brute. "These walls will drive you crazy as a eunuch in a whorehouse."

"At least the entirety of your humor isn't gone."

"Was I funny?"

Lôdumâ didn't bother to answer, instead glancing at his luxurious prison: Tables and chairs of burled walnut, ceramic vases filled with flowers, gold filigreed platters and basins, and a silver spittoon bejeweled with garnets and amethysts spoke of wealth in search of grandeur to spend it on. He couldn't help but wonder what sort of man commissioned such works; one might as well slap diamonds on a shit-house seat.

Life without a purpose, or at the least distractions, was proving unworthy of living. "What word from... I'll be damned. From anywhere?" Even within a dozen horizons of Gomjon and three weeks of riding from Bdein, they caught little news of the world outside their seclusion. Lôdumâ and his people claimed Noduhom Manor after the lord of its lands abandoned it to death and Rot; as far as anyone knew, the Noduhom family fled to find decimation at the whims of disease and would never return. Squatting in luxury wasn't so different than being born a lord; he didn't belong in either, but there was no way to stop him. Two weeks ago, Gimin and his riders left the grounds for the first time in six months, forays to villages they deemed safe. They'd settled into a game of Battlefield a candle ago, hoping the distraction would relax him before any bad news. The strategy might've worked if not for his bishop falling into a trap.

"You're sure you wanna know? You're running out of vases for flowers."

"There you go with that humorless humor again." He grinned but received a flat stare in return. "But not to worry, plenty adorn the lady of the manor's room if needs come to it." He eyeballed his bishop, surrounded by a knight and two archers. He used to love playing war, dreaming of the day it would be real, but now the tiny figures taunted him with the unlivable dream. "Bdein?"

"The bishop keeps the gates barred, no one in or out. Legal like anyhow."

"Five bedeviled years!" Lôdumâ surged to his feet with a flail, sending the pieces scattering across the room. At least they were stone instead of ceramic. The bishop caught his eye, the piece standing straight and staring his way. He cleared his throat before straightening with a deep breath.

"I've cheerful words as well. Duke Nevrin is dead."

The Ar-Bdêin cocked his head. "At least there is some beauty left in the world. Rot got him?"

"Executioner's ax by command of the bishop."

"Better if the roles were reversed, but we're forced to take what boons we receive. What for?"

"Official word is he smuggled a dozen young women into his castle for his pleasure, defying quarantine. Rumor is he sent assassins for the bishop."

"Who is on the block next, duke or duchess?"

Gimin chuckled this time. "The seat is vacant with most of the Marbôdun line burned and swept into the Mighty River."

"There must be some sycophant who wishes to keep their head. Titled positions don't go unfilled."

"The scuttlebutt is the bishop will seat some child of four years."

"The king's law is fourteen—"

"Precisely. A holy regent will oversee the seat until the child is of age and after a decade in the grips of the bishop."

Lôdumâ stalked to a window and gazed over the garden two stories below. The sun shown from a cloudless blue sky to glorify precise rows of blue, red, yellow, and white rose petals. Gardening was the one freedom he could give the people who followed him, as leaving the security of the manor walls risked the ire of the bishop's patrols. He opened the window, greeted by a warm breeze. "She's overstepping her own doctrine."

Gimin laughed, but it wasn't a happy sound. "And who to stop her? The king? The simpering fool hasn't set foot from Nardôk since he fled the Rot. He's the son of a bitch who signed the reins over to the demon bishop to begin."

Lôdumâ leaned on the sill, head ducked. "Tandunbô was a good man once. He might've been a great king."

"And you mighta been the Grand Duke of Bdein while I hand-selected your harem, but thus sings our follies. Hold. Lomik the Fourth is king, not Tandunbô."

"He took the name upon his crowning. We played together as boys. I bloodied his nose, he bloodied my lip, and I broke his arm. That was the last time our parents left us alone."

"But a good man, you say?"

His memories faded to grays over the years, his youth now more of an impression. "I believe so. A crown is heavy enough with the noble court fighting for and clutching your ear, and that without Rot ravaging the cities."

"And a bishop punching rings into every noble's nose. She's a tiny woman with a lion's desires."

Lôdumâ strolled to the bishop piece and its stone gaze and kicked it across the room. "We need the king in power."

"Power can't take the man; the man must take power. This king is unwilling."

"The quarantines must end."

"Or the Bishop is wise; fear of the Rot might be the only thing keeping Thôn from riding across the Humulîn."

"Agreed." The Rot didn't hit Thôn as hard as Hidreng if reports remained trustworthy. City gates staying closed might signal the enemy to stay away, but it was a desperate tactic suggesting the bishop feared Thôn. Fear was rational, but Lôdumâ imagined the woman's unwavering faith in Pulvûer might preclude fear of mortal and immortal enemies alike. "She is clever and the Hidreng in a bitter place, but I think hers is a play for power."

"Queen Ulmeen, you think?"

"No, she'd prefer a stick rammed up the king's ass to make him a puppet. What of the surviving numbers in Bdein?"

"Can't say, with confidence anyhow. Fifty thousand? Seventy-five? But the number dwindles, whatever it is, even if it means they're eating each other."

"Let's not speak of such sins." Lôdumâ wandered back to his seat but remained on his feet. "Nothing we can do for it, or anything else, whether rumors are reality or raving madness."

"True words." Gimin rubbed his forehead and ran fingers through his mop of hair.

"What aren't you saying?"

A gob of spit missed the spittoon, speaking to how little Gimin wanted to empty his thoughts. "There is word... A rumor that the Sword of Bdein returned."

Lôdumâ's breath escaped, and he flopped into his chair. Ivin Choerkin's theft rankled his memories year after year, unrelenting in his dreams. The witch, Meliu, blackened Gimin's eyes, but the sword's theft burrowed a hole in his heritage and pride. "How? In Bdein?"

"In Bdein, yes. Some southern king or another sent it north. They say it arrived by boat amid a shipment of wine."

Lôdumâ grimaced, chest tightening. "A celebration, no doubt, even as people wither and die. An insult to me and the Bdein name. Who holds it?"

"The Lady Stôltmor."

"A Stôltmor?" Lôdumâ couldn't recall the woman's given name, but the family name was all he needed. "Diunmo of Reshu. Somehow, that bastard got the sword from Ivin's hand."

"If the rumor is fact."

"Word was Ivin and the Silone reached the Dragonspans alive. How would the king of Reshu end up with it?"

A snorting laugh from Gimin. "I've never heard of Reshu, let alone its king."

"The witch's git is half Hidreng, his father banished by my kin."

"And the Stôltmors?"

"Them sods made sure the bloodline survived the journey south and were one of a handful of families to oppose the banishment."

Gimin stood and wandered to a rack bearing a dozen swords. "You've no lack of quality steel, but at least you know where it resides."

The notion of a Stôltmor gloating over an heirloom rightfully Lôdumâ's pinched his guilt over being the last of the Ar-Bdêin line. He picked up an archer and lobbed it at the man's head; it pinged off a sword's sheath before bouncing off Gimin's knee. "I've been meaning to take a ride."

The Thônian, a scowl darkening his face, said, "A ride?"

"To Bdein. An Ar-Bdêin should never stay away from home too long."

"Foolishness."

"It's inevitable. You've known it since first we met."

"Oh, aye, there was a plan. You reclaim Bdein and take the knee before a forgiving king, not go to war with Her Holy Highness in the middle of a plague. I've managed to keep you alive this long because the bishop didn't have an excuse."

"I need that sword back."

"The bishop wanted you hanged a decade past; not a thing to stop her now if you show your face."

"Technically, she wanted my guts stretched from a pole."

That, at least, earned Gimin's grin. "If these people bear a grudge, it could be a lie to draw you out. Either way, the bishop's people watch the roads, and every gate is closed."

"I am Ar-Bdêin—"

"*The* Ar-Bdêin, I remind you. If you die, there's no other except a stray bastard or two."

Lôdumâ pursed his lips and swallowed bitter words. "I am Ar-Bdêin; I will always be able to find my way into the city bearing my name."

"Let's say we evade the patrols, enter Bdein, and manage to retake your sword. What then?"

"I don't know, but it *will* be grand."

"The last time you concocted a plan in haste and with such deft details, you ended up humiliated by a red-head priestess and her Choerkin boyfriend."

Lôdumâ arched the brow over his left eye, squinting his right, and grinned. "You make a valid point, but the time to get there should count for time spent planning."

Gimin rubbed his cheek and sucked his teeth. "Should I have the horses saddled?"

"In three days, I've no desire to be rash." Only Lôdumâ chuckled.

ELEVEN

Destiny's Contessa

Sins to city and city to sin and spin to win the desperate sparkle in your eye,
the diamond glow of in love forever,
the burning coal of love in never.
Never was there a girl so pretty as the girl behind the pity,
Lost Puppy and Drowning Guppy,
a pity, the knife in your eye, a pity the knife in your gullet,
a party for the knife in your hand. Kiss miss amiss the long piss
bloody and desperate to die before the end of the sparkle in your eye.

—*Tomes of the Touched*

To say events followed Glimdrem's meticulous plan to reach the continent of Anduran would be to look at a glass window and call it a diamond ring. For starters, they didn't sail straight for the rising sun; with word of other Trelelunin wanting to join them, they traveled south. South meant sailing past his past. First, his true home, only horizons from the coast, where he spent over a century before the call of the Edan sent him to Sutân. When the Vale of Resting Winds rested somewhere on the western horizon was when the weight of leaving the Eleris forever weighed heaviest upon Glimdrem's unconscious heart—Banished—while his lips curled into a smile befitting the airy joy he forced into his conscious mind—Freedom. If he had died here, his soul would have traveled to the Father Wood, and children would have sung the memory of his name for a thousand years, forever tied to the death of the twenty-fifth archangel. Whenever they spoke of 'the luck of the twenty-fifth,' the name Glimdrem would've been in their minds.

Instead, he would be The Banished forever more. Never forgotten, his name cursed and unsung.

Three days later, he didn't care anymore. They stopped at the forested harbor of Reshimdolu, where he first met Lelishen four hundred years ago, and four ships waited to join them. Four ships of Trelelunin *would* sing his name if he led them to freedom and prosperity.

Another joined them in Shêlospidô, and two more in Fedisdîm so that by the time they passed from Trelelunin waters and the Iludetrê Highlands arrived on the southern horizon, the *Flaming Wing* led a fleet of a dozen ships. The trouble began when he realized that while hundreds opted to join him, thousands chose not to supply them. The Edan filled their ships at launch, but it was insufficient to feed so many for a journey across the Boxukolu Ocean. On reaching the lands of the Helelindin, he found no one willing to join them or fill their larders. Desalinizing sea water kept their barrels full, but they weren't fishing boats and needed to eat.

The threat of hunger forced them farther south, farther from their destination, and into waterways he never wished to see again: The sea lanes of the Gorotan. A haughty people he'd last spent time with two and a half centuries earlier, but they still left a bad taste in his mouth. Worse still, the raiders of the Boborun Nation frequented the Gorotan waters, and they were notorious for taking people's tongues so they never tasted again. The latter brought him to Berubondâ, the first Gorotan port city they reached.

He didn't expect to stay long, but that was another diamond turned to glass.

The Goro were ready and willing to trade, but Glimdrem had nothing to give them. And so his people did the last thing he would've desired, sailing at the bidding of Goro merchant houses to earn the gold necessary to bolster their supplies. Profits came slow and tedious, but then came the knock on his cabin door.

Glimdrem stepped into the sun to find Captain Nedefor Danik with a curious look on his face. "What is it, Captain? You look as a man who doesn't know if he drank wine or poison."

"*Senesor*, I've gotten word that a group of Mostulê traders seek an audience."

Ilsferu crept from the shadows of the cabin to stand behind him. "Another? These humans and their pathetic offers grow irritating."

Glimdrem frowned, though he didn't let her see it. Like many Trelelunin, she seemed to think people should hand them gold for being from the Eleris. "They wish to meet in regards to what?" He figured it a strange offer considering the captain's expression.

"They wouldn't say, but it's the who that's interesting. The Contessa of Mostul Ûbar."

His eyes flicked back and forth. "The halfbreed Contessa we've heard about?"

"None other."

Ilsferu spoke in repulsed tones, "They say she's dangerous. Sunk a dozen ships or more and murdered the nobles of Apreleû."

Glimdrem said, "They say she's wealthy."

Captain Danik said, "And bewitching with her looks."

And Glimdrem figured the Captain struck the chord of Ilsferu's discomfort. "Her gold is our concern. When does she want to meet?"

"Any time today. She said she'll be resting at Ibôl's Point until evening."

Glimdrem grinned; he'd visited Ibôl's Point for its views every day for the past week. "The lady has been watching."

Ilsferu said, "A safe and public place for all of us."

"Not us, my darling. Me." He turned and put two fingers to her lips. "If she's as rich as they say, the last thing we need is you spitting fire at a woman who doesn't compare to you."

"You are mine, nobody else's."

He kissed her and chuckled. "Is there even someone else who would want me?"

"They will."

"I am yours, forever, but no time like the present to discover what she wants." He turned back to the Captain. "I will walk alone but send a dozen of our finest archers behind. Just in case."

The man nodded. "It will be done. I recommend a sword or some other sidearm."

Glimdrem shrugged. "I have not carried a sword in this city since we arrived. This woman looks to make money off us, and we have no enemies here."

He strolled for the gangplank, crossed to the docks, turned north with casual strides, and his hands twined behind his back. He felt an urge to whistle, couldn't decide on a tune, and his puckered lips didn't make a noise before a random hum came to his throat.

The stroll to Ibôl's Point was one of the first walks he'd taken to stretch his sea legs after arriving in Berubondâ, and it proved so pleasant he worked it into his daily routine. The breezes rolled in warm off the ocean, and it wasn't long before the docks and ships gave way to a rising rocky shore with gulls riding the winds and sanderlings running the beach, with an occasional frigatebird or albatross out over

the waves. The path narrowed but remained wide enough for five shoulder-to-shoulder and climbed just high enough to serve as a popular location for the adventurous to dive into the swirling pool below without excessive risk. Most days, he would find several couples sitting alone for a picnic and romance, but today was different, perhaps because of the time of day and perhaps because of rapiers singing in a sparring dance. A handful of Mostulês draped in colorful silks stood and watched, but despite an attractive woman wrapped in a sarong, he knew the Contessa without seeing her face.

A woman in an ornate burgundy dress stepped this way and that with her back to him, her blade glinting as it caught the sun in her play fight with a man in blue silks, both sporting the peculiar dueling pose Glimdrem recognized as from the Nomnuvar region. He strode within a dozen strides and stopped to watch, appreciating the skill of both duelists.

After a wick of bloodless battle, she sheathed her rapier and turned to face him with a face glistening in sweat. The famed Contessa stood as beautiful as she was tall, a flowering wisteria amid the stolid oaks of her men, with cheekbones and lips to rival the finest Edan ladies, but it wasn't her smile that brought a chill to Glimdrem's skin. It was her words. "Hail, fair Trelelunin of the Mother Wood. I hope the winds found your sails on your journey." The highs and lows of her Edan, the inflections and breaths so precise he could have mistaken her for being inhuman. They'd been in Berubondâ for months negotiating for supplies and relying on dim-witted Goro, who spoke smatterings of Edan. Maybe it was this woman's halfbreed nature that improved her use of the Edan language, but this made little sense considering the Free Cities of Nomnuvar rested even farther from the Eleris. There was a singular human he'd met who spoke his native tongue so well, and his brow pinched with curiosity as he approached her.

'You are the Contessa of Mostul Ûbar, I presume?"

She curtsied rather than bowed, perhaps to keep her bosom in its southern-cut dress. "I am, good sir. When I sailed to reach you, I didn't expect to find you still in Berubondâ."

He repressed a groan at the reminder he hadn't intended to stay long. "In truth, the wind found my sails fine, but along the way, I tripled the number of ships and people wishing to join my exploration. My joy in discovering those like-minded hasn't assisted in my being able to feed them for the journey I intend."

"I see." She squinted with a grin. "Berubondâ is short of provisions? I wonder on that."

Glimdrem glanced at the short, stout warrior in puffing pantaloons, unlikely to be her consort, and reckoned him her personal guard. A young beauty draped in pearls who stood at her other hand was, no doubt, her handmaiden. The Contessa wasn't a title alone; in this case, rumors didn't lie. It meant wealth. "The Lord of the Edan, I confess, supplied me well enough in dried meats and freshwater to reach any destination, but they overlooked a real need for relations with so many mortal peoples: Gold." A blank stare from the human. "Coins."

"Yes. I understand. But I don't understand."

Glimdrem chuckled with a gentle wave toward her servant. "The Edan value pearls, as you do, and adorn themselves with gold, but they mint no coins."

"I've heard they trade with many peoples."

"And they melt and wear the coins they receive or turn around to trade them back." Sometimes, it proved difficult to explain being impoverished without stating the obvious: The Edan didn't intend to make him rich by banishing him and his followers. "They are a people difficult to understand even for we Trelelunin."

"Your ships are as fine as I've seen. You could sell one for a fortune."

His lips opened with a smack, but not a word until he bit back an insult about filthy humans owning a Trelelunin vessel, let alone one of Edan make from the hallowed timber of the Eleris. "It is an offer I have spurned from those so bold to make it. My people have taken on some voyages of trade, but none of my people speak Goro, and aside from you, I've yet to meet a Goro who speaks Edan well." He neglected to mention that he forbade his people from learning a language so beneath them, even if a few learned a handful of words. "Which begs the question, how do you speak my tongue with such eloquence?"

"I was born and raised in Vitolêô, much closer to the southern Woodkin."

"No." He blinked with a smile. "My cousins to the south speak with quaint mannerisms. Your words are pure and northern, like the Edan themselves and all who live within the Mother Wood."

Her cheeks flushed. "I cannot speak to that. My mother taught me as a child, and she died without my learning the answer."

Her mannerisms didn't suggest a lie but felt more like a truth she'd convinced herself of. The vine muttered, *How?* He ignored the question without a hitch. "My condolences." Something he'd learned to say among humans, as he didn't even remember who his mother was to understand the sorrow. "Your mother must have been a master of languages."

A real smile, now. "Hopefully, to both of our benefits. I would like to help you find the gold you need."

A playful grin. "Your lady's pearls would be a fine start."

"You know we humans better than that."

A dignified snort. "I do indeed. What can I do for you?"

"Since you won't part with a ship, I'm uncertain." Her grin was sly, and he doubted her suggested desire.

"What can you do for me?"

"I can make you rich."

"Wealth isn't a thing my people and I concern ourselves with." He rolled his shoulders. "Food and gear enough to laden our ships will suffice."

"Not for what I have in mind."

"Ah." He rocked heel to toe and back. "You fibbed earlier?"

"No. I'm uncertain, as I said, but I have an idea. The Boboru, what know you of them?"

A vision of Ûvîn flashed before his eyes, the living man rather than the dead, with a toothy smile. He squinted at her, a tingle down his spine without understanding why the hairs of his nape stood. Nor did he understand why the mention of Boboru would trigger such a memory, aside from the shark-like teeth. "A vile and dangerous people, but we have a few dealings with them."

"Do they extort your trade vessels?"

Glimdrem's head cocked. "Do they what?"

"They allow the Luxuns to sail unmolested but demand tribute from most merchants. They fear the Luxuns. Do they fear the Edan?"

"If they don't, they should. But then, Edan almost never leave the Eleris."

"But would they fear and respect your ships?"

He licked his lips, attempting to gain the measure of the woman's angle and failing. "If I am to understand your desire, you should speak straight to the point."

She fidgeted. "I need inside a city being blockaded by the Boboru."

He chuckled with a finishing whistle. "Now I see why you danced! The reputation of the Boboru would suggest not. Now, if I carried an Edan? The right Edan? Well, their ships are cumbersome, and they might be unable to stop us. We'd run a blockade as sure as any Luxun,

and I know of what I speak when it comes to Luxuns and their prowess with the winds." He nodded toward the broad-shouldered man who stood at her side. "This fellow, is he Darâ?"

"No, like me, he hails from Mostul Ûbar."

"A pity. A Darâ man once saved my life aboard a Luxun ship. A fine man."

"Some believe the peoples of Nomnuvar and the Ôlfindarâ islands are related, but to the point, would the Boboru fear or respect the Edan enough to free your passage?"

"They might, but I'd rather not discover the consequences of their declining. Our ships are not outfitted for battle, though I dare say it would be bold to attack us."

The Contessa exhaled, her eyes turning to the dock in disappointment. "I understand. I do. If you try and fail, I'll supply your ships with anything you desire. Succeed, and you'll have coin enough to resupply in any harbor in the world a dozen times."

Glimdrem flicked fingers in the air. "What is gold compared to lives? You humans trade them for cheap, but unlike you, death for we Trelelunin is a possibility, not an inevitability. Unless we take on stupid risks."

The woman met his grin with an acquiescent nod. "I understand."

"Do you? This time?"

"There are more traditional ways to earn what you need. I want to help you, and I will."

"If ever you wanted to help, you'd simply hand me the money or supplies. I wager you never lacked wealth for a day in your life. What you seek is profit. I have nothing to profit you with." He clicked his heels and bowed, ready to spin away.

"Wait. I have another question."

A sideways glance. "If knowledge could be your profit...."

"It might be. Does a human, a northern barbarian, share passage in your fleet?"

He scoffed. "A human? No." He cleared his throat, hoping to cover the flash of disdain in his voice. Then, Glimdrem's eyes refocused on the depth of her brown eyes. "A northern barbarian, you say?"

"From the island of Kaludor, a man named Solineus. He carries—"

"Two swords." The spark of disdain flickered into a hatred built over Lelisen's unnatural affection for the man. His face softened, and his lips parted in his broadest smile. "He's a friend I met in the Eleris. We traveled to Kaludor together." He waggled a finger in her face. "Is it he who taught you Edan?"

A breathtaking smile enlivened her beauty into something other, something inhuman, something both glorious and deadly, and for a flicker, her eyes turned green. "No, he didn't."

The vine said, *It's her. And he is him.*

Impossible, Glimdrem thought, but he knew it was a fool's reply. Impossible or true, he needed to know and couldn't let her go. "A friend of a friend is just a friend, but I owe Solineus my life and more than a few laughs. That makes you special. Come. Join me on the *Flaming Wing,* and we'll discuss how I can help you." His invitation was too quick, and he kicked himself as she looked to her man and spoke in Tôlk, another human tongue he hadn't bothered to learn. "I'm sorry, no. That's not possible. I grew excited and forgot my duties. But if ever I meet the man again, I could not in good conscience say I didn't try to help his friend. Might my lady and I join you aboard your ship for dinner tomorrow evening? We can talk then after I discuss possibilities with my people."

"Tomorrow isn't good. Give me a couple of days to settle some business?"

He raised his hands in smiling surrender. "We both have matters to attend to. Will the evening of the twenty-fifth suffice?"

The Contessa's smile returned in an instant. "Perfect. I'll be aboard the *Silver Willow*, docked south of your position. You will recognize her by the Hôduk mahogany and the star of Mostul Ûbar."

"I will." Glimdrem nodded with a crooked grin; even the Edan prized such a rare hardwood. "We will arrive at dusk. I'm sure whatever you have prepared for a meal will be exquisite."

"I have Edan wine."

He paused with a blink. Outside of treasure to purchase human kindness, he often reckoned the lack of wine as the biggest oversight for this journey. "Perfect indeed. It's been a pleasure meeting you, Contessa."

"Likewise." She curtsied with a smile and turned to leave.

"A quick question."

Dark eyes turned back to him as she stopped in stride. "Yes?"

"Have you ever heard of Gornite and Xanesu?"

Her lovely face peered at him with a blank stare, oh so feline. "No. Should I have?"

He dismissed the notion with a wave of his hand. "No, I suppose not. Someday, remind me to bore you with their tale."

"I will. Thank you."

Glimdrem stared at her lithe steps until a crowd of sailors parted like a wave before enveloping her. Impossible repeated in his mind, but every option he conceived raised doubts that ricocheted between dubious and fantastical. And the vine didn't say a word.

Twelve

Watcher's Worry

Brother Wolf sings into the wind
of your fears and leers and jeers,
"What have you eaten today, Sister Lion?"
Sister Lion sings against the wind
without peers and tears and seers,
"What have you drank today, Brother Wolf?"
Mother Moon swallows their winds
and blows fogging breaths upon their mirrors.

—*Tomes of the Touched*

Rains swept the plains that evening, and after soaking overnight, they rode toward the blood-red horizon of a rising sun, thankful at least they weren't at sea. No one could say when they lost the buried road, and with dripping clothes, no one cared enough to backtrack and find out. What they didn't lose were the six come and goes who'd watch them pass, then watch them arrive only to watch them depart again, as if watching the horsemen make great circles while Rinold thought they walked a straight line. If not for the sun and compass, Rinold might've begun to believe they were riding loops.

They reached the river two days after finding the road, one day longer than Rinold expected, and it brought on the wish that they had a Wayfinder with them.

The Mûulbon River was wide and swift and without a sign of a bridge, or for that matter, anything much that would serve as a marker. Muddy banks and nondescript scrub trees wouldn't mark the point of their arrival in his mind. The road was, more or less, due west from this position, so it'd be handy to know where to start if ever they tried to find it again.

He strode to the largest tree he could find, pissed, then used his ax to notch the tree three times on the river side and once on the west. He ignored the six men watching him from a hill when he turned and strolled back to Polus. "A man just can't get no privacy no more."

"Mmmm. Have you ever seen one take so much as a step?"

"Maybe once, or it mighta been the grass blowin'."

"We should send riders."

"And to the families of which men do you wanna explain how you got them killed?"

"We don't know that, mmmm."

"You're right, I don't." He gave his canteen a shake and headed upriver from where more men pissed, and Polus followed. "They're givin' me the fidgets, but what harm? They done come too far to be ghosts, from what we know. If they're Histê, what kingdom? If they're from a Wiirê tribe, we sure as hells don't wanna give them trouble. We need friends. And if they're somebody else?" He shrugged.

Polus snorted and licked his lips. "Mmmm, so we head on back to Endelêun. I'd feel better if we were on the eastern side of the Mûulbon."

"Oh, aye. Without a bridge, you're liable to feel like some lizard's lunch before making it to the other side." The river would likely kill

them all if they tried to cross, but this exact danger kept farmers who tilled the soil south of Endelêun safe from the Histê. At this moment, a picture of Endelêun formed in his mind, sitting at the branches of rivers but more like the center of a compass.

Northeast, a massive forest full of massive beasts and creatures looking to eat everyone. Northwest, a forest more normal, far from safe but from all reports, filled with fewer giants. Southwest, plains of chest-high grass blew with few trees and herd animals that might be considered giants, and the critters that ate on them remained large but weren't as aggressive as in the northeast. Southeast, the land started as plains with shorter grasses and plenty of shrubbery, but word from explorers spoke of more forests with wiry trees curling and twisting into haunting forms that some claimed would eat people. Endelêun, the pin of the compass, was a city empty of all but ghosts before they arrived. "What the hells is with Endelêun?"

"Mmm, what were that?"

Rinold waved a finger and shook his head. "Thinkin' is all. We've reached a damned weird part of the world?"

"That right? You seen the rest o' the world have ya?"

Rinold chuckled as he meandered farther north with half an eye on their visitors. Or, more apt, they were the hosts and Rinold, the guest. "Point made, big man, but you gotta admit...." A thicket of scrub brush like he'd seen a hundred times before cropped up on the bank in front of them, with yellow flowers and green berries shifting toward mauve, but the way branches twisted sent him to a crouch and stare into what might be an eye.

The warlord stood straight. "What ya peepin' at, Squirrel?"

A hushed breath before he pointed. "I'm thinkin' we got a skull staring straight at us. Damned well hopin' it's dead dead and not fixin' to eat us, anyhow."

Polus whistled and motioned, and half a dozen wandered their way with their hands on swords and axes, but Rinold arrived at the growth before any of them to put toe to skull. Leaves fell away to reveal cleaned bone, but the skull was still attached to vertebrae, so it didn't roll. He knelt a second time, snapped a stick, and poked. Grooves in the bone and clumps of black hair rested nearby in tufts of grass.

"A man. Somethin' toothy, along with bugs, helped clean him up. Scavengers either drug most of him away or dragged this part here." He stood, took two steps, and kicked at leaf litter. A second skull flipped to stare at the sky. "At least he didn't die alone."

"Them river lizards?"

"Nah, they don't leave bits and pieces, and they don't scavenge." He glanced at another covered lump. "Nah, unless we got a critter who collects their dead, people dumped these folks and covered 'em a little. But not so much to be reverent."

"How many, ya think?"

"Coulda been the three, coulda been a dozen with bones scattered here to the hilltop with them bastards." He brushed his hand through debris, and scraps of bones flipped in the air. "I'd wager them wolfish beasts ate on 'em. We got shattered bone."

"Any wound marks?"

Rinold rolled a skull. "Got a hole in the head here, bigger'n most bites, but no promises." He stood and circled the area, probing and kicking to find scattered pieces, and a stretch of faded fabric popped from beneath leaves, its zig-zagged colors faded. "Another jaw over here, and I'd guess they were Histê by the wrap's pattern." He looked to the hilltop and the unmoving who gazed their way.

"How long dead, you figure? A month?"

"Heat and critters in these parts? Two weeks, maybe. Could be more or less dependin'. I don't think our watchers are Histê."

"Thinkin' they killed these people?"

"It's making sense in my mind. The Histê might travel these plains, but they don't control 'em. Might be we got friends on the hill."

"Might be they're waitin' to kill us and fertilize another copse."

Rinold itched his cheek with eyes still trained on the hill. "Damned shame to come this far and not get an idea who these people are."

"Changin' your mind on sending six to see?"

"Nah. Hells, if anyone is gonna die, it might as well be us, eh?"

An arched brow from the Broldun. "I know yer lady, and my ass is a damned big target. And as warlord, I'm not supposed to be gettin' m'self killed."

Rinold spat in the grass. "Yer right, I'll go alone. I've got a chance to speak their tongue if they're Wiirê or trade with them, and alone, I'll scare no one."

"Your so damned puny two of ya wouldn't make no one piss."

He snorted at the Broldun. "Collect my body if needs be." Rinold walked a dozen strides.

"You're puny enough riding a horse shouldn't scare 'em much neither."

Rinold snorted, made his way to his mount, swung into the saddle, and kneed the horse into a sauntering walk toward their watchers. All the bastards stared straight at him; he knew it even if he couldn't see their eyes, but not a one reacted to his approach. A swirling wind danced the grasses in front of him in winding waves, and clouds drifted in rolling billows across the horizon, a world in motion, all except *them.* Standing on two legs or one with the other cocked to make a triangle, hands at their sides, or holding a staff, he couldn't so much as discern movement in the draping fabric of their clothes.

This final revelation brought a chill between his shoulder blades. Maybe he rode toward ghosts after all. "I'd see through 'em," he

muttered, deciding they wore leather or some other stiff gear. As he approached what he guessed within an archer's range, he squinted toward where faces must be and found only shadow. "Godsdamnit, the sun is right. I should see somethin' unless they're wearin' masks. Gotta be it."

Twenty strides later, he stopped, raised an arm high in the air, and spoke in Wiirê. "The sun greets you with warmth through the bows of the trees." He grimaced. If they understood him, he'd just made an ass out of himself with no forest for horizons. Good news or bad, they didn't react with so much as a twitch. "Greetings!"

He stared, and his horse stomped a hoof with a snort, but still, no one moved. With a quick squeeze, he rode forward a little farther. "My name is Rinold. I am of a people from far, far north, from beyond the forest and over the mountains." He pointed. "Far, far, far... I ain't doin' m'self no good here, am I?" Finishing in Silone was sure not to help, but at least no one pulled any weapons. "This is a pisser."

A nudge of movement as one raised his head, and in the sun, he thought he saw brown covering the person's face. *A mask.* Ghosts and monsters didn't need masks, so he was pleased. He reined his horse to a stop and tapped his chest. "Rinold."

A rattling noise came from the one who'd moved, and a flicker later, a hand rose, pulling a slip of cloth from a face. "Nok nok tubûku. Êt um."

Rinold smiled until rays of light reflected from ivory on the face. Rinold struggled to keep his smile as he muttered, "That ain't no jewelry." Tusks sprouted from cheeks hairy enough to shame the finest Broldun beard. "That's right, Rinold. It was damned fine making your acquaintance. I'll be seeing you later now. Later. Soon. Bye now." He smiled, waved, and backed his horse a dozen steps before reining into a spin to face his people. "Ride slow. No hurry. Don't hear 'em comin'

for me yet." He glanced over his shoulder. "Ain't a comin'. Ride calm." He patted his horse's neck all the way back to Polus and the other men and didn't break his smile.

The Broldun stared. "You look like a godsdamned idiot smilin' like that, Squirrel. What the hells?"

"They ain't human, and I swear it might have said it wanted to eat me. Probably not! But it sounded that a way."

"That were true, why the hells didn't they eat ya?"

"I said it sounded like it." He turned his horse and waved. "Thank you kindly for not eatin' me."

"You might skip tellin' Puxele about this genius move of yours."

"There's some advice I'll take. Let's get the hells out of here."

Within wicks, the party followed the river north. "Tusks. They had tusks and wiry fur."

"Sounds a bit like my auntie on the Moduru side of the family. Folks called her Truffles."

"Now yer full of shit."

"The woman made m'kin a mushroom fortune come every spring."

Rinold rode in silence for flickers, wondering if the man wasn't telling a version of the truth before he glanced over his shoulder to find the hilltop stood clear. His eyes whipped to the fore expecting the buggers to already be in the distance waiting for them. Nothing. "If I find you lie about this woman's tusks, you're gonna owe me your best bottle of whiskey."

"Didn't say nothin' 'bout tusks, did I?"

They rode northward with the sounds of wind and the rushing river on their right for company until six figures appeared on a hilltop to the northwest with shifted poses but otherwise standing still. "Ya know, I was starting to think someone was propping up statues to confuse and frighten us until one of the buggers spoke and moved."

"Mmm. I'd say they were leading us into a trap, except we aren't following them."

They both chuckled. "Aye, tempted my thinking too." His eyes shifted to the floodplain ahead, then jerked back to a rising hill north of the six. The hill the watchers stood upon appeared the same as thousands before, but Rinold thought maybe the next stood out. He pointed. "That there hill look different to you?"

Polus grunted. "Mmm, it's a bit less rounded. I've seen a dozen or so like it the past couple of days."

Rinold blinked. "You did? Why the hell didn't I see 'em?"

"Too busy staring at your statues?"

Rinold's head jerked before he chuckled. "From the mouths of idiots."

"What's that runt?"

"You're a genius."

"About damned time you admitted it; now tell me why."

He rolled in his saddle as his mind worked. "Ten to one says they disappear and reappear on yonder hill beyond the odd one."

"I ain't takin' that bet, Squirrel. You're sayin' they've been drawing our eyes from these other hills all along?"

"Aye, I am. An escort for distraction, to make sure we don't see what we ain't supposed to see."

Rinold stared at the six as they rode, and as before, the people faded and, this time, reappeared on the second hill away as predicted. "There they be."

"Proof it isn't, but you weren't wrong. So, what do we do about it, mmm?"

"Well, Broldun, the way I figure, if we keep our eyes right where they want 'em, then won't nobody have to explain to our wives how and why we died as fools out here."

Polus chuckled. "At least on this trip."

"At least on this trip."

"Why the hells ya think they're protecting a hill?"

"I don't care."

They rode and stared at the fading and reappearing six for a day and a half before the watchers miraged away for a final time. Nine days after that, they both kissed their wives in Endelêun.

THIRTEEN

One-Sided Conversation

Sing a song about singing? Write a story about writing? Paint a mural about painting? Do yourself a favor and live a life about living instead of dying a death for nothing.

—*From A Warning to the Artist*
by Ingred of Aburdine

Kinesee's original plan was to drive Alu batty searching for prophetic tomes, but it didn't take long to decide that a sister-in-law was fair game as well. Izilfer accepted the challenge with wide-eyed glee, so they found themselves first searching the area where the *Codex of Sol* was found.

People had rearranged the chairs and tables around the room into a tidy pattern, and the table carved as a map of the city still sat beneath a monstrous golden chandelier. The shelves along the walls still sat empty, with no way to tell if here had sat thousands of books or other treasures.

Kinesee kneeled, running her fingers along a stretch of cracked mortar, looking for anything out of place. At the same time, a half

dozen warriors stood guard, or rather, watched the three ladies attempt to prove themselves for the third day in a row while pretending to stand guard.

Izilfer said, "This is exciting. Thank you for inviting me."

Alu guffawed. "My little sis' folly is exciting? How boring must've your days been?"

The priestess tittered. "You have no idea. I promise. When I spent my days healing, well, to be blunt, broken bones and cuts get boring too, but you know what they have me doing now? Instructing this girl, Hulerê."

Kinesee said, "She's an impossible brat or a terrible healer?"

"Neither. She's so perfect! I was good, one of the best, my master's claimed, but this girl? The other day, we heard of a man with the Drowning Cough and went to try to help. She touched him and prayed."

"Healed?"

"No. But I told her to *feel* for the man's lungs. Not just his lungs, to... well, to feel for an infection not so unlike gangrene. It takes most adherents weeks to penetrate the secrets of the body, and most never learn to heal the Drowning Cough at an advanced stage. Hulerê found the infection." She snapped her fingers twice. "And healed him. Not just healed! Cleared his lungs of mucus! Like he'd never been ill. Even with my prayers, he would've taken half a day to be up and walking. The man could've jogged from the table."

"But this is a good thing. An amazing thing. A miracle of prayer."

"Yes, but how am I supposed to teach that?" She giggled. "And I admit, I'm jealous."

"Well, I guess we're three bored ladies in the end."

Alu said, "I wasn't bored. I eat fine foods, spar with the men, and... well, it isn't boring."

Kinesee flushed, aggravated with her sister. "I'm not some vase so easily broken. It isn't as if I don't hear your excitement most every night."

"I'm sorry... sorry's not the right word. I just—"

"I know. I sleep without my husband, but the twins do help me keep warm some nights." She grimaced. "I'm sorry, too."

"Neither of us is a vase."

Alu and Tudwan longed for a child, but even with the assistance of prayer, they hadn't conceived. "Let's just allow for both of us to be sorry and move on."

Silence ensued, broken only by the scratch and rub of fingers tracing mortar and knees crawling on rock, until Izilfer said, "Speaking of moving on, might we consider a new place to search?"

The three laughed as they surrendered to good advice and stood up one by one. "The palace is huge, and the city huger... more huge? This was the only place to start I could think of. My dreams haven't done me any favors this time."

They stretched their legs as they wandered to the wooden table carved into a perfect representation of Endelêun above. The last time here, Kinesee took the time to count the rings in the wood to four thousand four hundred and twelve.

Izelfer said, "Might a Kingdomer, a Wayfinder, have mapped the palace?"

"I think they walked the perimeter but detailed the inside? I haven't heard anything." She turned a circle. "The odds of two secret doors seems slim."

Alu grinned and said, "The odds of one seem slim to me."

Kinesee sighed, feeling worthless again. As a child, she had nothing but sand for a castle and felt like a queen; now that she lived in a palace, she felt like she was nobody. She snorted. "Focus. I knew the secret door's latch when I saw it, but in the dream, I didn't even go into

a hidden door. Here, there's a ladder down leading to a stair, but in the dream, it was a spiral stair."

Izelfer said, "Dare I ask how you knew about the secret door, then?"

Kinesee's head cocked, her thoughts flashing to Ivin for no good reason. She shivered and shook off the distraction. "Best I can figure, there was more to the dream, earlier pieces I don't remember."

"How many spiral stairs are in the palace? Fifty or more? Every tower along the walls of the tower and fortress has one."

Kinesee shrugged. "It's so vague, but I have the impression of, I'm not sure, but not like a guard tower. Brass fixtures on the rail, hanging lanterns for light? I could be so wrong."

Alu said, "We can't count on an old dream, but it's all we've got. Who knows the palace best?"

Izilfer said, "Servants?"

Kinesee said, "Children. If I was ten or twelve—"

"As if that was a long time ago?" Alu smirked.

She didn't dignify the truth. "I'd be everywhere exploring. Every nook and cranny."

"And everybody would be irritated with you."

"Haha. But true."

Izilfer said, "There aren't many children in the palace, at least old enough to be good explorers."

"Are there prayers to find secret passages?"

Izilfer's eyes widened. "I haven't a clue. Working with Elemental Minerals is a rare discipline. Stone, metals, and gems are solid and difficult to manipulate. To be blunt, I have no idea how it could be done."

"Couldn't a god just tell you?"

She giggled. "Oh, wouldn't that be nice?"

Alu said, "So instead of gods, we put our faith in children. How about ghosts?" Kinesee stared. "I'm only half joking."

"If I could talk to one, and they talked back, who knows? Might as well ask the gods, I suspect." She leaned on the table's stone, gazing at the unexplained gemstones scattered on the three-dimensional map. "I don't suppose this model here would give us any clues?"

Izelfer said, "A hundred people have spent hundreds of hours staring at the thing. Even Kurin, the Wayfinder, mapped the city above. It's precise."

"And we still have no idea about the latcu gems."

The three of them stared, and even Harlik took a glance before looking away, bored. Alu said, "No latcu in the palace proper."

Izelfer opined, "They'd make beautiful earrings."

They stared a while longer, but that was the extent of useful input with respect to the stones. Kinesee sighed and pulled up a chair. "The shape of the city is so perfect." People smarter than her called it an ellipse, but she preferred the word egg-shaped. Only a perfect egg, even when constructed straddling a river and overlooking a monumental cliff. "And if this is a map, we could find whatever we're looking for if searching for a building." She pointed. "The shape, the design, this is a bathhouse."

Alu said, "You're cheating because we've been there."

"Bathhouse, bathhouse, bathhouse." Her eye picked out their shapes with ease: the narrow, staired entrance leading to a broader building where arching roofs protected the bathers instead of the more typical peaked structures. "The builders wanted folks to know a bathhouse on approach. What about libraries?"

Izilfer raised her brow. "A common library?"

"Why not? They shared baths, why not knowledge?"

The priestess' eyes narrowed with a smirk on her lips. "The Church wouldn't allow just anybody to thumb through the *Codex of Sol*. Such books would be in temples."

"Maybe your Church, but the Codex of Sol was found right in this room. A most peculiar temple. And then, stuck in the drawer of a table."

Alu knocked on the table where she'd found the book. "My little sis has a point."

A disbelieving gaze on the pretty lady's face. "Fine. A point. What location is more safe than this one? If they had common libraries, they wouldn't leave such important tomes in them. They'd be kept safe for study."

Kinesee couldn't argue with the logic, but, "Safe, but not always in temples. How did the holy keep books on Kaludor?"

Izilfer pulled up a second chair. "I only know Istinjoln's library, but there was a main room where religious treatises were stowed on shelves for anyone to read—common books, sometimes with three or four copies, or even a dozen. If your studies led you to knowledge more arcane, the librarian would need to fetch the tome for you. If especially rare, say, *The Corruption of Unilis,* you'd need permission from a high priest to acquire the book. Or you'd have to be a scholar, like Meliu."

"Permission just to read a book?"

"*The Corruption of Unulis* speaks of Elemental Dark, and as such, no one was permitted to copy its pages, and few had cause to read it. It's a legend in Istinjoln, with spooky tales of priests sneaking in to read its pages, going mad, throwing themselves from the walls, or rotting their wits until they could speak no more. Children's tales, I'm sure, but what the book teaches is dangerous. But either way, no one has found a library at the temple of Tomarok."

Kinesee wasn't about to dismiss scary tales; she'd seen too many frightful magics, but the library's storage and retrieval system caught a more pleasant side of her imagination. "Let's suppose the city had common baths and libraries, and let's suppose they mirror Istinjoln.

An area with common books for everybody, but also a place where more valuable and rare books are kept. Do you imagine this one-of-a-kind tome was kept amongst other rare but less dangerous books, or was it in a place locked and separate?"

"Locked, of course."

"Secret. So, if there is a library in the city—"

Alu said, "Or libraries."

"Then it would follow suit that they would have secreted away places to store rare books. Hidden vaults, even." Kinesee's eyebrows danced over a broad smile as she stared at her sister-in-law.

"If, and I mean if, all your assumptions are right... Yes. Fine. But in this gigantic city that could house over a hundred thousand souls, we've found one! One book. The *Codex of Sol.* Have you heard of another, let alone a library?"

"We don't need to find a library full of books, just what was once a library. It makes sense they'd have vaults, hidden or otherwise."

Alu said, "Hells, something might even be found in a secret place in a noble's or wealthy merchant's home."

"Let's focus on common spaces first. There'd be fewer, I'd think."

Harlik cleared his throat. "There were scores of empty bookshelves in a building we cleared over here." He pointed to a broad, three-tiered structure. "Folks reckoned it some sorta office for storing records, but might just as wella been a library."

Kinesee smiled as her eyes alighted on the miniature building. "You see? I—" Her next words choked on her tongue as a dim green glow lit a tiny wooden street, her focus shifting to a round-cut piece of latcu smaller than her pinky. "Is everyone seeing what I'm seeing?"

Izilfer's voice came under her breath. "Yes."

The gem cast a weak shadow over a handful of buildings, a faint halo, but it twinkled. Then it flashed. The fuzzy ball of light reformed

into a beam illuminating Palace Road and the bridge across the Temirân River. The light grew in intensity until it cast a green tint to Alu's astonished face. "I'll be damned."

Kinesee's heart raced. "That's right outside the palace."

Alu stuttered, and Izelfer stood with her jaw locked open, but Harlik said, "It could be dangerous."

"Then you'll just have to keep up. It's a short run."

Alu said, "Wait." Kinesee's knees bent to run, but she stopped as her sister grabbed her shoulder and pointed: A shape formed in the tiny rod of light, casting a shadow onto the wooden road, so small there was no way to guess what it was. She looked up at the ceiling instead, and her breath escaped her. Other eyes followed her gaze.

Harlik said, "What is it?"

Alu said, "A paw print?"

Izelfer said, "A wolf's?"

The tiny shadow on the street was dark, as one would suspect, but the shadow—if it could be called a shadow at all—on the ceiling was white. A reflection? And unlike the print of a wolf, it showed no claws. "Gods bless us! No. It's a lion's paw." Whether she ran, walked, or managed to steal someone's horse, she might not make it in time to witness whatever made the gem glow and cast this image, but she ran anyhow, thankful she'd worn britches instead of a dress.

She remained thankful for her choice of clothing, but she regretted the optimistic declaration of how short the run was in quick order. First, the stairs, then hallways, then a ladder plenty long enough to make arms *and* legs burn, and by the time they made it out of the palace, they'd already run farther than a crow would've had to fly to reach Palace Road—all that to get a hundred strides closer to their goal. She felt worse for Harlik and the other warriors in their armor, who huffed poles behind them and tried to catch up.

Everyone dripped sweat by the time they reached the courtyard, and only Izilfer wasn't out of breath, but still the priestess said, "Stop." Guards stared in confusion as she bowed her head, muttered a prayer, and a flicker later, Kinesee's lungs opened, taking control of her gasping breaths with a rush of vitality. "Go."

They sprinted across the courtyard to the main gates, where a dozen armored men watched the wide-open entry. When they passed through the barbican to stand in the street, the only four men who acted as if they saw anything out of the ordinary stared at them, not some eerie light or mysterious threat. Dozens of people wandered the street, none of them paying them a lick of attention.

She glanced both ways down the road, then looked straight up at a blue sky with puffs of tranquil clouds. No green light. No white lion's paw.

A flash from the corner of her eye, and she leaped back from a team of horses pulling a carriage. It didn't slow or weave to miss her, and before she screamed at the driver, she realized that no one else had reacted at all. Alu and Izilfer stood straining their eyes at an empty sky with airs of disappointment, not shock at almost being run over.

Kinesee's mouth fell open when she realized she saw through the horses and carriage. She grabbed Alu's shoulders and shook. "You didn't see that?"

Wide eyes met her own. "What? Do you see the light?"

"No!" She waved her hands toward the carriage rolling towards the bridge in the distance. "That!"

"Sis? See what?"

"Horses! A carriage! Ghosts!" But as she blinked and looked closer at the people around her, it was like a hand grasped her heart. Four guards stared at them, but the other eight looked on as if nothing was

happening, and she could see the faint image of the wall or courtyard through them. Most of the people in the street... "They're everywhere. The ghosts."

Izilfer spun on her. "What? Where?"

Kinesee turned a circle, her heart slowing and thoughts congealing. "All around. Clearer than I've seen before. Their clothing is bright. Their skin flush. It's like they're alive, only I see through them. And yet, they're more solid than normal. Almost real."

"Do they see you? Do they look like us?"

"No. And yes. They dress differently. The women, their dresses are lighter weave. Fewer pleats. The guards wear breastplates with mail, and it is embossed with a lion."

"They are Silone, long dead. Old tomes speak of such armor during the God Wars. Can you hear them?"

She took a shuddering breath before she strode toward a couple walking with a young girl between them, holding hands. A pleasant and familiar scene that might've brought a smile to her face if she couldn't see Endelêun's skyline through their chests. Kinesee fell in stride beside them, listening close as their mouths moved. The words came faint with a mild echo, making it more difficult to understand, as if from a distance across an amphitheater. Kinesee repeated what she heard. "Suleerum..."

Izilfer said, "We'll see, my sweets, the price of chocolate has gone up. Please! Please, please! I'll sweep the porch for a week. Now, baby, you listen to your father. Mother? Yes. There is a strange woman walking beside us."

Kinesee paused her strides with wide eyes before trotting to catch up, then repeated their words with Izilfer translating. "There's no one there, sweets. There is. Her lips are moving. I think she's saying what we're saying." The family stopped, the adults looking around in con-

fusion, but the child stared straight at her, her translucent knuckles whitening as they gripped her parents' hands.

Kinesee knelt to meet the girl's gaze and smile, then tried her hand at what little Canonic Silone she knew. "Hello."

And she thought she understood what the girl said next.

"She says hello, but I don't hear her."

Kinesee repeated her words to make certain she understood before watching the couple drag the daughter away with worried glances Kinesee's way. "There's no one there. Come, Nutonu. Nutonu, there's no one there." She kneeled with Izilfer and the others by her side until the trio of ghosts passed from view.

Alu said, "The little girl, this Nutonu, sees you? But no one else?"

"Far as I can tell. In my room, the woman there sees me."

Izilfer sucked a whistling breath through her teeth. "Incredible. I couldn't sense them at all with my prayers. Nothing. Not Life. Not Spirit."

Kinesee stood. "I'm not imagining things."

"I didn't say you were."

"Good." She blinked, and when her eyes opened again, it took a flicker to realize that the street had gone empty but for a horseman riding their way. "There are so many more ghosts than we have people." She stood with a nervous chuckle. "So very many."

Izilfer said, "Harmless, at least so far. Better, they keep us safe from the Histê. Are there more close?"

"Gone. They're all gone now. In an instant, the street cleared."

Izilfer turned a circle. "Fascinating."

Alu said, "So what the hells was the green beam of light saying? Here there be ghosts? I don't mean to sound silly."

"I wouldn't call it silly at all. That's a question worthy of an answer." The priestess puckered her lips for an exasperated breath. "When these people built this city, gods knows when, why would they require a map that showed them ghosts? It makes no sense."

"It doesn't at all."

Kinesee nodded in agreement. "So what would make sense?"

They stared at each other, and Kinesee cast a glance at Harlik, but he shrugged. "Don't you be asking me nothin'."

Kinesee giggled and turned her gaze on the one person who might have a clue, Izilfer. "Well? You're the smart one."

The priestess' feet shuffled. "If I had to guess?"

"Please! Guess away."

"How often do you see ghosts?"

Kinesee shook her head. "Not often, and most of the time, it's just a woman in my cursed bedroom. Nothing like this before, not even when the Histê army arrived. I heard and felt them more, then."

She licked her lips. "All right. Fine. Don't bind me to a single word of this, you hear me? But—"she scratched her ear and cleared her throat—"my guess is the latcu gem's light, it probably indicates a surge in Elemental energy. A bevy of ghosts might trigger gems set to sense such things."

Kinesee wanted to accept the idea at face value, except... "But again, *why* have this carving with gemstones to sense the Elements?"

And again, they all stared at each other.

"Why? Why. I don't know."

Kinesee shook her head. "And if these ghosts are always here, why now? I saw nothing special. I mean, outside of ghosts, that would cause the gem's light if your idea is right."

Alu said, "Does it godsdamned matter? We live in a city of ghosts, but they don't give two damns about us. Let 'em be."

Kinesee wanted to agree but had to ignore her sister's outburst. "If the model city was built to detect Elemental energies, we need to know why."

The sound of hooves clopping their way stole her attention, and she looked to Roplin and a retinue of riders heading their way. Alu said, "Well, hells, men, to interrupt our fun. No offense, Harlik."

The man chuckled. "None taken."

They waited in silence, a bit like children caught stealing from the larder until the Choerkin reined in his horse and dismounted, giving Izilfer a quick kiss on the cheek. "What are you ladies doing standing in the middle of the street?"

Izilfer smiled with a flirtatious wink. "Waiting for you, of course."

"Of course. And, of course, I know better when these sisters are involved."

Alu said, "Would you believe we were chasing ghosts?"

The Choerkin glanced between each woman, then caught the gaze of Harlik, who shrugged. "I suspect I better."

Fourteen

Starry-Eyed Fear

The senseless sensing of things that aren't has long plagued the minds of mortals. A man's eyes might lie, a woman's nose, or their child's ears. Even the most intimate senses of touch and taste can lie. But the most damaging lies are often those of the senseless senses, emotions, such as believing there is love in someone's heart when there is only murder or contempt—or getting lost in a dream.

—Fredrûark of Nomundom

Ivin stood atop Choerkin Tower, gazing at the bright dome of Skywatch reflecting the orange of Eliles' eternal flames like a miniature sun. Indecision stroked his thoughts with bouts of shame and cowardice, and he wondered if High Oracle Meris trembled less before stepping toward the Road of Living Stars and eternity than he did at the thought of entering the stars a man could return from. Or had he already returned once from the Seven Heavens? The Twelve Hells? Or did Sol send him to the Forges to be hammered into a weapon?

He stepped left and looked down, and in his mind, he could see Meris lying dead on the rocks, body broken and gray hair mopped over rock in her death.

"Well, boy? Why do you think she did it?"

"Some said you pushed her."

A bellowing laugh. "I was already dead and gone, poisoned by that monk of yours."

"I thought he was a friend." Ivin turned to face his father, cringing at the sight of yellowing froth dribbling from the corner of his mouth and into his shaggy, silver-streaked beard. With a suck and swipe, the foam disappeared.

"Well, can't say we all didn't make mistakes, am I right?" He stepped to the edge and pointed. "But why?"

"We'll never know."

Broad shoulders turned on him, a snarl on Kotin's face. "You don't pity the witch, do you?"

"I did once, not now."

"Pity!" A head-rocking snort and his face eased. "Maybe we're all due some pity now and again, but her? Not from us. She took your mother and sister and then herself, the only godsdamned right thing she'd done in my memory. But it don't earn no pity, got me, boy?"

"I should've believed you all those years ago. I've regrets in life, and that might be my greatest."

"Shit, boy, you're just sayin' that 'cause you're here. With me. Now." He slapped his shoulder, and Ivin rocked sideways. "Give it a good thinkin', and you'll find worse to sweat yer soul over."

It didn't take a flicker. "My wife and twins. You're a grandfather, you know?"

The big man leaned against the parapet; despite the heat of the tower's flame and his bearskin cloak, he didn't sweat. "And that's a damned fine thing, though I wish I'd lived to see the day."

"Me too."

Ivin stared at his father until they both smiled and laughed. "There ya go, my boy. Laugh at death and regrets. Better than tears every day." He pointed over the edge. "But tell me why."

Ivin turned and looked again upon Meris, and this time, the dead crone looked back, her neck twisted until dead eyes stared at him. "Regrets?"

"Your dear mother and her... Peneluple prayed with that witch on every holiday and begged her to break bones for her every gods-damned year. Hells, Meris sat at my own table for dinner more than a dozen times over the years before you were born. Your mother was loved and called friend by many, but she didn't call more than a dozen people her friends. Meris was one."

Ivin raised his eyes to the Fire, and a ghostly image of dead eyes flickered in the flames. "Meris has a granddaughter on the island. Living in the stars with the holies."

Fingers pinched Kotin's chin as he stroked his beard. "That miserable old bird laying with a man is frightnin' enough without the notion of her birthin' holy brats."

"She seems a nice girl."

"What proof... Hell's, it don't matter none. Regrets matter."

Ivin's gaze returned to Meris. "You think she killed herself because of what she did to mother?"

"Aye, and why not?"

"Twelve years, why wait so long if she regretted it so much?"

A voice crackled behind him, and a chill ran his spine. "Living with a righteous regret is easier than surviving one born of a mistake."

Ivin blinked, the body below disappeared, and on turning, he stared into the very alive gray eyes of the High Oracle of Skywatch. "You admit it then."

"Holy sacrifice—"

"Becomes murder," said Kotin to finish her sentence.

"And murder is a sin worthy of the Seventh Hell."

Ivin clutched his face, forcing his head back and his eyes to the middle of the Fire's maelstrom. "I'm dreaming. Damn you both, I'm dreaming." He strode for the door.

"Where you think yer goin', boy? We aren't done here."

Meris said, "I only told you part of the truth when last we broke bones."

"To the Twelve Hells with the both of you!" Ivin shook his head, slapped his cheek as he entered the stairwell, and slammed the door behind him. "Wake up, damn it. Wake up."

But the grip of sleep refused to let go, and he could sense the pressure of a chair's seat on his shoulder blades. As he turned a corner, he passed Joslin with his smiling face wrinkled and mummified by salt. "Good day, Lord Ivin."

"Wake up!" Down and down he went until he stepped onto the main floor of Choerkin Keep without a clue where he was headed. He sighed, spun a circle, and walked toward the main hall, his strides shifting to a jog before erupting into a maniacal sprint with gasping breaths and desperation in every step until he burst the hall's door open to see himself sitting asleep in a chair. Peace, serenity, shallow breaths with his chin tucked to his chest above folded arms.

It was with conflicting senses of deep relief and resignation that he moved to the chair to sit in himself, but the moment he settled in, he awoke with a snort and gasp, eyes blinking and sitting up, and it wasn't as if he awakened at all. He stood and turned with hesitation, half expecting to find himself still asleep, but in the chair sat only empty air.

Ivin licked his lips, took a deep breath, and resolved to avoid yet another regret.

He needed to find Eliles.

He needed to see the stars.

The entry to Skywatch swung wide with a whisper on hinges he recognized now as fashioned from Îkoruv, Elemental Iron, and he stared into the darkness with trepidation before even seeing the stars.

"The last time I was here, Meris broke bone and spoke of my future."

Eliles stood by his side. "Cryptic, but haunting in how right it looks in hindsight?"

He chuckled. "You experienced the same?"

"No. Master Dareun always smoothed the bones to protect me."

"Smoothed?"

She sighed. "We feared that a true reading would reveal me as Defiled. With prayer and tools, the breaks could be predicted, aligned with marks, and made to break as the smoother desired."

Ivin snorted with a shake of his head. "All these years then, all of these fortunes from Bontore, false? The creations of priests?" He stared into the darkness ahead, seeing a house of lies instead of a reverent hall of futures.

"No, no, that's why your bone spoke the truth. Honest bones can reveal many truths."

He considered the words of the Meris in his dream and the real one's fortune before he sailed for Kaludor. While the portents remained fresh with his dwelling upon them for years, he'd almost forgotten the abrupt end to their meeting. He stepped through the doors and looked up at the wonder of the stars and could almost hear the echo of her nasal voice.

"A hundred cracks might mean a hundred things of which I will not speak, full of contradictions. It would take days to decipher. Leave now, young Choerkin. The bone speaks volumes which would serve to confuse and muddle your thoughts."

"Well, Meris, my thoughts are confused and muddled now more

than ever." Staring at the field of stars, he wondered how he'd been nervous to step beneath them again. So beautiful. So tranquil. So at peace. "Kotin got a good laugh when Meris stopped her reading short. She wasn't ready for what it said." He licked his lips and sighed, his mind wandering to what clues the bone might have offered to avoid what was now the past and what it might have offered for his future now. "She wasn't ready for how it broke. She expected a smoothed stone and got an honest one."

Eliles cocked her head. "Master Dareun trained in the Ways of the Oracle as a boy. The system of storing bones is precise, and mistakes brought whippings and worse. Here at Skywatch? Where only the finest oracles and attendants lived? It's unlikely."

"Smoothed or not, something went wrong that day." When two strides into darkness, a spiral stair with an angelic glow appeared in the distance, and he chuckled. "This is a bit like a peep behind the puppet show."

She giggled. "It a place few puppets are ever meant to see."

He reached the stairs and climbed. "A marionette on strings controls a marionette on strings; how high must we look to find the puppeteer?" Ivin stared when he reached the top. "Just step out?"

"Mhm. It's not slick. Or at least not especially so."

His heel touched and rolled to his toes, and sound rose into the air, reminding him of a string strummed. He stopped with a smile by his third step and turned to Eliles, who stood at the top of the stairs with eyes narrowed.

"Your feet stroke a harp."

"It's beautiful."

She stepped toward him, footfalls striking with echoing chimes. "I've never heard anyone's feet sound different except The Touched. He walked in silence."

Eliles strode past him, and he followed her song, the notes of his harp blending with her rhythm into a melancholy tune. When she stopped to face him, he couldn't help a grin. "We make beautiful music." He grimaced. " Sorry. That sounded...."

"Yes, it did."

Ivin settled to his knees after she sat. "So, what do we do?"

"It's simple enough. I just need the name of the person you want to see."

The *who* was simple; saying it aloud was the difficult part, so he stalled. "You said Solineus was still in the north? At New Fost?"

"Is that the town's name?"

"Yes. Show me Solineus."

Eliles bowed her head for a flicker. "Elinwe, show me the way to Solineus Mikjehemlut."

Ivin didn't know what to expect, but when the stars blurred into a vision of the world, it took only a flicker flying over water for the view to refocus on a Luxun Ship. "Holy hells, is that the *Entiyu Montoño*?" All doubts fled as the vision drew close enough to recognize the script on the bow, and flickers later indistinct figures on the ship turned into Solineus standing beside Captain Intœño who pointed at the horizon, and standing so close to Solineus' arm they touched, stood Alu. Ivin laughed. "That man's in trouble."

"What am I missing?"

"That girl there, that's Sîu. She's an islander with a keen eye for him. If she's still with him, I'd wager she has her hooks in him."

"Pretty hooks."

"Pretty everything. Sorry."

She giggled. "Truth is truth."

"How far away are they?"

"Close. Real close. With open water and such a short journey to grasp direction, I'd guess somewhere to the southwest in the Parapet

Straits. More west than south? This is as close as I've ever seen anyone off-island. As close as I saw you."

"Sailing west, no doubt back to Mulshahar and the Emudar farther south."

"Mulshahar?"

"A city on the west coast somewhere, red-gold domes... hells, I've never been there. Awake, anyhow. Take me to Rikis."

"Elinwe, show me the way to Rikis Choerkin."

Their view of the strait pulled back and glided east as expected, but not for long as their view of the world took a confusing spin on its axis. It took a flicker to realize their vision faced east before drifting forward, bringing ships into view. One ship was Silone, but he guessed the other three Edan make. They approached the mouth of a river with a city and, to the northwest, a fuzzy image he suspected might be a tower. Ivin leaned until his hands supported him with a light pluck of harp's strings."What? Where are they?"

"Your guess is as good or maybe better than mine. I spent most of my life in Istinjoln. They're east of us, is about all I can say. Not Northern Vandunêz?"

"The rivers in Hidreng flow to the Strait, south to north; we're looking at Kaludor." Ivin tore his eyes from the Edan and Silone ships to assess the landscape. Plenty of cities sat on the mouths of rivers, but this was close, and the buildings to the northwest... there stood only one answer that made sense. "Son of a bitch. Broldun Fost, and that there is Fermiden Abbey. " The sky tracked closer, the view of the city and shore disappearing as Elinwe's vision found Rikis sitting on a crate, chatting with The Wolverine and a couple of sailors. "There'd be no reason to enter Broldun Fost that I can imagine. They might be heading up the Kiubor River. It also... They're headed for Istinjoln. Godsdamn." His heart fluttered with excitement and aggravation, the

desire to run to the docks, dive in the waters, and see about swimming to freedom and Choerkin Fost. "Damn it!"

"What?"

"The Edan must've found something, some way to fight the Celestial Gate. To close it."

"If true, that's wonderful. It gives reason to hope."

"And reason to regret being trapped here." He cast a grin her way. "Not that I mind the company. Is there a way to hear them?"

"Not that I've found, no."

The drum of his excited heart faded to a dying patter. "Gods, I want to be there."

"Maybe I could get you off Herald's Watch."

"How?" A burst of thrill that died in an instant. "No. No, no. I can't."

"You said it yourself. Solineus came and went—"

"You understand it's not possible." He looked into her eyes and godsdamned if he didn't want to say *because after all these years, I made it back to you,* but the notion was a smitten child's foolish love note. An untenable fantasy dead for years if it'd ever had hope to start. "Your fires are the visible trap. If we lived in a heroic poem from the God Wars, the flames would be as much symbolic as real. The Fire of Sol's prophecy."

Her gaze ducked to her knees before looking at him again. "You know the prophecy."

"Probably better than you do, despite Meliu trying to hide details from me. You raised me with the Sliver of Star, but how can I be the king prophecy promised if I never leave this island?"

She stroked her chin, and he suspected she wanted to say something other than what came from her mouth. "I didn't raise you from the dead."

"You didn't? What the hells would you call it then?"

Soft eyes tugged at his heart. "I healed you."

He wanted to believe. "Healed an incurable poison and months of coma with the Sliver of Star; I'm not sure if it's worth arguing the meaning of *dead* with the *Codex of Sol.*"

She sighed. "You still remember nothing of, well, of *not* being dead?"

He turned his gaze back to the bird's eye view of the world that appeared so crisp and clear as to be approaching unreal. "I've called it a patch of darkness in my memories, a blank, but that's a lie. Meliu read a portion of the *History of Olô Nodustok* to me." He stopped. *Did she? Of course, she had to have.* "I think it's more a fable, but Olô's life story is sewn into a tapestry by the Fates depicting all his deeds from smallest to most grand—every memory. If the Fates did the same for me, there wouldn't be a stretch of black cloth or two pieces cut; it'd be my last and first memories stitched together with nothing possible between. If I didn't know better, I'd say I lost nothing. No time. Nothing. Does it sound silly?"

He felt her stare and feared she might express pity for him, apologize, or say something else trite. "What if you really are missing nothing? Instead, the tapestry was folded and stitched to hide the truth. If true, in order to fix your memory, we'd need to cut the stitches to find what's beneath."

He chuckled. "It's an analogy; don't take it too far." But his lips pinched in thought. How far off was she?

"From the look on your face, I'm not sure I did."

"If we could find my memories, I'm not sure I want to remember. Did I stand at the foot of the Road of Living Stars stranded? Did I fall into a hell, or was I driven into the Forges to be hammered into a weapon for Sol? Or did I laugh and dine in the comfort of the Seventh

Heaven, speaking with Sol about the great victories I'd earn on my return? Or was it the black cloth, a tapestry of nothing?"

She giggled. "It seems you've given it some thought."

"Too much. It needs to stop." He sighed and rubbed his forehead. "I'll want to keep an eye on those two."

"So, you'll be coming back to the stars?"

He turned a fake frown to face her honest smirk. "Aye. Maybe that's why I didn't want to come here in the first place. But since I'm here, let's check on an old friend. Rinold."

The world blurred, forcing him to squint as they passed over plains, rivers, hills, cities, and mountains to forests he figured familiar and back to an expanse of tall-grassed plains. A herd of horses appeared on a hill first, but as they drew closer, he saw men, maybe a hundred, but the vision stopped its approach before he could make out faces.

"As close as we get?"

"Closer than I expected."

Movement, and he caught a flash from a big man's back. Ivin blinked once, then twice. "I'd wager that's Polus Broldun with the latcu sword. They named him Warlord and gave him the Choerkin sword! Ha! It's best Kotin never hears about this." He chuckled. "And if your vision centers on a name, that's Rinold."

"Where are they?"

"Aye, well, that's a tougher call. The plains southwest of Endelêun roll for hundreds of horizons. At least they're safe for the time being. Show me—"

A rain of musical notes erupted from the universe around them, and he scrambled to his feet, reaching for his sword, but Eliles grabbed his wrist. "It's our young friend from the stars, nothing to worry about."

Ivin spun to face the music running their way and relaxed on recognizing her face for certain. "Good gods, girl, you damned near scared me to death."

She gazed at them with a panting smile by the time her run brought her to their sides. She slid to a seat beside him with a booming crescendo. "I can't believe you're both here!" She stared at their view of the world, where Rinold and Polus overlooked a massive herd of beasts crossing the valley below. "Woah. Wowee. Look at those critters! Who are these people? Where are they?"

Ivin sat back down with a groan, resigning himself to being pestered here on out. "The big bastard is a Broldun but a friend, and the little guy is Rinold the Squirrel, and they are far away to the south."

"Exciting! Where next?"

Ivin bit his lip; he'd been about to say Kinesee but hesitated again with a newcomer. Part of him declared his hesitance irrational, but his mouth wasn't persuaded. "Adinvan Mikjehemlut."

"Elinwe, show me the way to Adinvan Mikjehemlut."

Their vision swept west while pulling north, sweeping over plains, hills, and forests before waves and sea dominated everything beneath a wisp-clouded sky. An island appeared on the horizon, rugged and mountainous with white caps on its shores, and on the eastern and northern beaches, Silone longboats rode the waves and sat perched on sand. He counted two dozen boats before the view shifted, drawing them close enough to see people scurrying. If Adinvan was in sight, he wasn't close enough to pick him out.

"That island is gorgeous! The flowers, the trees, the blue waters... And we're stuck on this ugly rock."

Ivin glanced at Ieru. "I felt the same way growing up, only I didn't know anywhere looked like that."

Eliles said, "And this place is called what?"

"Pôn, I think. Sîu's home and her people live on a number of islands in the Medrisên Sea. They're busy, judging by the number of ships. They're supposed to be hitting the Histê kings to distract them from coming for the people in Endelêun."

"I don't know much, but wouldn't the Histê retaliate against their islands? It sounds risky."

Ieru leaned to steal their attention. "No offense, but girl from the stars here. None of that makes sense. Who are the Histê?"

Ivin chortled. "Next time we meet, I'll tell stories. For now, they're people who want we Silone dead. As for the islanders? That's our biggest fear, dragging them into the war, but Solineus might've done that already when he saved Sîu's brother from Histê priests."

"Saved him?"

"Blood sacrifice."

"Ewwww."

Eliles said, "When Kûmjotu-kî destroyed their temple? I think I was talking to her when she left to save him."

Ivin's head pulled back to stare. "You talked to the Great Kî?"

Ieru's eyes bounced back and forth. "The who?"

Kinesee said, "A dragon, though she looked like an old—and by old, I mean, long dead—priestess named Fudenu of Ulmor, who you, young lady, would appreciate because she's the one who brought the grapes to Herald's Watch centuries ago."

Ivin shook his head with a sputter. "How don't I know all this?"

"Because you wasted your time sitting in that godsawful tower sulking."

Ieru eyeballed him. "Yeah, you did."

"Whoa, ladies! No teaming up. You mentioned a dragon in the flames and stars—"

"In the stars?"

He and Eliles both stared at the girl, less from her words than the stressing pitch, and they asked, "What?" at the same time.

Her eyes bounced between them again before landing on Eliles. "That first day I met you, I felt something watching me as I slid through the Shower of Stars. Scary, a little. I knew it wasn't my auntie or anyone else, or I didn't think so. Would it have been this dragon? Tell me! That would be so fun."

Eliles straightened. "Scary? I doubt she'd look to frighten you. I'm sure it was just your imagination."

"Wrong and boring." The girl snorted. "Take us somewhere else."

Eliles caught his gaze. "Well, I think there's someone this man has been avoiding."

In truth, there were two, but Ivin knew of who she spoke. "Kinesee Choerkin."

"Elinwe, show me the way to Kinesee Choerkin."

Elinwe's sky shifted in an eastbound blur, passing over a coastal Histê city so fast a blink might've missed it, passing over forests and rivers again until slowing into focus over the massive city of Endelêun straddling rivers and overlooking the plains from high cliffs. But he didn't get the time to take in the busy roads leading into the city before Elinwe's vision jarred their senses by streaking into the city, straight for the palace, and passing through flashes of rooms and halls before entering darkness.

Ivin muttered, "What the hells," and then a room flashed into brilliant Light. *The* room, deep beneath Endelêun, is where the original copy of the *Codex of Sol* had rested in a drawer for untold centuries. His breath escaped at the sight of her, kneeling and feeling around the floor.

Ieru said, "She's your wife? She's young."

"I'm not that much older, and we were forced to marry."

"She's pretty! Too pretty for you, but I suppose the Choerkin thing counts for something."

"She didn't want to marry me, either." Though he uttered the words, he didn't know who he meant them for, Ieru or Eliles.

"Well! At least she's pretty. I'd like to be that pretty someday."

Eliles giggled and said, "You are far from homely."

"Eh! Maybe, but it'd help if I was ever allowed to grow boobs."

She slapped her chest, and Ivin raised an eyebrow Eliles' way. "I thought you said this one was being raised by holies?"

"Mmm, she has a mind of her own."

"I do." She pointed. "Who are these other people?"

"The one banging on the table is Izilfer, my sister by marriage with Roplin. The lady with the sword and scratching the wall with it is Alu, Kinesee's older sister, and wife to Tudwan Ravinrin."

"If I can be so bold, what are they doing?"

Ivin stared at their peculiar behavior, poking, prodding, and banging on walls, tables, floors, and ceiling. "I don't know. This chamber is deep beneath the palace. They found a copy of the *Codex of Sol* here."

Eliles said, "That table is a carving of the city. It's—" Eliles gasped and covered her mouth. "Heavens above. I've never got so close before! Not this far away."

Ivin grunted, and his breaths came faster. "How the hells didn't we notice? We're right above them."

"How? Is it her? Your connection to your wife?"

"The room?" A chill flooded his spine, and he balled his hands into fists. *Have I led them to her? Who?* "Get us the hells out of here."

"Where?"

"Anywhere! Now."

"Elinwe, show me the way to Master Dareun."

The world's view streaked away until their vision passed over the Dragonspan Mountains, then it spun to face north, taking them all the way to Istinjoln.

As their travel slowed, Eliles said, "Are you going to explain that?"

"I don't know. I can't."

"Well, you better try."

"A hunch. A gut feeling. Meliu mentioned—"*did she really? She must have—*"someone looking for Kinesee. Rin, the White Lion, or something. If we just showed them the way—"

"We didn't. They couldn't be here with us in the stars."

What she said made sense. They were alone. In a universe self-contained. On an island. Trapped by Fire. But all that meant was that anybody, anything, who could see what they saw was powerful beyond mortality. "I pray you're right."

Ieru said, "Is that Master Dareun?"

Ivin turned from Eliles' gaze to stare upon Istinjoln and a shadowy figure standing atop the monastery's highest tower. The blazing beam of light known as a Celestial Gate illuminated his transparent face beneath gray skies and rain passing through his form. When their travel stopped, Ivin said, "He's staring straight at us." No. He was staring straight at Eliles.

And she at him. "Master Dareun? Can you hear me?"

The haunt stood as an elderly man, gray and colorless to Ivin's eye, and bearing an emotion in his expression that stretched his features into what he at first interpreted as rage, then horror, before settling on desperation. Dareun's mouth opened and closed without a voice and too much like a fish for Ivin to read his lips.

"Did he say something?"

Eliles' head shook in a flurry. "I don't know! I don't know. Can you hear me, Dareun?"

Over and over, the man mouthed something. "Is he saying yes? More? What the hells?"

A blackness rose in the gray sky behind the spirit of Eliles' master, a man Ivin knew was the closest thing to a father she'd had in Istinjoln. A darkness climbed over the battlements and lumbered his way on froggish hind legs and tentacles of Shadow from its faceless head. "The demon Solineus spoke of. It must be."

"Run! Dareun, please, run!"

But the man stood still, mouth making three distinct, exaggerated motions with his lips. "One word. Two or three syllables?"

"Gods! Run!"

Shadow tentacles reached over Dareun's shoulders, coming for them as if they'd reach all the way from Istinjoln to steal their souls. Then, Istinjoln disappeared, and they stared into the stars. Tranquil. Silent. At peace. Until Eliles screamed.

Ivin grabbed her and pulled her into a hug. "What happened?"

"I don't know. I don't think... I don't think he's there anymore to show me."

She rocked back and forth in his arms, and he leaned his head back to stare into the stars. "He's fine. Shadows can't kill a ghost." She snuffled and nodded, but he knew neither of them knew if it was true. "What was he trying to say? It must've been important."

She shook her head against his shoulder, and when he looked back down, Ieru crept close.

"I think," she cleared her throat. "I think he was saying, 'Almost,' but it doesn't make sense. Does it?"

Ivin muttered the word aloud, "Almost," while paying attention to the shape of his lips as he stressed the sounds. "Almost. She's right."

Eliles' shaking slowed. "Almost what?"

Ieru hugged Eliles' back, and Ivin stretched his hands over her shoulders, too, holding them both tight. "Almost closed the Gate? The Queen is almost free? Almost." He clutched them both and wouldn't realize how natural it felt to hold them until days later because, at that moment, all he wanted to do was scream.

FIFTEEN

Questioning Numbers

Lord Êmoxuhoktu of Ôxêum Dedor raised the finest Popûêz Baboons in the land. Fierce, loyal, and angry upon his word and whim they guarded his palatial grounds. He rewarded them with a beautiful queen thinking to continue their bloodlines, but in this act, ended his own.

—*From Nibesêûmô,*
Legend of the Baboon Queen

"Is she what all the sailors say?"

"She is human, yes."

Ilsferu's eyes narrowed, bringing a smirk to Glimdrem's lips. "You know what I mean."

He did, indeed. A crew of Trelelunin babbling over the looks of a halfbreed human had done the upcoming meeting harm. "She pales to your beauty, but she is rich, and we need gold." He offered the crook of his arm as his love stepped from the gangplank, and she accepted with an appeased smile.

With the sun sinking over the bay to the west, the docks transitioned from the bustle of work to sweaty men either heading for

inns and taverns or making final preparations for the next morning's departure, allowing their walk a more casual and dignified gait without the need to dodge and weave. The sheer number of humans who swarmed Bonduborâ's wharf at the peak of the day brought a squirm to Glimdrem's stomach, realizing how outnumbered he and his people were. How outnumbered the Edan were, not that the Edan would bother to worry about such a triviality. In the case of the Edan, power was more pure than the simplistic relativity of numbers, but here in a human city, the only power on his side was perception—a fickle power on the breech of fading with the outstaying of a welcome.

He straightened and raised his chin with a half dozen Trelelunin warriors marching stiff-spined at his back and strode with a glide as close to an Edan's that he could manage. Perception. Guards didn't follow in his wake due to fear. Perception. He didn't lack steel at his side because he trusted the city's thieves. Perception. A psychological ambiance to tickle the human brain, to reinforce the notion that to touch him was to touch the Eleris and incur the Edan's wrath. It was what those who left the Mother Wood called *insetis neu Eleris*, the traveling threat of the Mother Wood, the promise of retribution.

If a single Goro suspected he and his people were outcasts, banished from the Mother Wood, it might be enough to crack perception's veneer, ending his welcome as well as his life. Or if not his life, at least his lifestyle. Glimdrem didn't know what reaction the Edan might have to his demise and often pondered the possibilities. They wouldn't mourn him, not for a flicker, but killing any who once called the Mother Wood home might be viewed as an unacceptable precedent. However curious he might be, Glimdrem had no burning desire to find out.

Ilsferu said, "You're far away."

He snorted with a chuckle, realizing that he hadn't even been paying attention to their route as they approached the dock's "T." He paused as horse and wagon rolled close down the main boardwalk with a clatter, then turned south without a second thought. "Musing on our situation."

"The *Turquoise Leaf* should return in the next couple of days. She might bear good news."

He raised her hand for a kiss. "It may indeed. Profits enough to survive on, no doubt. But this Contessa may be our key to the world without having to negotiate every step."

It was his love's turn to snort. "I don't see how one woman can be so valuable."

He couldn't share his suspicions with her. Wouldn't. But with or without the impossibility of Xanesu's soul having taken residence in the Contessa's body, there was opportunity. "We of the Eleris don't understand wealth and power as humans do. Power we understand: it belongs to the Edan. Always has and always will. Humans age and die. Power is a thing to be fought over and taken, and wealth is a branch of power. Never underestimate one human's ability to collect both."

"If she's so powerful, what need could she have for us?"

His lips wrinkled. "Power can defeat wealth, and wealth can defeat power. They work hand in hand, but the relationship is never simple. It is a dance I don't claim to understand in full, but it's one we need to learn."

"I do enjoy dancing."

"And you are stunning when atwirl on the floor." He kissed her hand again, and when his eyes raised, he spotted five blue banners in the sky ahead, their silk adorned with stars. "Mostul Ûbar. Five ships. I think we've found the lady we need."

"If you hadn't compared the Edan to pigs, we might not need her."

His words came as a reflex despite not believing them. "You might be right."

As they drew closer to their destination, he noted warriors with muscles that appeared as hardened and perfect as onyx statues and not a soul passed between them. It was peculiar until he realized the five ships held every occupied berth along a dock suited for eight or more ships. "Perception is power, my love."

"She does make a spectacle."

"Indeed." Even his Trelelunin ships had been forced to share space with foreign vessels. Rumors spoke to the woman setting pirate ships ablaze, bringing down a smuggling ring, and, in the process, bringing down the corrupt leadership of Apreleû, one of the most powerful city-states in the Monsoon Straits. Of course, rumors also said that a night between her thighs left a dozen men dead of disease, but Glimdrem figured her enemies spoke these whispers. Such was the way of humans, disparaging with words what they couldn't destroy in truth. "A woman who can command an entire dock for her retinue might be who we need."

"Let's make this quick."

They turned in their approach to find the dock behind the Mostulê guardsmen devoid of life. Empty of workers, sailors, slaves, or even more warriors. The two ships on the left of the dock were standard Goro craftsmanship, and on the right, larger ships of a lighter wood that he suspected native to Mostul Ûbar, but at the end sat the flagship. Even concealed behind the broad shoulders of the men in front of him, there was no way to mistake the deep amber of Hôduk mahogany with polished streaks as dark as ebony. It was a vessel that would bring whistles from even Trelelunin sailors.

He stopped strides in front of the central guard, though nothing about their appearances suggested a rank to him. "Glimdrem and

Ilsferu of the Mother Wood. The Contessa expects us." He expected the man to recognize only a single word, contessa, among his Edan words, but whether the Contessa had educated her guard or not, he bowed and stepped to the side.

"*Nobrûmî to,* Trelelunin. Welcome. She awaits you on the *Silver Falcon.*"

His pronunciation was understandable, more than Glimdrem could say for most humans who thought they spoke Edan. "Thank you."

They passed with courteous nods and strolled down the empty dock, with plenty of time to take in the grandeur of the ship they approached.

A tall, wiry-built Goro with a waxed beard and mustache greeted them on their arrival to the gangplank, a man who looked the sort to sail when and where he wanted rather than when authorities told him to. He, too, spoke in better-than-average Edan. "I am Captain Sandorelê. I oversee the Contessa's fleet and partner in her business."

Glimdrem whispered first to his love, "Be careful of using Edan; it's no longer safe to speak freely," then leaned into a slight bow while Ilsferu stood rigid. Without asking permission to board, he stepped onto the plank. "From your use of Edan, I suspect you prepared for this visit for some time."

"Aye. Sorry. Yes. We took our time reaching Bonduborâ. Uncertain if you had departed these waters, we checked every port on the way."

"Aye is one of the few Goro words I know." He approached the man and was pleased the captain didn't offer his hand. "I'm looking forward to our feast. I do miss Edan wine."

"That's *my* Edan wine we'll be drinking." He winked and nodded toward the cabin doors. "The Edan know how to crush a grape better than even the Goro, but the Goro *gropu* will get you drunk faster."

"Ironic, seeing as the Edan are incapable of intoxication. They drink it for the flavors alone."

The man strode in silence a flicker before rubbing his chin. "That is a shame. They miss out on good times."

"You have no idea," Glimdrem said with a smirk.

Ilsferu interrupted, maybe fearing he'd say too much. "Our stores of wine were shallow to begin with and have dwindled to nothing."

"Nothing? How the hell do you keep the crew from mutiny in the dead winds? Entertain them?"

Glimdrem glanced at Ilsferu's blank face. "A region where the winds often don't blow, slowing travel and raising anxieties amongst mortals."

"Ah! Trelelunin will not experience dead winds. Mutiny?"

"A crew taking the helm, casting the captain overboard or some such." The stymied look on her face left Glimdrem to speak with the captain. "Such things are unheard of on a ship of the Eleris." In fact, his banishment and the flight of his people from the Mother Wood was the first time he'd ever heard of anything resembling a mutiny.

"Well. I guess I should seek out a Trelelunin crew."

Ilsferu said, "They'd mutiny you, sir."

Glimdrem stroked the back of her hand with a thumb. "He was joking, my sweets."

The human chuckled before saying, "I take care of my men with an excess of gold, in particular since my partnership with the Contessa." Their stroll ended as Sandorelê opened the door and gestured for them to enter a huge, wide-open cabin set with three long tables with a dozen chairs each, but only the central table bore settings.

The Contessa sat at the end of the table with the same bodyguard and handmaid as when they first met, seated to either side. "Please, afford yourself the comfort of this hall."

Ilsferu's grip clutched his hand, and her voice came soft. "The quality of your Edan was not exaggerated."

Glimdrem freed himself from her hand, pulled a second chair to the end of the table, and motioned for Ilsferu to sit. "Never have I lied to my love, yet she suspected me. That is how rare your gift is."

A broad smile with perfect teeth. "Rumors didn't exaggerate the Lady Ilsferu's beauty, either. The grace of the Trelelunin bestows honor upon this humble vessel."

"Humble. I'm at least uncertain on that account, though there is no denying my love's perfection." He took her hand in his as he sat and kissed her palm. "The *Silver Willow* is spectacular, and sitting at the head of a dock reserved for your vessels alone... The statement isn't subtle."

"You noticed?" A wry grin before she flicked her hand before her eyes. "I don't impress the locals; I keep me and mine safe. I've stepped on uncountable toes over the past few months."

"I see. I don't wish to find new enemies by assisting you."

A humored grimace as servants entered through the door behind her, carrying bottles of wine and a silver serving bowl. "I don't doubt a few folks will give you a cold stare, but because of who I am rather than for what you can do for me."

"The Boboru not included."

She hesitated as a cork popped. "I'm not so sure. If the Boboru understood what I plan, well, in the long run, they might change their mind."

A serving girl filled his wine, then Ilsferu's. "Dare I ask?"

"The Boboru blockaded the city of Lultûhol, as I mentioned. This disrupts trade and raises the threat of war across the mouth of the Monsoon Straits, maybe farther. The needle in their eye is a pirate known as Red Skull for the flag he flies, and they claim he hides in

the city. And I ask myself, why would the Boboru risk a war, and why would Lultûhol suffer a blockade for a scoundrel?"

Ilsferu said, "And why should we risk entanglement for you?"

"Because I have what you need. Wealth. You have what I need: a position of neutrality with the Boboru."

Glimdrem smiled at his lady with a glance before turning back to the Contessa. "You're both right, as you well know. We're willing to entertain your proposition but only upon hearing an explanation and with the understanding that I'm not risking our lives or war."

The Contessa gestured for soup, and servants ladled. From the smell, he guessed a spicy dish with pork sausage.

"If the Boboru are adamant on refusing entry, you sail away. If you manage to get me to the docks, all the better."

"As I've mentioned, but Ilsferu needed to hear it from you. However, entry requires one thing: A reason. I haven't met with a Boboru in over a hundred years, but I doubt they'd let me through on a wink and goodwill." He spooned the soup but didn't bring it to his lips.

"I admit to hoping you could devise something particular to your people."

"A delivery is out of the question. Anything related to trade would raise objections." He sipped soup, an unobjectionable flavor that sizzled on his tongue and gave him an excuse for wine. With this, he took more than a sip. Dry currant with an earthy cherry. He blinked. "Novdoron?"

Captain Sandorelê answered, "You have a tongue worthy of the drink."

Glimdrem grinned at the unusual phrasing and raised his glass in salute. "I doubted your veracity, but this is legitimate. Not drained and refilled. But it doesn't help answer our question."

"We could offer something they want, a third party to confirm whether the pirate is even in the city."

"Too bold, too forward. That's the salt on the meal if they need further convincing." He ignored the soup and drank wine. "I don't yet know what you want."

She took her first drink of wine, a dainty sip. "How far can I trust you?"

Ilsferu said, "A Trelelunin's word is as good as an Edan's."

"From what little I have heard, the Edan are a peculiar sort." She raised a hand to halt any rejoinder. "But honorable to a fault."

Glimdrem said, "No argument from me. Your friend, Solineus, and I braved death together more than once."

"And I don't know him that well."

"We aren't childhood chums, but I would call him honorable to a fault. You can trust me with anything that will not compromise my people."

She rubbed her forehead as she took a longer drink. "I stumbled into a dangerous situation I thought I had resolved, but have since had my doubts. Have you heard of donu-honêsh?"

"The word is not familiar."

"It is an herb that brings visions and often death. They say a euphoria comes with its smoke, and people become addicted. I destroyed the trade and killed the only man who knew its secret."

"The problem does sound solved."

"Do you like coincidences?"

Glimdrem smiled. *Like the coincidence of you speaking perfect Edan?* "No, I don't."

"Someone looked to start a war in the Straits, between the Goro, the Free Cities, the Boboru, and who knows if they meant to draw in the Korômonê or others. There were gears turning that I can only speculate upon, but the blockade of Lultûhol is tinder just waiting for a spark."

"You think someone will use the situation to start the war you stopped?"

"Yes, though I'm not sure I stopped anything so much as slowed it. Simêum and Mostul Ûbar would be unable to stop the Boboru, but the war someone wanted needed Gorô cities. No one knows why the Boboru want this pirate so bad. If I can find out, I might understand both the risk of a region-wide war and who is trying to start it. My uncle was one of those who believed in war, but he wasn't alone."

"Your uncle won't answer your questions?"

Her eyes remained cold. A killer's eyes. A predator's eyes. "He is dead. By my hand. He meant to use Lultûhol and donu-honêsh to draw Nomnuvar and the Gorô into war against the Boboru. He would have had his revenge upon Aprelêu while freeing the Straits of the Boborun scourge."

Glimdrem swished wine around his tongue before swallowing, savoring the tingle. "Not wholly ignoble goals. The Boboru are a repulsive people."

"I'd prefer to break their grip on the Straits without sacrificing tens of thousands of Gorô lives."

"And you think this pirate can answer your questions?"

Her head cocked in thought. "No, I don't. Not directly. But I think he's a piece of the puzzle. If I come to understand *why* the Boboru and Lultûhol want him, I'll know whether he's a player, a piece, or a mere coincidence."

"Altruistic goals, a saint after your mother's faith."

"A stretch."

He leaned into Ilsferu's ear. "It seems odd, does it not, that she sought us out for such an unlikely outcome."

"I sought you first with the idea of trade to make us rich, but on arrival, I heard you were not a trading expedition. I expanded my notion of what to trade."

"An altruistic opportunist. But my people will not agree to such a journey without a plan."

The Contessa nodded to Sandorelê, and the captain removed a pouch from his waist and dropped it on the table. "This should buy you time to conjure a plan."

Glimdrem plucked the thick canvas from the table. "Too light for gold."

The Contessa smiled. "A friend, perhaps more an ally, taught me that gems are easier to carry. This bag alone should outfit your ships for a year's journey, and all you have to do is agree to my terms and try to get me inside Lultûhol."

Glimdrem forced the strings loose and peeled the pouch's throat open to look into its gullet by the cabin's ample light. Emeralds, rubies, diamonds, and topaz caught his eye in an instant. "The quality of the stones?"

"They aren't perfect, inclusions here and there, but the cut and polish are better than average."

He cinched the bag and dropped it back on the table. "I'm sure I have people who will tell me the quality, but the value? We know little."

"There are people in the city who can confirm their value."

In truth, he didn't doubt her word. Even inferior stones would buy his people a future. "And what are your terms?"

"As stated, but I have a few things to attend to before making the attempt."

Glimdrem blinked and sipped. Sipped again. "You give me a bag of stones and my freedom to sail away?"

"I will accept your word as a Trelelunin who bears honor to a fault."

"I'm no Edan."

"And one who desires the more I can offer. Sail to Simêum, and I will find you there. After that, we sail to Lultûhol. Succeed or fail, and you leave a wealthier man."

"I think my people can be convinced."

Ilsferu said, "I'm certain that is so. We can spare a couple of ships for the journey."

Glimdrem glanced at her with a frown, knowing she didn't want him taking such a mighty risk. He couldn't speak the reason aloud, but he needed to go, needed to learn if the Contessa was an impossibility come to life. "It will be discussed. I think it will make more of an impression on the Boboru with all of us there, and I trust no one but myself and Ilsferu with such an important task. I owe Solineus my best effort."

Ilsferu's hard squint softened in a flicker, but he understood he would hear about it later. "It will be discussed with all our captains."

The Contessa clapped her hands, bearing an infectious smile. "Good! How long until we have an answer?"

"A day or two." He lifted the bag and offered it to the captain, but Sandorelê refused.

"The Contessa said she trusts you; thus, so do we all."

Glimdrem grinned as he plopped the gems beside his bowl. "Trust is a rare trait amongst humans. At least in my travels."

"Special considerations for a special agreement with honorable souls."

"Indeed." He tipped his glass and nodded to a servant for a pour. "Let us feast and get to know one another."

The Contessa raised her glass. "To what I hope is a fruitful alliance."

Glimdrem raised his cup beside Ilsferu's and tapped with a ringing chime. He drank, smiled, and waited for some word from the vine, but nothing. He talked, laughed, drank, and filled his belly until sunset, and it wasn't until he lay in bed, half asleep and relaxed by Edan wine, that the whisper came: *There are twenty-five of them.*

This simple extrapolation of reality, if accepting the impossible premise that the Contessa was Xanesu, had not struck him until

now. She carried a rapier, though it wasn't the one from the Vale of Whispering Winds.

Only twenty-four. The twenty-fifth died in front of me.

Did he?

Impossible. But to which did he make this response, to having survived or to being dead? He chuckled aloud, and Ilsferu rose to an elbow beside him in bed.

"What?"

He cupped her cheek with a hand, gazing into those beautiful eyes. "Just musing over how this woman could solve our problems."

"Or get us killed."

"No. We risk nothing and gain everything." He snaked a hand around her neck and pulled her to him for a kiss. Laughter. And he pulled away. "You laugh at me?"

Even in the dim light, his Trelelunin eyes discerned her confusion. "I did not laugh."

He pulled her tight for a kiss to avoid explaining, and the vine laughed harder.

Sixteen

Swirling Minds and Wine

Dig a grave your friends. Dig a grave for your family. Dig a grave for your neighbor. Dig a grave for a stranger. Dig a grave for your enemy, if you must, but never dig a grave for yourself.

—*Codex of Sol*

While the first meeting of High Priests took place in a cave in wild mountains far from any holy site she'd ever known, the meeting at which the vote would be held on whether to vacate the Canon of Justef would be called to order at a site maybe more holy than Meliu would have imagined. The massive Pyramid of Tomorok, while impressive from the outside, held secrets in its interior that once laid bare, amazed holy scholars like her all the more.

Gods knew how the original builders achieved placing such massive stones with perfect seams, assembling its grand body with veins that led to its plateau and a few other chambers along the way, but it took months before someone stumbled upon an entry secreted away near the exit to the plateau. No one could open it, but once they knew there was a secret, it didn't take long to find an entrance they could open. What they found shocked everyone.

The pyramid was riddled with passages on five main tiers and descended at least seven more levels into the mountains. The impossibility of constructing such a complex system staggered their finest minds until they realized these halls had no seams at all. The pyramid's construction took place first—maybe built by a people not even Silone—then the secret passages were hewn from the stone with prayers. The answer held a certain satisfaction, but it also raised a number of questions about what Element was used to create such a masterwork. It also raised the specter of the Silone being conquerors who took another religion's holy place and made it into their own. Many worried that vestiges of foreign deities, maybe even those considered Vanquished Gods trying to return to the world, wandered the halls, something worse than the ghosts who haunted the streets of Endelêun.

Meliu strode these halls without a sense of wonder or trepidation, her mind besieged by petulance, until she reached a gold-plated doorway hammered with the image of the Lion of Sol with his mouth agape in a roar. Two priests stood to either side and shuffled to block her way without making eye contact.

"I swear to Kibole, move, or I'll send you Dancing Bastards away screaming."

They parted as they'd come together, without acknowledging she was there. Some days, this might've irked her, but today, she shoved the doors wide and prayed to illuminate the room. The Hall of Lord Priests burst into view as if never dark as the door closed behind her. Buffets lined the walls, chiseled from gigantic tree trunks, beautiful with their intricate engravings, begging the question of how the logs were brought inside and forcing one to wonder how much food had been prepared for ancient meetings held here. Or perhaps these exquisite and enormous pieces held more alcohol than food. Wine.

This was a theory Meliu approved of and wished to be brought into today's reality.

But it was a great oval table sitting in the middle of the room, inset with a massive sheet of white marble—glowing in her Light—a foot smaller than the table's top to leave a ring of polished wood that captured the eye's focus. It was surrounded by nineteen chairs crafted from the same dark hardwood as the table, a wood that no one yet had a name for, though they assumed it was locally cut. Nineteen chairs for the Seven Heavens and the Twelve Hells, the reason that Sedut and others chose to name this the Hall of Lord Priests. Within the histories written in the Codex of Sol, they'd found a passage stating that the seven Lord Priests often met with twelve High Priests; there was no stopping the assumption of this chamber's use when the pieces fit so tight.

Meliu wandered to her designated seat, one of twelve with seats and backs covered in black leather for High Priests instead of white for the Lord Priests. Despite discussions, no one had decided to push for elections to the Lord Priesthood just yet, so if a lord priest existed, it was Ulrikt. Or his face.

Meliu plopped into her seat, determined to show patience, but her tapping fingers betrayed the truth. She'd talked Sedut into allowing her travel to Mulshahar with a small army as an escort, but the damned woman managed to move up the vote that Meliu dearly wanted to miss. The trouble was, she didn't know whether it being moved up was a good sign or bad, in part because she didn't know which choice was good or bad. Some part of her prayed for gridlock and another vote in a year.

Footsteps approached from behind, and Sedut's voice ruined her already questionable mood. "You're early."

"Only because I'm late in leaving. I should've been two weeks out by now."

"A fifty-year-old Woodkin bottle, which I suppose they still consider young." Sedut plunked a bottle of wine on the table but didn't open it. "You've duties here, to me and the Church, beyond whatever responsibility you feel for the prisoners and that damned... blessed Codex you tote around like some sort of totem."

"You could find another for your vote."

"No one with the respect you've earned. They fear me to the core of their marrow, but you?"

Meliu giggled, though with a dark humor. "They fear me as well."

"They do. They should. Truth be told, they should fear you more, but with your cutesy smile and demure tones, they don't. And the common folk? You're a hero for the ages."

"A hero? That's worthy of a laugh."

"You who killed a foreign witch, a Breath Stealer, while trying to save Silone warriors? You who rode into the teeth of a Tek charge with Darkness withering our enemy? You who demands to chase after the captured and enslaved the flicker we know where they are? It's no godsdamned wonder you and Ivin got along; neither of you has a clue of how the people see you."

Ivin's insertion into the conversation did little for Meliu's mood. "I seem to recall you at that battle with the Tek."

Sedut snorted and said, "Scattering shit, blood, and brains all over your friends wins fights but doesn't make people easy with your presence. People like you, and they don't understand that what your Dark does might be worse than the artifact's mess."

Considering the swath of destruction Sedut left in a couple of fights, the assertion seemed farcical on its face, but having felt the madness of Dark creeping into her soul, she found it difficult to dismiss the notion even if she wanted to. "What the hells do you know about the Dark?"

"Nothing you haven't told me, and that's more than I needed to know. When we're drunk and swapping tales, mine are of revulsion and gore, the stench, the hardening of my mind and gut. Yours are of the madness of the mortal body facing the horror of the immortal soul shredded to tatters, the dislodging of the two into chaotic insanity where the tortured soul may never control what its body is doing ever again. Some treatises speak of Dark's taint following the soul into the hells."

"Foolishness."

Sedut shrugged. "Is it?"

Meliu tugged her ear and shook her head. "It sounded like you had that speech ready."

"I admit, I've wondered about the power of Dark for a while now. Elemental Lightning is dangerous, and you know what? I never killed no one until I held the artifact. Just a wolf in the mountains once to scare away the pack, and a few Wakened Dead around the tombs of the Steaming Lakes. All right, a few dozen. But killing somebody for a second time doesn't count."

"Forges, I'd only fantasized about murdering a couple of folks once or twice before all this. I scared rats away from library books with my Light." They shared a laugh. "Then the world changed."

"No, no. The world didn't change; our *lives* changed. The cursed world around us hasn't really changed since gods know when. The Age of God Wars. The Age of Warlords. The commonality is?"

"War."

"Someday historians will name our age, and I'd wager the name will have a familiar ring to it. War has always been there, just waiting to find us. And speaking of wars, might I ask which way you'll vote today?"

"You know."

Sedut eyed her with a grin. "I didn't bring an expensive bottle of wine I had carried over five hundred horizons as a bribe because I thought you jumped off the fence."

Meliu sighed but said nothing.

"You've heard of the marvelous things Hulerê is doing under Izilfer's tutelage? She cured a man in the final stages of the drowning cough without—"

"If the council goes my way, Hulerê will be on her way to the priesthood. Satisfied?"

"Tell a lady the truth; it was the wine, right?"

Meliu scrunched her brows. "Of course it was."

"Good! So long as you share, it wasn't a waste of gold and favors."

A *swish* from across the chamber caught Meliu's ear, like robes rushing across the floor, and she turned her head to see no one. "What the hells was that?"

"What was what?"

A thrum pounded Meliu's ears, and maybe she screamed; she felt the burn in her throat but heard nothing. She lost the grip on her prayer, and the room shifted from pure Light to deep-cave dark in an instant. The boom in her skull died into silence, then sounded as if a gong vibrated between her ears. As her ass slid from the chair and hit the stone floor, the realization struck her consciousness: Elemental Sound. She cupped hands over her ears in desperation but knew the instinct was folly.

Silence.

Gong.

And she wilted with palms slapping the floor, forehead leaning into the backs of her hands, and consciousness slipping from her. *Elinwe. Elinwe. Elinwe.* A repetition like an echo as further words refused to come to her prayer until the silence came again. "Elinwe, bring me

Light." Rejuvenation struck like a rod surging through her spine, straightening her body until she leaped to her feet, gasping for breath and opening her eyes to the brilliant Light of the goddess.

She spun, seeing nobody except Sedut, the woman on her knees and hugging Meliu's chair. "You all right?"

"I think so." The grimace on Sedut's face told a different story than her words.

Meliu leaned, seeing no wounds. "You're hurt. Where?"

The woman gritted her teeth through hissing breaths. A hand shook the chair into a quake. "Everywhere?"

"Help us!" Meliu dropped to a knee, grabbing her shoulders. "Where? Tell me something." No words came, and she grabbed Sedut's robes, stood, and pulled them over her head, yanking her until she kneeled naked. Meliu stared. "Nothing. I see—" A speck of blood beaded on her back near her spine. Another appeared on her left shoulder, and as Meliu ducked, another dripped down her left thigh. She had no idea what was happening, but no one made this sort of assault without the intent to kill. "Shits! Help us! Elinwe, hear my prayers. Bring me Life for this servant of Sol."

A wave of energy surged from the heavens, through her body, and into Sedut; the shake of her hand eased, but her jaw remained locked in a clinch.

Meliu sprinted for the door, slamming it open to have it rebound into her face. She pushed again to find herself shoving the limp bodies of the two priests guarding the entry. "Help us!" Her voice echoed in either direction, and she turned to run right, but moments later, she heard sandals coming from behind. She spun with a prayer for Dark in case it was the enemy, and she saw two young postulants in white robes running her way. If their robes weren't a lie, there was no way they had headed this attack.

The two men dropped to their knees as Dark swirled behind her. The first said, "High Priestess?"

She eased the prayer but kept a grip on its power, letting it swell to protect her rear. "Izilfer! She should be nearby."

"Her and her—"

"Go! Get her! High Priestess Sedut has been attacked and is dying in the Hall of Tulule. Go!" Both men stared. "You need past me."

"Yes."

She drove the power of prayer to the ceiling, and to their credit, the men ran beneath it without a moment's hesitation. Meliu stared until they disappeared around a corner, then trotted back into the hall to find Sedut lying on the floor, naked and trembling, one bead of blood already coagulating into a ball of scab.

Meliu slid on her knees, refusing to release the Dark but praying for Life and Light. The energies sang through her body in a disjointed chorus, the old euphoria raging her will into indomitable heights that could only lead to godhood.

Impervious mind. Immortal soul. Unbreakable body.

The trouble was Meliu didn't need saving. She laid her hands on the woman's ribs and felt her wounds in her own body, four pricks, one more than she'd seen, and at each, a burn radiated. *Poison.* She was out of her depths by a horizon. "Sedut. I don't know what to do." Life. Light. Dark. They combined into heady confidence, a surge of powers that didn't leave room for doubt. "I will save you."

Meliu's fingers dug into Sedut's ribs as she unleashed the powers of prayer into her flesh and bones. A god-fueled rush as she murmured, "Elinwe, save her," over and over again. Eternal Light. Eternal Darkness. Eternal Nothing. Not stopping even when Sedut's eyes flew wide and Darkened as black as glistening pitch, blood trickling from her nose and spattering from her mouth as she screamed.

"What are you doing?" The yelling jarred into Meliu's consciousness but didn't slow her prayers or the flow of Elements.

"Elinwe, save her."

Meliu's body leaned, and she dragged Sedut with her. It took flickers to understand that fingers dug into her armpits, trying to pull her away from Sedut's dying body.

"Stop! Now!"

"I will save her! You will not kill her!" Dark flooded her soul unbidden, a torrent destined to destroy the eternity of whatever enemy stood near her. She glanced up and into Izilfer's steady eyes and swallowed the Dark back into herself.

"I'm here now. Let go of her."

Meliu tried. Fingers locked. The world turned black except for Izilfer's eyes, such brilliant blue eyes. "I can't." Life and Light blazed in a flurry around her, but Dark seized her body and soul.

"You can and you will."

Life and Light fled from her, driven away by Dark. "I will save her."

"No, I will save her. You need to save yourself."

A voice within Meliu laughed even as she spoke, "I am immortal."

Izilfer's hands rested on Meliu's, a peaceful touch on top of hardened claws. "No. That's the touch of the gods. Bringing delusion. You've gone too far. You need to come home or never come back."

Izilfer had lost her mind if she was Izilfer at all. "Liar!"

"Don't just listen to my voice. Hear my words and follow them back to the girl who loves books. Not codices and tomes, simple books with simple stories about talking mice and dancing fireflies of your childhood."

Her mind fluttered to her mother, and her voice muted in bedtime tones as she read sheets of cheap parchment folded into a handwritten book. *But the mouse had eaten too much bread and drank too much water, so his*

belly no longer fit through the hole! Meliu knew the cat would pounce soon and that the mouse would talk his way out of trouble. *My drunken pa wrote me a story. I won't cry.*

"Don't let the touch of the gods consume you." Izilfer's fingers—or were they her mother's?—tugged at her hands that hooked into the claws of a hungry feline, and her predator's grip loosened. "Meliu, come back home. Come back to you."

The rush of energies faded, and Meliu's head spun as if whipped into a whirlwind. "I'm dying." With those words, her soul reached out for power, but her hands flopped limp.

"No, you're coming back to you. Back to rest." Fingers gripped her armpits and dragged her, and Izilfer followed, holding her hands. "Rest. Sleep as a child in your mother's arms after a bedtime tale."

Meliu's eyelids wore weights; were they stones to hold shut the eyes of the dead? "Don't let her die."

"I will save Sedut."

"Mother. Don't let my mother die." There came no answer, or at least not one Meliu heard, but even as she slipped into a dream of a hearth-warmed bedroom in a ramshackle cottage in snow-covered mountains, she understood the demand's impossible desire. Mother died days before father sent her to Istinjoln. But it didn't stop the soft caress of a hug nor the words that brought the fattened mouse nose to whisker with a hungry cat, and Meliu nuzzled into her mom's cheek to hear the end of the story. But she fell into slumber too soon.

Meliu knew she lay on a bed, arms and legs sprawled beneath heavy covers, what she didn't understand was why twitches shook her fingers and toes and places that never twitched before. *How the hells does a rib twitch?* Eyelids fluttered into abject darkness, moistened by the

stale heat of her breath, and her eyeballs itched, but no matter how hard she tried, numb arms wouldn't raise shaking fingers to scratch them from her skull.

Panic. "Nyah! Nyah! Neeeahh!"

Feet scrambled her way, and a flicker later, light invaded. A face stared at her, and not one she expected. For a moment, she wondered if she still dreamed. If maybe she gazed into the eyes of her childhood self. Except the hair was all wrong.

The girl smiled. "You're awake. That's good."

With a face and a voice, Meliu knew the girl was Hulerê, and she wanted to say the name, but her pasty tongue and cracked lips would have nothing to do with saying it right. "Ularê?"

Hands touched her face, and Life tingled into her lips and cheeks. "Sorry. If I'd known you were going to awake, I would've taken care to make your first moments more comfortable."

"Sedut?"

"Alive but unwell."

"How many bugs have I eaten?" She tried to laugh at her own joke, but a chain of twitches ran from Meliu's pinkie to her thumb, then shivered up her arm until cocking her head hard enough her neck popped. She groaned and plopped her face into the pillow. "How many days was I unconscious?"

"Three candles at most."

If the girl said a year, it would've shocked her less. "I feel like I was dead for weeks." Her foot cramped from heel to splaying toes, and she stifled a scream. "The meeting? You and Izilfer... what happened?"

"Nothing. Without Sedut to call the meeting, well, I guess they're all sitting and waiting to see whether she dies."

"Heavens, girl, what are you doing here with me? You should be with her."

Hulerê cast her a blank stare. "There's only so much I can do. I'm a healer."

Every muscle except an annoying quiver in Meliu's cheek froze. "What does that mean? She doesn't need healed? Or are your abilities a lie?"

A hesitant smile and the girl scratched her head. She sighed, and Meliu feared the worst, but what she got confused her instead. "There are witches in the woods, right? So the stories say. They brew herbs and cast magic and sometimes heal people."

"That isn't you."

"No, but there are other stories. Of the Defiled, Touched by the Vanquished Gods, who take the wounds of others, and I heal myself from there. The people call me an empath."

"So, go and take her wounds."

"I can't."

"The more you say, the more confused I..." Meliu's twitches returned in a flurry, and she collapsed back to the pillow to rattle the frame.

Hulerê touched her head with her right hand and put her left on her spine. Muscles relaxed at her touch, but she didn't feel a surge of Life. "The damage you suffered is in your brain and spine, and Izilfer can no more take your affliction from you than I can do what she does to keep Sedut alive. We are both where we need to be."

Meliu took shuddering breaths to recover, muscles easing enough to prop herself on an elbow once again. "Is it poison? Sedut, I mean."

"Yes. From what I understand, similar to that which sent Ivin Choerkin into a coma."

Meliu's heart sank. "She's dead then; a matter of time."

"Maybe not. I wasn't here for the Warlord Choerkin."

"You said you couldn't heal her."

"I did. Not yet. Do you know why Izilfer wouldn't be able to heal you? Have you ever thought about it? Twitches from prayers too powerful for the body to handle."

Meliu giggled, and her lips shook. "No."

Hulerê touched her again, and the twitches eased more. "Prayer heals by driving Life into the body, and Life heals, *but* it's also an Element. At best, the healing will offset the damage being done by feeding your body more Elemental energy. As likely, your twitches get worse, and if someone pushes too much Life into you, well, it might kill you."

Meliu's mouth gaped. "Son of a... Gods." The ramifications took flickers to even begin to penetrate her thick skull. "But you take my wounds and heal them yourself. Perfectly safe for me, but not you."

Hulerê grinned. "Yes, so you'll forgive me if healing you takes time."

Meliu couldn't resist a chuckle even as this new reality burrowed deeper. "I've been healed of twitches before. In Inster, a town in Tek Hidreng."

"I heard of what you and Sedut did there."

"Before that, I... Lord Priest Ulrikt, he healed me." She looked at the girl now closer than she had ever before, and her heart bounced at the notion this girl could be a Face of Ulrikt. A shiver ran her spine. "He, uh, healed me." *But why would he hide from me now?*

The girl stared, eyebrows raised. "I've heard rumors of a Lord Priest's Face. Didn't know to believe it."

"Sedut was right." Ulrikt paid for Defiled children not to kill them but to turn them into servants of prophecy. *I am one of the Defiled.* Her head spun.

And Hulerê touched her. "Is something else wrong?"

Meliu's lips straightened into an awkward pause, torn between laughing and wailing. Instead, she said, "Just thinking."

"A Lord Priest's Face using empathic healing might be bizarre to you, but it gives me hope! Izilfer swears I will someday learn healing with prayer, and then, I can heal anybody."

Meliu's brain still struggled. "That'd be wonderful."

Meliu's muscles relaxed again as a flurry of twitches passed with the girl's touch. "You see, Sedut's poison is so strong... If she'd been bitten by some common snake, well, I could handle that."

"You can pull out her poison?"

"No, but I can keep healing what the poison attacks until the body defeats the poison on its own. So to speak. Not too different from prayer. But this, this poison is Elemental. It won't fade. But?"

More twitches faded Meliu's fingers, and her brain awoke. "Because it's Elemental, you can pull it into you."

"Right. I pulled a small amount from her and almost died. Once we connect, the flow isn't easy to stop. But, once inside of me, it is just another Element, and it's turned."

"Turned?"

"Izilfer told me to think of Life as a coin with two sides: healing and killing."

"I've never considered Life for killing."

"You've experienced it, except it was twisted into pain, unable to kill. The Maimer's Lash."

"Twelve Hells." This child knew secrets beyond her years, and once again, she wondered if she wasn't The Face. "Izilfer taught you all this?"

"Mhhm. Well, sorta! Sedut, too, and a few others." She shrugged. "We think we're right. Maybe. Who knows? Anyhow, when the Elemental poison enters me, my body is strong enough to flip the coin back to healing."

"Like you did with the Maimer's scar?"

"Yes. But you see, I can't pray for Life to keep healing Sedut's wounds. Only Izilfer and others with prayers can keep her stable. I can only pull small bits of poison out and slowly save her."

If the Face of Ulrikt could heal Meliu's twitching, he could've healed Ivin's poison. *Only if it was still alive.* Her eyes clenched tight. *Only if he wanted him alive and here. Prophecy needed Ivin on Herald's Watch.* "Godsdamnit." Meliu struck her palms to the matress and her legs over the edge of the bed, damned near screaming as a torrent of twitches shook her from toes to thighs.

"You need to rest."

"No. You need to get me to the meeting hall."

Seventeen

Angels, Demons, and Ghosts

An advance in my apologies,
wounding your soul
with such a gentle blow,
the bumping in your phrenologies,
wetting your face, and ignoring the toll.
Ha ha! Go to hell, I say,
for I've already been there.
The irony oh the laughable irony!
Your offense in being told to go where you want to take the rest of us.

—*Tomes of the Touched*

Ivin awoke as he did every day: Uncertain of the time. It might be the same as sleeping in a cave except the opposite of the oppressive nature of utter darkness; it was the oppressive nature of constant light; the tower of Fire that swallowed the island gave no reprieves. In a cave, he could sleep beside a fire, and in the morning, at least embers might still glow. He could dim the blaze to a glow with blankets over the windows, but true dark could only be found in the recesses of Choerkin Keep, and in those places, sleeping became like resting in a tomb, a place he'd already come too close to making a permanent home.

He sat up and spun, bare feet falling from the bed to caress a floor warmer than it should be. As a child, he dreaded mornings and their cold, few things being worse than the chill of feet warmed by blankets settling on icy stone. He missed the tingles on the soles of his feet now, wishing to relive some piece of his past, but the Fire robbed him of even this tiny pleasure.

Warm feet carried him to the window, and he pulled open the curtains, the eternal Fire greeting his vision, a concave wall of rushing flames ever-changing yet forever the same. *How long did I sleep today? How long was I dead?*

Neither question held a satisfying answer.

His mind clung to a last memory and a first memory. Telling Kinesee that he loved her, and awaking on Herald's Watch to the face of Eliles, the beauty of which he'd dreamed for years, and finding not a tear's drip of pleasure in an old dream coming true. Instead, confusion and panic, his body too weak to scream.

Solineus watched him awake from death, or coma, with his unforgettable smirk. Pleased by the favor he'd done for Ivin while never realizing he'd delivered a friend to an eternal prison. Ivin recalled the final words he had spoken to Solineus before the man left the island, and the words fell from his lips in sorrowful tones: "Tell her I love her—my children. I won't ever know their names. Tell them." With a wife and twins growing up thousands of horizons away, not even a dream come true could compare.

A knock on the door and Ivin turned with a shake of his head, stepping into boots and throwing bearskin robes over his shoulders. "Enter."

Hinges creaked, and a shy young woman opened the door. She wore plain gray robes, and her long hair was pulled back in a tail. She didn't smile. "Lord Choerkin wishes you to share breakfast with him."

Ivin groaned and wiped the crumbles from his eyes. "Best not disappoint him, I guess."

The girl bowed as he stalked from the room, irritated at his summons but unable to deny the Lord's wishes. Ivin entered the Great Hall of the keep, a lone hulking shadow waiting for him.

Lord Kotin Choerkin squinted from beneath his thick brows. A frown hinted through a beard so bushy it shadowed the lips from further interpretation, whether Ivin's old man mocked his dour mood, enjoyed a private and biting joke, or was annoyed at gods knew what. "What the hells you looking at, boy?"

"You look younger than I recall." His beard was dark and shaggy, without so much as a hint of silver.

"Your mother has ways to keep a man young. But you, you're older and more piss-tongued than ever."

"Unfortunate that I'm not as honey-tongued as my sire."

Kotin folded his arms over his belly. "Keep your tongue sweet, or your mouth closed today. We've important godsdamned visitors."

Ivin's mind cleared as if the sun burnt away a fog: The Ar-Bdeins arrived at Herald's Watch today. How he could forget such a momentous moment escaped him, and of a sudden, joy overtook his melancholy.

Ar-Bdêin. The name is important. A twitch in his neck kicked his face to the side and raised a corner of his mouth. *Why important?* But the question faded before his consciousness found the answer. "I look forward to greeting the Ar-Bdeins. Very much." Even if he didn't recall why.

His father's glower mellowed. "That's a good lad." He stood and wrapped bearskin robes tight. "It's a cold one out there, boy. Let's go."

Snow struck Ivin's face with a biting sting for the first time in what seemed an age as they stepped from Choerkin Keep. He smiled as he strode to the street with a bounce in his steps. Some part of him

missed the icy chill of winter on Herald's Watch, just like some part of him had missed his father's sharp tongue. *But my feet were warm.* "A beautiful day."

"Is it?"

"Every day that's different may be beautiful." A part of him knew the snow shouldn't be flying. A part of him knew that the sun rising over the eastern Strait wouldn't be visible in the unchanging days in which reality lived, but a part of him didn't accept what he knew.

They meandered down the winding streets, and Skywatch's dome appeared to his right hand. "So, tell me, boy, did you learn your lesson about that cursed building at last?"

"I haven't been there since." *Since when?* Recollections of Meris reading cracked bones scattered his consciousness. He ran away. He walked away. He smiled. He shivered. "I think Meris is dead."

His father laughed. "I think yer dreamin', boy, the crone will never leave the stars. Never."

Gray hair and a fractured body flashed in his mind as the echo of a scream he never heard reverberated in a fall he had only imagined. "Maybe you're right."

Their steps never missed a beat. "She murdered your li'l sister and mother. Never you forget that."

Ivin sighed. "I believe you."

A grunt before Kotin said, "You do? Piss tongued, but wiser."

Ivin chuckled. "Maybe more accepting of the darkness." *Meliu. Dark. Love.* His mind turned to prophecies that Loving Darkness had read to him. *Loving Darkness? A name earned?* "I think she killed Peneluple seven years too late. I was the prophesied child she meant to murder. The one who looked the most like mother."

"My dear Peneluple." Kotin clucked his tongue, taking this theory calmer than Ivin had expected. "You might be right." He pointed at

the harbor as their altitude gave them a view over the Watch's main gates. "The Ar-Bdêin await."

A royal blue pennant with a golden tower flapped in the wind. *Bdein. A tower.* The city and an image of a tower and a broken stool flashed in his mind, but he couldn't pin down why before, in a blurred flicker, they stood on the waterfront waiting.

The Ar-Bdêin ship sat moored to the dock, and a stocky man led the way toward them with three slender men with clean-shaved faces in his wake. The Lords Ar-Bdêin, or at least three of them were, and it was the one who wasn't that interested Ivin most. He was in his twenties and walked with strides more haughty than the true lords, and he wore a smile to oppose their earnest, diplomatic demeanors.

Kotin rested an arm over Ivin's shoulders. "Him there, that's Gier Ar-Bdêin, ruler of the city of Bdein. Wave-born rumors say another family has risen to knock the bastard from his perch. He needs a safe harbor, and we enjoy his coin and trade but never confuse him for a friend."

Kotin stepped forward when they drew close and clasped Gier's forearm. "Welcome to Herald's Watch. It's been too long."

The man grinned. "Only a Choerkin would invite snow for an old friend." He clapped Kotin's shoulder with his free hand. "Kotin Choerkin, I'd like you to meet my brothers, the Lords Erumô and Hibôltu Ar-Bdêin. This is Lôdumâ, my nephew, by way of a sister."

Kotin gestured, and for the first time, Ivin noticed his brothers standing beside them. "These are my boys, Rikis, Roplin, and Ivin."

Gier smiled at each in turn, pausing when his eyes lit on Ivin. "You are the spitting image of your mother. My sympathies to you all for your loss."

As the two patriarchs spoke, their words blurred, and Ivin stared at the young Lôdumâ, the man who later captured him and Meliu while

planning to sell her to Thônian priests. Awkward. More awkward, considering Lôdumâ stared at a twelve-year-old Ivin and not him.

Ivin blinked when looking at himself, so young, so innocent, so soft.

In a blurry blink, he stood in the Great Hall of Choerkin Keep. Kotin sat with a mug of ale talking to Gier with Lôdumâ sitting mute by his side, while Rikis sat with feet propped on the table closer to the other Ar-Bdêin lords playing a board game the Tek called War against Eremô. Roplin and Hibôltu sat close, studying the game. The young Ivin lay sprawled on a bench by the fire, asleep or faking it to avoid the foreign company.

Ivin strolled close enough to overhear what he might've heard if not asleep as a boy.

Gier Ar-Bdêin said, "The simpering Turlid have always been a cowardly lot, but I always suspected they had designs on *my* city. It's a holy alliance with unholy intent; may Pulvûer's eagle eat their eyes and leave their hearts dying for the buzzards."

"I've got m'own holies I'd enjoy gutting, I promise you. What says your king? Surely he don't condone this war."

"The king is old and withering and making sure his favorite son doesn't join him on the funeral pyre before becoming king himself. When the throne isn't secure, the jackals gather. King Fedinhœ can't risk the disfavor of the Rînmod Bishops."

"Godsdamned unfortunate for you, friend." Hearing his father call a Hidreng friend brought a twitch to Ivin's lip. "But why'd the bishops align against you?"

The Ar-Bdêin barked a humorless laugh that raised the hair on Ivin's neck. "I erred a decade past, a killing I thought long forgotten if not forgiven until Postrel rose as heir to the Bishop of SinMedor. The stink rose from that old corpse, I fear."

Lôdumâ leaned close. "The Rînmod also frown on the familial inheritance of the wealth of Bdein. Replacing our line with Turlid would be a step closer to the Rînmod controlling Bdein."

"My nephew does not lie. The Rînmod continue to consolidate power. Someday, they'll move on all of Hidreng, but not while I breathe. Not while I hold Bdein."

"Aye, aye. I hear your words, and I sympathize, by the gods I do, but what the hells would you have me do? I can't sail to Bdein without starting a war with all Hidreng. No matter how rich the spoils—"

"Nothing so dramatic, my Choerkin friend. All I need is ships. A score of longboats."

Kotin laughed. "A score! What good is a score against the walls of Bdein? Even if I had them to spare."

"I have the treasure of Bdein, but I lack men and ships to carry them. You have the longboats, and I know this to be true."

"Aye, *we* do."

"With them, I will sail to Thôn and shower their mercenaries with gold."

Kotin slunk in his seat, an incredulous stare. "You'd bring down the demons of Thôn to regain Bdein? But even then, they wouldn't be enough."

Gier's eyes grew intense as he leaned his elbows on the table. "When we sail straight into Bdein, forces loyal to me will rise. I will have my city again! Do not doubt me."

Kotin straightened and picked a tooth with his pinky. "So says you, and by our long-standing friendship, I believe your words."

"Twenty longboats?"

"Are yours if your treasury is generous."

"Gems, jewels, and gold are yours, along with my undying friendship when I retake Bdein. A treasure worth a hundred such ships. A thousand."

Kotin sat unblinking, then nodded once before grabbing a scroll and dipping ink. A wick later, he rolled the parchment. "Roplin. Take this along with our esteemed guest to Captain Uldmun. Make damned certain there's nothing on them boats to prove they were ours." Kotin's eyes turned to the Ar-Bdêin. "Your generosity best not be a ruse."

Gier stood and bowed as Roplin took the scroll. "You will be satisfied long before we sail." He turned to the game of War. "Brothers, let us visit the harbor, shall we? Lôdumâ—"

"May stay here. We will speak of the treasure you carry."

Gier hesitated, maybe thinking of his nephew as security on a loan. "As you wish."

Roplin led the party from the room, and when they passed from hearing, Kotin spoke to Rikis. "Keep an armed eye on them. A noble son can become a son of a bitch when desperate, follow me?"

"It'll be done." Rikis waited several flickers before following, leaving Lôdumâ and Kotin alone with the youthful Ivin asleep strides away.

Kotin clapped his hands, and a servant rushed into the room, Jermin, father of Joslin, the serving boy killed by the Face of Ulrikt. Jermin refilled the men's mugs and stood to the side.

"So, Lôdumâ. I've heard word of you. They say you're a bright boy."

"I'd like to think so, Lord Choerkin." His smile was smug and familiar to Ivin.

Kotin took a long drink before speaking. "Then tell me the truth of what I am seeing."

"The truth, Lord Choerkin?"

Ivin pounded fists on the table. "This man is a betrayer! Whatever he says, don't trust it." But no one heard him.

"Aye, the godsdamned truth. If you don't know what I mean, then by the hells, you aren't as smart as you think you are."

Lôdumâ took two breaths before draining half his mug, then two more. "My uncle will get us all killed while making you rich."

"You're so sure?"

"He sees what he's up against but refuses to accept it. Even if Thôn delivers and your ships carry them to Bdein, there aren't enough loyal to our name to carry the day."

"No doubt?"

"None. We will all die. Turlid and Turgin and the Bishop's priests. We will sail to our dooms."

Kotin drained his mug, then held it to the side for Jermin to fill. "I'd hoped for, well, hope. Yer kin and mine haven't always been friends, but we've reached a profitable peace for two generations."

"Believe me when I say I wish I could answer differently." He shook his head. "We will fight to an honorable end if we avoid knives in our backs long enough to reach Bdein." He saluted with his mug.

"If you're as smart a boy as folks claim, chums with the future king?"

"We were friends in our youth, yes. "

"Aye. If you see no hope, as you say, stick a knife in your uncle's back when it suits you best and live long enough for your friend to become king... then take your godsdamned city back."

Lôdumâ blanched at the suggestion and cleared his throat as Ivin stared at his old man, surprised by his advice. "My uncle is a good man. I will talk him out of this suicidal ploy. I promise."

Kotin said, "I wish you the best, boy, but I've never known your uncle to take a slight lyin' down, let alone taking what's deemed his."

Lôdumâ sat staring into his mug of ale as Ivin took a seat beside his father. "You planted the seed of his betrayal."

Kotin turned to him with an arching brow. "Did I? There ain't no man who can say that for certain, is there?"

Lôdumâ looked up, his eyes landing on Ivin for the first time since the meeting at the docks. "We'll see each other again. Ask me."

Ivin blinked. "We will never... well, we will see each other again, but in a different time, not after this dream."

"There is a saying in Hidreng, *îstok nûor emetu hemen gîirim.* A man is only trapped when he believes it is so."

"Your saying never saw the Fire surrounding this island."

"We will meet again." Lôdumâ shrugged before his head drooped, staring into his mug as if never looking away.

Kotin bear-slapped Ivin's shoulder. "Never you mind the Ar-Bdêin, boy. He's a liar, just as you said." His shoulder rocked again, but Kotin hadn't laid a hand on him this time.

Ivin caught himself from falling from the chair in the great hall with his legs splayed and arms outstretched. His eyes were wide open, but his father, Lôdumâ, and Jermin were gone. Damned sad considering he could use a mug of ale.

He blinked and glanced around the room: the dark fireplace, the empty table, and the years of dust without fresh prints. The constant light from the Tower of Flame was the only light in the hall. "A dream." Except he wasn't groggy, no fog from waking. "Had to be a dream."

Dozens of candles in the candelabra above ignited in unison, and as his eyes snapped upward, the cindered remains of wood in the fireplace burst into a flame so strong the metal grate glowed orange as if it'd been ablaze since dawn.

Before he could ask how he noticed a man adjusting the flume of the hearth. "Good morning, young lord. You've awakened late."

"Jermin?"

"Indeed, who else?" The man turned with a smile, younger than moments before, when serving Kotin and Lôdumâ. "I'm sure there are still biscuits and gravy in the kitchen if you'd like me to fetch you some?"

Ivin's mouth watered. "Demeu's biscuits?"

The man stared. "Who else? Are you fevered, my lord?"

Demeu died soon after his sixteenth birthday, and he'd suffered the loss of her cooking since. "Gods, yes. Biscuits. And anything else she has."

"Very good." He laughed as he strode from the hall. Before another voice rang from behind.

"I feared you would miss breakfast again."

Ivin's heart seized, and his mouth parted with a single word before going dry: "Mother." Tears welled in his eyes before he turned all the way around. And there Peneluple stood. Young. Beautiful. Alive. So *damned* alive. Blond hair tied in back but still draped over her shoulder, and her smile warmed the room beyond the heat of the hearth.

He ran toward her, ran and ran and ran, the planks beneath his feet shifting, slowing him as if he were running up a hill of marbles, but nothing would deny his reaching her outstretched arms to press his face against hers to mingle their tears. Her hands grasped his, and he lurched forward into a hug.

And fell through empty air. Collided with uncaring maple hardened by hundreds of years of dry air and footsteps. Rolled onto his back, wailing, screeching, crying in an infant's fit but with man-sized rage and tears. Clenched his eyes shut. Hysterical pleas in his mind drowned out by his repeated scream of "no."

But when his eyes opened, there were no tears, and he stared at the ceiling with its dark chandeliers whose candles hadn't burned in years. His tight chest and rolling heartbeat numbed his sense of touch, gifting him with the terror of feeling afloat in reality. He managed to whisper, "No. Mother. I'm going mad."

Eighteen

Short Comfort

She loved him. She killed him. He loved her forever.

—*Tomes of the Touched*

Sometimes in life, being short stood as a benefit, in particular when standing beside a child who acted as her crutch. Meliu grimaced. Leaning was more accurate, stumbling or lurching, maybe. Meliu would've hollered at the first adherent in their path to help speed her journey, but Hulerê did more than lend her shoulder. On her twelfth stride from bedside, her knee gave way in a quivering flop, and she fell forward with one hand on a wall and the other landing on the girl; flesh bore the brunt better than stone as Meliu regained control and straightened her leg.

Coincidence, or so she had first thought, but the pride driving her to walk on her own brought her back to the girl time and again, and the weakness precipitating her coming fall disappeared with the strength to continue on. She didn't call out for help on seeing a young priest, but neither did she keep her hand on Hulerê's shoulder. At first, the reason was pride, but by the time they rounded the corner leading to the meeting hall, it was like a test to see if the girl's uncanny powers worked every time. They did.

"Do you need to sleep?"

The girl giggled. "What?"

"The Edan don't need to sleep. Some say they are so steeped in the power of Elemental Life that they don't need to sleep nor eat."

"Well, gracious. I sleep and eat, I promise."

This was a modicum of comfort; Meliu would've been as jealous as the Twelve Hells. She'd lost so much scholarly time to sleep it vexed her, not to mention all of the dreams and nightmares she could have avoided. "Are you consciously healing me?"

"Hmmm?"

Meliu smiled. "That answered my question, I think. Could somebody heal themselves by just touching you?"

They strode a half dozen strides before Hulerê answered. "I expect lots of questions from common folk."

"I'm as common as they get, but among the holy, I have the uncommon ability to admit I don't know something by asking for answers." She grinned. In her youth, she'd been the opposite.

Another dozen strides of silence. "I know too many stories about you to say you are common. I like you, even if the modesty is false."

"Some days it is, some days it isn't."

"No."

"No, my modesty is false?"

"No, people can't heal themselves by touching me. When I remove your wounds, our lives are attached. Mingled." She scrunched her face when she looked at Meliu. "I wouldn't want to say our souls connected, but maybe, in a sense. I've spent half my life thinking on such things, you know?"

"All of what, five years?"

A smirk. "Six and a half. Even when I stop touching you, we remain in contact, so when you touch me, I take your wounds more by... by instinct. Like the first time I healed my mother."

Gods, what a gift this girl was given; if Meliu had been gifted with Life instead of Dark, what might she have done for her mother instead... she shook her head. "If it's easy, why not remove my twitching altogether?"

"Easy?" She stopped and turned to Meliu. "The damage the Elements done is in your head and your spine. I don't understand it any more than I understand the poison killing Sedut. So I take all the time I need. It's not so different than what you did. It's too much energy, but in my case, it's too much wound. If I go too far, I die. Never think it's easy." The girl turned, and Meliu struggled to keep pace.

"Slow down. And I apologize. Of all people, I should know how *not* easy the Elements can be." Hulerê calmed her strides, and Meliu put a hand on her shoulder to ease a twitch in her neck. "You don't talk like most any child I ever met."

"I'm thirteen, and I found that you old folks don't take so kindly to being healed by poorly-spoken brats."

"I'm not old."

"And I'm not a child."

Are you a Face? "Fair enough, I suppose. But if you healed me faster, I'd have less time to irritate you on this walk."

"You have a solid argument. But still, I like you."

"Good. I like you too." They reached the meeting hall's entry, and Meliu stopped in front of the door to stand straight and take several breaths. "No matter what I might say inside this chamber, remember that."

With a steady hand, she opened the door and stepped inside to find the gathering of high priests still there. Their conversations hushed the moment she entered, with all eyes turning to her. Meliu locked eyes with the woman she figured held the most influence with the group without Sedut's presence. "High Priestess Jelodu, it is good to see you and the others are still here."

The woman stood with a face of emotionless stone. "It is good to see you up. We were led to believe you were close to death."

Meliu glanced at Hulerê. "Was I?"

"Depending on how you define death, yes. Madness brought on by Dark? Izilfer believes it so, with the... It doesn't matter. Izilfer and I brought her back from wherever she was headed."

Jelodu nodded. "You have done the Church a great service, young lady. And what word of Sedut?"

"I've heard nothing for the past candle. Izilfer will keep her alive and maintain equilibrium until I can reverse the poison."

Olum of Benet, from the territory of Clan Tuvrikt, stood and said, "We are to believe this miracle? This thing no one achieved to save the southerner's precious Choerkin Warlord?"

"My gift and Izilfer's prayers will slowly purify her if I don't kill myself with the effort."

Meliu said, "The fight to heal us goes on. What should be debated in this chamber should begin. The Canon of Justef."

High Priestess Lizel didn't bother to stand. "Without Sedut and you, there wasn't a point. You represent Istinjoln in her stead, but she who proposed the change in canon, by tradition, must be here."

Meliu hobbled to her chair with Hulerê at her hand and braced herself with both. "Does tradition dictate that we allow an attempted assassination to stop the hearing? That would seem odd, in particular, seeing as we can assume that was the assassin's goal."

Olum sat down. "Are we so sure? The woman had enemies."

"Your suggesting the timing is mere coincidence makes me wonder if your people weren't the attackers."

He snorted with a chuckle. "Curious, as it's well known amongst our colleagues that I intended to vote for vacating the Canon of Justef."

She glanced around the table to see nods from several high priests. "Also convenient, to shade you from suspicion." She raised a hand to halt his protest. "Not that I am suspicious. No, as you noted, she had plenty of enemies, but most wouldn't be capable nor bold enough for this assault. But, the fact is, I find it difficult to figure out *who* could've done this."

Olum stood with a nod to the empty head of the table. "I believe High Priestess Meliu shows wisdom; though she is young, she has proven herself over and over the past several years. We can not cower before threats. I move for the Council to move forward."

If his backing vacating canon didn't take her by surprise, his being bold enough to move forward did.

High Priest Bekid, whose position she couldn't guess, stood. "Mmmm. It isn't ideal. No way to claim it's so, but I don't see why we shouldn't proceed. Clan Broldun nor Fermiden Abbey cower from a fight."

Meliu squinted at the man. Judging by his tone, he also backed the end of the Canon of Justef. "Do we have a consensus?" Glances passed around the table as everyone stood. "Then let us proceed."

As everybody else sat, Jelodu remained standing. "We of the Citadel of Rokan spent months searching out and studying those that the Canon of Justef names Defiled. There is a danger with these people; I don't think anyone can deny this potential. Most, well, their abilities without prayer are mild. A wisp of wind. A spark to start a fire. A glow to keep a child company at night. Harmless and simple, but there are the rare few who have hurt people."

Olum stood. "This risk with the gifted could suggest a need for training in the ways of the most holy gifts of the Pantheon of Sol rather than as a cause for naming them Defiled."

"Indeed, as with many arguments, there are two rational sides."

As Olum sat, Runker of Mulharth stood. "These people with minor gifts aren't our prime concern. This child here who takes wounds and achieves things unknown, aye! That's the sort of folks I want word of."

Jelodu gave a sage nod. "Most with profound gifts, though we found no one to rival this girl, Hulerê, are healers of Life or Spirit. I do not know what this suggests. Or rather, I'd fear trying to interpret the meaning of this fact. Does this mean the Goddess Erginle is closer to reaching the mortal realms? Does it mean the pantheon sees our need for healing? Or perhaps it is the Goddess of Fertility, Tulule, gifting us both with more children and the gifts of Life and Spirit."

Meliu stood. "The *Codex of Sol* notes that the Elements Life and Spirit are the most natural prayers, as we were created from these energies. I'm uncertain of your holy schools, but in Istinjoln, it always appeared there were more adherents studying Life and Spirit than other Elements." She sat and met Jelodu's gaze.

"I'm not privy to official numbers, but anecdotally? I agree. Lizel?"

The High Priestess stood. "I... Combined, no doubt. Many consider Life and Spirit of a single discipline. Others consider Fire, Stone, Water, and Wind all related. Combine those four, and... I don't have the numbers. I can only guess that Life is the most common discipline."

Runker stood in a huff. "Piss on comparing numbers. What did you see when interviewing these people?" Then plopped in his seat with crossed arms.

Jelodu shrugged with a smirk. "I suspect we found the same as the rest of you: There were no signs of harm intended nor dealt. If the only question we had to consider was whether to accept those gifted

with Life and Spirit, I wouldn't be able to make an argument against them. The question arises with respect to anyone who still hides from us. Let us say, and I mean no offense to High Priestess Meliu, someone adept in Dark is accepted?"

"I am a Priestess of Light, you will remember."

A nod. "Yes, of course. Dark, Fire, Lightning, and others can be deadly. The question is, do we risk allowing them into our ranks?"

Meliu bit her tongue regarding her conversation with Sedut; it would be a star too far.

Lizel stood and ended Meliu's temptation. "It would be difficult to vacate the Canon of Justef's ban on just Life and Spirit, though many outside this hall would accept the logic. She leaned and rapped the table with knuckles. "There is a bigger issue I cannot allow to be skirted without debate."

Jelodu said, "Please, do tell."

"While you and I reckon many others sought out Justef's Defiled, I delved into what tomes and histories I could discern what precipitated the Canon of Justef. I found nothing."

Meliu said, "Could the basis simply have been fear and prejudice?"

Merduun stood, "Are you suggesting that any who vote nay today act out of fear and prejudice?"

She smiled, believing exactly that of him. "No, not at all. Just stating an obvious possibility."

He grunted and sat while Lizel cleared her throat. "The fixtures of Canon were *not* chosen without some evidence. Some proof. Something perceived as wisdom even if it is later deemed false. In a sense, we are arguing against Lord Priest Justef without knowing his argument."

A pang of fear struck Meliu's intended vote for the first time, and her arms goose-pimpled. "The Canon Debates were documented."

Lizel sighed and bowed her head. "Seventy-two volumes, but as far as I know, only twenty-eight survived the journey to the Rôemhîen Pass. Justef is among the missing."

Another twinge. If Ulrikt sought to vacate Justef all along, he wouldn't have hesitated to make sure the book disappeared, but he would only do so if there were a strong argument against it. *A strong argument against himself? Against me?* "What are the chances of it being anywhere we can reach it?"

"I traveled north and found nothing suggesting it's hidden or lost in some collection."

A twitch rocked Meliu's leg, and she put her hand on Hulerê's shoulder and felt it fade. *How can I argue my own salvation?* "Well, High Priestess Lizel, I think you've found that the strongest argument against vacating Justef is, in fact, the lack of an argument for Justef." Several chuckles from around the table brought a grin. "Funny, but no joke. If we vacate to find our decision wrong, we tear down a dam difficult to rebuild."

Runker said, "You're suggestin' we'd unleash the Vanquished, are ya?"

"I don't know what I'm suggesting."

"Here's a thought for ya, little lady. Sorry, little high priestess lady. When was the last time a Defiled has been captured and killed?"

For a flicker, Meliu's chest seized, wondering if he'd put pieces together in the manner Sedut had. She swallowed hard. "I heard of Defiled marched into Istinjoln—"

"Nah, nah. Since we fled Kaludor. A hundred? Ten? One? I'd shout to the Twelve Hells no, the answer is none. I did my own thinkin' and researchin'. The Canon of Justef doesn't say the Defiled can't join the priesthood, well, not in so many words, mind you. It states they must be exterminated to save the Pantheon of Sol. These past years, the Canon of Justef has already been vacated! In deeds, but not words."

Meliu looked to Lizel, embarrassed to admit she hadn't bothered to read the Canon of Justef in full. Ever. But what the man said made sense, though she hated to admit it. "Lizel?"

The woman stood as if hesitant to speak. "He is correct. Death is the ban that keeps the Justef's Defiled from the Church."

Runker laughed before looking straight at Meliu. "You folks thinkin' I'm from the north makes me stupid is gettin' old. To follow Canon, we have to start killin' folks like that little lady keepin' you upright. If we vacate Canon, we might open the doors of the Church to the Vanquished." He sat with a smirk.

Jelodu looked around the table before saying, "I doubt anyone here would suggest we start hunting the Defiled. Am I right?"

Meliu muttered, "No," along with every other High Priest.

"But is that a vote to vacate?"

A moment of silence ensued before Runker, Olum, Merduun, and Bekid all said, "Aye."

Dancing Bastards. One more, and the Canon of Justef was vacated. "Wait." All eyes turned on her, and she questioned her own wits. "I want what I have to say to be found in the Debate on Justef, sure to be written soon." A glance to the back of the room showed seven scribes with quils in hand staring at her. "I walked into this room determined to make history and vote for vacating Justef, but serious doubt arose in my mind. Then, I feel the healing powers of this child beside me, and it is erased. I sense no evil, nothing of the Vanquished in her touch or soul. But still, I am troubled." *What of the people like me?* "What of the others? We've been able to reach out to the gifted in Life and Spirit because they know they are needed, but others may still hide. If Justef is vacated and we allow those with Life and Spirit into the Church, I feel justified, but if we take away the fear of Justef from the others, might we learn more of them? Perhaps a two-year moratorium on them joining the Church as postulants and priests. Until we can speak to them, learn more of them, then meet and vote again two years hence?"

Lizel's brows scrunched. "There is no such lore to suggest this possibility. Vacating Canon is final and complete."

"Says who? We're high priests making a decision meant for Lord Priests. Can we be blamed for hedging our decision?"

Runker said, "Justef, the extermination of the Defiled would needs be declared vacated for eternity in order to make these people feel safe."

"I understand. My vote is aye either way, but I would prefer this provision added."

Jelodu took a deep breath before speaking. "This addendum would ease my doubts as well. Without High Priestess Meliu's provision for a vote come two years, we have a quorum already, but with the provision, do we have unanimity? My word is aye."

Brisk nods from Lizel as she said, "Aye."

"Do the four who favored vacating agree to these terms?"

A flicker later, the vote was unanimous, and Hulerê stood by her side with a satisfied smile.

The bad news was that the vote, in part thanks to her provision, only started the lengthy process of rewriting Canon. The good news was that she didn't need to speak, so she got to sit the whole time. That said, sitting was more of an exhausting challenge than she'd ever imagined, this both despite and because of Hulerê.

"What is Dark like?" the girl whispered in her ear.

Meliu imagined being so skilled in Life wasn't so different than Light, always wondering what it was like to have *real* power, the kind that made other acolytes step wide around you in the hall instead of

shoving you against the wall. But no, Life was unlike Light; healing afforded a different respect that Light didn't. Meliu tried not to answer but, in the end, surrendered to the girl's patience. "Terrifying. What is Life like?"

"Mmmm, exciting at first, then methodical."

"Be happy. Dark is terrifying, then horrifying, then it tries to drive you mad and kill you."

"Would you trade? If you could, I mean."

"On a personal level? Hells, yes." It sounded good to say, but she questioned it. Ivin in the tower of Bdein. Killing the Breath Stealer. Playing the role of a monster under a bridge. The mission to save the Silone slaves she'd soon depart upon. "But considering the people Dark has saved? I'm sad to say it's a trade I couldn't make."

"We both save lives, but in different ways."

Meliu grinned. "Very, very different ways."

The girl leaned in close enough her lips tickled Meliu's ears. "I've been thinking. If I can—"

Jelodu stood, clapped her hands once, and everyone at the table stood as if pulled by strings, except Meliu, who groaned and put her hand to Hulerê's shoulder, her muscles gone stiff as jerky after sitting so long.

Lizel intoned, "The gods be praised, for we have finalized vacating the Laws of Justef from the Canon of Sol."

Jelodu said, "Our day here is almost complete. Our scribes hold seven copies of the scrolls dictating the end of Justef and the provisional vote in two years. You are free to leave when you have signed all seven copies."

She took a single step toward a scribe before Rusker bellowed, "Woah, High Priestess. What makes you think you should sign first, mmm?"

The woman smirked. "Are we really going to bicker over who signs in what order?"

"We're about to, aye."

Jelodu's mouth gaped, but it was Lizel who spoke. "High Priest Runker has a point. Whereas the Lord Priests of old had a hierarchy, we have none. We are all equals here."

Jelodu glared for a flicker, but she nodded. "Your recommendation?"

"Each scroll has been scribed for the seven clans. The first signature on each should be from the priest representing that clan. We shuffle around from there until finished."

Murmurs of agreement from around the table until Meliu said, "Considering the state of my legs, I'll sign the Choerkin scroll first, but after that, I'm happy to sit and sign the rest last."

Runker glared at her. "So you'll be famous for signing last?" Her jaw dropped before he smiled. "Shittin' ya. I'm good with that plan."

And for the first time since meeting him, Meliu held a smidgen of respect for the man. "If it helps, maybe you can sign last on the Choerkin scroll?"

"Done!" And he laughed before eyeing the others. "If there's no dispute." Meliu wagered that on some days, someone would've accepted his challenge, but today, folks were eager to get out of here.

Hulerê looked up at her with a big smile. "That was too easy. I thought it was going to get interesting."

Meliu whispered, "We aren't done yet."

But the process was smooth as silk, smoothest for her as she signed once and took a seat to smile as the others shuffled one past another to sign here or there, with Runker making certain to sign the Choerkin scroll last.

It wasn't until the high priests were shuffling out of the room that Meliu stood with Hulerê and hobbled to the Emudar scroll first, then

Ravinrin, then Broldun, and then she looked up, seeing a man with bright blue eyes holding the rolled Choerkin scroll at the end of the row of scribes. She signed Mulharth and Bulubar before daring to stand before the man.

His voice came as strong as the first time she heard him preach as a child, with a tongue wrapped in silk and dripping honey. "My dear, you look as if you've seen a ghost."

Meliu stared but didn't know why; some part of her knew the man wasn't dead all along. She raised her voice so everyone remaining could hear. "Lord Priest Ulrikt."

She glanced around. Scribes rolled scrolls as if nothing was out of the ordinary until one strolled their way with a smile, nodding. "Good to see you again, Rothbert."

Ulrikt tapped the man on the shoulder with his scroll. "Likewise. I'll see you in the archives next month."

And like that, the scribe from Emudar passed him by. "How the hells—"

"Hulerê!" An acolyte sprinted into the room. "Hulerê! Izelfer needs you with Sedut. Swiftly."

Hulerê's eyes bugged as she stared at Meliu. "I can't just leave you here."

"You can and you will. Just get me back to my chair first."

They turned and stumbled as her toes caught, and Ulrikt gripped her arm to steady her. "I have her child, go and do what needs done."

"Thank you." The girl dashed from the room with the acolyte in the lead, and Ulrikt's powerful grip took her to her seat without a second threat of a fall and not so much as a twitch in her lip. She settled into the chair, less comfortable now despite being less stiff, as she watched the last people in the room meander into the hall. "I suppose I have you to thank for my little healer's departure?"

"You know my games so well. You won't need her any longer."

Meliu rolled her eyes with a sigh. "Well, I guess the gods are pleased that at least one lord priest made it to this meeting."

Ulrikt chuckled, blue eyes twinkling in the room's Light. "Witty, it's good to see so much Dark didn't ruin your humor." He reached beneath his robes and pulled out a bottle of wine with a corkscrew already inserted. "Shall we celebrate?"

"No." She squinted at the turquoise-blue glass and the etching on the bottle. "Trelelunin?"

"Edan."

"Shit. Open it."

He popped the cork, pulled two glasses from other pockets, sat them on the table, and poured as if cozying up to an old lover. "You didn't think I'd miss this moment, did you? Brilliant move with the two-year moratorium vote, I must say. The votes were there, but you made it unanimous."

"Don't make me regret my genius." She reached for her glass, but her hand trembled.

Ulrikt grabbed her shaking fingers. "Let's take care of that, shall we?"

When she touched Hulerê, the quivers went away, and so too did they disappear with Ulrikt's touch, but with him, she could *feel* the pull of his energy taking the damage in steady, rippling waves of warmth and chills. Her lungs sucked an involuntary breath, and she gasped as the energy gripped her chest, slithering into her spine and racing for her head. The hairs of her neck stood with a chill even as sweat beaded on her brow, breathless for flickers that felt they could stretch into eternity.

He let go of her fingers, and her hand collapsed to the table as her held breath escaped in a rush that spun her wits in a whirlpool that

might have felled her if she was standing. Four deep breaths before she looked up to see him sipping his wine without a hint of a nervous twitch. "Dancing Bastards, be kind. Who needs wine to get drunk?" Still, her hand moved to take the glass, steady and without a whisper of weakness.

"It's too delicious to pass up, even if it isn't Thônian Whiskey. A dreadful people, but a wonderful drink."

"I'd rather not think on anything Tek, thanks." She sipped the wine, and her eyes rolled into the back of her head with the hints of honey, raspberry, vanilla, and the most subtle ginger of what must have been a luxurious vintage. "Good gods. Don't ruin this moment by speaking." She took another drink, then another, savoring each through her teeth and over and under her tongue. She leaned back in her seat. "Where in the hells did you get that bottle?"

"I can not take credit for acquiring this *Emushuwon Nêevê*, no. Perhaps I should, but I prefer to sing the praises of those who are due the honor. Lord Priestess Sadevu gifted this bottle to me when she realized she was dying and told me I'd soon be Lord Priest." He raised his glass in salute.

"This is some old stuff."

"Perhaps the only bottle left to the world after all this time."

She eyeballed him with a grin. "You are forgiven for some of your trespasses for so long as this bottle lasts."

"Then I suggest we sip and enjoy."

She rested the glass on her lip and dribbled wine onto her tongue. "Ooooh, I'm spoiled on other wines. Sedut will be so jealous." She inhaled the fumes before glaring at his smile. "So tell me, who died atop Tomarok that obviously wasn't you?"

"Someone who forgot their own name a long, long time ago, so don't bother to learn it yourself."

Her glare hardened. "And *you* poisoned Ivin."

His brow arched as he sipped and swished. Swallowed. "No. The Ravinrin boy, I'm afraid. It isn't up to me to decide which forks in the road fate takes. I just nudge the curves and maybe build a few bridges."

"Some said so, but I always found it difficult to believe." At least she now knew he was there. She took a bigger gulp, indulging in a full rush of flavor. "Would you have selected a different path?"

"Yes, I would, but it's similar to what you whispered to Hulerê. You would change it if it were a personal choice. I would have had him chosen as king and, maybe more importantly, choose to accept the offer. On the other hand, the boy has surely suffered as few have before and will live from the experience like no other. Perhaps it is his destiny's route that saves the most lives."

She shook her head. "I don't know whether to hate you or... hells, I don't even know what to call the other option."

"Your father loved you, yet he sold you for gold."

She clunked her glass on the table. "My father was—"

"A worthless drunkard with much cheaper taste in booze than his daughter and a terrible cook, everyone I ever spoke to said it so. But, he loved you. I know how much his love for you was worth to him, but how much was his love worth to you?"

"Nothing, not a godsdamned thing. The son of a bitch was—"

"Heartless as a blizzard with the temper of lightning. Too literary for a child, I assume your mother said this of him?"

"She did. And she was right. There was no love."

He sipped with a smile. "The value of his love for you was that he could not *kill* you. That evil man who punched and kicked your mother, who never had a kind word for no one not paying him, carried his Dark-stricken daughter from the mountains all the way to Istinjoln, begging us not to kill you but to save you. He thought you possessed,

but I realized I'd never seen anybody like you. I promised to save you, to care for you, to turn your demon toward the Light, and gifted him with gold enough for a dozen Defiled children."

Meliu's lip twitched from anger this time. "Liar. He would've dumped me off a bridge. He sold me! The son of a bitch sold me to you!" Ulrikt sat in perfect solemnity, enraging her further. "That bastard never loved no one but himself! I know now. I do hate you."

"Sold you might be a matter of semantics, and no doubt he was a worthless son of a bitch, a whoreson, and whatever other lowborn name you'd like to give him. I won't argue against those accusations for a flicker. He barely made it from Istinjoln with his gold before finding a tavern to drink his treasure away and died in a knife fight two and a half months after delivering you to Istinjoln."

Meliu slumped in her seat. She'd assumed the man dead for a decade, but— "I swear I saw him... It was you?" She shook her head, refusing even a flicker of grief.

He shrugged. "A daughter shouldn't feel abandoned, should she? But, he was unworthy of your forgiveness. Now, how much was his love worth to you?"

"What the hells do you mean?"

"He could've left you in a blizzard or dropped you into a river, but he brought you to Istinjoln. You were healed—"

"And you healed me even then."

"I did; how do you think I got so good at it? A child, maybe no one, is meant to handle Dark." He chuckled into his glass. "How do I know you pray for Light to shelter yourself from Dark? Because I spent hundreds of hours poring over tomes trying to find how to keep you alive. Light. That's why we trained you in Light until you forgot all about the horrors of your past. We saved you, we sheltered you, we raised you into a brilliant scholar and one of the most respected High—"

"A tool! Shaped me into a tool."

His cheeks raised in a scrunch. "We're all tools of the Pantheon. You who knows the intimate touch of Elinwe and Etinbine must know this truth, my child."

Teeth bared. "I'm not your child."

"You and Eliles are as close to daughters as I have."

Meliu's eyes rolled, and she slapped the table. "Please! How many times have both of us almost died because of you?"

"I'd die for either of you—"

"Then kill yourself. Now."

His growing smirk infuriated her all the more, then came his words. "Not what I meant, but I appreciate your keen wit."

"Maybe my father should've left me in the snow to die."

"I disagree, and so do you, or you would never have been able to taste an *Emushuwon Nêevê* well over seventy-five years old."

She planted her face in her hands, wanting to scream or cry, but instead came out with a muffled laugh. "Point taken." She sat up with a sigh and took her glass for a drink, and the two stared at one another in silence for a couple of wicks and enough drinks to demand another pour. She set the bottle down with reverence. "You win. I'm not better off dead."

"There are texts to suggest you might not have died if abandoned, and... shall I spare you the stories?"

"If I would've become some sort of mouse-eating demon haunting people's barns or some such, no, I don't want to hear about it." She gazed upon him over a sip, and his mouth remained shut. "Right. That's enough of an answer for me."

He laughed. "I missed our talks."

"We never spoke that often." He tilted his head with a grin. "That I knew about." He tapped his nose. "Do you have any godsdamned idea how irritating you are?"

"I have a notion."

The conversation was too much to grasp with a single bottle of wine, but her thoughts shifted. "The *Codex of Sol* came to an end. What games do you play now? You've seen more prophecies, you son of a bitch."

"I have."

"Ready to share?"

"No."

Another drink of wine as her head buzzed a little, loosening her tongue more. "You weren't the boy who kissed me on my thirteenth birthday?"

"No."

"Elinwe be praised." She laughed. "But you're here for more than reminiscing about my father and to gloat over vacating the Canon of Justef."

"There was a rare wine to share with a friend."

"As much as I appreciate the wine?"

"So suspicious of my ulterior motives."

"Forever and always. Here to tell me to rescue Ivin from another tower?"

"That is my girl, and that is her tongue."

"How's this for tongue? I should shout to the world you're still alive."

A concessionary nod. "I can't stop you, but I prefer you didn't. If I'm to keep Kinesee and her children safe, it will be easier with everyone thinking I'm dead."

She slouched. "You son of a bitch. Godsdamned son of a bitch."

"For speaking the truth?"

"For shutting me up so easy." She sipped wine. "Why the hells have you come to torment me?"

"To share wine and words."

She sat up straight. "Answer questions?"

"Only the right ones."

She chuckled and clutched her head. "You aren't here to tell me what to do, and you aren't here to answer my questions."

"I've answered questions. You can't deny me that."

"All right, you have, but only the questions you came to answer. To earn my trust, maybe?" She leaned back and, in a flicker, figured she had his game pegged. "You wanted me to know you're alive. Needed me to know. Why? No, never mind." She stood and snagged the remnants of the bottle of wine. "Seeing as I can walk again, I'll walk while I can still do it straight."

She'd reached the door with a swaggering step while musing on the alcohol content of Edan wine when Ulrikt said, "I've another vintage at least as rare; I'll be sure to share after our next great victory."

His smug confidence grated her nerves and tempted a childish retort to the fore of her mind, but then, she figured he'd heard it before. So she stopped, raised the bottle high, then drank. "You do that." And she meant it, turning into the hall and saluting the guards with a bottle owned by two lord priests. Irritating and devious Ulrikt might be, but his taste in alcohol was impeccable. Plus, she wondered now if the man wasn't the closest thing to a father she'd ever had. This wasn't high praise; the bar was set somewhere between a snake's belly and tongue, but it *was* praise. She muttered at the bottle as she walked. "You must be damned strong. Damned damned strong."

Nineteen

Empty History

Paradise in the rise, paradise in the fall, paradise in the constant motion and rotation of us all, spoke the poet Ilumdisus. His wisdom stood beyond the common. People dream and pray for static perfection as paradise, unrealizing that every hell is based upon a static state.

—*Codex of Sol*

Meliu waited a day for Sedut before finishing the Edan wine, figuring its flavors would lose character, and Izelfer didn't plan on forcing Sedut to awake for a week. Meliu was right to finish; the faded notes of the vintage proved that at least something Edan aged into weakness.

"I'm leaving today."

Sedut groaned, trying to sit up straight. "I figured you gone soon as I heard how long they had me down."

"You also missed an amazing bottle of wine, but I kept you a souvenir." She brought the bottle from her sack, and a snarl spread the woman's face.

"An Edan bottle? You drank a whole Edan bottle without me?"

"Not alone. I had a special guest." She sighed and glanced around the room to make sure they were alone. "The bottle was a gift."

"Who would?" Her brows pincered. "I knew it."

"We both did, even if I wanted to believe otherwise."

"He asked me not to tell anyone, but I couldn't do that. If anyone can keep the secret, it's you."

"But should it be? You serve the Church, but?"

"It should depend on whether I believe in his mission, but... even when I sat there hating him, I wondered if things would be worse without him. When I thought him dead, it terrified me. I find him alive, and it terrifies me. He confirmed your ideas on the Defiled. Us. Which makes me think he's been watching us."

Sedut groaned. "You're serious? How?"

"I don't know. He's famed for Fire and yet heals me with a skill beyond Izilfer and Hulerê combined, and he can shift his flesh to look like anyone. What can we say he can't do?"

"I wish I knew."

"No doubt he has eyes and ears everywhere. We know now that more than one Face existed. Is he the last, or is there a dozen more? Oh, and Lord Priestess Sadevu is the one to thank for the wine. You pieced that together, too."

"I appreciate being right, but if you tell me she's alive, I'm going back to sleep."

Meliu giggled. "No. Not that I've seen anyhow, but I bet he could make her look alive."

Sedut shook in her bed. "What the hells do we know about anyone?"

"Or anything. There are more prophecies, and our friend already said he'd open another bottle to celebrate our next win."

"Perhaps it's best no one knows, after all. What good would it do?"

"The person I want to tell most is the one he asked me not to tell, Kinesee. If I told her, she'd suspect everyone until it drove her mad."

"Or she'd be like us, so used to it that you forget him and go back to your life. I think that's the way of most people."

"But what good does either do? He claims he needs to protect her children, and if she knows—"

"Whose children?"

Hulerê slipped into the room with a grin. "Are you two talking about who healed you? I need to know. He could—"

"No! You little sneak."

"Hey, I was guarding you both so no one else heard."

Sedut grinned. "There are some answers in life you're just best off not knowing."

That's when Meliu noticed the girl's white robes. "You're an acolyte now? Jelodu isn't wasting time."

Hulerê beamed. "I am, though I plan on high priestess by eighteen."

"Your ambitions are admirable, but not even Ulrikt achieved this."

"Who is Ulrikt?"

"The last Lord Priest of Istinjoln. Lord Priest by thirty-two."

"Hmmm. Lord Priestess by thirty."

Meliu laughed, and Sedut said, "Careful what you wish for, postulant."

Hulerê said, "Izilfer and Roplin are looking for you; that's why I'm here. They'll be waiting with the others in the courtyard."

Meliu stood with a nod. "It's well past time to head for Mulshahar." She patted Sedut on the knee. "You rest, and don't be surprised if you get a visit."

"Thank you for the notice."

Meliu nodded before turning to Hulerê. "You be good, and don't be too eager to rise in the ranks."

"Eh, one of you will be lord priestess before me, and you're both young. And with me around to heal you?" She shrugged, and Meliu ruffled her hair.

"I'll miss you, my little healer."

Meliu smiled as she strode through the door, but within fifty strides, her lips flat-lined, and on reaching the courtyard, she wore a frown.

Kinesee stood beside Izilfer and Roplin, and not too far to the north stood fifty armored warriors holding their horses. Her little trip would grow bigger when joined by six priests, a dozen monks, and two Wiirê guides after leaving the city. This didn't include thirty pack horses for supplies.

Meliu curved away from Kinesee and toward Roplin in her final strides. "Just how the hells are we going feed and pay for all these people when we get to Mulshahar?"

"If you run out of coins, I guess you hope to find her wealthy pa."

Kinesee added, "I'm sure you'll manage somehow, with or without him."

Meliu grunted and turned to her, wrapping in her a hug that took flickers to be returned. "You just keep them little ones safe." If they were alone, she might have broken her silence of Lord Priest Ulrikt's reappearance.

"I will. And we'll keep looking for books. If they're in this city, we'll find them."

Meliu nodded with a grin. "I don't doubt you. And say goodbye to your goat for me."

She smirked. "I think Tenkur is going deaf, but I'll be sure she knows."

"And be sure to send word to Mulshahar, so your father knows we're coming."

"It might take a month or more, but Solineus will know you're on the way, assuming he's there."

"It's all that can be hoped for." Meliu sighed and stared at the girl. "Remember that trinket I gave you? The necklace?"

"Of course."

"Don't lose it."

Kinesee's face squirreled in confusion. "I won't."

Meliu figured this single clue was the most and least she could do but figured Kinesee was bright enough to piece it together. She turned next to Izilfer. "You make sure Sedut is up and ready for a fight."

"A fight against who?"

"I don't know. I felt good about leaving when I had the idea, but I feel like a storm is coming, and maybe I should be here."

A giggle. "What enemy could breach these walls?"

"The enemy within. An enemy we don't yet know. If I knew, I'd name it. Be careful."

The healer's twitter faded into a sage nod. "We're comfortable but not complacent yet."

"Good." Meliu eyeballed Roplin next. "And you, be smarter than your little brother. No getting poisoned."

"I'll do my best."

The clop of horse's hooves drew Meliu's eyes, and she smiled anew as a familiar face approached. She walked to greet the rider, bowing as the woman dismounted. "Wayfinder Kurin, I didn't expect the Ironwing to send his finest."

"I dunno about the finest, but the old man does seem sweet on you two. I'll be riding with you, but I also brought Nêmorum to help Kinesee map this city."

Meliu glanced to see Kinesee damned near bouncing. "Someday, I will repay your king's favor."

Kurin said, "The city looks grand! Still empty as a gambler's pouch, as the saying goes, but looking more lived in."

Meliu said, "It'll be scores of years before we have enough babies to fill this place."

"And you won't be helpin' the cause?"

Meliu smirked. "No plans to."

"The Broldun bloke seemed sweet on you."

"If he wasn't married, he'd do his damnedest to fill half the city himself. Thank the gods he's married."

Kurin chortled. "I'll be honest. Half the reason I'm here is to reach Mulshahar and find out how the trade agreements progress." She looked at Kinesee. "Your father hasn't sent word in some time and seems easily distracted."

"I've heard nothing myself, but I'm sure he'll handle it as soon as possible."

Kurin nodded and said, "I'm ready to ride when you folks are."

Roplin stood tall with an appraising eye for the collection of men and horses waiting for orders. "Aye. There's no reason to keep you here any longer. You be safe out there, priestess. And be sure to send news when you have it. Our pigeons from up north will be flying soon."

Meliu nodded in silence, spoke her final farewells, and mounted a roan five-year-old gelding she'd learned to love over the past few months. She'd named him Three-blazes for the white streaks on his face, and he nickered as she swung into the saddle. She reined the horse toward Kurin, and within moments, they were joined by Commander Florinz Ravinrin and Edlmir. She glanced at the big man with a grin. "I'm surprised to see you here."

He snorted as he adjusted his ass in the saddle. "I've a godsdamned way of drawing the short straw whenever a suicide party rides."

"Woah, now!" She glanced at Kurin, recalling the man's bridge-destroying trip with Solineus. "You didn't bring any stonebreakers, did you?"

"Not a one."

"See? It's all good."

They laughed and rode from the courtyard and onto the barren streets of Endelêun. It felt peculiar to be in the saddle again and knowing she'd be stuck there day after day for months to come, elation to travel and surrender to the fact that the easy sway would turn into bone-jarring, muscle-cramping bouncing before settling into a comfortable numb.

TWENTY

Missing History

No promises,
as I hold your bleeding heart in my hands,
your tearless cries without blame,
your tamed shame grown accustomed to its cage,
pumping lump, crimson pumping pain
Forgotten to futures not, a knot tied in Rot
unbreaking but forever killing,
thirteen wraps of the noose,
killing the goose to plump the pillow
of your lying head so dead,
oblivion staring, torment blaring, hell unerring,
smiling curses inward with no one else to blame.

—*Tomes of the Touched*

To say Kinesee was thrilled at the arrival of Nêmorum Dûldelâ, a Wayfinder handpicked by the Ironwing of Helmveline to help her map the city of Endelêun and its palace, was to understate her optimism by a horizon. She imagined them exploring the palace together step by step, making marks and studying the map for peculiar shapes and unexplainable gaps. What she got was a cranky old man who demanded to work alone. Of course, he probably didn't expect to be

working with a woman who'd dash off to tend to twins, either. She spent two days tagging along as much as she could without feeling she'd abandoned her children, but when the man spoke so little that she missed the whining and crying, she admitted defeat.

She awoke before the twins did without a care in the world she could do a thing about except boredom. It seemed right and proper that a person should be able to combat this nebulous state of mind with the declaration to "do something," but the battle cry, though simplistic, proved difficult to obey when she couldn't think of anything to do. With toddler twins, perhaps bored wasn't the right word at all. Cabin fever might be the more accurate term. Kovin and Neesebelu grew close to eleven months old. They waddled around the room, going everywhere they shouldn't until she called her handmaid for help. They tried stuffing anything that might fit into their mouths until she moved everything out of the room or up high. They jibbered and jabbered to each other as if sharing a secret language, and considering all the mystic phenomena she'd seen in the last several years, she did more than consider the possibility before laughing at herself.

Yep, that's what life has become: sitting around thinking about gibberish in circles. She stared at the table she and Ivin sat around most every morning and glanced at the box of enchanted dice. She opened the case, nagged the dice, and gave them a roll. Loaded dice. Perfect in their cheating, these cut and pipped bones stole even the entertainment of random chance, so she stuck them away and slapped the lid shut. Started by the *clack* of the box, she glanced toward the twins. Sighed in relief that she hadn't awakened them. Sighed again, figuring this might be the highlight of her day.

She blinked and looked back into the bedroom, and a chill struck. A translucent woman sat in the chair against the wall. It wasn't the ghost who had visited before. This one appeared younger, maybe

closer to thirty, and left the impression that she had hair light enough to be blond when living. Kinesee grinned at the stranger.

And she smiled back.

A fresh chill pimpled Kinesee's forearms—rare to garner such a personal reaction from a spook. Kinesee glanced from the cribs and sleeping children to the ghost, then back and forth again. "Well, at least you break the monotony."

The ghost raised a finger to her lips to shush her, and Kinesee's eyes widened. "Did you hear me?" When the apparition didn't respond, she smirked. *She doesn't want me to wake the twins.* Rapid blinks, and she stood straight. *She can see the twins.* Most of the time she saw ghosts, others couldn't, and many ghosts didn't seem to see people other than her.

The haunt stood and sauntered toward the crib, and despite the languid, unthreatening steps she took, Kinesee dashed to the crib to block the ghost's path. The spirit's chest rose and fell in what might be a huff or a sigh, but if anything, the youthful features of her face showed understanding. Kinesee stared. What good could she do if a ghost wanted past her? She softened her gaze and stepped from her path, and the ghost stepped forward with a smile, leaning over the crib like an adoring cousin or aunt. When she reached out with a finger, Kinesee flinched to grab the woman's wrist but caught her own foolishness instead.

The finger never reached Kovin's forehead; instead, it mimicked brushing a stray hair from his eyes. "*Sosdolu imêm tidin.*"

"His name is Kovin Choerkin." Kinesee had seen dozens of ghosts since that day in the street, but this woman was the first who she'd heard speak since the little girl in the street.

The woman straightened fast to look her straight in the eye, and with only a pace between them, it startled her. "Shits."

Her head cocked, "Shits?"

"Sorry. You spooked me. Shits! Did you hear?" Kinesee's heart beat even as first Neesebelu, then Kovin stirred with whimpers.

The spirit stared with uncertain eyes. Even if she heard her, she shouldn't understand her. She glanced to the crib, the children already awaking, and stomped her foot while shouting "Shits!"

The spirit nodded and laughed, "Shits."

The door opened, and Budoe said, "Is everything well, m'lady?"

"I'm fine, yes."

Izilfer sped through the door. "What's wrong?"

Kinesee laughed. "Nothing. You don't see my guest?"

The priestess flashed her gaze all around the room. "A spirit?"

"Mhhmm. Right beside you." The ghost stood still, except her eyes trailing up and down Izilfer's robes. "She sees you. Is the word shits the same in Canonic Silone?"

Her brows headed for her hairline. "Did you just ask? Yes, pretty much."

Kinesee grinned. "She knew what I was saying. For a flicker, I thought she heard me. She can see the twins, too." She hefted Neesebelu from her crib for a hug while Kovin raised his hands to her with a spit-soaked gurgle from his lips before saying, Mommy.

Izilfer waved her arms, hands passing right through the ghost. "The same woman you've seen before?"

"You just fondled her breasts, and no, a younger woman."

Izilfer jerked her hands away. "Was that a joke?"

"No, but she didn't seem to feel it any more than you did."

"Well, thank the gods for small favors." She bowed her head in prayer and looked back up. "Nothing. All the tales I've heard of ghosts, even those that proclaim themselves lore, none of them explain this."

"Rinold said ghosts killed Wiirê in the forest."

"Violent ghost stories aren't rare, though I wouldn't have believed them until he spoke of it. But then, I'd never seen demonic possession until... Well. Why is she still here? Don't those who see you leave?"

Kinesee shrugged, turned to the spirit, and grinned. "I don't know. Maybe she likes children?"

Neesebelu gasped and reached a tiny finger toward her hazy form. "Wady."

"Gods above. Lady. She sees her." Kinesee clutched her tight and turned; she glanced at Kovin, the boy quieter than usual, and no wonder why. He, too, stared at the ghost.

Izilfer lips puckered. "I'm not sure that's a good thing."

"Me neither."

"*Mêisotu nastuô.*" The spirit smiled at Neesebelu and blew her a kiss before walking around Izilfer and through the closed door.

Kinesee tracked her with her eyes, and Izilfer followed her look. "She's leaving?"

"Yes. *Mêisotu nastuô.* She said that and blew a kiss. What's it mean?"

Izilfer grimaced. "Meliu is better with this sort of thing, but I think *Mêisotu* means baby girl, or a term on endearment for a baby. *Nastuô* is maybe something like, see you later, but literally means 'in the time of moons' if my memory doesn't fail me. Ask Meliu when she gets back. I haven't studied Canonic Silone in a decade." Izilfer picked up Kovin. "You all alone, little boy? How's our future warlord today?"

Kinesee rolled her eyes as Kovin said, "B'Nana."

"Ah! Hungry! Let's see what Auntie Izilfer can do." She stood him on the carpet and pulled a banana from her robes. "Magic!"

"You know his belly well enough."

"Knowing a man's gut is the best way to shut them up. A good stew works on Roplin every time." She grinned as she peeled and handed Kovin half and Neesebelu half. "Why do some ghosts see you and

some don't? Why can you hear some but not others?" She sat in the chair where the ghost had been sitting.

"Is the seat warm?"

"No."

"Might've been too long." She stood Neesebelu beside Kovin and took a seat across from Izilfer. "I've wondered about the ghosts too. What if it's like a mirror?"

"A mirror?"

"Sort of. I mean, Sîu said I had a gift—an ability to see them. I can see them sometimes, but not all of them. I know that. But what if other people who were like me when alive, their ghosts can see me, but not the others? The street the other day, with all the ghosts you both could see? I can't explain that."

"And the Yellow Eyes, I mean the Wiirê, can see them all the time?"

"And be seen. We need to be talking to Rinold and Nehek."

"Rinold is still in Endelêun—not sure if Puxele is letting him out the gates again—but if Nehek is here, he's outside the walls."

"I heard he's close."

"Roplin and Tedeu want to send him with a few of our people to Wiirê tribes in the northeast, so it's likely."

"Well then! After these two lay down for a nap, we'll see if we can drum up some theories."

Kovin smiled at her. "Thweory!"

Izilfer giggled. "He's a bright boy, taking after his mother, I'm sure."

Kinesee stood and wandered to the door, opening it to find Budoe. "See if you can have Rinold tracked down and see if he knows if Nehek is nearby. And make sure Besthu is around for a nap; I need to get out and stretch my legs."

"Aye, m'lady. Consider it done."

Rinold searched for Nehek amid an encampment of Wiirê on the Endelêun side of the Mûulbon, but well away from the city gates. He didn't know why Kinesee wanted to speak with them both but figured he best take every chance to get his ass outside the gates that came his way. The camp was a place where tents had turned into huts, and huts were beginning to be replaced by stone and mortar. It didn't have a proper name as far Rinold knew, with most Silone calling it The Village, or The Bridge Village, descriptive but not very catchy. He'd once suggested to Nehek that they call it Puxele—to make up for the whole river naming failure—but the man refused to take the suggestion to the elders. His next try was Squirrel Town, but this genius notion got skewered by laughter and didn't so much as earn him an official refusal.

Packed dirt paths led between structures now, where once there had been grass, and he guessed a hundred Wiirê made their homes here while at any given time, this might balloon to three hundred as merchants, trappers, and hunters came and went. Every bit of trade between Silonê and Wiirê staged itself here, and a massive block of the trade was for iron goods. The smiths of Endelêun were likely the busiest and wealthiest people in the city, thanks to their hunger for steel and other metals. Even Ilpen Gurer, Eliles' friend, who was a tinker—specializing in copperware—had hired help to keep his fires burning all night to expand into iron goods.

He tracked down Nehek within wicks of arriving, and the two meandered to the field in front of the northwest gate of Endeleun to wait for Kinesee, and as they walked, they talked. "This here place still needs a name. You didn't like Squirrel Town, so I thought on it and figured you might warm up to Squirrelyville."

"Squirrel Town is better."

Rinold clapped his hands in jubilation. "You've seen the light! Squirrel Town it is."

"No."

"You've a way of destroyin' a man's dream." Rinold grunted, and they strolled twenty strides before breaking the silence with a severe change of subject. "You ever see disappearing men on the plains? Men with tusks in their cheeks?"

"Like bones piercing their faces?"

"No. Like tusks proper and stiff beards. More like a peccary or boar."

His silence spoke volumes but was difficult to translate. Nehek scratched his brow. "I've heard rumors of a thousand things in the wilds, and I have heard of a people some claim to live in the forests to the southeast. No reason they wouldn't visit the plains but disappear? No. Not as you describe."

"What do them rumors say?"

Nehek laughed. "Some mentioned tusks, but I guessed it decoration like shamans sometimes wear. But mostly that they're there and dangerous. "

"Aye, I don't doubt it. Puxele has me locked in the city; she'd likely as not spit and cook me for steppin' outside the gates. Stories true about you headin' out to find hidden Wiirê tribes?"

"Why, lookin' to go so your woman kills you?"

He pondered for a flicker. "Don't suppose it's worth dying for. You think you can bring a few tribes to the table to talk?"

"It won't be easy. They are people more used to hiding than talking to strangers. The journey will be wet and dangerous. You'd love it."

Rinold didn't doubt that a bit, but the look he got when spouting off to Puxele about the disappearing boar-men and dead Histê earned

him a look that spoke to his not leaving the city until his daughter reached maidenhood. "I'm stuck between these walls for a time. It could be worse!"

"Yes. You could be living with ghosts."

"Better than demons, my friend, at least if you don't have yellow eyes." Four horses road from the gates of Endelêun, and it took less than a flicker to pick out Kinesee's white gelding. "Looks like they're eager to chat."

They strolled forward until they met the riders, Kinesee, Izilfer, and two guards, Budoe and Yulmin. Yulmin unloaded and set up folding chairs in a circle. Rinold never did get used to how the canvas of the things hugged his ass and hips but accepted the gesture anyhow.

After an opening round of niceties, Rinold said, "So! What brings you away from your twins?"

Kinesee leaned with a smile. "Ghosts."

Nehek poked his forehead with a thumb, a gesture to ward off the dead, and Rinold said, "What the hells about 'em? I see the spooks now and again, and they don't bother no one."

"Have you ever heard them speak?"

"No. But I'm sure the one in the forest, the priestly bastard who done killed a friend, he heard me. I'd swear it."

"Heard you?" Kinesee glanced to Izilfer and back. "Every now and again, I hear them, but they never hear me."

"Well, I never done heard a peep out of that haunt. I've tried to talk with 'em here, but they ignore me or don't hear a thing I say. In the forest was a different place and a different ghost. It was ruins, where the roof came and went." He shrugged and turned his eyes to Nehek. "He was there."

"I was, and this man saved my life."

Kinesee shifted her gaze to the Wiirê. "What do you know about them?"

"You would be better off seeking a shaman of my people. Ghosts and haunted regions are more to their liking than mine." He grunted. "Me? I know a few places to avoid because they will murder me. This city being chief among them. Until the night a ghost killed Jitô, I'd never seen one."

"Is there a shaman here?"

"No, they don't travel so often, though I've seen a couple pass through to bless and remove curses."

"I will do that." Kinesee sighed, then looked over her shoulder. "These ghosts of Endelêun, you can see them now?"

"I can. They walk the walls and man the towers beside you Silone. I don't think they see. Sometimes, I will see a group leaving through the gate, but they fade and disappear on passing the walls."

"I see nothing but our people. Is there ever a time you see no ghosts on the walls?"

"No. It's like any guarded city."

She sighed with a groan and turned her eyes back to Rinold. He half expected the conversation to be over. "Have you ever been to the Codex Room?"

He blinked in confusion. "The what?"

"There's a secret door in the palace leading down to a room, a room where we found a copy of the *Codex of Sol*."

He cocked his head back and leaned in his seat. Jerked and planted his feet to keep from falling over backward. "I weren't ever invited." In fact, no one had told him where the rumored second copy came from.

"Nêmorum, a Wayfinder the King of Helmveline sent, is searching for more passages, but my point is more this: There's a table carved to duplicate the city, and one time we were there, it glowed along a street. When we got there—"she shook her head"—ghosts made an empty road look busy. You two are part of a handful of people who know about this; I'd appreciate it if you kept mum."

"Ohhh, so I'm one of the special folk now."

The girl smiled, and he forgave her for keeping secrets. It wasn't like they'd grown close in the time they shared in Ivin's life. "More special than I ever imagined, if there's even a chance at you talking to them."

"Talking to 'em. Aye." He folded his arms and crossed his legs, and the canvas squeezed his hips. He squirmed and damned near fell over again. "Stupid godsdamned chairs anyhow." He squared himself and managed to remain sturdy in his seat as he crossed his arms. "And let's just say I speak to a ghost; what the hell am I gonna say? Hey ho! Squirrel here! Please don't kill our yellow-eyed friends?"

"No. You're going to ask her to lead you to a hidden library somewhere in the palace or city."

"A library, you say? What kinda library?"

"One with books." She smirked, and he glared. "The *Codex of Sol* sort of books. Meliu said the *Codex* was probably one of many. It could be the biggest discovery since we arrived in this sweltering place."

He stared. Grunted. "I'm supposin' Puxele only threatened my balls if I left the city. She didn't say nothin' about talking to spooks. I was gettin' bored anyhows."

"Me too. I wish Nehek could join us."

The Wiirê's eyes widened, and Rinold stepped in. "I saved his ass once, that was enough."

"No! Not the ghosts, not why..." Nehek pointed, and they all looked, but where his finger led, Rinold saw nothing.

"Where? The wall? The sky?"

"The ground before the wall. A white lion stalks the length. It's huge. No ghost."

"The hells you say. I see…." Nothing, except the tall grasses and weeds, bowed as if something huge strolled through them. He eyed Kinesee and her gaping lips. "You see it?"

"No. I feel it."

He took her word for it, but his gut suggested the girl lied or hid something from him.

Twenty-One

Bridging Islands

A dead silence amid absolute defiance,
dead obeisance amid absolute reliance.
Kill the Killer Queen by feeding her tongue
and starving her mind.

—*Tomes of the Touched*

Pikarn kicked a helmet so hard his big toe hurt for a week after Solineus jumped ship and sailed away. Rikis slapped him in the head for being an idiot, and all the Wolverine had for a response was, "He was the only son of a bitchin' human who can do more than piss at 'em!" All the more aggravating that the Choerkin laughed at him instead of taking his point for serious.

But his toe healed, and so did his mood by the time Inslok and his people arrived. Three ships, three Edan, and a whole mess of Trelelunin to keep the Shadows off of him and the other fool humans who might join them. The Singing Dolphin led the Edan ships up the Kiubor and Harumin Rivers to the island of Berul, but the journey was slower than expected as the winds seemed to fight them at every turn. From the sounds of it, Neseldun could guide a single ship upriver

with or without a favorable wind, but that would have the rest of them cussing and maybe a week or two behind. So Pikarn cursed his luck while trying his damnedest to practice the patience of the Edan until Berul appeared in the distance.

Oldenu's refuge was a changed place since Pikarn first arrived, and he was impressed but not surprised by the advances made with the manpower and supplies moving in from New Fost. Here, where the river ran so wide and slow that some considered it a lake, Berul was the largest island, but several smaller pieces of ground popped above the water's surface as well. Stone walls, crude but mortared and effective enough, surrounded five of Berul's closest neighbors, and bridges connected them all. With the stone outcroppings safe from flood and attack, they'd ferried loads of soil to the islands that had only grown weeds, moss, and lichens. Oldenu told him that names came next, accidental like and lacking creativity, but so far, she hadn't been able to talk people into more proper and impressive names. Pig Island, where a sounder of twenty or so hogs lived; Horse Island, the largest and most hospitable ground for many of their riding horses; Hay and Grain Islands, two smaller pieces of ground where the walls bore roofs to give them the appearance of buildings sitting on the water, and Chicken Island, where a large coop housed over two hundred of their vital feathery friends.

Pikarn stood atop Berul's reinforced wall with his arm around Oldenu's shoulder as she finished pointing out their greatest improvements until, at last, her eyes turned to stare at the Edan ships. "When we head inland, I want you to stay here." He'd figured it was the perfect time to let his feelings be known, seeing as she stood in awe of Inslok's glow as he stood on the bow of his ship like some statue. On top of that, he expected his out of nowhere pronouncement to catch her off guard. He was wrong on all counts.

"You're a piss-headed half-a-man if you think I'm letting you go without me."

His stomach muscles clenched in case she punched him, but she must've been in a better mood than the last time he arrived. "At least I didn't wait to say it til after I got you in bed."

"You smug son of a bitch."

"You're right. Apologies. After you got me in bed."

"I should dump yer Choerkin lovin' ass in the river to see if you still float."

"I'm right certain I don't, so I'd appreciate your refraining." Her eyes remained hard as stone, but her lips fought against a grin. "Besides, you don't even know where we're headed as yet."

"Does it godsdamned matter? I'm goin' even if it's straight to The Forges."

"Aye, well, maybe it's a crooked road to the hells at the least. I'm taking the Edan to the Chanting Caverns."

Her nose scrunched. "The place you spoke of? Where Shadows took Suvarn?"

"Damn my luck to be the only one around to know the cursed way. They've got 'emselves an Edan who's right famous for closing a Gate and entrapping a Forges fired demon."

"That's good news."

"Exceptin' she don't remember two shits about how she did it." He didn't want to laugh but couldn't help it.

"That does sound like a joke. I assume it isn't."

"Gods, I wish it were. If the Gate's still there, they wanna study it, see if they can close this little one before even trying the one in Istinjoln."

"At least it's a plan."

"It is." He clutched her shoulder. "All's well here?"

"Our diet keeps me skinny, even with Colok bringing in meat now and again, but we haven't lost a soul since you left."

"Small wonder and hard praise. The Colok are our next goal now that we've done reached Berul. We've over a hundred and fifty Trelelunin under Edan command, but if blood hits the whirlwind in the Chanting Caverns, we'll be wanting them beasties by our side."

"Our side?"

"My side. You aren't a goin'."

"We'll see about that. A party of Colok passed through about twelve days ago, but I think I know where they're holed up. And when I said we didn't lose a soul, I neglected ta mention we gained a few."

His brows knitted, uncertain whether to be nervous or intrigued. "You did what now?"

"Round about two months back, a boat came floatin' down the river with six aboard. Holies."

He wanted to celebrate survivors, but uneasy worms squirmed in his gut. "Useful or pieces of shit?"

"Half dead at first. Injured and starving, too damned weak to heal 'emselves. We've fed 'em up best we can, but one is still close to dying from the Drowning Cough. They keep him alive with prayers but can't seem to break the fever. We've got 'em separated just in case. Come on, I'll take ya."

"You tryin' to kill me with a cough?"

She ignored him as they stepped down crude and wobbly stone stairs, then crossed the village's square heading north before speaking. "They say they're from Nedudîk Temple."

"You don't believe them?"

"I've no cause not to. They're none too fond of me, and Broldun's in general, seein' as their high priest was in the running for Lord Priest. Like a great many folks, they saw Dunkol Broldun's ascension

as something closer to betrayal or even a heresy rather than prudent politickin'."

"It was a vote that pissed off more'n a few around Choerkin fires too."

She strode several strides before saying, "I dunno what the hells it was, mmm? Politics, sure as shit, but me and more'n a few Broldun figured it stupid politics. Figured he had somethin' on someone to make it happen."

"Way I heard it, Lord Priest Ulrikt pulled strings, but ol' Ulrikt done killed him in Istinjoln with every other Lord Priest."

She cast a sidelong glance. "The rumor is true?"

"Oh, aye. Folks I know saw it all. And I saw your Broldun lord priest Taken by a Shadow of Man. No godsdamned accident, I'll guarantee that. Where's Nedudîk? I only heard if it afore."

"Up the Harumin River and into the foothills. Never been there m'self."

She pointed to a stone hut puffing smoke from its roof and strode toward its door. She opened it without a knock or announcement, and they walked into a space with six crude beds, little more than sticks tied together with sinew and blankets stretched between. Two small tables and rickety chairs were all the furniture beyond the beds, no surprise since the last he'd been here, the building stored grain and textiles, but a pleasant enough fire burned in the middle of the room. Four holies sat around the blaze, two priests and two priestesses, while another priest at the back of the hut tended to someone sprawled on a bed.

No one rose to greet him, so he stood with his hands behind his back, rocking on his heels.

A priest across the fire said, "I heard shouts announcing boats."

Oldenu answered, "Not just boats. One is Broldun, three are from Eleris Edan. This is Pikarn of the Estertok Patrol, though that hardly seems to matter no more."

"The Wolverine?"

"Aye, that's me. I hear you folks boated on down from Nedudîk, can't say I ever been there."

The priest stood and strolled to stand in front of him. "Outside your range, no doubt, and you wouldn't have been welcome. You'd be less welcome now as the Taken overran the temple." He extended a hand. "Kîjun of Yulôk."

Pikarn shook his hand. "Pleased to meet you. Is there anythin' I can do for your wounded?"

"I fear not unless some god owes you a miracle. None of us here are healers, but I fear no amount of prayer would heal her."

"Drowning Cough? We've Trelelunin healers who could take a look, maybe. If they're willing. Herbs, salves. We brought plenty for the folks on this island, which counts you."

"It isn't the Drowning Cough. We, well, when fighting our way out of Renonis, a village south of the temple, we killed a Taken. A tentacle of shadows reached out and struck Iminêu of Ilonumar in the chest. Long as a whip and no bigger around, but it almost took her life."

"A man of mine, one of my oldest and most loyal of friends, was struck by a Shadow, and he walked the Starry Road. It's no way to die, I promise. The Trelelunin might be able to help."

"I don't believe they could."

He squinted. "The Edan aren't healers, but they know things others damned well don't. You should let somebody have a look-see."

"The Trelelunin and Edan do not follow Sol. It would be sacrilege to be healed by them."

"Come now, your priestess is dying." He'd never heard of a priest refusing help from anyone, not that holies in different regions didn't take on a variety of beliefs, and this stubborn streak sounded plum foolish enough to him that he believed priests from Broldun territory might believe it.

"It would break her oath to Sol."

Pikarn sighed with a glance at Oldenu, but all he got from her was a shrug. "We're headed on to the Chanting Caverns, and heal her or no, might they look at her? The wound might teach them something about these Shadows of Man and how they take and kill."

"I must insist, no. Any healer would be tempted to soothe her wounds and trip her into the Twelve Hells."

He snorted. "The Edan ain't no healers, and trust me, they wouldn't give two shits about her dying or not."

"Infidels will not touch her."

Pikarn raised his hands in defeat. "Then you might as well stick a knife in her to speed her journey."

Kîjun bowed his head. "You might be right, but I'd prefer we all pray for a miracle. All of us who praise Sol as king of our gods."

"Well, priest, I'll say a few words and ask them kindly."

"We all appreciate your sentiment and prayers."

Oldenu said, "Tell him what you told me, Kîjun."

The priest balked, head twisting to the side. "I don't know what I saw."

"Spit out what ya mighta seen."

"I suppose we are your guests." He shifted his weight and sighed. "When we were floating down the river, starving, and maybe our vision not so clear, we saw packs of Taken and Shadows, all normal like, you know? Standing, staring, following us down the river a ways before disappearing into the wilderness. It might've been a fever dream, but I swear I saw... one Shadow faced a group, and I know they don't have a mouth to see moving, but the manner of motion, if it was human, I'd swear the demon was talking. It

pointed, and Shadows and Taken went where it told them before the Shadow vanished."

Oldenu caught his gaze. "You've seen more Shadows than me. You ever seen anythin' like that?"

Pikarn licked his lips and puffed warm air into his hands. "I have not. I always figured they kinda, dunno, seemed to be readin' each other's thoughts. Just a sense of what the others were thinkin' like birds in a flock swoopin' and divin' together. I've never seen one point or gesture, either, best to my recall. Hungry and tired, you sure you weren't seein' things? The sun and snow can do things to a man's mind, too."

"Veru and Môdêk will back my words, even if they know the truth no more than I do. But the Shadow did disappear in a blink. All three of us will swear on it."

"Aye, well, that's a new godsdamned bone to chew on for sure. You see anything else unusual when you were up north?"

"Everything or nothing, depending on how you look at it." A weak grin and a shrug.

"Aye, I know what you mean. Well, Inslok's ship should be docking soon. He's an Edan. I'll see what he makes of what you said." He turned but stopped, looking back. "One last thing. Might I ask how you survived so long?"

"We hid until we couldn't no more."

Pikarn waited for something more, then chuckled when it became obvious the priest wouldn't offer. "Fair enough." He strode through the door with Oldenu by his side. "Odd bugger, that one."

"From what I gather, they had no easy go of it. None of 'em speak much of their days before getting on the boats."

"Hard times forge a harder camaraderie... or they start stabbin' one another. But I doubt it's a pretty tale." He looked toward the docks and spotted Inslok stepping from the ship. He waved, and, no surprise, the Edan spotted him and waited for them to arrive.

Inslok said, "You've turned a small cluster of islands into a formidable shelter from Shadows of Man."

Oldenu smiled. "I thank you. It's been a chore, no doubt."

The Edan turned to face Pikarn. "I assume you had something to say."

"Aye, that I do." He repeated the priest's story and got the exact reaction he expected. A stare. "Any idea what the hells that might mean?"

"We assume the Shadows have some communicative connection with the Queen. Whether they speak in a means more typical of corporeal beings doesn't change our plans nor, I would suggest, make them a greater threat."

"That right? How about them disappearing? Because if they can disappear, what's to keep 'em from appearing right next to me, and the next thing we all know, I'm Taken. That'd make your finding the shrine a might more tedious, am I right?"

He blinked. "I suppose."

"That's somethin', at least. But there's another issue." He shuffled his feet. "Were you the one who done snuck into that Tek tent and took heads?"

"No."

"No?"

"I left heads, though I took heads elsewhere."

"Aye, my mistake. There's a priest in yonder building who was hit by a Shadow of Man, a tendril into the lungs."

"I doubt any of us can save her, from what I've read of the historical texts. Prolonging life is the most anyone has been known to achieve."

"Well, that ain't the thing." He sucked his teeth, uncomfortable with what he was about to say. "They don't want you to heal her. They seem to think your healing her would insult Sol or some dumb shit."

"You expected me to take insult."

Pikarn snorted. "Ya should be even if you aren't. Anyways, I thought maybe if you slipped in and took a look, on the sly, like, you might learn somethin' from the wound. See if you might be able ta heal it, 'cause I'm tellin' you now if a Shadow pokes me, don't you give two shits for my eternal soul and insulting Sol. You save me, got it?"

"I can look."

"Don't be seen."

The statue-stare with a blink made Pikarn wonder if the Edan wasn't insulted at last. "I'll let you know what I learn."

Pikarn reached high to slap him on the shoulder. "Thank you." He turned and strode toward Oldenu's home and took her hand.

Which she shook free of. "Speaking of odd buggers."

"Oh, aye."

"What was that about heads?"

He took several strides in silence before relenting to the stare burning the back of his head. "As the story goes, the Tek Hîdreng were wantin' to wipe we Silone off their continent, but that Edan went and collected Hîdreng heads from around the kingdom and delivered 'em to the leader's tent as a warning. Without wakin' not a soul." He opened her door, and she walked in, turning to watch him close and lock it.

"He's polite, at least."

"Don't never mistake his being polite for caring."

She kissed him on the cheek. "I prefer rude but caring."

"Don't get me wrong about that Edan. Without him, we mightn't have a chance in Istinjoln. He, they, care—"

"But if we all fell over dead, they'd just move on. Like a hog."

He chuckled. "You got 'em figured pretty quick. I suspect they'd be aggravated over failing more than begrieved over our ends." He grinned. "Ah hells, no matter. I need a week of sleep after winds in the Strait and riding the rivers before I'll think straight."

"Not sure I can stand more than a day in bed with your hairy face and stink."

He stripped his axes and set them on a table beside the bed. He knew he was exhausted when the blankets and pillow looked better than Oldenu. He muttered, "Damn, I'm gettin' old."

"What was that?"

He turned as she dropped her sheepskin cloak, and he smiled. "Nothin', now get over here."

Inslok didn't let him sleep for a week, a day, or until nightfall, as a heavy knock rapped Oldenu's door. "Pikarn."

Sunlight streaking through shutters blinded him as he threw off wool blankets and found clothes. "I'm comin', I'm comin'. Sleepless son of a bitch anyhow." He tossed Oldenu clothes and stumbled toward the door, having tripped over his own boot.

The door creaked open. "I woke you."

"If I didn't know better, I'd say you're gloating. Come on in."

Inslok stepped inside. "I made it inside to see the woman."

Oldenu said, "They left her side so soon?"

"No, I used alternate means. I am confused."

Pikarn sat on the bed and stared. "How so?"

"You told me she was a priest."

"You're saying she's not?"

"She is neither a priest nor Silone. She speaks Tekite. Thônian dialect."

"A Tek! What the hells is she doin' here?"

"She isn't well enough to say. The wound is incurable by any means I know. I'm uncertain how she is alive. Shadow didn't just pierce her lungs. It pierced her heart."

"They said it was a tendril. Sounded like the thing was still escaping the body it'd Taken. They killed the Taken, and a seeping piece struck her."

"I suggest it would've Taken this woman if it wasn't still attached to the dead body. Instead... I'm uncertain what the Shadow of Man did to her. There is no precedent spoken of in the histories I read."

"What did this woman say?"

"Unulk umineninê Fîkêzê vrâ gubor."

Pikarn grunted. "My Hîdrêng goes so far as sayin' I don't speak Hîdrêng. My Thônian doesn't even go that far."

The Edan's lips pursed for a flicker. "Fîkêzê, Virgin Holy Mother, please forgive me. She repeated this and said nothing else in my little time with her."

"Is she a Tek priest?"

"No. She would have three scars at the jugular notch of her throat if she were."

Oldenu said, "We don't have trade with godsdamned Thôn. What the hells is she doing on Kaludor?"

"Thôn is over a thousand horizons from the Mother Wood, little concern of the Volvrolan's, so I can't speculate."

Pikarn said, "That's a curiosity and all, I won't argue it ain't, but you're telling us she should be dead is a bigger worry."

He blinked and cocked his head. "I said that I didn't know how she was alive, not that she should be dead. Something is keeping her alive, so by that measure, she should be alive."

Pikarn rubbed his forehead and grabbed a hunk of jerky, ripping until his right cheek puffed with peppery meat. "Their priestly prayers keepin' her alive?"

"Unlikely, but possible. The Pantheon of Sol is powerful. If a god took an interest in this girl, they might keep her alive. But why would they care about a woman from Thôn?"

"Sure as shits, they'd have a good reason."

"Sure as shits?"

Pikarn grinned. "You don't need to sleep, but don't tell me you don't shit."

"I do."

"So it's sure, am I right?"

"I suppose you are. The more reasonable explanation, though not sure as shits, is that the wound itself keeps her alive."

Pikarn's head twitched. "Come again?"

"I sense no Shadow in her, but the wound will not heal. Hence, one would suspect her to die. The wound, despite feeling like a hole through the lungs and into the heart, does not bleed."

Pikarn shared a glance with Oldenu. "Call me a pessimist if you like, but this don't sound good."

Oldenu said, "Sounds spooky to me, and I'm no scaredy white."

Inslok shrugged. "I suspect it will kill her soon enough, so not good for the woman."

Oldenu clucked her tongue. "Why the hells is she begging forgiveness from her god, then?"

"Foolishness, as Fîkêzê forgives no one, but as you humans say, it doesn't hurt to ask."

Oldenu glanced at Pikarn, and he shrugged with a grin. "What Oldenu and I are saying is that she's done something to forgive. And she's kept alive by a wound that should kill her?"

"You're suspicious of a hidden motive or meaning?"

"Godsdamned right, I am."

A curt nod. "You should kill her then."

Oldenu said, "Hold a flicker, Edan."

Pikarn raised his hand. "Sweets." She frowned, and he blew a kiss. "Why the hells are five priests of Sol keeping a Tek woman alive? Or pretending to. Anythin' odd?"

"Dunno. Not so much. They stay mostly to 'emselves, but aren't shy or nothin'. Rare they leave the one alone."

"Then we should never leave them alone." He looked back to Inslok. "You're telling me that with five hundred years of learnin' in that noggin of yers, you have no ideas?"

"I will tell you this: You are losing focus. I entertained seeing the injured woman because I might learn something useful. I did not. What I learned turned out counterproductive because it distracts you."

Oldenu said, "He's an odd bird, but he has a point."

"Aye, all right."

"I'll have people keep an eye on them. We maybe shoulda been all along, mmm."

"I'm focused, Inslok. What do we do next?"

"A night of rest, then we seek out the Colok. Agreeable?"

"Aye, agreed, so long as you or no other woodkin knocks on that door again before sunrise." He grimaced. "Unless it's right important. Agreeable?"

He gave a sharp nod before he turned and exited, shutting the door with a gentle click.

Pikarn rubbed his forehead and scratched his beard. "He might be right. Might be we should kill her."

She rose to rub his shoulders. "If we went around killin' everyone that might need killin' there'd be a lot of dead folks."

He flinched as she rubbed a kink in his shoulder. "I want you here watching them when we go to find the Colok. I don't trust no one else."

"That worried are you? Not just tryin' to keep me here and safe?"

"Both, but the Tek woman makes me nervous, no lie on that. Only other I'd trust is Rikis, and he won the damned arm wrestlin', so I can't get him to stay."

"You arm wrestled the young Choerkin? No wonder your shoulder's sore."

"It weren't my brightest moment."

"I'll stay, but no promises I'll do the same when you make for the Chanting Caverns."

"Wrestle for it?"

She grinned. "I'm as sure to win as the Choerkin, but you'll enjoy it more."

TWENTY-TWO

Honor's End

A symbol, you say?
When is a symbol a symbol,
and when is a symbol the Cat's Tail or the Ocean's Whale?
What use when a symbol means whatever you wish?
A dish and a spoon,
a rooster and a raccoon,
a feather and a sword;
which are you, Dainty Deceiver?

—*Tomes of the Touched*

The *Entîyu Emoñô* was a week beyond Purdonis Bay when they rounded the *Veveshûon id Nederñô*, the Horn of the North, when they spotted Thônian ships to the south and swung wider out to sea before tacking south-west. Without signs of pursuit, they pointed the prow due south a day later. It was then that Solineus could no longer dismiss the Captain's probes about his secret package.

They locked the captain's quarters and slid the wrapped weapon from the ceiling, a panel with impossible seems to spot and a trigger to release beneath a table most would figure nailed to the floor. Maybe the Luxuns didn't smuggle elicit goods, but they were prepared if it came to it.

Solineus tugged at the wrap, untwining its folds with reverence to reveal the waved flamberge blade with blue-gray swirls in its black Ikoruv-alloyed blade and hilt with polished silver wrapping the grip, though he couldn't say if it was common silver or not. Considering the nature of the weapon, he suspected it was another infused alloy.

"Noboru nosên!"

"I think I agree, even without knowing what you said."

He wiped his mouth and pulled at his nose. "I thought I'd never live to see a weapon to compare to your two swords, and you show me this?"

"I don't know if it compares or not." He considered how the whorls flowed along the blade to shift the balance and chuckled. "Yes, it compares. No voices."

"That is a good thing, I don't doubt. No story told of weapons possessed ends well for the wielder."

"Well, we all end dead, don't we?"

He chuckled as a finger crept close to the blade, but not its edge, and with a poke, touched a swirl. Traced its shape. "I half expect it to move, like cream in tea."

"It moves, but only when you swing the blade, putting the weight toward the tip for a powerful blow."

"Ah. I see. Amazing. The black metal is Ikoruv, but not pure. I'd guess a ladle of Therêt in the alloy and other infused ores. The wire wrap, Ofdolus and Ermôlên?"

"I don't have a clue. There's a smith at the Sun Forge in the Dragonspans I want to take this to. If anyone knows more, outside of the Edan, she's the one."

"Ah." He smoothed feathers and broke his stare at the weapon to look him in the eye. "You didn't ask the Edan?"

"No. Something in my gut... They were leery of the Twins, and I wasn't in the mood to explain how I found it." The Luxun stared at him with twisted lips. "I found it buried on Kaludor."

"Where you buried it? Where someone told you where it was? A treasure map? That would be fun."

Solineus sucked a breath and stared at the sword instead of the man, deciding how far to go. "A vision told me to dig there."

The man blanched and backed away. "Sent by your demon swords."

"No. They aren't demons, and the vision was from someone else. Now you see why I didn't want to talk about it."

The Captain tapped his eyes with two fingers, then his chin before kissing the fingers in a gesture Solineus hadn't seen before. "Beware this man, sweet Sîu. Even a good man can only run with devils for so long."

She smiled. "His aura is clear."

The Captain's feathers fluffed and settled as he regained his composure and courage, approaching the blade again. His curiosity returned as well. "Your demon swords are latcu blades, yes?"

"They are."

"Have you tried marking this blade with latcu?"

The notion hadn't occurred to him. "And risk damaging it?"

An exasperated slump in his chair followed by a low chuckle. "I'd wager this sword has survived centuries of war in a time we scarcely conceive. Go on."

Solineus stood, flicked the latch on his harness, and the Twins slipped to his waist. Palm and fingers wrapped Sister, and a familiar hiss whispered in his mind, but when he tugged, the blade didn't budge in its sheath. He pulled hard, then jerked to no avail. He huffed at Captain Intœnô, embarrassed. "Did you know this would happen?"

An innocent but bemused expression spread the man's smile. "How could I?"

"Come on, Sister, it's just a test." The blade slithered a hand's length free of the sheath and stopped. Solineus glanced at the duo, who stared at him as his cheeks reddened, and as the flame rose to his forehead, the sword loosened to slide free at a grudging pace. The notion of the Twins being able to exert such a force had never occurred to me. "You ever do that to me in a fight, and I'll throw you in a river." A nonsensical hum thrummed through his mind.

The Captain glanced at Sîu. "He speaks to them often?"

"Not that I've heard."

Solineus groaned, wondering if people would soon think him as crazy as The Touched. "In my defense, they talk back even if I don't understand them. He brought Sister to hover over the flamberge. The two-hander needed a name, but he guessed it already had one. "Until I know your real name, I'll call this new sword... What was it you said?"

"*Noboru Nosên?*"

"Yes. Perfect."

The Captain laughed. "You'll get a chuckle or stare from every Luxun."

"Aye, well, what's it mean?"

"Mmmm, close enough to say *holy pissing shit.*"

"Like I said, perfect." He lowered Sister toward Noborunosên until within a finger and leaned close to look. Unlike the iron in the Eleris, the latcu didn't etch or mark the Ikoruv alloy, and even when touching, they might as well have been mundane metals.

"What are you doing? Letting them kiss?"

Solineus smirked. "This latcu can plumb cut through a steel sword, even mark metal just by being close."

"You're serious?"

Solineus nodded to a tray on his table. "Hand me a spoon." The man did, and Solineus brought Sister close; she didn't just scratch the silver; a notch formed in an instant, and in a flicker, the spoon dropped in half without the two ever touching.

Captain Intœñô hissed through his teeth. "That was part of a set."

"You wanted to know. Now you do." Though in truth, he hadn't expected more than a scratch. He tapped Sister on the flamberge. Not even a scratch appeared, and a pulse wavered through his arm. He tapped harder, and Sister sprung from Noborunosên and took his arm with it. "It's like Sister bounced off a spring." He sheathed the Twin, wondering if Sister was trying to send him a message when she wanted to stay in the sheath. "We're playing with things we don't understand."

"As much as I want to know more, I agree. I have seen marvels today." He picked up the two pieces of spoon. "I will keep these as a memento."

Sîu grinned. "Pass them down to your children."

"I will! With some great story to build on the truth."

A shout from outside. "Krâtôxêu!"

Sîu asked, "What does that mean?"

"It means we sailed farther west than I meant to. Krâtôxêu is an island."

From outside: "*Ivhonêu nûê!*"

"And that means a shipwreck."

Solineus wrapped Noborunosên and handed the sword to the Captain to hide, and within flickers, they stood on the quarterdeck staring south. The Sailor in the crow's nest and the Captain shouted back and forth before bothering to explain. "A ship has grounded on Krâtôxêu."

"Luxun?"

"No, but it's flag fallen. Tek would be most common in these waters, but even then, it could be of six kingdoms."

Sîu said, "None of our concern, then. Sail right by."

"No, the Ocean's Honor compels us to look for survivors. The wreck isn't old."

"It's risky and apt to be a waste of time."

"A funny thing for a man who was once lost at sea to say."

Solineus shifted his weight with a defeated grin. "Does he at least see survivors?"

"No, but it isn't a tiny island. As I said, the Ocean's Honor demands our search. But if we see signs of any hostile ships or a creature who might have done such a thing, we'll leave."

"Creature?"

He chuckled. "Not all dragons fly. Toswoûl, a giant octopus, can crash a ship to shore if the vessel is too big to drag under. Most beasts so big leave signs we Luxuns can see, but there are plenty of dangers in these waters."

"I was better off not knowing."

The two laughed at him, and Sîu said, "A child of the land."

Solineus snorted. "And damned glad for it. I'm none too fond of water. I tolerate boats because I need to get places."

The sun sagged a couple of candles past midday by the time the *Entîyu Emoñô* brought them to the broken body and protruding ribs of a cog missing her prow and name. Half the ship's officers, in addition to Solineus and Sîu, stood staring with spyglasses in hand, looking for signs of survivors, but they didn't spot the living or dead.

The Ocean's Honor called, and they answered. Sîu spoke for Solineus' heart when she said, "We should be moving on."

But his gut disagreed. "We detoured this far and dropped anchor."

His response brought a glare from the woman. "To what end? This island is a barren rock. If anyone survived, for how long?"

"If they got supplies off the ship, long enough."

But their disagreement didn't matter as the Captain ordered a rowboat into the water. Solineus glanced at the crow's nest where four Luxuns stood as eyes of the compass surveying the waters and horizon for threats, then back at the lifeless, boulder-ridden beachhead. "I want to see this ship."

Sîu's mouth opened, but Captain Intœñô answered first. "Ill advised. Let my people go ashore."

"Ill advised, why? There's nothing there, and there's nothing on the horizon. How much safer can it get if you're willing to risk crew already?"

"You are a paying guest while we are honor-bound."

Sîu said, "What is your gut telling you? It seems to like fights."

Solineus put his hands to the Twins; soft whispers swirled. "My gut tells me there's something misplaced about this wreck. The Twins are calm."

"If you go, I go."

"I'd rather you didn't, but I know better than to argue."

The Captain gazed up at him, feathers puffed. "What does this mean with the demon swords?"

"If danger is close, their voices will be more anxious, tense, warning. Something."

"And they are always right?"

A head-rocking snort. "No, but more often than not." Eyes spun as a seal broke the water's surface and dove again twenty paces from shore. Solineus chuckled.

Sîu said, "Well, at least she didn't seem scared."

With the seal's approval, Solineus and Sîu joined six Luxun sailors. As they drew closer to the wreckage, his nerves tingled, and he wondered if he shouldn't have slipped into some armor. He blamed the choppy rhythm of the wave for unease, hands resting on the Twins. Their voices remained tame.

Sîu said, "All quiet?"

"So far."

Solineus turned his eyes to the ship ahead, gazing over Gûvron's shoulder. The Luxun was the third officer on the *Entîyu Emoñô* and the Luxun onboard who spoke the best Edan. "See anything out of sorts?"

"Nothing that sets my eyes afire. Hold your oars."

The boat stopped to bob on the surf, and Gûvron stood for a better view, so steady he might as well be a goose riding a wave rather than a man standing in a boat. Solineus followed his gaze the best he could, and as their boat drifted, scorched planks came into view. "Fire."

"It appears so. This ship ran aground hard and fast, not drifting after its crew died from Rot like I thought it might have. Ghost ships from Rot have ridden the currents as far south as the Monsoon Straits. The fire could have started after the wreck, and people have been known to burn their ship so others can find them."

Solineus hadn't heard of ghost ships from Rot until now, but it made sense. So did setting its hull on fire. "If the blaze attracted friends, the survivors were rescued."

"I doubt it was caused by an accident, yet it is just as possible or more likely from an attack." He spoke to his men, and oars dipped the waters, taking them an easy fifty strides east of the wreckage. Two Luxuns splashed into the surf with bare legs, oblivious to what must be bone-jarring cold, and dragged the keel onto shore. The other Luxuns hopped to the beach, slung bone bows from their shoulders, and notched barbed arrows.

Solineus stepped to the rocky beach with one hand on Sister and the other clutching Sîu's arm to assist her over the prow. Icy waters splashed higher than her sealskin boots, and she jumped farther ashore with a soft giggle. "Gods, how I miss the south."

Gôvrun strode to stand beside them as others fanned out with their bows. "This is not a Tek vessel. I'd wager it is Goro make."

"Goro? That's a long way from home."

The Luxun grinned. "Not so far as I am. But yes, I've never seen a Goro ship in these waters. If drifting, it would have to have ridden the currents from Sutan. The Goro don't trade past Mulshahar, far as I know. They must have been exploring trade farther up the coast." He pointed and spoke, and two archers made their way toward the wreckage, and they followed a dozen paces behind.

Sister murmured as they approached, the first hint of caution from the Twins. Where the prow and forecastle should be was a massive hole leading into the hold, which meant what remained was more or less the middle of the ship. "What the hells would do this?"

"Seas are unforgiving, and storms sweep away everything in time. But I've not seen anything quite like it before."

"Crashed ashore under attack, and storms stole the pieces."

"No way to know yet."

Sîu asked, "Any guess as to how long ago?"

They stopped to wait as archers gazed into the vessel's gaping wound, and one stepped inside, disappearing for a flicker before returning to shout and wave them forward.

"It's difficult, but the breaks in the timbers show little weathering. Less than two weeks, I'd say. Bodies would give us a better idea, but my men say there are none."

"Washed away as well?"

"Less likely." They approached the hull and looked inside.

Solineus said, "Empty." Scattered shards of crates, broken glass, tattered canvas, and other simple debris, but nothing of value or use. "Scavenged? Pirated?"

Gûvron shrugged. "Or if the fire was a signal, their people took any cargo and bodies to bury at sea. We may never know."

Sîu slipped from his side, heading inland, and he followed. "I don't suppose a dead ship has an aura?"

She grinned at him. "Yes, a wild blur of yellows and greens and blues. Do you know what it means?"

"That you're sick of my aura jokes?"

"That we're fools for being here."

"That would've been my second guess."

She surveyed the steep and rocky rise of the island, a field of stones that'd make beautiful trebuchet ammunition, and his eyes followed her gaze and landed on an outcropping of growth. "That runt of a tree there. See that?"

Life aside from moss slicking the stones was scarce, so the bent and twisting shrub with less than a score of branches stood out. "Aye, I see it."

"Does that look like a path to its right?"

"Whereabouts to the right?" But as soon as the words came out, he saw a barren stretch climbing higher. "Never mind, I see it. Damned well could be, but it could be a trick of the eye or a natural formation."

"If it's a path, it means something lives on this island."

Solineus turned back toward the ship. "Gûvron! Is this island populated?"

"Nothing says so on any charts I know of." He trotted their way with the other Luxuns closed behind.

Solineus pointed when he arrived. "What do your eyes make of the area just right of that tree?"

He clucked his tongue and shifted his weight. "Let's find out."

The party picked its way across rough stones and skirted pieces of wreckage, with the Luxuns in the lead, but a piece of plank caught

Solineus' eye. In two strides, he flipped the wood with his toe to find words painted on it. "Gûvron. Know what this says?"

The Luxun gazed back. "Very good! It's Goro for *Blue Vixen.* Never heard of her, but it is a Goro vessel for sure."

Sîu sighed. "It's almost worse, knowing the ship's name. How many souls were lost?"

The wreckage was devastation, making it hard to imagine most of the crew walking away. "Maybe none, if their people rescued them." Too hopeful by a moon's leap, but it eased the horror of his thoughts a touch.

They turned back to follow the Luxuns farther down the beach, but their only frame of reference was a scrub tree that appeared and reappeared as boulders blocked their view. Then, a quick whistle from a scout up ahead.

A stretch of cleared stone led uphill, though it didn't go far before disappearing into a turn. Solineus' gaze wandered the slope, and he huffed, uncertain whether to be worried or hopeful despite Sister's controlled whispers in his mind. Mold covered plenty of stones, but several laying off to the sides of the possible trail were bald on top, and others nearby bore scars in the green. "Those stones have been moved and not long ago."

Sîu said, "Surviving crew?"

Gûvron trilled a whistle and spoke to his archers, who knelt and eyed the hill above. "It does not fit the story in my head, but it is possible. Big stones."

"We should leave."

"Ocean's honor."

Solineus looked at her with a smile and shrug. "Ocean's honor."

"Honor my father, don't die stupid." Gûvron joined Solineus in a quiet laugh. "No joke. If these Goro are up there and want rescued, why not call out?"

Their joviality fizzled, and Solineus said, "She does have a point."

"They could be sick or dying."

Sîu rolled her eyes. "And moved these stones maybe days ago?"

"Asleep."

"Don't die stupid." She planted her palms on her hips, and the Luxun fidgeted.

Gûvron spun to look back up the hill. "She does have a point, doesn't she?"

Solineus said, "If we crashed ashore and climbed high, taking all the supplies, why? To keep watch for ships. It's broad daylight, and there sits a ship flying the Crown and Moons. Why hide?"

"I will discuss it with my people." He stepped toward his men and called them together.

Sîu said, "I'm not going up there."

"I'm with you." She arched a brow, and he cleared his throat. "I swear it." His fingers clenched the wire grip of Sister, and he sucked a pensive breath; standing still wasn't his strength, and it gnawed at him.

The Luxuns jabbered for more than a wick with some disagreement until two of the men turned and leaped onto rocks to the left of the trail. Lithe, sure-footed steps carried them upward, their bare feet undeterred by bare rock or lichen. The archers who remained behind spread out with narrowed gazes, looking for any threats.

Gûvron said, "A quick search. The Ocean's Honor demands it."

Sîu slipped her blowgun from her belt and dipped a dart in poison. "Let's hope honor doesn't cost lives. What does Sister have to say?"

The whispers hummed, nothing concise, but when he put his hand to Brother, his head twitched from the rumble in his mind. "Brother is nervous, I think."

Gûvron's hand went to his bow, and in an instant, he had an arrow nocked. "Your demon swords?"

"Yes. They aren't agreeing. That's unusual." Sister buzzed in his ear, a whistle next. "Shits. Something's up there." He crouched and drew the swords.

Gûvron shouted something to his men, and bows stretched bone, sinew, and glue, creaking into severe curves.

No one moved above or below. Nothing came for them. A saltwater breeze was all he could smell. *What if it comes from behind?*

He spun to stare at waves lapping the rocks and turned back to the hill and its silence.

"Could they be wrong?"

Hisses ricocheted from ear to ear. "No. Something is coming for us." Mutters from Sister and an impression of meaning tickled his fear. "No. They're here. Somehow."

Gûvron shouted to his men, and Solineus' eyes darted one to another and back and forth as they crept backward in retreat. Left, right, left, and right again when he saw the flash, the waver in reality as a Luxun scout turned his head to watch his step onto a lower stone.

"In front of you!"

But the man didn't understand Edan, and his eyes rose to look at Solineus instead of the rocks ahead of him. A steel bar drifted into existence like a chameleon coming out of hiding, swung by hands big enough to crush the Luxun's head. The scout lifted into the air, flung like a doll toward the beach. A bellowing roar as the attacker appeared from a mirage of camouflage, and Solineus' mind leaped to Lord Captain Ushtrûôk. "Boboruns!"

A tip of steel lurched from the chest of the second scout. The Luxun stood gawking into the air, into an unseen enemy, until a massive foot rose and kicked him in the chest, freeing the spear and tumbling the scout down the stone face of the hill. An eight-foot Boborun with bare arms appeared, howling in its guttural tongue. Arrows

thrummed from the archers, streaks soaring into the shark-toothed men, fletchings bobbing from shafts without penetration enough to kill. And stones rained from higher above.

Solineus' feet threw gravel as he charged headlong toward the Boborun spearman bounding down the hill, the Twins a distant scream in his ears. Too long since they sang. Too long since they bathed. Too long since they fed on blood.

Driven by their lust, he leaped atop a boulder, a spear pointing at his chest before he jumped into a crevice, the spear passing over his head. Momentum carried the giant's weight, no way to stop, as Solineus planted a foot on a stone and jumped, planting the other foot to jump higher and swiping the Twins in desperate arcs. Sister flinched with a bite, but Brother hammered higher, slicing the patella before the spearman's leg flopped free. A bellowing scream as he tumbled, crashing into a boulder to break his spear, his head cracking into a cluster of small stones.

Solineus stood with splayed legs between two massive stones, watching the spray of blood, when Sister hissed. He slapped his heels together and dropped, gazing up as a steel staff left a trail over his head. He should've been looking down.

His right ankle bent and twisted on landing, and only clenched teeth and the fire of battle kept him from screaming. He ducked lower, and steel clanged stone above his head. A thrust nicked his shoulder as he dodged, then his attacker flinched, swatting at his neck, before taking his staff with both hands and swinging.

Sister caught the steel and bit deep, but the force of the blow slung him deeper into the crevice. His ankle forced to bear weight, he stumbled and hopped before crashing to his shoulder face down.

Brother screamed, and he rolled left. Steel rang right. Sister hissed, and he rolled right. Steel rang left. He kicked with his good leg to

crawl, slithered right, and steel rang left. He rolled to his back, and the Twins crossed in front of him as they sang and caught the steel shaft a foot from his face. He scrambled back, staring as the monstrous man took the staff overhead for another swing. His head struck stone, no farther to retreat, and he bellowed in defiance as the Boborun came for him, wide-eyed and mouth agape. Falling until broad shoulders wedged a couple of feet above Solineus.

The steel staff clanged the bottom of the crevice and slid downhill. White froth foamed and dripped onto Solineus' chest, the Boborun staring with dead eyes. Solineus' gaze fell on a dart in the dead man's neck. Not a dart, three darts. "Sîu."

He smiled until he realized he still needed to get out of there.

Stones sailed overhead, and he heard shouts both above and below. He sat up and lifted himself on his knuckles to throw his legs behind him and started crawling the best he could. Shoved past the Boborun's tree-trunk legs. He guessed fifteen strides stretched between him and the beach. Not so far, but too far. He needed to make a run or, more apt, a hop for it. Whatever his body could manage. If he sheathed the Twins, he'd move freer. If he sheathed the Twins, he'd be without any warning.

Clear of the Boborun's body, he rose to his knees, sheathed the swords, and took two breaths before surging to stand. His one-legged jump was more pathetic than he hoped, and he climbed with silence between his ears, but the sound of arrows rushing overhead and his hands and elbows slapping and scraping stone.

He reached high, and a blue hand caught his wrist; a flicker later, Gûvron's feathered head looked down on him with more a grimace than a smile. A kick, a shove, and a pull, and he lurched onto the boulder's crown as stones crashed around them. The Luxun brought him to his feet and lent his shoulder, the shorter man stouter than he

looked, as they stepped, stumbled, and damned near careened down the rocky slope.

Solineus dared look up to see rowboats in the surf and a dozen more Luxun archers sending arrows over their heads and Sîu's head poking from behind a boulder waiting for him. He hobbled and gimped with Gûvron's shoulder, and she leaped to his side as they approached, arm snagging him around the waist in a desperate attempt to help him reach the surf.

A Luxun officer on the boat shouted commands, and two of the Luxun archers they arrived with ran past Solineus, diving into the surf, bodies wriggling and arms waving through the water toward the boats with uncanny speed. *Shits, this is gonna be cold,* was all he could think before splashing into the surf. But Gûvron was there to help him swim. Then, he wasn't. He felt the impact, the shake in the man's body before his grip disappeared.

"No!" A stone splashed the water after bouncing from his savior's shoulder. Or was it his head?

Sîu slipped and fell beside him, his weight tipping her with Gûvron's loss. A gurgle and a scream as the Luxun flailed. Icy waters soaked his clothes, but with a shove, Solineus was deep enough to take his own weight easier, and he reached back, snagging the man's collar and falling toward the boats with a push of his good leg.

Splashes from the boats, and flickers later, as he spat saltwater and struggled to keep Gûvron from drowning, hands took hold of them both. Lifting, pulling, and driving them from shore. He relaxed in their grips, spitting salt water that splashed into his mouth, and after making certain Sîu was by his side, he stared at the rocky hill. No more stones sailed through the air, and if the Luxuns still sending arrows high onto the island could see a target, he'd be forced to admit their eyes were better than his own.

Solineus sat on the deck of the *Entîyu Emoñô* wearing one mule-eared boot and a linen wrap strapped tight to his other throbbing foot and ankle. More important, still, he and Sîu sat wrapped in a heavy blanket with wineskins filled with hot water cradled to their chests by fingers wicks ago, numb but tingling now.

The Luxun healer aboard took Gûvron straight to the cabin they'd been bunking in with the Captain right behind.

Sîu leaned into him. "On the bright side, I know how many darts it takes to kill a Boborun now."

"On the bright side, I can feel my toes now."

She giggled and stretched to kiss him on the cheek. "Next time, don't charge the enemy by yourself."

He rolled his eyes. "The Captain lost four men to the Ocean's Honor today, so I'll count myself lucky."

"Five, maybe."

The door in front of them opened, and Intœño stepped out with choppy strides. "It remains four, for now. Nostodyu thinks Gûvron will live."

"Thank the gods."

Solineus shivered. "What the hells were Boboruns doing on that island? The ship was Goro."

Sîu added, "And why attack us? Why not ask for help? The Luxuns aren't at war with them, are they?"

The Captain sighed and sat on a coil of rope. "Boboruns shouldn't be here, no more than a Goro ship should be. Boboruns hate the cold and avoid Tek waters. Why they'd attack is simple. The Boboru don't ask; they take. They needed our ship to escape, so killing us was what they needed to do."

Solineus said, "From what I've seen of them, I'd agree. But they're sure the hells here."

Intœño pulled a flask from his hip pocket, unscrewed the lid, and took a swig before offering it to them. When they both declined, he took another drink. "The Boboru have fleets traveling to and from Sutân. Some folks believe these are treasure fleets, a bevy of smaller vessels protecting larger cargo ships laden with gold from Sutân's ruins. The Boboru are a practical people. I'd wager they commandeered this Goro ship as a tax some time back, and it served as an escort in one of these fleets."

"Hells of a theory."

"Right, except why in the names of the Wave Dancers would they be this far north?" Intœño crouched as he took another drink and tapped the deck. "Here we are, and Sutân is over here. If the ship were wounded and riding the currents—"he traced a circle"—they'd come around hereabouts, but odds are high they'd end up in the Parapet Straits with the icebergs, not crashed here on Krâtôxêu. Not a thing I can wrap my wits around explains why they'd be here."

"Bad luck?"

A snort. "Say what you will of the Boboru, but they're some of the finest sailors the world knows. They were under sail to reach this far north, and maybe, maybe, they wrecked in a storm, but it still doesn't explain being here."

"The ship was named the *Blue Vixen,* and she bore scorching along the hull. We thought maybe someone burnt the ship to call for rescue, explaining seeing no bodies or survivors. But now?"

"Attacked by someone."

Sîu asked, "I've heard of Tek using Wyvern's Flash."

Intœño said, "No. There would be more than scorch marks if Wyvern's Flash were to blame."

Solineus said, "Unless someone here speaks Boborun, we may never know the answer."

"The bigger question I must answer is whether to risk more lives killing them all."

Sîu's eyes widened. "Are you mad? We don't even know how many of them there are."

"The Ocean's Honor demands it. We of the Crown Islands do not take attacks lightly."

Solineus licked his lips and questioned his thoughts before speaking. "I want nothing more than to gut every one of those big bastards, but I can barely hobble."

"Nostodyu will have you ready for battle by tomorrow's dawn once finished with Gûvron."

Solineus groaned. "Ocean's Honor got your men killed."

"An assault on the Ocean's Honor demands blood."

"Like I said, I want nothing more than to gut them all but, *but* Sîu is right. We don't know what we're up against. They hide like snakes in a bush, and gods know they probably have a thousand stones to throw at us. Just how do you think you're going to make it up that hill to kill them?"

"Ocean's Honor demands blood."

"If we die here, they'll take the *Entîyu Emoñô* and sail free."

The Captain spat before taking a pull on his flask, then he stood with feathers flaring on his head, reflecting the sun with brilliant blues and purples amid the black. "I will sleep on it and decide come morning."

But morning came without a decision, and without a decision, their anchor still rested on the floor of the sea. Then, a night to think turned into three, and Solineus found himself pacing the deck and biting his tongue to keep from venting his impatience.

Captain Intœño strolled from his cabin as the sun rose a finger above the horizon, and with a pause to click his heels, angled to cut off Solineus' path. "I realize you wish to leave."

Solineus glanced at Sîu walking their way, and on seeing them together, she rolled her eyes with a smirk and changed course for their cabin. Apparently, she wanted to remain a neutral party. He sighed and decided to play on the man's merchant goals. "I reckon I'm eager as hells to get ourselves south and make our fortunes. Isn't that what Luxuns are famous for? Prompt trade for high profits? We're throwing gold to the waves every day we sit here."

"This is so, but Luxuns dance the waves unmolested because we have a reputation we maintain. Letting those cowards live would speak the wrong words to the wrong people."

"To fish." The Captain's feathers ruffled in confusion at his words. "Who the hells are they gonna tell? Fish. No one else."

"Another ship will arrive. Another ship they will try to take. And if they succeed, they can spread word of our weakness. The Ocean's Honor."

"Yeah, I heard you before. What will it take to satisfy the Ocean's Honor? And I mean the least."

"All of them, dead."

Solineus sighed, still surprised by the man's tenacious drive for revenge. "The least."

His feathers flared with his blue nostrils. "At sea, their ship would burn, and all would die. That is Ocean's Honor."

"Burning a ship doesn't mean everyone dies."

"The ocean decides."

"I reckon there isn't no way to drive them into the ocean, but if we burn their ship? Drag it out to sea to burn or sink? The island and the ocean then decide how many live or die. And in the end, they will die here."

"Another ship—"

Solineus had spent the past days thinking of ways to defeat the Boboru without sieging the rocky island and losing more lives. "Would

we have come to this island if not for their ship? Would anyone else who knows these waters?"

"No. Unlikely."

"You sailors wave flags at one another; isn't there some symbol for danger?"

"They are common, but there is no one flag to warn people away."

"Leave buoys painted with these symbols or nothing at all, and the first chance you get, tell the Luxun navy to come up and send the bastards to whatever hell their gods demand. Damn it, man, we can't waste forever to decide or die for Ocean's Honor."

His feathers fluffed and fell, and he stared at the toes of his boots. "There is wisdom in your words. We will send their ship to hell with a Barrel of Storm. A message." His feathers stood tall. "A good plan."

A candle later, longboats rowed to the remains of the *Blue Vixen* with a single Barrel of Thunder, and Luxun sailors slicked the oil onto boards and placed the barrel in the hull while others stood with arrows nocked in case of attack. They sailed away soon after, and Captain Intœño insisted on standing with them to watch as a film of oil caught fire on the waves and raced toward the island.

Solineus blinked and waited; fire burst as high as the island's mountain with a plume of black smoke and flickers later a pulse of warm air brushed his skin. "I reckon the ship is gone." The Captain grunted. "How many of those do you have onboard?"

"Two dozen."

Solineus whistled. "Then I reckon that's a reason folks don't pirate your ships."

He chuckled with a grin. "It's one."

Twenty-Three

His City

Fîkêzê the Virgin waged war upon sin, not the sinner, upon the liar not the lied to, upon the complacent not the defiant, and upon the holy not the innocent. In so doing, the sinners, the lied to, the defiant, and the innocent waged war upon her, a group of fools best known as The Deceived.

—*Thônian Tome of the Hokandite*

Lôdumâ worried that he and his three most trusted men would stand out as painted statues in a burnt-out forest wearing clothes only bearing dust and horsehair and considered rolling around in grass and dirt before entering, but the secret tunnel passing beneath the Fulgar River added so much filth that by the time they reached the entry to the city he feared they would look as beggars instead. Dusty cobwebs and their too-alive inhabitants infested most passages, but more than a few dripped slime and forced them through stale pools with mysterious squishes beneath his feet, forcing him to ponder if he'd stepped on something alive.

Gimin and Yovun leveraged rusty hinges to squeal in defeat after a half-candle of shoving and shoulders while Kworgin and his narrower frame squeezed through the entry first.

Lantern light waved to and fro before hushed words. "Safe."

Lôdumâ slipped through the door, spotting several empty crates and a pair of rat skeletons that were new to the room since the last time he'd been here. Then, his father was smuggling him and his brothers from the city for a trip to Herald's Watch, the Silone island sailors claimed was swallowed by a tower of Fire, and now he returned as the last Ar-Bdêin. From sneaking out to sneaking in, a depressing fall from the days of his forebearers riding victorious into the city with the heads of their enemies on pikes and wives and children in chains.

Gimin forced the door wider for his armored shoulders, and Yovun followed. Gimin peered around the room, eyes landing on the hallway opposite their entry. "It's been a long time. You know where we're at?"

Lôdumâ snorted. "If you gave me a map of the city, I couldn't tell you where we are, no. But I never did know. The important thing is I know where to go."

He glanced at the men and their confident grins and wondered if he shouldn't have brought more people. Thirty-four more warriors hunkered in a gulley a couple of horizons east of Bdein, but he'd reckoned too many would draw attention.

Yovun's hand rubbed the brass pommel of his sword, a nervous habit that had kept it polished since Lôdumâ first met him twenty years ago. "Right then. Where do we come out then?"

Lôdumâ nodded toward the hall and led them into the darkness. "The paths I know bring us up under Mordijô's Stable or inside the palace."

"The Ar-Bdêin planned an exit?"

"All smart men do, but the tunnel was from before the Great Forgetting. Maybe it dates back to when the Hokandite walked the lands. The story I heard spoke of the tunnel staying hidden until some servant's boy hid from his mother down here, and it was found while looking for him."

Gimin said, "No question, the exit at the river is a masterwork dating to the God Wars."

"I agree, except perhaps on whether questions could be raised. I doubt we need to worry about being heard, but better safe, eh?"

The musty passage turned once before the corridor led straight to stairs carved from granite that wasn't native to the region, perhaps the only clue of a secret passage lost in the depths of the shadows above. With a ladder, they'd be able to climb into the shaft that led to the palace, but it was a route more apt to get them killed. He climbed the stairs without pointing out the hole above, and on this level, they passed more turns that led to places he'd never bothered to explore. He counted six such corridors on their left before taking a right turn, and a hundred strides later, they arrived.

The room was maybe twenty paces square, empty pallets lined the floor where once bags of wheat and oats were stored, and several looked as if they'd been converted into beds. Lôdumâ's eyes flicked from corner to corner, but he saw no one. A ladder still led to a trap door above, the opening large enough for a platform attached to a pulley to raise and lower supplies.

Gimin stepped to his side with a lantern in hand. "Am I right to guess people didn't use to bed down here?"

Yovun said, "Likely as hell, the stable above is used for something."

Lôdumâ exhaled as he poked an empty bed with his toe. "I don't like it, but this is the only exit I know of we can reach unless one of you can fly. Let's be honest, did any of us expect to live this long anyhow?"

Chuckles from Yovun and Kworgin.

But Gimin's tone remained flat. "And if the trapdoor is barred?"

"I guess we wait for these folks to return and give them a fright."

Kworgin cracked his knuckles and strode for the ladder. "I'll give it a check and see." He gave the ladder a hard stare on arrival.

"A touch of rot, but looks sturdy 'nuf." The man damned near scampered up the rungs despite the weight of his armor and gear, hooked his left arm, and gave a shove with his right. Trickles of dust caught the light in flutters, and a soft squawk echoed before he eased it back in place. He glanced at Lôdumâ and shrugged. "Quick or quiet?"

Gimin drew his sword, and Lôdumâ and Yovun followed his lead. "Make it quick, but don't get yourself killed."

Kworgin re-gripped and planted his feet a rung higher for spring, his free hand rising to the door. Legs and arm drove up in a single motion, the door slinging up and open, and by the time it banged on the floor above, he landed on the ground in a crouch. Fingers tickled the hilt of his sword with eyes locked on the hole above.

Dust fell as they stared at a distant ceiling dominated by a massive beam, the light of day dim above.

Lôdumâ strolled closer to the ladder. "If anybody is up there, we mean no harm."

No response and he took a step closer, but Gimin grabbed his shoulder. "Me first."

Lôdumâ scowled but understood the man's sentiment. Gimin owed Lôdumâ a blood debt beyond saving his life. "So long as no one thinks me a coward."

"This is a joke?"

"Yes. A poor one, it seems."

Gimin sheathed his sword with a nod and set foot on the ladder, waiting until halfway to say, "I am coming up in peace." A moment later, his head disappeared through the hole, glancing left and right. "Safe. But the decor is uninviting." He hauled himself up, and Lôdumâ followed, and as soon as his eyes rose above the floor, all sense of relief disappeared with a quiver.

As he remembered, the room's location was central to the stable, with doors exiting north and south and the only windows high above, but then his eyes followed Gimin's stare. "Bless the Fields." A dozen skeletons stood shackled, all but one with its nose facing the western wall, their bones wearing a metallic sheen. "Copper?"

Gimin tapped a skull. "I'd say so."

Yovun and Kworgin arrived and drew swords out of reflex.

Lôdumâ strode to place a hand on the back of one's skull, a woman, by the shape of the pelvis. Smooth and chill to the touch. "Someone wouldn't have cast these? Like statues?"

Gimin said, "They'd need twelve molds."

He marched down the row, stopping in front of the one facing forward, and stared into his empty eyes. "Why coat bones in copper? Drop a criminal into a vat of molten metal, and it might make others think twice, but these folks were long dead. And why leave them here, in a stable?"

Kworgin eased the trap door shut. "Only way to know is to ask."

Lôdumâ's head rocked with his snort. "You're right, my friend. I'm a thinker, and you're a doer. I should learn from you."

"You keep right on thinkin', Ar-Bdêin; it's kept us alive this long."

Gimin said, "There's no rule against doing and thinking at the same time."

Lôdumâ rose to tiptoes and leaned to peer through the skeleton's eyes and into its reflective interior before heading for the northern exit, which would've been lined by stalled horses on either side in years past. He guessed most were eaten long ago, along with cats, dogs, and vermin people might catch. Flickers later, he led his men onto Narudâ Street, the main thoroughfare of a bustling district that boasted three caravansaries and a half dozen luxurious whore houses along with a multitude of wealthy homes and businesses in its heyday.

"Son of a bitch." Lôdumâ licked his lips as his eyes followed Narudâ Street up and down, a road wide enough that four carriages could pass without rubbing wheels and didn't see a soul. Buildings once painted in vibrant colors to celebrate the Hokandite and the wealth of their people bore a patina of sooty gray that bleaked hope from his vision and robbed him of the joy of being home. "My greatest fear had been being attacked the moment we stepped into the street."

Gimin said, "Don't dismiss it yet. I sense eyes on us."

Lôdumâ didn't retreat into the stables but took the man's hunch to heart. The Thônian read situations before enemies inked words to the page, and if he'd listened to Gimin about the Choerkin and his Silone witch, Gimin's eyes wouldn't have been blackened by Dark. "How many eyes?"

"Two pairs at least." His gaze drifted and narrowed. "One's roundabout the third or second-floor windows. The second is gone."

They stood filthy as stray hounds, but the packs on their backs would suggest food and supplies to the hungry. "Went for friends?"

"They felt young. A street urchin, maybe, but that doesn't speak to motive."

Kworgin asked, "It's still a big damned city empty or no, and I'm unsure where the devils I'm at. Where'd you plan on taking us?"

"I hoped for inspiration once inside, but we're not so far from the Fulgar River as you might think. Question is, do we seek people out or let the curious come to us?" He stepped into the street, kicking at flowering weeds growing through the cracks, then turned north, figuring that standing around looking lost or confused invited more suspicion than picking a direction. "Trouble is, I didn't know who my friends were before The Rot, and now I don't even know who's alive."

"As it stands, I'd be happy to find folks who talked to us before eating us."

"Don't bow to rumors." Stories of cannibalism abounded far and wide, too many to discount, but he preferred not to think on it.

A haze of smoke drifted over Lîulin's Way as they passed, making it an unattractive route off a main road like the Narudâ. Except old rules needn't apply. In a city turned upside down by plague and quarantine, any side street or alley might be the most important and powerful in the district.

Two *clacks* echoed from the roofs above, and in the distance, three clacks answered.

Gimin inhaled and thumped his chest with a huff. What he lacked in humor, he made up for with melodrama. "If we were deer in a forest, I'd swear we were being hunted."

"Sounds more like we're being stalked by bucks in rut to me."

More clacks, but instead of sticks, it sounded like jars rattling together this time. "What if they're talking to us?"

"Then they damned well know we don't speak their language by now." He grinned but didn't look to see if anyone shared his humor.

Sticks clacked to the east, and jars rattled to the west, sticks south, jars north, jars southeast, and around and around, driving needles into his nerves.

Kworgin said, "Unless they're ventriloquists, we're outnumbered."

Lôdumâ laughed, quivering more than he'd like. "At last! Someone with a sense of humor."

Gimin said, "Too many eyes. A hundred pairs and more."

The clacking and jangling intensified, and the hairs on Lôdumâ's neck stood. "I'm not—" Something struck his pack, and he stopped in his tracks; no one was close enough to touch him.

He glanced behind.

Not a hundred pairs of eyes ran toward them, but it was more than enough ragged city folk to cut them down with machetes and

spears, and a few carried bows. "Run!" An arrow struck a cobble not far from his feet, and he leaped though it served no purpose.

The sound of sticks and jars died in the air as they sprinted, the only good news being their pursuit had been running longer than them. They passed Menou Street, then veered toward a nameless alley before remembering it came to a dead end. Sticks clacked ahead loud enough that his ears picked them out over the shouts of their pursuit.

"Follow the sticks!" He barreled ahead with his men on his heels to protect him from arrows more so than being slower and ringing glass caught his ear. He glanced ahead: Tubûlu Alley. His gut tightened as he veered. He knew the alley as narrow, one popular with street thugs in the drunken hours after midnight, but they couldn't run forever.

He turned down Tulûlu with terror in his heart, passing between empty crates stacked on either side and slowed to kick a broken wine case from his way, its boards splintering and bouncing from a wall like so many drunkard heads had done in days past. He thanked the gods for an otherwise clear path and sprinted hard as shouts echoed between the walls that felt like they tightened. If the enemy appeared on the other end, they were dead.

Twang. The sound kicked in his brain as a bowstring, but the incongruity of hearing a string... A crash from behind and screams. He didn't dare look back, but a blur drew his eyes upward to see archers raining arrows upon their pursuit. He denied his legs their desire to stop and lean against a wall, forcing them to carry him from this trap in case it next turned into their doom.

They rushed into the open air of Myindôlu Street, escaping the dying echo of their feet to find themselves staring at pikes like those carried by patrolmen throughout the city's districts, but there was no mistaking most of these folks for officers of Bdein law.

He slid his burning thighs to a stop and raised his hands. "Whoa! Peace!"

A woman stepped forward as the sounds of dying faded behind them. She kept her black hair pulled back in a bun, and her weathered, gaunt face spoke of someone who'd seen too many hungry days and too many deaths. "Who the hell are you?"

"My name is Lôdumâ, most recently of Noduhom Manor, where we lived until a couple of weeks past."

She blinked and stared at him as if it was the craziest thing she'd ever heard. "Nobody is goddamned stupid enough to enter Bdein if even they could."

He grinned through panting breaths. "Smart enough to know how and damned fool enough to do it."

She turned and shared whispers with a pikeman before nodding east. "You can keep your weapons, but don't touch them. Follow me."

The woman didn't offer a name, and he didn't ask. In fact, he didn't utter a word and imagined Gimin praising him for rare silence. Their hosts led them east as Myindôlu Street curved, and it didn't take long before he recognized the building they headed for: The Constabulary of Nodurâ District. She marched them inside, the doors barred behind them, and here they surrendered their weapons and offered their hands to be tied before the woman led them down a hall. The good news is that he knew the jail cells sat in the opposite direction. From experience.

The chamber she marched them into must once have served as the regiment's dining hall, judging by the size of the room and the count of tables and chairs. It'd been six years since he spent a night behind bars here after a scuffle outside a brothel, then spent two more days playing cards and dicing with the soldiers.

At least three dozen men and women stood scattered along the room's edges, faces of one and all harder than any of the soldiers he remembered. The middle of the room stood as a wide open path to a round table circled by heavy oak chairs, sturdy and simple as befitted the building and its purpose.

Disarmed and with wrists tied wasn't how Lôdumâ had planned to start a conversation. "We stand in the armory of the Nodurâ District unless I'm lost. By law and courtesy, my men and I should know who we address."

A scrawny man with a twitching left eye said, "What, you were some sort of barrister?"

"Good gods, no. I was never so good at lying to make the law my livelihood."

A man in maille armor strode into the room, clean-cut and shaved. He was tall and likely a big man once when food wasn't scarce. He matched the furniture, mundane and lacking ornament, but his aura suggested anything but simple. By the way he carried himself, straight-backed and self-assured, he wasn't just an old soldier; Lôdumâ figured he'd found the leader of this band. "The law don't carry much weight anymore."

"Hence, I mentioned courtesy."

The feet of a chair squawked as the man spun it to take a seat. "You first."

A deep breath. "As I said, I'm not much of a liar. My name is Lôdumâ Ar-Bdêin." He paused to let the name sink in.

It took flickers before a response. "Am I supposed to be impressed?"

"I am—"

"The last true Ar-Bdêin, male or female, outside of an unknown count of your bastards scattered up and down Hidrêng."

"Eight, last I knew. But I am the last Ar-Bdêin, and this is my city."

He glanced at several of his men with a smirk and shrug. "My name is Lundar Ilsôfin, and my claim to this city is worth as much as yours. Nobody gives a shit for your name."

"I'm arrogant and determined, not delusional. Tell me who claims the city now."

The man chuckled. "Were those people trying to kill you because of your worthless name?"

"No. They didn't give me a chance to impress them like you did."

"Do you so much as know who they are?"

"Less than I know about you, and all I know is the name you claim."

Lundar leaned his elbows to his knees with a smile. "And that's why you're alive. Sort of, anyhow. You call Bdein yours; I call Nodurâ mine, most of the district anyhow, and yet I get word there are four men in my tunnels. Nobody knows who they are and, more importantly, how the devils they got there. My people collapsed every entry leading into our Nodurâ tunnels over a year ago."

"And yet here I am." Their capture and questioning started to make more sense, but he wasn't sure whether to feel safer or not.

Lundar opened his arms wide in a grand gesture that brought chuckles from the gathered forum. "Here you are in our luxurious home. Lôdumâ Ar-Bdêin if I'm to take your word, and that's a name most would find shameful to take. Most think you betrayed your kin, but I don't give a bedeviled damn for your family history. No, sir, because there's another thing I know. If Ar-Bdêin you are, you would've been strung from a bridge if you were in *your* city since The Rot came, though I can't say by whose order, the Palace, the Bishop, or some other fortunate enough to stumble on your hidey-hole. Seems peculiar, don't it, you being here and alive?"

"You underestimate my ability to go underground."

"No, sir. I think I estimate just right. Nobody gets into Bdein without the say of the Palace or the Bishop. You know what that means?"

Lôdumâ stared until he'd blinked four times. "That was rhetorical, wasn't it?"

"No."

"The Palace or the Bishop let me in?"

"Wrong. The both of them want you deader than they want me, and that's pretty damned dead, right? No, what it means is you know a way into this city and, for some godsdamned unfathomable reason, chose to use it."

Lôdumâ squinted at him, recognizing now that he wasn't dealing with a stupid man. Quite the opposite. "And no lie I concoct will convince you otherwise?"

"Is that an admission?"

"I need to admit nothing. You have me all figured out. Except, of course, one important thing. Why I entered Bdein."

"I've no doubt it's only important to you."

Lôdumâ smirked and rolled his eyes. "Got me again." He raised his tied wrists. "Is this necessary?"

Lundar gestured, and twitchy-eye untied the knot. "And my men?"

Lundar shook his head. "The man with black eyes, I don't trust him."

"He is of Thôn, but his eyes were blackened by a Silone witch, not by practicing witchery."

"I heard stories of your stealing the young Choerkin from the Bishop and his witch. If you thought she wanted you dead before that?" He shook his head with a broad smile.

"I didn't steal him. He escaped, and I caught him again, so I planned to sell them both fair and square. It didn't work out as planned."

"Your plan for this city is going just as well?"

"I'm still alive, and I have something you want. My question is, what do you want it for?"

"Any entrance is a threat."

Lôdumâ laughed. "Oh, please. Spare me. I'm treating you as an intelligent man. Return the courtesy."

Lundar snorted, fingers twining in a grinding grip. "So be it. If you can pass the Quarantine Patrols to get into Bdein, I can get out. Food, arms, medicinals, everything I need."

"Maybe not so smart after all. A wise man would say to escape and run for the hills."

"Like you did?"

"Fair enough. I can show you a way out and in, but everything you need for what? To feed the starving? To end a grudge? To proclaim yourself king?"

"There's only one thing nowadays: survival."

"I can't argue with you there. I could show you a place to survive that's far more comfortable than this."

He shook his head. "More comfortable than the great city of Bdein as it was and can be again? No. I was born here and will die here. Ridding the city of rats begins with you telling me how to get what I need."

"I won't give you what you need—"

"Then you die."

"Excuse me, you didn't let me finish. There's something I want, and rumor speaks to it having entered Bdein not too long ago."

A hard stare before speaking. "You shittin' me, Ar-Bdêin? You came here for your family's sword?" He leaned back and laughed.

Lundar belted a sincere and hearty laugh that grated on Lôdumâ's nerves and didn't seem to be ending soon. "So pleased to amuse you!"

The man brushed tears from his face. “I’m proud to have lived long enough to hear someone say something so stupid.”

With the laughter gone, Lôdumâ’s spirit returned. “The sword *is* here, isn’t it?”

“Oh, it is. Sardôn Stôltmor stood atop the palace gates waving the fool thing like some conquering hero, proclaiming its return proof of Pulvûer’s godly favor for his family’s rule of Bdein.”

Lôdumâ spoke through grinding teeth. “Stôltmor. They rule Bdein now.” His head cocked. “What happened to the Turlid?”

“The Rot, most of them. The last of the youngsters were put to the Bdein sword from what I heard.”

Knots twisted in his gut as he fought against a twinge of pleasure at knowing someone ended the Turlid line, even if it wasn’t him. He should empathize more. Some Turlid hiding somewhere might be the latest version of Lôdumâ himself. “How sad.”

“For another laugh, tell me, how do you plan to get the sword back?”

“I will stroll into the palace and take it from whatever bastard holds it.”

Lundar shifted his gaze to Gimin without laughing. “Are all his plans so well thought through?”

“They are, and most times they somehow work out.”

Lôdumâ said, “I’m best thinking fast and on my feet, but there are things I need to know.”

“If you think your family’s sword gives the Stôltmor rule of Bdein, you’re wrong.”

“It’s just a sword, but it *is* my sword. Answer my questions, and I will answer yours.”

“So simple?”

“Did I say my questions would be simple?”

A grunt. “I won’t help you retrieve your sword. However you lost it, you can get it back on your own.”

"The Choerkin stole it."

"No shit?"

"It was a distressing few days all around, but more to the point, I don't need your help getting my sword back. At least, no more help than you freeing my men and answering my questions. A place to hide."

Lundar stared with a humored smirk. "You don't remember me at all."

Lôdumâ's face scrunched, and his heart pounded, hoping he didn't bed the man's wife or sister... or mother. He swallowed his fear and took a breath. "Should I?"

"I arrested you outside the Golden Curtain and ended up knocking you in the head before dragging your ass here. Didn't need to mind you, as you were too drunk to give a good fight. But it felt good putting a little crack to your skull."

Lôdumâ scratched his head with a chuckle. "I was pissin' my third bottle of whiskey and don't remember nothing past my second whore until I awoke behind bars."

"Now that I believe! You made us keep you jailed for two days to recover."

At least it wasn't as embarrassing as having slept with the man's mother. Or maybe it was worse, recalling his retching and the smell of his clothes when he walked free days later. "I apologize for making you hit me, though I lost plenty of coins gambling with the men while hungover."

"You were a drunken sod but not the devil so many spoke of." Lundar gripped a chair and gave it a heave, its legs and back clattering and bouncing across the floor before sliding to a stop at Lôdumâ's feet. "Least I could do for a true son of Ar-Bdêin."

"Appreciated." Lôdumâ flipped the chair upright and sat. "Who rules Bdein?"

"The Stôltmor hold the Palace, and the Bishop's people hold the Temples District. Outside those walls, the city is run by people like me."

Lôdumâ nodded, keeping his face solemn, but inside, he chuckled. "A city version of the Hundred Nations, in a sense."

"Huh. Yes, but simpler, I suppose. Those who meant to kill you live in the Kîgern District, headed by Mîkêl Polark."

"Rinwel's son?"

"Yes."

The Polarks sided against the Ar-Bdeins in the uprising, so their fall from the palace to the streets didn't upset him. "Rinwel was a twat on his best days."

"He's a twat with soldiers now and dangerous. His people overrun my streets, but we hold the buildings and tunnels. So far. I'm an honorable man, and I mean to control honorable streets. I hope you can see that by how I've treated you."

"How many kings does this city hold?"

"Gods only know. But no matter, really, as the priests hold the ultimate power. They keep the gates and say where the food goes. But, outside the holy grounds, they let things be, no matter how bloody it gets. Sometimes, I wonder why they don't let us starve if they care so little."

"Why not just take control, is what I'd ask." The politics in Bdein were complex when his family ruled, simpler under the rigid reign of the Methrên, and chaos now. But why nurture disorder? "The Bishop has a reason for everything she does. The skeletons covered in copper, some message from the Bishop or Stôltmor?"

The man sucked a breath. "No. When first they barred the gates, and Rot ravaged the city—"he stared at the ground before his feet, speaking in hushed tones"—we delivered wagonloads of dead to be burned outside the gate every day, and later, they stopped opening the

gates so we threw them over the walls to burn, and when that became too much, we dropped them in the river. Sacrilege, but what else could we do?"

"Pulvûer will forgive the trespass; their souls have reached the Hokandite Fields."

"I pray you're right, Ar-Bdêin. Many questioned the Hokandite, blamed the Hokandite, and plain lost faith. The harder we prayed, the more who seemed to die day after day after day. A year and a half back, or thereabouts, a boy dreamed of twelve skeletons covered in copper—a vision from the gods. Folks were so desperate they believed him, so instead of throwing the next twelve who died into the river, they stripped the bones of flesh and covered them in molten copper. Stood them against a wall like in the boy's dream."

"Eleven facing away. Why?"

"Devils, if I know, Ar-Bdêin. Next thing you know, not a blessed soul who came to pray to the skeletons died. You can guess what happened. And you can guess, people made more skeletons."

"Not waiting for The Rot."

"Murder in the streets, pots and pans boiled down to cover bones. Funny thing is, people kept right on dying from Rot. But not in the River District where the original twelve stand."

"No Rot at all?"

"Not a single soul succumbed since. Turns out it wasn't the skeletons alone. River folk prayed to the skeletons and received the blessings of the boy prophet. No prophet, no cure."

Lôdumâ rubbed his forehead and relaxed in his seat. Glanced at Gimin, the man's dark eyes unreadable. He turned back to Lundar with a sigh. "You've seen this boy?"

"I have. A normal enough lad if you ignore the line of people bowing to kiss his bare feet, and I'm one of the humiliated sods. I pray

at the shrine whenever the streets are safe for travel. Most do, and why wouldn't they? A simple gesture of faith and humility to save their lives."

Lôdumâ found the notion difficult to grasp. The teachings of the Hokandite said there had been no true prophets since the Great Forgetting. He wanted to believe such a blessing was possible. It made sense that the gods would help their people during such horrifying times. "What do the holy say about him?"

Lundar's hands rose in a plaintive gesture. "Devils, if I know. The priests melted down several of the dozens and burnt the bones before people started hiding them in buildings, but as far as I know, the holy never made a move on the River District's skeletons."

"And people whisper into their ears?"

"Yes. After the Prophet blesses them."

"And no one dies?"

"Not of Rot, no how, unless they miss his blessings for too long."

Lôdumâ blinked. Popped a knuckle. "Another reason to control the streets, to keep people away."

"People stopped dying as often anyhow, immunity some say, but if anything, anything at all weakens the body, Rot is quick to take hold and kill. I hadn't lost anyone to Rot for a month and a half until Polark started running our streets. Folks are scared to make the journey, and two have died since."

The man's sincerity left Lôdumâ with no doubt he'd gotten lucky to find him, but the story he told was unnerving. Prophets held power, and power attracted all sorts. "Who leads the River District?"

"As far as anyone will say, the prophet himself."

"You believe that?"

"Nah. He's a boy, ten or eleven. I mean, everyone does his bidding, don't you doubt it, but he's still a child."

"My money is on the Bishop, directly or not." Lôdumâ stared wide-eyed at the ceiling for flickers before remaking eye contact. "I think you're a good man, Lundar, despite or maybe because of the knock to my head. One I deserved, even if I don't remember it. I've one last question, and I'll show you how to get out of this city."

The man leaned forward with intense eyes. "Ask."

"Do you have a ladder?"

TWENTY-FOUR

Touch of Shadow

Autumn rise and Spring fall,
to skewer the Whisperer ten feet tall,
the Summer Dancer and the Winter Rider,
stare all day into the eyes of a spider,
looking for answers and looking for lies,
finding old mysteries and finding corpse flies.

—*Tomes of the Touched*

They were seventeen days out from Berul when they arrived at Snow's Eye riding all but a dozen horses available to them, a party of two score Trelelunin, three Edan, and two humans looking to talk to Colok. An odd lot of allies that struck his funny bone whenever he bothered to think about it. Pikarn spent decades hunting Colok in the Estertok Mountains, a challenge on the best days, but he figured it would be easier now, seeing as the Colok were no longer enemies.

Turned out he was wrong.

Snow's Eye stood empty, and not even the keen eyes of the Edan spotted Colok tracks on their way. They didn't even see prints left by Taken. Life felt scarce in general.

Trelelunin collected firewood, and before sundown, a roaring blaze lit the main hall of the remnants of the gate's tower with their horses stomping in the makeshift stables the Estertok Patrol threw together ages ago. Sitting in this place brought back agonizing memories of Modan dying from Shadow-inflicted wounds. Of sitting cozy around the fire with Tokodin, the godsdamned monk who'd later murder Kotin Choerkin, his lord and childhood friend. So many good people lost. "And somehow, my old ass made it here alive," he muttered to no one.

Pikarn glanced at Rikis. The Choerkin stood talking to Nevon Iminler, the commander of the Trelelunin. With memories of Modan writhing on the floor dancing in Pikarn's head, he couldn't bring himself to care what the two spoke about. He needed out of this hall, freezing fresh air to clear his thoughts, but there was no way in the hells Inslok would let him walk out the door.

He stood and moseyed to and put feet on the stairs, surprised no one stopped his climb until he squeezed through a ruined door to find a half dozen Trelelunin and Limereu Lesedreden, the Edan archer, eyeing the surrounding terrain. Pikarn puffed the icy air and made his way to the woman's side. "Mind some company?"

"You are welcome here, Wolverine."

"Any Shadows?"

"I've spotted twenty-three, but no more than three at a time. So, no way to know how many watch our broken tower."

He plied his eyes to rocks, snow, and trees in the moonlight, and though hundreds of shadows caught his eye, not a one could he call a demon. "Any threats? Or better, sign of Colok?"

"No to both."

"Always been Colok in this stretch of the mountains. Even when we couldn't find them, we saw tracks aplenty. They should've seen us."

"You are worried for them?"

"Nah." He shifted his weight; old hatreds died hard. "I worry for them because it makes me worry for us. Our peoples killed each other for a lot of years, but they'd be useful come to a fight in the Chanting Caverns and Istinjoln." Motion in the distance caught his eye, the snowy terrain well-lit by the light of the moon, and when he looked around, several Trelelunin stared in the same direction. A wind kicked up snow, but he didn't feel a breeze even standing here exposed. He pointed for no good reason, a flicker of hope in his soul. "What do yer eyes make of that? Maybe Colok sleds and Tundra Wolves are kicking that up?"

"A whirlwind." She turned to a Trelelunin. "*Holu* Inslok *and* Neseldun."

He only knew a smattering of Edan but recognized *holu* to mean something akin to "summon" or "go get." Flickers later, his eyes widened with understanding, and his hands clenched the hafts of his axes. "You think that's a godsdamned Daevu?"

"A *Mokotu-Xê?* I think it's possible. It could also be wind."

The only time Pikarn had encountered a Daevu was when he was under thirty and in his prime, or he wouldn't have been fast enough to still be alive. "My patrol was caught in a blasted storm some years back. I couldn't even see the thing killin' us. Daevu and snow all looked alike. Ain't too proud to say I showed it my tail, and so did the only others who survived."

"Running can be a sign of wisdom."

His laugh croaked nerves. "Aye, wisdom."

Pikarn about jumped out of his boots when a voice said, *"Mokotu-xê?"*

He glared at Inslok, but the Edan ignored him, so he turned back to a whirlwind that might be a monster that trappers and miners nicknamed doom-snow. "You killed one on the tundra, am I right?"

"We met one, yes, but Solineus killed it."

Pikarn snorted. "Now that godsdamn figures. That bastard is probably stripping his furs and bitchin' about the heat by now."

"He wouldn't have killed it without me."

"Now, that's good to hear. First things first, is that one of the bastards or no?"

It was Neseldun's voice that startled him this second time. "Tough to be certain from this distance."

Pikarn grumbled before saying, "It'd be right peculiar for one to be down this far into the mountains this time of year. Any part of the year, in truth. Most we heard about came around in Velôbrâ and Tôlpol, sure as hells not in the month of Beldrên. Not once." It was true and sounded good, but felt optimistic.

Neseldun stepped to the edge of the wall, leaning his hands to the stone and staring. "Could you get an arrow close enough to get its attention? If it's *Mokotu-xê* at all."

Limereu huffed. "I could drop an arrow into the wind, but even if there's a *Xê*, there's no guarantee it notices."

"You shittin' me? That there's a quarter horizon away or more. And even if you do drop an arrow in there, I'm pretty sure I don't *want* its attention."

Inslok said, "If she can see it, Limereu can reach the target with *Motu Ênsâ*, but you have a point."

"Damned right I do. Those things have been known to kill hundreds of men without leaving a body behind. If a Daevu is here from the tundra, it might explain why the Colok are scarce."

Limereu said, "Some *Xê* are known to claim a range. If it calls this region home, staying away would make sense. My memories are vague with respect to defending against such a creature, but without the proper arrow, I know *Motu Ênsâ* would do me no good. The Elements are best for dealing with an Elemental, one might say."

Neseldun said, "The *Xê* of the Eleris trend peaceable, but I have subdued a few in the past."

Pikarn snorted and spat. "Subdued? I wanna hear killed."

"There is no call to kill them in the Eleris."

"Well, by gods and be damned, wander your ass out there and give it a try. And make sure to circle it so it don't see you coming from this way."

Inslok said, "There is a saying which translates to, if you see the bear from behind, don't shoot it in the ass."

Pikarn laughed. "And I thought you didn't have no sense of humor."

"I thought it was good advice."

Pikarn choked his chuckle until dead. "Right. It is."

"We came unprepared for such a meeting."

Inslôks owl-stare gave Pikarn the feeling he was being blamed. "Don't you go puttin' that on me. It's late Beldrên, not the warmest part of the year on Kaludor, but headin' on towards it. What I want you wise Edan to tell me is, what the hells is a Daevu doin' here outside of the Treaty Lands?"

The three shared glances before Neseldun said, "Like some animals, maybe once humans go away, they move into the territory."

"Oh, ho! That's all fine for a bleedin' wolf, bear, or mountain lion, but those Daevu slaughter us, not the other way 'round."

"Might the priests have had a hand in defending the mountains?"

"Can't say it's impossible, but not that I even heard rumored."

"It's gone," said Inslok.

The Wolverine looked in a hurry as if he doubted the Edan's word. "And may it never come back. But how lucky have we been so far?"

"We are lucky to know it is out there. We'll at least know to be looking for *Mokotu-Xê*."

Pikarn pulled jerky from his pouch and offered the slab to Inslok. Shook the meat at him and then the other Edan when he declined. "It's good and spicy, and chewin' it helps keeps yer face warm. Right, you don't get cold. So don't none of you try to take my meat when I ain't lookin'." He grinned. "Nope, no sense of humor yet. I'll just head back to the fire and let Rikis know about our new friend."

TWENTY-FIVE

Puzzle or Maze

Send me the lovers amongst the losers. Send me the warriors amongst the dead. Send me the impassioned amongst the poisoned. Send me the hateful amongst the blessed. Bring me these and I will raise an army worthy of hell.

—*Book of Nokumdontulus*

Kinesee strolled into the third-floor lounge in the southern wing of the Palace of Endelêun and spotted her quarry. The room was one of six identical halls in the palace that she thought of as commons for gathering, though in truth, she didn't know how they'd been used. A dozen round tables suited to seat four stood aligned in neat rows with stained glass windows providing ample light most of the day. A couple of these rooms had become social hubs for those in the palace, bringing people together morning and evening to chat, but this one sat distant from most of the occupied rooms of the palace, and no doubt, this was why the chase led her here.

Wayfinder Nêmorum sat with the posture of a grizzled old vulture and the personality to match while poring over a broad parchment, which she assumed was his map in progress. She couldn't guess his age except to say that his youth had long ago expired. He was an ageless old anywhere between a weathered fifty and a spry seventy-five, and now that she witnessed his sour stare for a drawing, she questioned whether it was worth the trouble to bother him. She grunted and strode onward; after all, the twins didn't nap as much as they used to.

She stopped at his table and glared. "The Ironwing did send you here to help me, you do realize that?"

He didn't bother to look up. "Yes. He seems quite fond of you." He glanced her way before putting quil back to parchment. "Pretty, but I'm too old to give a wit."

"You're an aggravating man."

"And your children are menaces."

She gasped as she fought the urge to strangle him. After three breaths, she calmed. "You're a crotchety old bastard."

"I call it honesty, though I can't argue the bastard thing."

She grimaced. "Sorry about that."

He shrugged. "I accept honesty."

She pulled out a chair and flopped into its seat. "If you're so fond of honesty, tell me about your work."

He sipped a steaming drink before spinning the map her way. "I find the words offensive, but in your tongue, the palace is a gods-damned puzzle or maze."

Her brow furrowed as she stared at lines so neat and orderly that it became repetitive. The south and west wings sat as identical rectangles, and every room in one appeared to match the other. The rooms inside each were no less orderly, like someone had stamped them into existence. She twisted her brain to decipher what he meant, to spot a puzzle or maze. "I'm not sure you're using the right word in Silone."

"Oh, aren't I? Every room a twin of a dozen others and all in neat rows, the last place you'd expect a puzzle, am I right?"

"Fine, but a maze?"

He shrugged. "I think it is, but I can't prove it. Not yet. Lookee here." He pointed to a room. "Here is where the secret door leads to the Codex Room with the table carved as a map. The size of the room is normal, but the rooms below are shorter to allow for the passage down. Follow?"

"It makes sense."

"The rooms in the opposite wing measure the same right down to a fingernail, but there's no secret passage."

"Yes, we looked."

"This means the builders anticipated what I'm doing. Coy bastards to make sure all the measurements matched in the mirroring wings, even if they didn't drop a shaft into the tunnels below. See all these darker lines? These are the walls thick enough. I'd guess there might be a shaft or something hidden. One hundred and twelve."

"Good gods."

"And it's a pattern, I'd swear on it—a puzzle on top of a maze. There could be a warren to put bunnies to shame beneath this palace, sitting here on granite where no quake could shake its walls and tunnels down. And the one shaft we know of? Smooth as a baby's belly, meaning whoever dug it used Elemental energies. It's too perfect."

"Huh." It was all her tongue could muster to say. Kinesee had learned bits and pieces of lore surrounding the Elements, but she knew nothing of working stone with magic.

"Aye, huh." He banged the map with his finger a dozen taps as he said, "And I can't prove this either! But I'd wager every blessed block of this palace was cut by the Elements, and gods damn me for saying

it, but they carry a blessing of some sort, an enchantment. This place was built in the Age of God Wars, and here it stands: perfect! Flawless. Who has ever heard of such a thing?"

She shrugged. "I guess we all have now."

He flopped back in his seat and laughed. "So we have. So we have."

Rinold's voice echoed from behind her. "Hello, friends! Learnt anythin' new?" He pulled up a chair and looked at the map. "It's gods-damned beautiful even in ink."

"This palace is a master's work of art. The whole city is."

Kinesee said, "You've seen the aqueducts?"

The man blinked. "More works of art. The grade is immaculate. I couldn't have planned them better, and I couldn't have built them. Purifying the water." He shook his head with a smile. "The gods had a hand in this place."

Kinesee appreciated the man's sudden loosening of his lips, even if it wasn't helping much. "Have you started mapping the city?"

He leaned his forehead to two fingers and stared at her. "As your people say, are you shitting me?" He tapped the map again where marks she didn't understand rested. "This here room is twenty by nineteen, right? Except it isn't, oh no, not everywhere. Over here, the wall shrinks by half a foot."

Rinold said, "An error?"

Laughter as Nêmorum slapped the table. "Mistake? Half a foot? No. They guided the wall with an angle so slight you wouldn't notice unless measuring for carpet or some such, and there are hundreds of these all over the palace, and the wings, again, mirror one another. Nah. They were playing games with me. With anyone trying to do what I'm doing. Like they *knew* a Wayfinder might someday try my tricks."

Kinesee grunted and stared. "Let me guess. They form a pattern?"

"Seems to, aye. But I didn't catch on to the trick at first. I'm not done, and if they did this with the palace? The city? I might die before finding every peculiarity in a city so big."

"Endelêun could be a giant puzzle sitting atop a maze."

"It pains me to say so, but yes."

"I would understand if you chose to leave and go home."

Nêmorum smirked. "The builders set a challenge I intend to solve, so if by chance I meet one in a heaven somewhere, they'll owe me a drink."

Rinold chuckled. "I like yer idea of heaven."

Kinesee folded her arms and leaned back in her seat. "No ghosts want to come out and talk, and we can't find our way into the maze."

Nêmorum grinned. "We might find a dozen passages before finding the one that takes us into the maze, but I promise you, it's there. When I have all the pieces to the puzzle, I'll solve it. This, too, I promise."

She stood and bowed to the Wayfinder. "I thank you. Feel free to *not* make me hunt you down next time."

He grinned. "I doubt that, but we'll see."

"Mmm. Then expect to see me soon."

He raised his still-steaming drink but didn't say a word as she turned and strolled away with Rinold joining her. "Well, m'lady Choerkin, we straddle failures thus far."

"Don't I know it?" She puffed hair from her eye, but it fell back for her to swipe away this time. "We've stumbled into a thirteenth hell."

He chuckled as they stepped onto a spiral stair and headed down, her stomach grumbling for lunch. "Two plans struck us down to this new hell. What next?"

She snorted. "We don't have a next. We have what we have."

"There's always pick axes."

"Don't tempt me." She laughed and stomped the final steps to the ground floor. "No. From the looks of his map, it'll be months or years before we find Endelêun's secrets, and then, we don't know what we'll find! Every library might as well be empty. We need to speak with a ghost. We need someone who knows the palace's secrets, and they're our only hope."

"Unless you dream it."

She faced him with a growl even as her stomach grumbled. "Don't tease me again until after I eat."

They walked in silence as they approached the kitchens until he sucked his teeth and said, "I've been giving that a think. After the twins go to sleep tonight, send word, and I'll sit with them. See if someone shows up after dark."

"I've never seen a ghost in the room at night." She smirked. "That sounds funny to say aloud. But you're sure Puxele won't mind?"

He chuckled. "She knows yer too young and pretty for me. And that Kovin would chew my kneecaps off if I touched you."

Kinesee laughed. For some reason, Kovin took an immediate dislike to Rinold. "All right, so long as she doesn't mind. I don't need rumors setting off some feud."

He grimaced with a nod. "Your handmaid should sit with us to squelch any gossip."

"Good thinking." They stepped into the hall outside the kitchens, and the scent of cinnamon rolls and fresh bread filled her nostrils, and if she were a dog, she'd drool.

Twenty-Six

Icy Greetings

The darkness in the dawn and the light in the sundown are two truths that must be understood to grasp the teachings of the philosopher Nerkinditî, but does understanding his meaning make him right? Nerkinditî would say it so.

—*The Oxeum Codex*

They fired smoke into the sky for three days in hopes of the Colok seeing and answering the beckons. All they saw were Shadows of Man slipping from shadow to shadow amid the trees and boulders and a pack of Taken who stared at Snow's Eye for the better part of a day. It was bitter to see no Colok but sweet to see no Daevu, a trade-off the Wolverine wanted to call positive but couldn't quite bring himself to say so.

Come the dawn of the fourth day, they faced a decision: move onward or go back as the number of enemies skulking the perimeter grew every day. The Edan and humans sat around a fire inside the tower, staring at one another after Inslok asked, "What think you of reaching and holding the Chanting Caverns without the Colok?"

Rikis said, “I’d say we need a camp, a base, a defensible position, something, more than ever without them.”

“Aye to that,” said Pikarn, “and there’s nothing to say we won’t be findin’ Colok deeper in the Estertok Range, maybe even beyond Omindi Pass.”

“You’re still optimistic?”

“Oh aye, take it from someone who hunted the Colok most of his life, it’ll take more’n Taken and a stray Daevu to destroy them. They hide like wind in the beans.” He grinned, but the damned Edan still had no sense of humor. “And the Shadows can’t touch ‘em. Hiding? Moved on to safer ground? Aye. But they’re there, and they’ll fight if we find them. Fightin’ and killin’ is in their blood.”

Rikis said, “Our smoke spoke to all the wrong bastards. We got maybe a hundred Shadows out there watching us; could be more just over the hills with a thousand Taken. My question is whether to send for the rest of the Trelelunin or to go back and get them, let things settle, and then move forward again. The third option is going forward.”

Inslok said, “So long as Marukane stays in Istinjoln, Shadows are of little concern. We will surround you. I ranged a horizon in every direction before dawn. There are a few scattered Taken.”

“That alone makes me nervous. Why not more? Are they hidden in some cave? Behind another wall or just buried themselves in the snow?”

“We will keep you safe.”

Pikarn wanted to ask how Inslok traveled so far in so little time, but it was on the tip of his tongue before he said, “I don’t doubt yer intentions none, you Edan. Yet... I’m with the boy, though I don’t know of no caves too close. There’re just too many Shadows for there not to be Taken. I’ve no doubt they could be hiding somewhere near... No.

No, no." He should slap himself for not seeing it earlier. "What keeps the Colok away, harmless Shadows, and puny Taken? No, the Daevu like I was sayin' the other night. The Taken would want no piece of that monster, either. Shadows fear water but not snow and ice. What could a *Mokotu-Xê* do to a Shadow?" He raised his eyebrows and met the looks of the Edan one by one.

Neseldun said, "A *xê* of Elemental Cold wouldn't be able to melt snow into water, nor might it even understand to do so to kill a Shadow. Two beings incapable of harming one another. The theory has merit but no proof."

"Do I godsdamned need proof?"

"No."

"There you go!" He laughed. "Tell me anythin' else that makes more sense."

Rikis said, "So, let me get this straight. If right, we're safe from Taken so long as we're in the territory claimed by a Daevu? Why doesn't that make me feel better?"

A Trelelunin rushed down the stairs and to Inslok's side, speaking so fast Pikarn didn't catch a word, let alone understand the jibber jabber coming as fast as rain on a tin roof.

Inslok nodded to the warrior, then said, "Come. There is smoke rising to the west."

Smoke indeed rose in the west, a solid black pillar drifting north. Pikarn leaned with his hands resting on a broken stone that once would've been part of a higher tower. "Too small to be a forest fire, and nobody right-minded would build a fire to make so much smoke considering all the beasties it'll attract."

Rikis chuckled and said, "Like our fire."

"Aye, someone wanted us to see it. The question's their message."

Inslok said, "No humans who survived this long would make that fire."

"Best we know, Shadows and Taken don't start fires."

Rikis said, "Nor Daevu. Our smoke was for the Colok. This could be theirs."

"The odds are with that, I'd say. But then again, our holy friends back on Berul swore they'd seen Shadows talkin' to one another. Taken following their directions. If true, and we didn't know about it, why not start a fire to draw us out?"

Inslok asked, "Where do you guess that fire is?"

"Oh, a guess that'd be. I'd put it north of Istinjoln and not so far from Omindi Pass, but that's a damned big area, and I could still be off by horizons. Zjin's tribe hales from the region. It'll take two days at least to reach wherever that is."

Rikis cleared his throat as he stared. "If Inslok says we're safe, that's the best we got, and this smoke is *all* we got for finding Colok. We have to go."

The party marched from Snow's Eye a half candle later. Pikarn and Rikis insisted on walking at the lead with Inslok, but every time Shadows of Man got too close, Inslok moved them to the middle of the group with a quick reminder that Pikarn knew the way to the Crack of Burdenis. Turned out that feeling important and feeling smothered were one and the same for a man used to riding in front, and the Wolverine grumbled through chewing his jerky, griping loud enough he hoped to irritate the Edan, but he only managed to annoy himself.

They camped for the night and prayed smoke would still rise on the horizon come morning, and it did, welcoming or luring them onward. By midday, Pikarn figured he had a bead on where the fire sat, somewhere near the base of the Nerbendi Mountain on the eastern side of the Omindi.

Winds drifted the column of smoke into a fading slash of gray against a crisp blue sky, and mild temperatures kept the ride pleasant

while melting snows into shimmering streams for the horses to splash and slosh through. In normal times, Pikarn would celebrate the weather, but every brook of flowing water and every warm breeze coming in from the coast made him wonder why a Daevu would be down from the Tundra.

He always looked forward to the spring and summer months on Kaludor. With greening fields and game aplenty, the Colok and Silone sparred less often, Tundra Wolves and Fever Snakes kept to the highest mountains, and the Daevu weren't even a worry for miners and trappers. It should be the most peaceful time of year, with farmers beginning to break ground in the hills to the south and lumberjacks sending the first logs downriver.

Rikis broke his ruminations. "Shittin' hells."

Pikarn's eyes snapped to, focusing in an instant on a blur of shimmering snow and wind ahead, and he drew his reins tight as Inslok called a halt.

"Hold your horses!" The Edan looked him in the eye. "This time, there's no doubting what we see."

The column of swirling snow and ice swelled, maybe thirty feet high and twenty across. "Does the thing see us? Or does it even have eyes?"

"The *Mokotu-Xê* is a small piece of living Elemental power in the eye of the wind. How and what it senses is a mystery."

"What I'm askin' is whether I kick my horse and start outrunning you now or not."

"I suspect it knows we're here. What you want to know is if it cares we're here, and I can't answer that either, except to say it isn't coming at us."

Rikis licked his lips, and Pikarn wagered the Choerkin's mouth was drying out as fast as his own. "I've heard tell of trappers standin' still to watch them pass."

Pikarn said, "An old timer... watch it, Choerkin, older'n me, said he and his party stood stone still, and a Daevu passed half the group before attacking and killing four of 'em for no reason. All kinds of godsdamned stories, and you don't know which ones are true and which are whiskey-driven horseshit."

Limereu said, "What knowledge I have of other *xê* suggests the possibility of these stories being true. Such a powerful being might destroy those in its way without knowing or caring of the death it deals."

Pikarn grimaced. "You tryin' to say it might kill us without even knowing we're here?"

"Like you stomping on a beetle, or more apt, slapping a wasp to make sure it doesn't sting you. Other scholars' thoughts, not mine."

Rikis said, "Like I would destroy a hornet's nest in my home, while I might pass them in the wild if they don't buzz me?"

"Or ignore one who buzzes by."

Pikarn said, "Well, shits for sure, that's some sorta genius that does us a spit's worth o' good. What the hells good does it do us? We're standin' round yappin' while it's figuring on whether we're a threat worth stampin' out, or maybe such pussies we aren't worth killing, or it don't care at all leaves us be. We turn these horses and circle around, I'd say."

Inslok said, "Retreat could be a sign of weakness."

"If the godsdamned thing was human, aye. It ain't. It... It's a son of a bitchin' headin' our way."

"It seems to have taken an interest in us, indeed. No one attacks unless I give the say. Keep your horses steady. Stay calm. We want to appear a hornet's nest capable of stinging if provoked but unaggressive. Limereu and Neseldun, if it attacks, I expect you to hold it off until I can kill it."

The Daevu's whirlwind almost didn't look like it was moving as it grew closer, shrinking the size of its storm in a trick of perspective, an illusion meant to deceive. Pikarn muttered to no one, "Godsdamn, the beast is a thinker, all right." He reached into his pouch to snag jerky, took a bite, and handed it to Rikis. "Last meal?"

"Let's hope not."

By the time the creature approached within twenty strides, its swirl of snows was little taller than a Colok and no wider than a horse's length. The *Mokotu-Xê* stopped, then swirled left several paces before moving to the right. It hovered in place, and Pikarn imagined it was staring at them as much as he stared at its brilliant display of dancing ice crystals in the sun. Despite being closer to the Daevu than he ever imagined, he saw nothing of the supposed *Xê* at its core. His horse fidgeted, and he patted the gelding's neck. "Easy."

Inslok leaned in his saddle, extending a hand to touch Pikarn's horse's forehead, and the animal soothed, muscles relaxing, and breaths slowing.

"Do that fer me?"

Inslok grinned but didn't speak, a rare expression from the Edan.

Limereu raised her arms above her head, spread them like wings, and then brought her hands back around to her chest. He glanced at Rikis, the man sitting as a statue except for his mouth working the jerky faster than a cow with cud. He swallowed his own peppery meal and licked his lips with a sigh as he turned his attention back to Limereu and her circling arms. *What the hells is that crazy woman doin'?* The only thing he wanted more than to voice the question aloud was to stay alive.

The Daevu hovered a foot closer for every one of Pikarn's tensing breaths, and for the first time since his youth, he felt the chill the creature brought, a cold that seemed to skip the skin to burrow into his meat

and bones, a freeze to make the goose pimples feel fevered. Fingers clutched his reins as memories rekindled in his mind, of screams fading as brothers in arms disintegrated into crystalized powder in the midst of a blizzard, of turning to run with no prayer of surviving the day, of the ache of a seizing cold in his throat and lungs until he could run no more and accepted death, falling and rolling to his back to face the Daevu's doom and discovering the storm gone.

He sat paralyzed on his horse, staring, and then he saw the flash, the hint of something more than snow, ice, and wind. A gleaming nothingness, like the reflection of a mirror dancing on the ceiling, twirling, insubstantial, and beautiful. Mesmerizing. *The Daevu.* The swirls slowed, and a pattern emerged, sparkles of ice collecting in tendrils... no, arms, imitating Limereu's motions.

"Son of a bitch." He wasn't certain if he thought the words or muttered them aloud.

Limereu stood in her stirrups, raising her arms higher, altering her movement patterns, and the shimmers matched her motions like a mirror delayed by a flicker in time. She sat back in her seat and, with a flourish, brought her hands to rest on the horn of her saddle. The Daevu's arms followed and, on coming to a stop, faded back into the swirl.

The burning cold in Pikarn's bones eased as the creature hovered, studying them, he suspected. Flickers turned to a wick, and then, without warning, an arm of flowing ice reached out to touch Limereu's cheek. An instant later, the Daevu withdrew at a speed no horse could ever match, moving east five hundred strides or more in three beats of Pikarn's heart.

A heart that beat even faster now. "We didn't have a prayer of outrunning that thing." *I didn't outrun it back then.* Guilt gnawed at him for years after surviving that day on the tundra, and it gnawed at him again. *Pure chance. Why was I so lucky to survive? Better men than me perished.*

Rikis' voice came raspy and dry. "How the hells did you do that?"

Pikarn shook off old pains best forgotten and straightened in his saddle. "Aye, what was all that arm wavin'? Weren't no mating dance, I hope." He shivered and scrubbed the remnants of the past from his mind.

Limereu reined her horse to face them. "I was speaking with the *Mokotu-Xê*, I think."

"That right? What the hells did you say?"

Her head cocked. "I don't know. I sensed its curiosity but also a growing tension as we sat and did nothing. So, I did something."

Pikarn ripped a fresh hunk of jerky as he watched the Daevu hover in the distance to the east. "I'm supposin' we should take advantage and—" As his head turned to the west. A flurry of whirling snow fifty feet high swelled on the horizon. His eyes flicked east, and the Daevu that had just passed them was still there, growing larger. The roar of blizzard winds echoed down the valley. "Oh, shittin' hells, this can't be good."

Limereu said, "Ever heard of two *Mokotu-Xê* together?"

"Nope." Pikarn's gaze flicked back and forth. The one in the east approached the height of the other, a high-pitched wail warbling from the rush of its winds. They were like two rams squaring off and rising for the charge. "We're in the middle. Ride for the tree line! Ride!"

He heeled his horse and wheeled south, his eyes on the western Daevu, the creature blurring into a streak before a flicker later, a detonation louder than any thunder he'd heard threw him from the saddle. Daevu storms crashed in a brilliant and blinding explosion, a blizzard of shimmering ice as he somersaulted before hitting sloppy snow and crashing shoulder first into the base of a pine. His ears rang, his body throbbed, and his face, where unprotected by beard, felt like a dozen needles had poked his skin.

Pikarn crawled three paces before braving to stand and lumber forward. A riderless horse thundered by, bucking and kicking, and stumbled after the animal, hoping it knew where the hells it was going. He covered his eyes with the crook of his elbow as painful snow brought tears to blind him further. Faint screams to his left. Another horse running to his right.

He tripped over something, his arms buckled and slid, and he fell face-first into the snow, a log or rock cracking his jaw. He spit metallic blood first, then what he reckoned was a molar as he scrambled back to his feet. Thirty or forty aimless and blind strides later, his swinging arm hit a tree, and he clutched tight as the pain in his face faded into frozen numb. "Rikis!"

In the howl of a warring storm, it was a fool's call. He hugged the tree, hiding his face. *Gods know I'm not a praying man, but if you hear me, let us survive this day. Survive it whole. Your people need us to succeed.* He decided that praying to the gods was a step more foolish than calling out for Rikis; if anyone would hear him, it would be an Edan. But what the hells was the point? He gripped his new best friend tight, shut his eyes, and counted to focus his mind.

But memories of death on the tundra rushed into his vision of a Daevu storm in the middle of nature's snowfall. Were they the target then, or like now, were they in the wrong place when two devastating forces collided? Chance. Bad luck. His luck was better than so many who disappeared without a trace or who were left in frozen pieces.

A thunderous crack and a wave of energy swept across him, and he wondered if one had killed the other, but the wind howled, and a dozen more explosions ensued. Flickers and wicks passed with the feeling of heading toward eternity, his fingers numb, clutching bark, when everything went still and into silence. He opened his eyes to the cloud of his breath and a clear blue sky then slumped to his knees

before turning his back to the tree to sit with his ears ringing from the explosions.

Twinkling powdered ice clouded the air, floating to the ground like a god had blown the fresh powder of a snowstorm, reminding him of a flour fight with his mother in the kitchen as a child. Only here, the death was real, even if sanitary. A horse lay dead in the snow without its hindquarters but with the legged boot of its Trelelunin rider by its side, yet there was no blood staining the pristine snow all around.

"Rikis!" A bare hand appeared before his face, and Inslok pulled him to his feet when he took its grip. "Where's Rikis?"

"He's behind us."

Pikarn turned and trotted toward a fur-covered heap on its knees. "You're all right?"

Rikis shook his cloak from covering his face, revealing dazed eyes and a bleeding nose. "I think so."

Trelelunin shouted names around them, identifying themselves as alive as Inslok strolled toward stand beside them. The Edan said, "We've lost at least three with their horses. We can take solace in their ends being swift." Inslok offered Rikis a hand and hefted the big man to his feet with the ease of helping a child.

Rikis squinted at Pikarn. "You've specks of blood on your face."

"Hmm?" He wiped around his eyes, leaving red streaks on his leather gloves. "Musta been ice. Them Daevu don't leave blood. Your nose is leakin'."

"Thought it felt funny."

Pikarn looked to Inslok, spotting Limereu coming their way, never having left her saddle or she'd already caught her horse. "You Edan see what happened?"

Inslok said, "A cock fight of sorts."

"Is one dead then?"

"I don't believe so, but it was difficult to see."

Neseldun came from around a broad cedar tree. "Two energies arrived, two departed." He looked at Inslok. "They are not *Mokotu-Xê.*"

An owl's blink from Inslok. "Meaning what?"

"A *xe* is a single Element. I suspect these are a hybrid of Elements, Cold, Water, Air, and Lightning. The Minister of Knowledge will need to note this and likely name them as the Silone have. Daevu."

"Daevu. Discovering how long the name has been in use will be fascinating. Impressive beings. Bred during the God Wars. We got lucky to lose so few."

Pikarn's eyes flicked between them both. "Bred? You mean like the Shadows of Man?"

Inslok whistled, and horses neighed from the woods around them. "Not like the Shadows, no. *Noko,* demons, and *xê* are not the same. During the God Wars, from what we understand, *xê* could produce hybrids in nature without the guidance of the gods. The Shadows are a product outside of nature." A horse trotted to Inslok's side and offered the Edan its reins.

Pikarn snorted at the horse, annoyed until his chestnut arrived, standing calm mere feet away. "Well, good to see you alive." He stepped to rub the gelding's forehead before looking back to Inslok. "We should tend the dead."

"There are few remains, and the Daevu didn't go far. The friendly one won the confrontation and still stalks the area it's claimed, but we can't rely on its remaining friendly."

"They're your people, so I won't be arguin' with that logic. I'd rather never see a Daevu again, friendly or not."

Rikis plugged a nostril and blew blood into the snow. "I second that notion. Where's my damned horse?"

TWENTY-SEVEN

Red-Domed Profits

A sinner fears a saint the same as a loser fears a winner, and a hater fears a lover. It isn't a matter of positions in opposition so much as positions of failed possibilities.

— *The Book of Leds*

The red-gold domes of Mulshahar gleamed in the light of the rising sun as the *Entîyu Emoñô's* gangplank struck the docks, and Solineus led Sîu ashore with a Luxun escort. Mule ears flapped on his boots with prideful strides, Sîu's elbow hooked with his and every eye on the docks stared at them. Two humans with an armed Luxun escort—just as Captain Intœnyô promised—brought wide eyes, gaping jaws, and clucking tongues. Plus, a few shaking heads.

Without spotting the *Fefemor* or Emudar ships docked in the harbor, Solineus reckoned his best bet on word about Captain Edmordô and their trade scheme rested at the Mulshahar Exchange. The massive building stood as he remembered, with wooden signs painted with four coins, but when they stepped inside, the decor was all the more grand than before, with new paintings hanging on the walls to compliment the hand-carved rosewood detailings of the walls. He didn't wonder long if the bankers would recognize him as four pretty young ladies strode his way with a bottle of wine and a bowl of fruit.

Flickers later, Sêeloru Ledun scuttled from a door down a hall and squealed at seeing him. "Solineus Mikjehemlut! It has been too long." She bustled their way, the hems of her silk dress dragging the plush carpet. The woman smiled on stopping in front of him, giving Sîu a glance. "I see you chose an island beauty over me! Alas, my dreams are squashed."

"Sîu, this is Sêeloru, the woman who handles my smedên here."

"Pleased to meet you, my lovely little dear, but he exaggerates. Monzulor Melehît manages his investments, but unless needed, I am the go-between. Please, please. Have a seat here at this desk."

Solineus settled into a double-wide chair two men carried to the desk so that he and Sîu could sit side-by-side. "Thank you for this welcome."

Sêeloru sat, propping her elbows and staring over knuckled hands. "The most talked about man in Mulshahar arrives again, and with Luxuns in his wake. A far less subtle arrival than your last, and sure to have tongues wagging a second time."

"Well, I arrived on the *Entîyu Emoñô* this time, having struck a partnership with good Captain Intœñô."

"You make amazing friends, I must admit. When I suggested you seek out Edmordô for a map, I didn't suspect for a flicker what you were up to."

"I take it that Edmordô has spoken to you?"

"Oh, he has. He caused quite a stir."

The fact she didn't giggle brought an unease. "My investments are safe?"

"Quite. Half the original deposit is in reserve, while the rest works in several grain and spice markets. Special sorts of markets which rarely fail, meaning a rare few may invest in them. Your arrangement with Helmveline is sound?"

"Back up. What do you mean that a rare few can invest in?"

She squirmed before standing and spoke to the lad holding the bottle of wine. "Murêshu, let *Kor* Monzulor know that Solineus Mikjehemlut and I are coming for a visit. Now."

"My people with me."

"Yes, of course. And guests."

Murêshu dipped her head and sped away, stepping into a hall and disappearing around a corner.

"Follow me, please."

Sêeloru led them in a slow chase of the bottle of wine, a casual saunter. "*Kor* Monzulor will explain the situation far better than I could."

The name rang familiar, but the title did not. "Monzulor is the man handling my gold, the same who learned Silone?"

"Indeed. He has since been promoted, in large part due to your investment and making him your signatory."

"I see." Suspicions prickled the hair on his neck, but he didn't dare raise a question. "Nothing bad, I hope?"

"You came to our bank as a rich man, and now you are richer." She giggled before lowering her voice to say, "The rest is up to interpretation."

He shared a glance with Sîu, and she gave him a crooked, amused smile. If someone had tried to take his swords or stop the Luxuns from joining him, he'd be more worried. Still, he didn't expect the coming conversation to please him.

Mahogany double doors opened into a plush office with animal hides on the walls and a man with a horseshoe of hair on his head

with his nose buried in a ledger. Murêshu gestured to two fur-covered chairs as the Luxuns spread out in the back of the room.

"My most famous depositor. It is good to meet you after so much time." Monzulor spoke in near-perfect Silone and looked up at them at last. Wide blue eyes, so brilliant in color that they felt unnatural, and yet he appeared human.

The doors behind them clacked shut by Sêeloru's hand.

"I've heard my investments are doing well."

"They are indeed. Half of the original sum is secured in its original coinage. Let's see, two hundred and sixty-four thousand *smedên* and some odd *saguts*."

"Three thousand and twelve *saguts*." After finding the purity of the Timôu in the Ironwing's coins higher than expected, the amount of his original deposit doubled Sêeloru's quick estimates before he'd even sailed from Mulshahar.

"Yes. Correct."

"And you were to invest the rest in safe markets."

He grabbed a spectacle from his desk and examined the ledger. "You were at a profit of ten thousand four hundred and eight *smedên* when the tides changed."

"You mean it lost value?"

He lowered his seeing glass and smiled. "No. I mean, your investments became safer while earning more."

Solineus scratched behind his ear and squirmed in the deep plush of his seat. "That's the opposite of how things work, from my understanding."

"Most often, yes!" He laughed, a croaky sound more creepy than lighthearted. "Captain Edmordô lifted your positions with his announcement of your partnership in bringing goods from Helmveline to Mulshahar by sea."

"Did he now?" It was difficult to hide his aggravation despite not knowing the details.

"Don't be angry, good sir. No indeed. Unlike this room here, the desks of the exchange have ears. And don't be angry with Sêeloru, she said nothing. Nor did I. The Patrons of Mulshahar heard of this wonderful news and invited your investment into their rather elite and rather private markets where you've almost doubled your value."

"Doubled? Doubled over two hundred and fifty thousand *smedên* in such short order? I reckon that sounds too good to be true."

"Well! I understand it sounds as such, but I assure you of the validity. As per our agreement, the original sum continues to be invested. At the same time, the profits have been deposited as hard currency, bringing your total at hand to some five hundred and seventy-one thousand *smedên.* I've seen the vault with my own eyes as I signed for its reception."

Solineus squinted at the man, turned his gaze to a wide-eyed Sîu, then back. "What do I owe for such fortuitous profits?"

A croaky laugh ensued, but more nervous this time. "I assure you, all taxes were taken off the top."

"Doubled? After taxes?"

"I understand your suspicion, but there is nothing nefarious involved, just the generosity of the Patrons of Mulshahar to invite you into their auspicious trades."

"Aye. The Patrons of Mulshahar." Smiling Men almost rolled off his tongue, but he didn't want to risk insult in this company.

"All is well. I assure you. This Captain Edmordô, he did not lie? Nor did you fail, did you, to achieve trade with Hemveline?"

And in that moment, he realized that the Smiling Men had their hooks in his ribs. No doubt his *smedêns* doubled, and no doubt the Smiling Men doubled it whether through legitimate investment or not.

He owed them. In a sense, they'd purchased a share in his business without asking. "He didn't, nor did I."

"Well then! The Patrons of Mulshahar will be well pleased. And so will you, I assure you."

Solineus concluded he'd never been assured of so much so often in such a short amount of time on one subject before, and a temptation to punch the man brought a tickle to his knuckles, even though he shouldn't and couldn't blame the man for the bind he found himself in. "I feel mighty assured, I reckon. When can I have a word with these patrons of Mulshahar? I'd like to thank them in person."

"I can assure you, that won't happen."

A smirk spread Solineus' face. "Details of these investments? I'd like to know where my *smedêns* are at play."

"Confidential. I myself only know the basics. Grains—"

"And rare spices. Yes." He leaned and snagged the bottle of wine from Murêshu's startled hand, then smiled at Monzulor. "You don't mind, do you?"

"Of course, it is yours."

"Do you know if Edmordô is in Mulshahar?"

"He is not. Last I heard, he sailed to Pôn to await your return?"

"Ah, well. Yes. We arrived from the north on the *Entîyu Emoñô* after business with the Edan." A fib, but no doubt it would make the man and any ears of the Smiling Men wonder.

"The Edan? Gracious, you do get around. Another trade opportunity?"

"A different sort of business." Solineus stood, and Sîu joined him. "Knowing everything is in good hands, we'll take no more of your time."

Monzulor stood and bowed. "Any time I can be of assistance, reach out to Sêeloru, and we can meet."

Solineus gave a curt nod and strode from the room, Sêeloru falling in by his side opposite Sîu. Her words carried a note of nerves. "As I promised, your treasure is in capable hands."

They strode in silence until reaching the main lobby, giving her time to stew, where he stopped and turned to her. "I do hope they took good care of you?"

The woman relaxed, face mellowing into a soft smile. "I am without want. Thank you for asking." She curtsied and stepped away, but they weren't alone for long as Murêshu bustled to reach them.

The lady handed Sîu an empty glass, then placed the other in his hand, leaving a piece of paper gripped in his fingers. She spoke in Kingdomer. "Glasses for your bottle, courtesy of the Exchange." She, too, curtsied, then backed away with a beautiful but devious smile.

They strode through the exit to stand on the boardwalk, stepping aside to avoid blocking the door. Good fun to watch the eyes of the street glance at their feathered friends while taking advantage of their bottled gift. He poured Sîu's wine first, then his own, glancing at the paper and its words written in crude Silone: *Buy me.*

Sîu said, "I do hope she didn't invite you to her bed."

Solineus sipped his wine with a grin while glancing around for ears too close. "You are a jealous one, aren't you?"

"You have no idea."

"She wants me to buy her."

If Sîu had feathers on her head, Solineus wagered they'd be standing on end as she glared. "A whore? A slave?"

"Mulshahar has plenty of one and none of the other, but I don't think it's what she meant."

"What then?"

"I don't know, but we'll find out."

"Because she's pretty?"

He lifted her wrist with his own until her hand reached her lips, and she sipped the wine with a grin. "We'll need to stay in Mulshahar for a spell and get word to Pôn that we are here and safe."

She deflated as she swallowed wine and his words. "Why? This girl?"

"She's the least of my curiosities. We need to arrange an introductory trade between Mulshahar and Helmveline, and we need to know how deep the Smiling Men have their teeth set in our trade."

"The Patrons of Mulshahar?"

"Yes, one and the same. And we need to know where the grinning Patrons of the other cities stand. Who wants us alive, and who wants us dead."

"Lovely. And this girl?"

"She might be useful, or at least she'll try to convince us she will be. But for now, we should find an inn for our stay."

This time, they tracked down the Golden Swordfish, an ostentatious inn painted alabaster white with gold-plated statues of its namesake jumping in a row all the way along the gutters until reaching the downspouts. He paid seventy-five *smedên* up front for five rooms for a month with a boisterous flare to ensure the Smiling Men knew he wasn't going anywhere soon and maybe prove he appreciated their generosity. He figured that the girl, Murêshu, would know, too, where to find him.

Twenty-Eight

Old Acquaintance

The wolf who leads lambs into war will be eaten.

—Kobutûwonê's War, *Oxeum Codex*

Lôdumâ kept his promise, leading Lundar out of Bdein by way of passing beneath the river, and Lundar gave him a right sturdy ladder. But he chose not to use it right away. Blundering into the palace felt like a risk on top of risks without knowing the city's political landscape. In truth, once he'd come home to witness the withering reality behind the city's walls, the Sword of Bdein wained in its priority.

This was still *his* city. Lundar's city. A city once the envy of a hundred nations.

He owed this place and its people something, even if he couldn't put a finger on what.

So it was that he spent three weeks traversing the Nodurâ District, learning its tunnels and dashing between buildings when the streets were empty of enemies. The way he figured it, a mouse should know every hole in which to hide in case a cat comes calling and best to know which hole held other mice with pointy sticks.

Lôdumâ could remain patient for only so long, but to his surprise, the palace wasn't the destination beckoning him most. The boy prophet drove his curiosity to the summit so he could go nowhere else until he climbed down that mountain.

He and his men stood in a building that was once a bakery on the outskirts of Nodurâ District. On the roof here and across the street, ten of Lundar's archers watched the street with quivers full of fresh arrows purchased on one of Lundar's forays outside of Bdein.

Gimin stood beside a window as he stared into an empty street. "You're sure this is worth risking our lives? We're here for a sword."

Lôdumâ scoffed. "Here I thought getting the Sword of Bdein was my folly."

"Oh, it is. But, we can get into the palace backdoor like while this here is walking in the open. Changing plans gives me the jitters."

"You agreed I think best on my feet."

"Strictly speaking, I lied."

"Name one..." Capturing the Choerkin and Silone witch was too easy. "Two." There was that time at the Reswonu Ford. "Three! Name three times my changes in plans didn't work out."

At least it gave the blackened-eyed man flickers of pause before answering. "The virgin witch, that time you bought the roan mare for a race, and when you kissed the Ruwelê sisters to get even with their mother."

Lôdumâ's mouth gaped in search of a retort but found none. "Your keen memory is frustrating."

"Give me time, and I'll have a dozen more."

"No need. How many times have I bowed to your advice?"

"Not often enough."

Lôdumâ smiled. "Seriously, I'm not sure why I keep you around. We go see this prophet, we get his blessing, and we come back to get my sword."

"And then?"

"Then? I don't know, but somehow, we're going to free this city of the Bishop's grip."

Three knocks on the barred front door, a signal from Lundar's people that the streets were clear in every direction.

Gimin stepped to the door and lifted the oak beam from its perch. "Time to find out how we survive this next foolishness."

Lôdumâ took a deep breath and strode for the door. "With aplomb." He stepped onto Red Fern Street with his head held high and in time to see the knocker disappear into a door down the street. Pigeons cooed and watched them from peaked roofs, and sparrows hopped along the road, but this was all the life in sight. He took strides down the road, his eyes watching the doorways and tangles of vines where a crossbowman could hide with ease, while Gimin focused on the rooftops. Kworgin and Yovun spread their eyes all around, including turning to look back.

They walked west in silence, no distractions, and within ten wicks passed from the district they now called home without sight nor sound of an enemy and only blocks from reaching their destination. Lôdumâ dared to speak. "If our host Lundar is right, these streets belong to the prophet and are safe."

Gimin said, "We had surprise on our side with this trip. Let us hope our luck stays strong on the way back."

They turned north as directed and startled at the sight of people exiting what Lôdumâ recalled being a tavern he might've gotten kicked out of once or twice. If it had booze, he could use a drink about now, but the group of three men and two women only glanced their way before heading down a side street, the same one Lôdumâ meant to take to the river. Voices echoed between the buildings, alerting them to more people before they reached the turn.

Gimin said, "Sounds crowded."

They turned the corner to find the narrow alley filled with milling people chatting and laughing in groups, leaning against the walls as if the Rot hadn't ravaged Bdein. For these folks, if they lived in the prophet's river district, maybe life had returned to something more normal. Lôdumâ passed them by, smiling and nodding at everyone who made eye contact; several returned the gestures, others didn't, but either way, Lôdumâ was joyous none of them wanted to kill him.

The narrow passage passed into a broad courtyard where once merchants set up tables and tents to sell their wares, fish and grain being the most common, but on any given day, he could wander here for a meal and the cure for a hangover. People had arrived, though not as many as in the old days, but there wasn't a merchant in sight. No tables, no tents, no wandering barkers, just a single wooden stage as the focus for the gathering's host.

The boy prophet sat in a high-backed chair suited for a fisherman more so than a king, with crooked wood held together by aging fishhead glue and creaking nails. To the boy's right stood a row of copper-clad skeletons in a neat row.

The prophet was nondescript, ordinary as hell from a distance, with dull brown hair and attire that might've held potatoes in a past life. What wasn't ordinary was the line of hundreds of desperate people, ranging from half-starved orphans to aging nobles, waiting to kneel at his feet and receive the blessings of Pulvûer.

Lôdumâ conceded to himself that his judgment was simplistic and perhaps tainted by a hint of jealousy or flood of cynicism. Even from far away, the boy possessed a demeanor, straight-backed and stolid with an air of importance that might result from being chosen by the gods or arrogance, but whatever its cause, you wouldn't mistake the

child for a nobody despite his impoverished clothes, no matter whether he stood alone or in a throng of thousands.

Here was someone special. Calm eyes never emoting. Hand on the head of those in prayer. Throwing a kiss into the sky to find its way to Pulvûer. Slapping a sinner before raising a foot to be kissed. Tugging the ears of the righteous. Every perfected gesture projected control over himself and others.

Gimin leaned in to whisper, "Should I leave you? Before we reach the boy?"

Lôdumâ pondered the man's words. No doubt a Thônian would find himself uncomfortable in the presence of a Prophet of Pulvûer, and maybe he considered that the prophet wouldn't appreciate his past worship of Fîkêzê, the Virgin Whore. "You don't wish to see the boy close up?"

"I wish to not distract him from speaking with you. My heritage. My eyes."

"And it wouldn't be the first time servants of Pulvûer struck down a man of Thôn who came in peace."

"It wouldn't."

Lôdumâ pursed his lips as the line crept forward several paces before stopping again. "I think you're safe. Peace is kept here by the boy's men. Breaking this even for you would be bad form. Besides, his reaction might tell a story we'd otherwise miss."

"Hell of a story if it ends with my head at your feet."

"Yes, well, so many great Thônian tales end that way, why would you pass up the chance?" He smirked, but Gimin wasn't amused.

The line continued forward, making progress wick by wick, and after a time, people arriving at the docks were turned away by the guards, having arrived too late to receive the blessings. A candle passed,

and then another, and at long last, Lôdumâ could make out the words of the soft-spoken child.

"Pulvûer bless this man and his family. May Pulvûer shower mercy upon his requests and drive his mighty admonishments into his open ears." The prophet leaned to grab both of his ears and gave them a disturbing stretch. Lôdumâ's hand wandered to rub a lobe of his own until the boy punched the prayerful man in the nose. "Spread your blood on the lips of the Righteous Fallen Who Forever Stand and speak your prayers."

The man stood, wiping his bleeding nose and taking strides to the statuesque skeletons, stepping river-side and raising his hand to smear blood on their lips. Finished with the eleven, he came around to the one skeleton facing the crowd and stood on tiptoes to whisper in an ear.

Lôdumâ wondered how many noses this boy broke every day and wondered how he'd keep from thrashing the lad if he were dealt the same.

The next four kneelers prayed with the boy's hand on their heads and received a more typical reply that he'd expect from any priest on any given day before the Rot arrived: "Pulvûer hears and blesses you, adherent to his righteous wrath. Whisper kind words and expect kind replies."

This left Lôdumâ next in line, and he froze, staring at the boy prophet as if he might be some sort of monster come to life from a childhood dream. *Your eyes are familiar. A dream or a nightmare?* He blinked, and the boy was a mere boy again, not some demon or haunt.

He stepped forward and kneeled on a stretch of hardened leather studded with brass to make the knees ache, then bowed his head. "Prophet of Pulvûer," he intoned as instructed, "find my sins and absolve them so that the mighty Pulvûer might heed my prayers."

He expected a hand on his head so he might continue his prayer, but instead, he was left untouched until the boy said, “No.”

Chills swarmed Lôdumâ’s skin, and he struggled to remain still. “Prophet of Pulvûer, I beseech you—”

“You are no servant of Pulvûer.” The boy’s voice rang with gentle tones, but his words cut deep.

“I received the Blessings of Monmour when born and again on my third birthday. I bathed in the Font of Jesup of Demunour on the day of manhood. I have shared prayers with priests and bishops—”

“Lôdumâ Ar-Bdêin forsook his vows and his blessings and his holy favors when he chose himself over his family as well as his city and his people.”

Lôdumâ paused for a dozen beats of his racing heart before raising his eyes to stare into the soft brown orbs of his accuser, so gentle despite his words. “You know me?”

“I know you.”

Was this boy a true prophet or just well-informed? “Don’t be swift to judge a man whose sins lay in a time before you were born.”

“I do not judge you on your past; that is for Pulvûer. But I may judge you in this now. Have you been sinless in these eleven years of my life?”

Murder, kidnapping, and debauchery flashed through his mind. “I have been but a poor sinner my entire life, but this doesn’t mean I’m not a servant of the righteous Pulvûer. Even if the Bishop of Sin Medor would deem my death proper.”

“The Bishop is a mendacious servant of Pulvûer.”

“Then on this, we can agree.”

“But still, a Servant of Pulvûer, even if power has drawn her astray from the truth.”

He bowed his head. “I *am* a servant of Pulvûer; I swear it on the wings of Kîholu. On the dying bosom of Argîn.”

"You, a servant in faith, when you bring this black-eyed monster before me? A Thônian whose bitch queen bled her father, Argîn, into his grave? By what witchery are his eyes darkened?"

The boy knew more than he should, no doubt, so the notion of lying to him was swallowed to burn in his gut. "A Silone witch, Holy Prophet. I captured her, but in her escape, she used the forces of Darkness to kill many and torture others."

The boy swept a hand across his face before tapping the middle of his forehead to shield himself from evil. "The Thônian cur you bring before me would be dead but for the favors of the patricidal Fîkêzê. His evil spellcraft saved him from this witch."

This was an argument he'd heard from his own people and one hard to deny. "I do not know how he survived, but Gimin has forsaken Fîkêzê for the righteousness of Pulvûer."

The boy leaned close, staring into his eyes, his voice solemn and unthreatening. "No man whelped on the blood of virgins may ever truly forsake his unholy mother."

Lôdumâ's gut stirred. Whelped on the blood of virgins was a phrase he'd heard before. When the priests of Fîkêzê sacrificed virgins on the altar, on important occasions, a pregnant woman gave birth in still warm blood, a practice deemed a blessing in Thôn but heretical in Hidreng. Could this boy know such a thing to be true? He sputtered before finding words. "I cannot speak to his birth. But he has been true to me."

"True to a man forsaken, to a man no longer a servant to any god? Can this be?"

"Except I *am* a servant of Pulvûer."

The boy prophet leaned back in his seat. "You don't need my blessing to survive the Rot, this I promise. You and your men are here; not one will the disease touch. Do you still beseech the Blessing of Pulvûer?"

"I do. More than ever after these accusations." He didn't lie, despite having lost religion years ago. Of a sudden, it stood important. Because he had been challenged? Because he needed the solace? Because deep down, he believed?

The boy stared with the same soft eyes as ever. Sullen, as if he pitied the godless man before him. "You came into this world a Servant of Pulvûer and blessed a hundred times over what the poor folk behind you received, and yet you spat in your god's ear. If you wish to regain such status, if you wish to prove yourself a better servant than the Bishop you so hate, and to be blessed again, you must earn his forgiveness."

The prophet threw a rope into the river of Lôdumâ's sinful life, and where in years past he would have laughed as he floated downstream, at this moment, he wanted nothing more than to grab hold and pull himself to the shore of redemption. "How? Name it, gentle prophet, and I will die before failing."

The boy smiled with yellowed teeth, but his breath smelled of roses. "Retrieve that which you came for and slay the darkened-eyed demon with the blade."

Lôdumâ froze, staring at the ground as a drip of sweat wetted the stones beneath his face. "Pulvûer's will be done." He stood and strode away without looking again into the prophet's eyes, turned away from the holy skeletons. Turned toward the palace where the Sword of Bdein rested dangling on the hip of his enemy.

Gimin stepped to his side. "I am the Darkened-eyed demon. Will you strike me down?"

Yes, but he couldn't speak the words, and in thirty silent strides, he wouldn't have meant them. "No. Absolutely not. Betraying you would be..." He almost said betraying family, but he'd betrayed his every blood kin decades past. "Unthinkable. We'll prove the prophet wrong about you."

Silence as they walked until Gimin said, "He did not lie. I don't know how he knows, but I was born in the blood of virgins."

"Son of a bitch, Gimin." His best friend in the world and most loyal ally was the chosen of Fîkêzê. "What the hell does that make me?"

"A good man... good of a sort anyhow, and my friend."

"Well, the good news is we might not make it back alive anyhow. It's a long walk, and they'll know we're coming."

They made their way along the safe routes of the prophet's district at an ambling pace and without fear, but when they approached the border of the Nodurâ District, they stopped to stare. "This is where it gets dangerous."

His words still rang in the air when he saw a man enter the street, and that one turned into a dozen in the matter of heartbeats.

Gimin snorted. "So much for being ambushed."

Lôdumâ wanted to think they were Lundar's men, but he knew better, and any doubt died the moment a voice shouted, "Lôdumâ Ar-Bdêin. I'd heard rumors, but I didn't dare to believe them true. Did you get so drunk you stumbled back into the city?"

"Any man who speaks my name should show his face."

He pulled his hood back with a smile Lôdumâ remembered, even if he couldn't see the gaps in his browning teeth. "That suits you better, does it?"

"As I shit and piss, Mîkêl Polark! I'd heard you were one of the highborn rats living in the sewers of Kîgern District."

"Better a rat in the sewer than a corpse in the river, eh? Your friend Lundar knows it well now that I own his streets."

Lôdumâ strolled up to the district border alone, and Mîkêl sauntered close enough to see the fine scars on his cheek given to him by his wife a decade past. "You're still an ugly son of a bitch."

He chuckled. "Here I thought we might be friends, but an Ar-Bdêin never changes. Even when they lose their family sword."

"What do you want? If it's to murder me, I'm unsure why we waste time."

He rubbed his stubbled chin. "Don't you doubt I didn't consider it, but after all these years, I'd feel the smaller man."

"Always were, always will be." Lôdumâ put his hand to his sword.

A sour expression with a raised brow, but Mîkêl didn't reach for his blade. "An Ar-Bdêin never changes, which means you're still my better with a sword. Soon enough, I might kill you, but not now. Not by my hand. Bad luck to kill the last Ar-Bdêin in Bdein, wouldn't you think?"

"Bad luck to be standing so close if I decide to take your head."

"My head isn't the one you want, now is it? And neither is that sword at your hip. You want, want, want, but can't reach your desires. But I've done you a favor, not passing along the rumor of your being here, so if Stôltmor knows, it wasn't from me."

Lôdumâ took his hand from his hilt and licked his lips. "I appreciate that."

"I figured you would. Look here, Ar-Bdêin. We don't need to be enemies, you and me and Lundar. That Stôltmor prick ran me out of the palace not long after slaughtering the Turlids. Sardôn is a no good son of a bitch, never has been; you and I both know it."

"Best I recall, everyone in his family wasn't better, except maybe Gôbulis' youngest daughter. What was her name?"

"Ênrid and she's dead more than a year now."

"Always the gentlest who pass on."

"Ain't that the truth, which is why you and me are still here. But let's be honest with ourselves: we aren't at the top of the heap. That there prophet you went to see may not control the city the way of a king, but he don't need to. Damned near a quarter of my

people have slithered away to his district, and I'd wager Lundar has suffered the same. Food and supplies? He controls everything the Stôltmors don't. In a wicked and unpleasant way, this here city mirrors Hidreng: A king with a crown and holy with a scepter. Them are the powers that be."

"And you don't like the arrangement."

"Tell me you do?"

Lôdumâ stared at a man sounding more reasoned than he'd ever imagined from their past run-ins. "What do you want, Mîkêl?"

"I want what Lundar has, and he wants what I got."

Lôdumâ frowned. "The tunnels of Nodurâ District?"

The man laughed. "No. I want the way out, and you damned well know it. No horse kicked your drunken ass over the wall. Tell me I'm wrong."

Lôdumâ smiled. "You aren't wrong."

"No way I was. It's simple. Lundar's picking up supplies so his people won't be leaving him, while mine leave me in a trickle until someday I'll be dry or kissing the prophet's toes along with everyone else. I will leave Lundar's streets, and then you let me know how I can reach the outside."

"There's over yonder, or you die and float down the river."

His head rocked with a snort. "Funny, Ar-Bdêin. Funny enough, I'm tempted to kill you now, for old-time's sake, but I won't. This city right now is a two-king town, and at some point, stories with two kings never end well."

"The one is but a boy."

"The most powerful boy ever who never wore a crown. Stôltmor don't like it; I guarantee that, but he's in a pinch."

"And what would you do if I told you? Collect supplies to become a third king?"

"Hell, man, maybe. But maybe I just get out of here. I never wanted to be no mighty lord or king. I just wanted a belly full of food and ale and a bed full of women. Gotta be villages and cities better than this."

Lôdumâ nodded, thinking of the plush manor and gardens he'd left behind. "There are places better and worse."

"Aren't there always? I don't expect you to say yes. Just say you'll take the offer to Lundar. I'll clear the streets here and now. Say no, and there's no tellin' if you make it back alive." He shrugged. "These streets can get ugly fast."

"Not too many choices in life are so easy. I'll take your words to Lundar to see if he trusts them, but if a man of yours so much as glares at us on the way back, the deal is off, and I'll kill you the next time we meet."

"Fair's fair." Mîkêl raised his hand and gestured, and for a flicker, Lôdumâ thought archers might rise from hiding, but instead, his men turned and walked away. "I'm a man of my word. The streets are his once again, no strings attached. Take my gesture for what it is: a kindness."

Lôdumâ squinted. "No strings, you say?"

"Well, one string. I'll know if you don't make the offer, and we'll be back. But if Lundar turns me down?" He slapped his hands together as if clapping away dust. "The streets are still his."

"You want out of Bdein so bad?"

"There's a storm coming, and if I'm not in a position to weather it, I'd rather not be here. Whether for a week or forever, I *need* out of this city." He winked and pulled his hood back over his face before turning and walking away. "Until we meet again, Ar-Bdêin."

Lôdumâ watched the man depart, heard the footsteps of his men coming close, and he turned with a smirk. "I guess we don't die quite yet."

Gimin said, "What the hell happened?"

"An offer of peace."

"And you trust him?"

Lôdumâ spun to gaze into an empty street. "No, I don't think I do, but I've been wrong before." He led them down the street with winds drifting dried leaves into piles. Not a soul watched them that he could see, and he felt safer now than when standing beside the boy prophet. "On the other hand, my gut seems to be saying to trust him. At least for now."

Twenty-Nine

Sixth Surprise

Send the babies where the devils fear to cry,
send the mothers where the demon's blood runs dry,
send the fathers where the saint's mortality goes to hide,
send the forefathers where the god became a bride,
and at last, send me, oh father of ice and snow, to the home of the pride.

—*Tomes of the Touched*

"Soludaru Emestrâ is pregnant. That's the fifth woman this month. The seventh overall."

Glimdrem stared at Ilsferu while refusing to say "impossible" but still noted he thought it. He drummed his fingers on his desk in the main cabin of the *Flaming Wing*, surprised not just by her words but her excitement. Did she want children? "Five. You are certain?"

"Our empaths know a pregnant woman when they touch one."

A stupid question, and he berated himself. "Of course they do. Sorry. It just, well, catches me off guard." Maybe it all made sense, with so much time spent at sea. But no, it didn't. While the Edan bore no children at all, Treleunin didn't breed like humans, like two-legged rats. Five pregnancies in five years for this number of people would

have been more expected. "It's wonderful news! But I don't want to get our hopes up for the future. It could be luck. Chance."

"I'm pregnant."

Glimdrem's mouth had dried into a winter's leaf so that his tongue peeled from the roof before speaking. "You're certain?"

Her smile beamed. "There you go again."

"Six. Eight." He blushed, feeling like an idiot for counting. He rushed to her for a kiss, lifted and spun her before settling her back on her feet. "I am going to be a father?" He'd had numerous relationships the past five hundred years, but he hadn't allowed himself the dream. "A father."

"I suspected but did not... I cannot believe it."

He put a hand on her belly and put his lips to her forehead. "I don't want to leave your side for a week. A month. Until the baby comes."

"It's me that will be tortured, watching you leave, but you must. I'll be fine."

"You can sail to wait beyond the blockade."

She shook her head with a laugh. "You think I will risk our child to a Boborun ship?"

"No, of course not."

Her lips came to his for a deep kiss, and they parted in a mutual sigh. "Go. Find out what the Contessa has found."

"Must I?"

"Yes." A quick kiss, and she shoved him away.

He stepped from the cabin but didn't take his eyes off her until the door closed. Three steps backward, and he still stared at the door. His arms raised as if of their own volition. "I am going to be a father!" Every Trelelunin within earshot cheered, and as he strolled to the gangplank, he met hugs and handshakes.

At the last, he met Captain Lendinim and his serious gaze. "Congratulations."

Glimdrem wrapped him in a brief hug. "It's a glorious day."

The Captain stepped back. "How many guards would you like?"

"Is Simêum dangerous?"

"It is said this Contessa killed half a hundred men the last time she was here and that before blowing five ships to Goro hell."

"I guess the city is safe since she's our friend." The same cold stare he was used to. "Four should suffice."

The Captain nodded and gestured to four Trelelunin Glimdrem knew well, including Neoburo, who was with him on Kaludor. He smiled at the warrior. "I am going to be a father."

The man chuckled as he straightened his jacket. "So I heard. Your heir will be the talk of our fleet."

They crossed to the docks and headed for gray streets in a city of massive orange walls. Simêites stared as they passed, with their height, pale skin, and angular jaws setting the Trelelunin apart enough that it wasn't only children who stared. They passed into the street moments later and turned north, heading for dock forty-two, where the *Silver Willow* and the Contessa's other ships sat docked. An overturned crate lay in the road with sailors scurrying to and fro and a crowd of people swarming to make their way past. They stopped to stare at the chaos, a delay that any other day he would have cursed, but on this day, his smile refused to die.

As soon as a gap opened, Neoburo used his height, armor, and sword to intimidate Simêites from their path, and they made their way past fishmongers and sailors until reaching Dock Forty-two, where the Silver Willow stood out like the sun in the night sky. Its beauty never failed to impress him, and this time, he would promise to ask who had built the vessel.

They stepped aboard with a hearty welcome from the Mostulê sailors, and within flickers, the Contessa herself stepped into view, her arms wide. "Welcome aboard, my friends."

Glimdrem walked to her with hasty strides that widened her eyes and wrapped her in a hug that brought weapons a finger from their sheaths. "I'm going to be a father."

She laughed then and patted his back. "Congratulations."

He stepped back to see Âvorê and other Mostulê tapping swords back into their sheaths. "Thank you. Ah! It's a glorious day."

"It will be more glorious when you smooth my return to this city. I think you can help."

His head cocked. "I heard you killed a lot of people the last time you were here. And blew up a dozen ships."

"Three ships and fewer than a dozen thugs who belonged to a smuggler who dreamed of pirating."

"It seems deserved, then."

"Yes, but having you by my side will help clear up the situation." She walked for the plank back to the docks. "The sooner it's cleared up, the better."

He followed. "By all means. I assume all went well with your plans?"

Silence until they reached the docks. "No. It did not. Not true. What I went to do got done, but I was accused of reneging on my word."

"By whom?"

"By a man I hope is still my friend. You remember me mention donu-honêsh?"

He didn't just remember it. They'd heard rumors of the herb in every port they stopped. Deadly, addictive, and running short in supply. People were killing each other for pinches of the stuff. "Of course."

"Well, the last of the donu-honêsh... He was going to destroy it after I told him where to find it. Trouble is, someone took it before he got there."

They turned north on reaching the main road. "That someone is rich or dead."

"Yes, and I can only hope the latter."

"And this friend thinks you betrayed him?"

"Or maybe he betrayed me, but I don't think so. This means there's enough donu out there to kill thousands."

"Or start a war."

"Yes." They turned down a narrow street that ended at a massive, square building that rose five stories high. She strode straight for the guarded door without making eye contact, and the guards swung the double doors open. "Lultûhol is more important than ever."

Glimdrem nodded. "I sympathize with your situation." Even if he didn't give a fig for human lives.

A wick later, they stood inside a constable station with a dozen armed men staring at them. A desk sat in front of them, and to either side along the walls rested a wooden bench not unlike pews he'd seen in churches. Not a single guard spoke a word. He leaned to her ear. "Who are we waiting on?"

"If we are lucky, Lord Emerus Shinî. His family is well-situated to be the next Yostul of Simêum. Otherwise, one of a hundred constables, I guess."

"They do not speak Edan?"

"Unlikely. I've never met Lord Emerus, but he sent word when I arrived that I should come here. It's been some time since I've had fresh word of the politics in Lultûhol and Simêum. Gods know ill winds might've blown in since last I was here."

A door in the back of the room opened, and a man in a frilled leather vest walked in with his nose held high in an attempt not to have to look up at his guests. His mustache danced as he spoke. "I am Constable Termaror Dûplânt, and if I had my way, you would be seized and thrown in chains."

The Contessa shot the man a curt nod and haughty glare. "Dûplânt. Yes, I imagine a man born so low would adore imprisoning me, but my father would frown on such a thing."

Glimdrem grinned at her fire, a different side of her personality than he'd seen before.

"Your father holds no sway for his halfbreed kin in Simêum." The man's heated gaze turned on Glimdrem. "And what is this... man?"

"I'd be cautious. This Trelelunin speaks Tôlk."

Glimdrem flashed a grin. "I do indeed."

The Constable snorted and slapped his desk. "What do I care about insulting a woodfiend? But it's you, you murderous creature, that I want."

She strode to his desk, and his guards loosened weapons in their sheaths. People feared the Contessa, and he wondered how many stories were true. "Last time I was in this city, in your district, I'm guessing by the smoke from your nostrils, I was accosted by pirates and almost killed. I should be the one demanding your head."

His eyes flashed wide. "You pompous witch—"

"Shall I demand the right of combat with you, Constable?"

His lips flapped, "There is no such right in Simêum."

She clucked. "A pity. I was hoping to speak to Lord Emerus Shinî to clear up this matter."

Glimdrem stepped forward, figuring she must have brought him for a reason. "I can end this now. I represent the interests of the Eleris Edan, and this woman guides me to Lultûhol."

The man snickered. "Lultûhol is under blockade."

Glimdrem did his best to make the man feel like an idiot with his stare. "The Boboru will not stop me."

"And you'll just force your way by?"

He did his best to mimic one of Inslok's owl blinks. "Stopping me would be a mistake. Just as depriving me of this woman's help would be a mistake."

The Contessa held up a hand, and he stepped until his chest came close. "There's no need for threats, is there Constable?"

The man stared from behind his desk with a sneer. "There's need for only one, mine to you. I've been told not to interfere with you, but if you so much as bloody a nose!" She punched him, and blood sprayed his desk. "Whore!"

"You'll do what? I'm here for reparations or at least an apology from you and your city."

Glimdrem stood straight as weapons loosened in sheaths for a second time and, for the first time in ages, wished he carried a sword.

The man leaped to his feet, still clutching his dripping nose. "Reparations! Are you insane? Seize this woman!" Not a man moved, let alone rushed her.

Glimdrem glanced at Neoburo. "The results of a fight?"

"A slaughter."

Glimdrem turned to the constable. "You should accept my commander's judgment. He's fought demons that would make a meal of your soul. Now, we need to speak with someone with authority. That isn't you."

A man's voice boomed from behind, "Simêites! Sheath those weapons."

Tangs clacked sheaths, and the Contessa spun to the newcomer. "Lord Emerus Shinî?"

"I apologize for my being tardy. Constable, you and your men will leave. Now."

The guards disappeared in an instant, but the Constable glared and slow-walked his way out.

The Contessa strolled around the desk and sat in his seat. "At last, someone worthy of speaking to. My father has nothing but goodwill for your family."

"The feeling is mutual. Did you need to bloody my constable?"

She shrugged. "The urge struck. He should consider himself lucky."

Emerus turned to Glimdrem. "I was a boy the last time I saw a denizen of the Eleris in Lultûhol. Trelelunin, yes?"

Glimdrem smiled. "I am."

Emerus whipped a handkerchief from his pocket and spread it on the desk to soak up the blood. "Your reputation has earned you friends and enemies far and wide. I need to ask what brings you to Simêum."

"I'm on my way to Lultûhol."

"Why?"

"How close is Lultûhol to dragging all of the Free Cities of Nomnuvar into war? I've been away for a time. Speak true."

He cleared his throat. "Too damned close."

"So tell me, Lord Shinî, do the Boboru want war? No. Does Lultûhol? No. Do you?"

"I do not, nor does the Yostul."

"Mostul Ûbar doesn't want war. I guarantee that Aprelêu doesn't either. They've got troubles finding a new leader."

"A trouble caused by you."

"A trouble caused by his desire to profit off donu-honêsh after murdering my mother. But that's irrelevant now. Tell me, who wants this war?"

He stood silent and, after flickers, shook his head. "All wars don't start because someone wants it. Stubborn souls and grievances, just like we have in Lultûhol, are enough. Hot tempers sparked at the wrong moment."

"Someone *wants* this war, and they're doing their damnedest to start it. I'm here to slow the war and sailing to Lultûhol to learn how to stop it."

He pulled up a chair and sat. "You have my attention."

"My father, by now, the *Kontzul* Juvileus, desires peace. We need you to be a cool head in Simeum. We need you to do what you can to calm the furies of lords of the other cities of Nomnuvar who are here. I can't have a war starting while I'm in Lultûhol."

He chuckled. "That would be awkward."

"Mostul Ûbar is secure, but Simêum? Your city is the northern neighbor."

"There is plenty of anger within these walls. We are more cut off from the rest of the Free Cities than anyone other than Lultûhol. Only fools speak of war, but to stab the Boboru in the eye?" He shrugged.

Glimdrem stepped up and said, "I will get her into Lultûhol and back out again."

"I will do my best to keep the peace, but when people get hungry enough, they will want the war. It's Lultûhol, maybe, that you should worry about."

The Contessa said, "The north worries me most. If donu-honêsh makes it this far south, be wary. Crush its trade before it starts."

He nodded with a skeptical squint. "It's never moved so far south. Our people are too strong to surrender to its temptation."

"I pray you are right."

"I am. How long are you in Simêum?"

"Water and provisions," she glanced at Glimdrem, "but I think our friend from the Eleris would like to celebrate with his beloved for a few days."

Glimdrem squinted at her with a grin. The woman speaking now seemed a world apart from the one who split a man's nose with a lightning fist. "I would." He turned to Lord Emerus. "I'm going to be a father."

He didn't miss a beat. "She's staying in Simêum, I hope?"

"She is. Yes."

The Contessa said, "Make sure she has anything and everything she wants. No spared expense."

"For the future *Kontzulê* Juvileus? Anything."

She laughed. "My father is still young."

"And well on his way to Yostul of Mostul Ûbar."

"You're getting ahead of yourself. And I'm half Goro."

"If you bring peace to Lultûhol, will a soul care who would say so?"

She grimaced, then laughed. "I will. My home is the sea."

Glimdrem pondered this relationship anew. Pondered what it might mean if this woman really was Xanesu. Or part of her. *A third-breed,* he thought to himself, who might someday be a step away from ruling one of the wealthiest cities in the world. "One step at a time. Let's break the blockade and bring peace."

THIRTY

Bought Not Paid

A tearing line in fabricated time,
the dented tin that is my skull, ha ha!
The Whiskey Worms burrow the keg,
leaking holes before reaching my leg,
blurring my pain into Craven Raven's
green-blacked reality. You think?
I don't know but hurry to decide!
Is patience still a virtue when given no choice?

—*Tomes of the Touched*

Captain Intœñô sat across the table from Solineus with a full glass of wine in his hand, an expensive vintage the Luxun had become accustomed to over the last month. "Gathering a cargo for Helmveline is proving more bothersome than I figured." The words were different today, but the sentiment was the same for the past week. Solineus reckoned it would be easier to choose a gift for the Ironwing, a king with without want, than to find what trade goods would excite them. If they couldn't impress, it might boil down to bulging their coffers.

"I don't even care what... We can't leave here with nothing. The Smiling Men are watching."

Sîu sauntered into the room, already tipsy with a glass of wine in hand and wearing an outfit that made her happy. Which meant almost nothing: topless with a short silk skirt. "Kegs of this wine should make anyone happy."

She strolled to Solineus' side and sat across his lap with her wineless hand around his shoulders. Pleasant and awkward as the hells at the same time, as the Captain tried to keep his eyes locked with Solineus'.

Intœñô cleared his throat. "There is trade with the Kingdomers, yes, but few seem to know what goods reach so far as Helmveline. Whether we bring something they always buy or something they want but never heard of, either one works, but if we show up with something they produce already or don't care two poops about, we'll whistle into our empty pouches."

Solineus grinned at the attempted Silone expression. "Two shits. But I understand. Exports from Helmveline will be snapped up. That's the good news."

Sîu whispered in his ear, "This wine is too good. Get rid of him and take me to bed."

He did his best to ignore her, but no doubt the Captain wondered what she said as Solineus fought a smirk. "As Sîu said, this wine might be a good option."

Intœñô's feathers fluffed as he swirled his glass and sipped. "It is at that, but kegs? Maybe a dozen cases, and that's fragile cargo for our first run. And best in a chilled space. We need bigger and simpler and safer."

"Their wealth is in ores and raw latcu, but they're already getting wood from the Helelindin. What spices move into the Kingdoms?"

"Plenty, and that's the trouble. Pepper, cardamom, cinnamon, anise, nutmeg, cloves, and dozens more. Long term, we can supplant their current suppliers, but we don't know what they're aching for."

"Sugar?"

The Captain gave an acquiescent shrug. "Sugar always carries value. We could take a sample, but I'd prefer more value for our limited cargo space."

Sîu said, "Nêerêp?"

Solineus said, "What's that?"

She took a drink and smooched his cheek. "A spice. A fermented liquid spice. Very spicy. Like me."

"If it's like you, there's not enough to sell."

"I'm worth more." She licked his ear. "Pôn and some of the other islands make it from the pistil of a flower. I'm not saying which."

Intœñô squinted her way. "I've never heard of it."

"We don't trade it, but you've eaten it every time you come to Pôn." She eyed Solineus. "You've had it too."

The Captain's eyes widened. "Is it the burn in your mother's red sauce?"

"Utukwu sauce, yes, some but not all of the burn. It's also part of the sweet, along with honey. The difference is raw and cooked, one sweeter, the one spicier."

Solineus recalled a sauce drizzled over pork with a sweet burn. "How much could we get?"

"None. I told you, we don't trade it."

Intœñô groaned, "Who brought the drunk to this meeting of the minds?"

"Be nice, now, good captain. Or I'll never feed it to you again."

Knuckles rapped the door, and a Luxun spoke. "A lady from the Exchange is here."

Solineus glanced at Sîu in his lap. "I don't suppose you'll put on clothes or at least stand up?" She shook her head with a grin. "Let her in."

His first guess would've been Sêeloru, but instead, Murêshu strode through the door with her slender shoulders draped in a silk sarong. Sîu tensed on his lap, her arm tightening around the back of his neck, and he knew the day just got more interesting. After this many days, he'd given up on the girl seeking them out.

"I'm sorry to interrupt your... meeting." Eyes that lit first on Solineus fell a nudge to no doubt land on Sîu's bare chest.

Intœñô came to Solineus' rescue. "And you are?"

She met the Luxun's gaze and curtsied. "Murêshu Nâ Merdelôn."

"You're from the Gorotan?"

"My blood is of the Gorotan, yes. My father moved his family to Mulshahar for the Notoholis Aprelêu, my mother was a servant, and I was born here."

"You know the city well, then."

But Solineus said, "Have you seen the Smiling Men?"

She grinned. "The Patrons of Mulshahar? Only a glimpse of a face a few times at the Exchange. Scales. Reptilian. A soft-spoken people who don't appreciate repeating themselves, so people listen intently."

He decided not to waste their time with small talk. "What did you mean, buy me?"

Sîu said, "Yes. What did you mean?"

"I... nothing unusual, I promise. My father put me under contract with the Exchange when I was seven."

"You're a slave?"

The woman blushed and frowned. "No. I was apprenticed as an interpreter but showed a gift for numbers as well as legal matters. On turning fourteen, I signed to continue my studies. I speak ten languages, including Goro and Kingdomer, with a variety of dialects, and though I know little of criminal law, I know more trade law than many barristers."

Solineus said, "It still doesn't explain your words: Buy me."

She stared as if he was an idiot. "My agreement extends another five years, but you can buy my contract. It is standard practice in the trade houses of Mulshahar. I'd expect an increase in pay, but I could assist in a multitude of issues you are destined to face."

"And it took you a month to come to us?"

The *you are an idiot* stare returned and hardened. "Contracts don't allow for soliciting buyouts."

"And yet here you are. Languages and numbers?"

"And trade law." She straightened her back with a prideful stance. "A dozen trade houses have offered me buyouts, but you offer a unique opportunity, and it's almost painful to see how much you need my help."

"Your boasts are impressive, and so is your nerve, suggesting we need help from a girl who totes wine around a lobby."

She shifted her weight but kept her veneer of calm. "I turned down those offers as my legal training isn't finished. When it's over, my pay will go up. Taking a new contract would've undervalued my services. I serve wine because... because they trot out pretty faces for esteemed guests. And with foreigners, I'm likely to understand things they don't intend to be understood."

"For a moment, I'll pretend all your boasts may be true. What, then, would you help us with?" Solineus grinned. "Enlighten me."

"For one, you will need to establish a trade house, physical and legal. Where would you buy a building for your operations?"

"Somewhere near the docks."

"Wrong. Where doesn't matter so much as from *whom* you buy it. Your two captains? Edmordô can negotiate the Monsoon Straits and knows every cove along a hundred islands to hide from pirates. The esteemed Captain Intœñyô can track down almost any good the

Helmveliners will covet from the Crown Islands to the Eleris, plus he carries Luxun clout, but neither man knows the ways of this city like I do. Both law and etiquette."

Intœñyô gave her a smiling appraisal. "She has a point. And she shows gumption."

"She does." Solineus adjusted Sîu's seat and smiled at his paramour. "What do you think?"

She puffed and cocked her head to stare at the girl. "I want to know what you want to know. How much of our business will she report to the Smiling Men?"

"Excuse me?"

Sîu sighed. "Don't be coy. How long have the Smiling Men held a side contract on your services?"

Solineus met Murêshu's fidgety stare. "The Patrons are curious about our business, and why the hells wouldn't they be? If it isn't the Patrons of Mulshahar, it would be the Patrons of Ôfelun or Înlark. How many cities are on the peninsula?"

"Six."

"Right. One of six. Which is it?"

She released her breath. "Mulshahar. My apologies for wasting your time." She turned for the door.

"Did we dismiss you?" Murêshu spun on a toe with a sheepish look on her face. "If everything you claim is true, the Exchange apprenticed you at the age of seven. They took you back on at fourteen, and at some point, the Smiling Men reckoned you an asset. Do you know what that tells me?"

Her face scrunched. "I can be bought?"

"No. It tells me you're one of the sharpest swords in the smithy, and that's the sort of person I'd hire."

"You would?"

"My hiring you might send two messages. One, it might say I'm stupid, too naive, or smitten to realize a pretty face works for the Smiling Men. Well enough. Being underestimated is one of the best ways to enter into a fight. Two, you tell them I know you report to them, meaning I have no secrets to keep. I'm an open book who doesn't mind hiring the first seed they try to plant in my business."

"Shrewd. Which do you prefer?"

Sîu said, "Stupid."

Solineus chuckled and jabbed her rib with a playful poke. "Aye, she's right. I don't get underestimated often enough."

"Oh, sweets, you're always underestimated." She kissed his cheek.

"My question is, can you be deaf and mute when you need to be?"

She smiled. "Absolutely."

"Well, what do you think, Sîu?"

"I think she can keep a secret, and she's smart enough to know I'll kill her if she touches you."

Solineus shrugged. "You're that smart, aren't you?" The girl nodded. "So be it then. Welcome aboard."

Murêshu licked her lips in the ensuing silence. Shifted her feet. "I'm hired then? For what position?"

"Well, we'll need to buy your contract. Make it official. Your first job will be to tell the Smiling Men that we're in the market for property to establish a trade house. I assume we'll stumble upon the ideal location soon after that."

"You will."

"When we arrive at the Exchange for a writ to buy the property, I'll be looking for someone with the wits and legal knowledge necessary to establish the trade house."

She smiled with a twinkle in her eye. "Me."

"Of course, we'll need to confirm what you've said on all accounts. Your talents included."

"Naturally." Nothing dented her confidence; she told the truth or could cover her lies. Solineus liked her; there was a devious behind her demure innocence and beauty that would make her a formidable tool. "Serve us well, and I'll make you *very* rich at a *very* tender age. More than rich, influential. Powerful. Prove you can handle it, and you will oversee our Mulshahar business dealings."

She blanched. "You could get me killed."

Sîu said, "That's the game we play. Are you in, or are you out?"

"Once you advanced me to such a title, they wouldn't believe I report to them anymore. But I'm in."

Solineus smiled. "Good. Now, straighten that smile and go back to work."

She nodded as her face eased into the workaday solemnity of a banker. "I look forward to our future." Her sarong spun with her turn and flickers later the door closed behind her.

Solineus' eyes turned to Sîu as she sprawled and finished her glass of wine. "Do you truly trust her?"

"Her aura is surprisingly clean of lies. Trust her without reservations? No. But I trust her enough to use her."

A long, chirpy whistle from Captain Intœñô as he eyeballed them. "A risky play, but you two make one hells of a team."

"We do, don't we?"

"Half drunk and half naked in his lap, take every meeting like that, and you'll throw more than a few negotiators off balance."

Sîu purred and curled into him. "I like it."

Solineus chuckled. "Oh hells no. That was embarrassing."

"I humiliate you?"

A smirk with a roll of his eyes. "Shush."

Intœñô nodded with a devious smile, and his feathers flared. "If we figure out what to bring the Helmveliners, and we don't die first, we'll swim in gold."

"Sounds painful." Solineus didn't trust the girl for a blink, and his gut gurgled with so much attention from the Smiling Men so early in the game, but it was hard to deny the temptation to believe in a dream. Wealth wasn't his goal, yet the notion of covering Sîu in gems teased him. "If we don't die. If our fortune doesn't sink to the bottom of the sea. If the Smiling Men don't steal our trade. If, if, if, and more ifs. And on top of it all, wars are expensive."

The captain said, "Not my war if there is one.."

The real question wasn't whether there would be war, but war in how many directions. "You'll be swimming in gold; I reckon I'll be trying to keep my head above the blood."

Thirty-One

Dangerous Bargains

The rains are the same, yes, in a devastating way;
oh, the fool who prayed for a drought, the lout,
oh, the fool who prayed for a flood, the dud,
and oh, the fool who didn't bother to pray,
washed away!
Ha ha!
What lesson here for the common man?

—*Tomes of the Touched*

The forests northwest of Endelêun held two major advantages to those due north: the clouds ran low on rain by the time they reached them, and the critters trying to eat them were more pedestrian than the hideous giants of Roemhien Forest. Oh, and a third advantage: she already had a name to put to these woods, the Lelibotun Forest between the Elumîsênê River and Tebûul Rivers. To reach these woods, they'd already passed through the Temuwolo Forest, which rested between the Lodhonu and Tebûul Rivers, and the Isiludlêmun Forest, which stood between the Lodhonu and Mûulbon Rivers. Even if she didn't really know where she was, being able to put a name to things eased her mind. On the downside, if they met any Histê in numbers, the odds of a fight were high.

They were a month and a half into their journey, and their northwest trajectory was bringing them into thinning woods and a sharp rise into the mountains to the north when their yellow-eyed guides first warned of Histê ahead. They hunkered down for half a day until they decided to camp for the night, and when morning came without the Histê moving, they turned due north for a stretch.

She figured the Dragonspans rising ahead of them belonged to the Kingdom of Œrinklîn, but not even Kurin knew which of The Eight Kingdoms claimed the mountains. The cagey woman insisted they could belong to either the Kingdom of Danlok or Œrinklîn as the borders amongst the peaks tended to wind in both directions. Even if both kingdoms agreed on the border, mines beneath could confuse the situation further. Until the moment she heard this, Meliu had never considered the possibility of a country's border being three-dimensional.

On the one hand, it was fascinating for her; on the other, she figured it frustrating for both sides involved and map lovers like herself. Candles later, she figured out that if she had a third hand, it would be worried whether she'd missed details in the histories of the *Codex of Sol's* disputed territories because of her misplaced thinking.

Five days later, after circumventing the Histê and curving their path northwest again, Kurin announced that she knew right where they were and declared the Elumîsênê River flowed in a valley just over the next ridge of mountains. She didn't prove it, however, as she turned them north to avoid a region where she said the Histê held a dozen fortresses that may or may not have once been part of the Kingdom of Danlok.

This time, they continued north until they reached the base of the Dragonspans and headed west into territory indisputably Danlok, which she proved when the walls of the Yusdelên City appeared on

the horizon. From their vantage in the south, the city was a wall sitting atop a ridge with umber and orange tile roofs sprouting from behind the parapets. Lush green forests grew all around, even up the steep slope leading to the wall, but if there was a road and a gate, it wasn't in the south.

They camped for the night still horizons from the Kingomder city, and Meliu munched on undercooked roots and jerked meat as Kurin eyeballed her. "The Kingdom of Danlok isn't so friendly as Helmveline."

"No doubt they'll love us if Solineus passed through to charm them."

The woman gazed with hard eyes. "I can read a wolf's three-day-old prints and their scat after a week, but you, I can't read if you poke fun or not."

"Half-poke, half-serious, but I know if I have to eat another one of these stringy roots with a smile, I'm going to hurt someone."

"Now you poke fun."

"Now I'm serious as the hells. I need a meal I don't need to pick my teeth after, a bath with incense and perfume, and a wine worthy of a hangover. And I don't care the order they come in."

"You are a strange woman." She snorted and sighed.

Edlmir plopped his ass on a log across the fire from Meliu with a plate of stringy roots. "Ain't no woman I ever met I wouldn't call strange."

Meliu said, "That's because you're too stupid to realize we're the normal ones."

He leaned in with a smirk and waggled his fork at her, a disgusting tangle of root skewered on its tines. "That might be right and so, but I know for damned sure you are strange."

"Tell me you don't want a real meal, though you'd skip the bath even if offered."

"Now, I've smelt as perty as a Choerkin before, I swear on it, but you're godsdamned right about that meal. The critters in this neck of the world have keen ears and don't wanna give up their meat. That said, I don't think Commander Florinz is gonna go traipsing into a Kingdomer city if our friend here warns against it."

Meliu shifted her stare to Kurin, and Edlmir followed. The woman groaned. "I can't advise for it. Your yellow-eyed friends would need to stay outside the walls, and the chances of something happening to them in the wild by themselves?"

Meliu rolled her eyes. "Those two can see a green snake on a green tree from a hundred strides. What the hells is gonna get them?"

Kurin spat into the fire and watched it hiss and pop on glowing embers. "Maybe so, but the Danlok would parade their heads and scoop out their eyes for alchemy in a flicker if caught."

Meliu grimaced at the image of spoons digging her friends' faces flashing in her mind. "We could use word from the world as well, and it wouldn't hurt to pigeon back a message to Endelêun to let them know where we are."

The squat woman tapped her plate. "I could send a pigeon to the Ironwing in Molikîn, telling him to send the message onward. I don't think we'd want them to know you Silone sent it and to where. The rulers of Danlok are grudging allies of Helmveline, but even that friendship rides the currents like an eagle. You Silone?" She shrugged and shook her head.

"So, which is it, a shrug or shake?"

Heavy stomps cracked a branch from behind, "A curious cricket sang to me that you folks were thinking of making for Yusdelên." Commander Florinz took a seat on the log.

Meliu said, "We've kicked the idea around."

"And?"

"I'd say we're inclined to visit."

The Ravinrin warrior looked to Kurin, who fidgeted but didn't say a word, then back to Meliu. "We've eaten our way through more biscuits and cured meats than I'd hoped, but we aren't so desperate as to risk our lives. I'm willing to barter with these people if and only if it's safe. Talk to me."

Meliu licked her lips. "Nowhere is safe once you leave your mother's womb. I think we learned that lesson well enough these past years, but I don't see them killing us with Kurin as our guide."

Kurin said, "It would help if more of your people spoke Kingdomer. Danlokians take offense with a wrong word."

"I'd wager over half these men don't read Silone, but at least half the troop speaks Kingdomer enough to keep from a fight. These Kingdomers would kill our Histê friends, so only those with more than a passing knowledge of Kingdomer and the wits to keep their calm ride with us."

"We might survive."

"A dozen who speak Kingdomer best and we trust the most. The rest hang back and guard the pack animals we don't bring with us."

A droning moan came from Kurin's chest. "I am sick of these nobu roots."

Come morning, they rode north as a group of fifteen with a dozen pack animals with empty packs and barrels. They skirted the forested base of the Yusdelên's cliffs, moving easterly, and by noon, their path led them to a road heading southwest and, from there, to the massive towers of the gates. They approached with Kurin in the lead, and three guards blocked their way.

A broad-shouldered man wearing a gold-gilt breastplate and a white plumed helm stepped forward, but his manners didn't match the beauty of his armor. His voice was dull, scratchy, and disinterested in them, even his eyes following the flight of a hawk instead of meeting Kurin's gaze. "And what's your business in Yusdelên?"

"I am Kurin, a Wayfinder of Helmveline, escorting these good people to Mulshahar. We seek supplies for our journey."

"That right? A strange Wayfinder with even stranger folk. Nah. Turn around."

Kurin straightened in her saddle and said, "See here, we are on the business of the Ironwing's," even as Meliu reached into her pouch.

Meliu lofted a golden coin the man's way. He caught it and stepped from their path. "Welcome to Yusdelên"

Meliu grinned as she passed Kurin. "I'm sure you would've talked us in eventually, but I want a bath."

They were thirty strides beyond the main gates when they reined in their mounts to avoid a train of monastics covered in black robes. At first glance, she thought their faces hid in shadows, but as they passed close, she realized a thick black veil covered their features. She leaned in her saddle. "How do they see?"

"They say that Hîmr, the Eye's Hammerfall, blesses them with sight. If you ask me, it's some simple trick." The woman gazed up and down the line. "I didn't know the Black Waters had grown so large in Danlok."

"The cult who stole the medallion from Solineus?"

"None other. Some are saying those thieves reached Hîmr, and they are awaiting help to free the god. In Molikîn, we've heard little, but rumors speak to hundreds or even thousands joining across The Foundations. After several hard winters in half the Kingdoms, people have grown desperate for hope."

"Not a worry for the Ironwing, then."

Kurin snorted as the end of the train approached. "The biggest concern. The more influence they hold, the more likely they try to steal the other half of the medallion."

"What happens if they succeed?"

"They won't, but if theft fails, a larger assault looms." Kurin jiggled her reins as the last Black Waters marched past, and they rode south into a broad street trafficked by only a handful of folks who avoided their tiny caravan.

Meliu licked her lips, the story feeling a touch too familiar now that she witnessed the followers. "At least your people haven't opened a Celestial Gate to summon a horde of demons."

"No, they only seek to unleash a god tricked into a millennium of imprisonment, a god known for war, a god bound to be angry, to conquer the world."

Meliu chuckled at herself. "You believe it's real? I guarantee they would've summoned Sol if they could have."

"I don't say it's true, nor do I say it's false, but consider the difference between bringing a god from their heaven to freeing a god already here." She smirked. "And don't forget they were interested in Tomarok just as you were.

"I didn't forget." Again, she'd been missing something important with her narrow thinking: The Pantheon of Sol might not have been the only people interested in the alignment of the Twelfth Star. Something happened in a place called The Vale of Resting Winds, something bad even if she didn't know what, and it was days before the Eve of Snows. Solineus' recovery of the medallion was a couple of years later, but might the ball have started rolling at the same time? "Did anything strange happen around the time of the Autumnal Equinox in five hundred and two? An event? Even talk of a celestial alignment?"

They rode in silence for half a wick. "I'd never heard of Dark Waters until that summer, with their faceless preachers appearing in town squares throughout the Foundations to spout foolishness. Claiming the return of Hîmr was nigh. It all settled down for a time when nothing happened that year." She paused, her gaze rising to the sky. "Seems a high priestess in Œrinklîn died young. Word arrived that her death was an accident, but people I know swore she was assassinated."

Meliu decided she was finished with coincidences when it involved people and their gods. "I've been a fool. The comet we called the Twelfth Star may have had repercussions around the world. Remind me to send a pigeon to Endelêun raising this question."

The party took quarters at an inexpensive inn dubbed the Mountain Wind, a rather bloated and romantic name for a place that sported one scent for its baths: local mineral with a delicate hint of sulfur. It sufficed for warriors and priests alike after so much time in the wild, but its comforts weren't enough to keep Meliu in her room. When Kurin said she was heading to the market for supplies, Meliu slipped her boots back on and followed.

When they stepped onto the boardwalk outside the inn, a haze of woodsmoke drifted on a breeze, carrying a hint of spice and meat that brought water to her mouth. "We're headed in that direction, right?"

"No. We follow the wind."

Meliu sighed. "You're as disappointing as the bath water in these parts." A group of hairy men bearing decorative scars on their arms squinted their way. It was hard to forget a time in life when he would've feared their looks. "Yusdelên has a different feel than Molikîn."

"Your hair draws attention, as does your walking by my side. They wonder who you are. But, I admit, it feels different than the last time I was here. Angrier. Darker. And fewer people on the streets, I'd swear it."

"Dark Waters? I'd say we've seen as many of them as common folk."

"I'll tell you this: if true, we'd best be out of Yusdelên soon as our packs are full."

Dirty clothes and dirty people bothered Meliu none; her earliest years were spent with folks caked in dust from mines, but the manner and repetition of glances carried an edge she didn't like. "I'll be happy if we're gone come sunrise."

"That means we don't wander on down to whatever feast was smoking up the street."

"Unhappy again, but my stomach will manage."

They crossed the road and continued south for two blocks before they entered streets more trafficked with guards at the corners and populated by more women and children, families from a higher strata of society.

Kurin must have noticed the look on her face. "We're staying at the inn closest to the traders we need, but if you think it was scraping the barrel, you're wrong."

"I did not say a word."

The ring of hammers on anvils caught her attention, and when her eyes strayed toward an oncoming street, coal smoke rose above the buildings. She stared at the rolling billows so long that when Kurin hissed, she didn't know why. Her eyes flicked back and forth on returning to the road ahead, and she prayed she remained stone-faced on spotting two men draped in vibrant silks that paled against the gold and jewels on their fingers and wrists while their ears, noses, and lips

were pierced to flout golden wealth in the form of rings and dangles. *Histê?* Any doubts faded when her eyes caught a dozen bronze-wielding guards behind them.

They stepped from their path with downcast eyes, and Meliu caught the lead noble speaking to the other in Histê, "Flame-haired demon whore."

The second Histê laughed, and Meliu's mouth opened to spring a retort when Kurin's elbow caught her ribs. She bit her tongue and watched them pass. "You understand Histê, too?"

The woman grinned. "And I know you too well. I've never seen Histê in a Kingdomer City, let alone so bold, though I confess to not being in this city often."

"They share a border, more or less. They're headed down that street of forges. Shall we follow?" Her feet didn't wait for an answer, and Kurin fell in by her side.

"If they recognize you as Silone, our time here could get interesting."

"I'm just a flame-haired demon whore. Beneath them."

"Which is something that will stand out after having seen you once."

Meliu didn't bother to deny it; she pulled her hair back, tied it, and pulled up her hood. "Better?"

"You're a magician."

She smirked. "If I made myself disappear, people would notice... and run like the hells." They left twenty strides between them and the group of Histê as they traversed the street that rang loud with hammers and roared with bellows and fire loud enough to crowd orderly thoughts from her mind. "A busy street at last!"

"Danlok is known for quality goods, though not at Helmveline's expertise."

They followed the group to a smithy with a giant of a man pounding a lump of glowing iron and a slender woman facing the

street—impressive labor behind a glib, haggling tongue, no doubt. The woman cut off the Histê's approach to the door.

She smiled and spoke, but there was no way to hear her over the din. At least until Meliu prayed, *Elinwe bless me with the wolf's hearing* and focused her eyes and ears on the conversation.

The woman's words still hid amid the bangs on the anvil behind her, but focused, she understood. "I repeat, the Norfîn Smithy is unable to deliver your order."

The plump bastard who'd called her a demon whore spoke in stilted Kingdomer. "Unacceptable. We paid; you deliver."

"His Eminence, King Barkôlk of Danlok and the Lord of the Lokêun mountain mines has denied your purchase under Paragraph thirty-four of the Writ and Treaty of Bonduborusî by request of the Ironwing of Helmveline."

Meliu muttered, "A treaty of Bonduborusî and a request from the Ironwing."

Kurin nodded but didn't say a word, and Meliu listened further.

"Unacceptable!" His next words grew angrier as they slipped back and forth between Kingdomer and Histê. "In the name of King Fesûduwolê the Fifth of Nargolis Dynasty, I demand delivery!"

"There will be none."

"You will add a hundred spearheads for this insult."

"You may file a request for a refund with the king, but he is away in Barkûsh and may not return for a month or two."

"Refund?"

"Norfîn Smithy has spent your gold in ore and forged your weapons and armor per your contract. You own every piece but can not take delivery without leave of the king. Consider the hardship of the smithy, having to store your gear until such time—"

"We will take what is ours!"

The woman cocked her head. "I'm sorry, I don't speak Histê well. Was that a threat?"

The man grabbed her collar and pulled her to his bulbous belly. "Threat! We will take ours! Burn!" Bronze swords rang from sheaths as he lifted her a finger from the ground, heaved, and Meliu heard a thrush through the air before she landed. A quarrel entered the side of the Histê's head and exited with a splash on his colleague's expensive silks.

Hands struck Meliu's back, and she soared toward the ground as men tromped past and over her. She curled with hands on her head, praying for Light and Dark, but when she opened her eyes, she saw Kurin's outstretched hand instead of enemies. She leaped to her feet with the surge of energy from her prayer, and the sounds of battle registered. She turned, ready to unleash the hells on anyone coming her way, but not a soul spared an eye for her. People who had appeared as ordinary folks from the street swung swords and axes, butchering the Histê in a fight that could go only one way.

Meliu turned a circle looking for threats, then released Light and Dark, shifting her feet to stand closer to Kurin. "What the hells are we watching?"

A flicker after her words faded from the air, the last Histê warrior fell. "A gambit. A very dangerous one. The Writ and Treaty of Bonduborusî was signed by all Eight Kingdoms; if there is a reason to call our people the Eight Kingdoms, it is this treaty. I'd wager when this smithy took the contract, they sent word to King Barkôlk and he to the Ironwing. Sînhôlar then requested that the contract be canceled to stop our enemy from getting quality arms."

Meliu watched as the woman, whose words had started this whole tussle, brushed herself off while speaking to a Danlokite guardsman. "But killing them?"

"I don't know. I'm guessing as is."

The woman craned her neck as her eyes landed on Meliu and shifted to Kurin. She strode their way with a dozen men behind her.

Meliu muttered, "Dancing bastards."

"Easy, priestess."

The Danlokite woman stopped a stride in front of Kurin. "You came to witness our loyalty to the treaty?"

Kurin bowed. "I did not."

Eyes crinkled, and she licked her lips. "You are a Wayfinder from Molikîn?"

"I am, but I've been south of the Dragnspans and wasn't aware of any dealings with the Histê."

The woman snorted, and Meliu doubted she believed Kurin's words. "When you speak to your Ironwing again, tell him we did everything but make King Fesûduwolê's decision to wage war for him, but a nutless king might sulk instead of fight."

Kurin bowed a second time. "I will tell him."

"Good. I hope your Ironwing knows what his will has wrought." The woman turned to Meliu with a satisfied grunt. "You, I cannot place."

Meliu's brain scrambled into a freeze, with their prepared lies inadequate for this unexpected meeting. She took the path least expected. "I am Meliu of Kaludor, from the far north. Kurin is my guide to Mulshahar."

Eyes widened. "A northern barbarian? We had one pass-through two or three years back."

"Solineus Mikjehemllut."

A hesitant nod. "I didn't meet him, but it sounds right." The woman studied her. "I am Têujaru Medalôn, Voice of the King in Yusdelên."

Meliu bowed. "Well met, Têujaru."

"You won't think so for long." She smiled. "If you're heading to Mulshahar as you say, I just threw a canyon in your path. The Reshmuhar Road will become unsafe once word of this spreads, and it will spread fast."

Meliu stared, and her mouth clucked open. "Shits."

"Indeed." She gave them both a curt nod. "Lucky travels to you both." With those words, she turned and led her entourage back to the slaughter staining the street.

Kurin said, "Our need to leave fast just grew." She turned, taking them back the way they came.

"How deep is the shit we're wading through?"

"I can't say, but we'll be slowed. Risking the Reshmuhar Road is a fool's bet, and there's little doubt we were seen speaking with the Voice of the King."

"That's bad?"

She turned left at the street's corner. "It's bad enough. Anyone listening knows who we are, and even if friendly, tongues have a way of rattling faster than a sidewinder's tail. We'll stay off the road and hug the southern face of the Foundations. Once we reach the Utumwu Forest, we make northwest to the coast and pick up the Reshmuhar Road there, where it'll be safe all the way to Mulshahar."

"You think it'll be that dangerous that fast?"

"Dunno! But what's the point of this journey if we end up dead part way?"

Meliu matched the woman's pace with extra steps as Kurin sped down the open road. "Is there a faster way?"

"The Reshmuhar Road." She smirked, then shrugged. "Maybe. We could take the Harberdên Pass into the Kingdom of Barkûsh; Helmveline is on strong terms with their king, but once you leave the mountains, you're in Ilu lands, and if you step on a crunchy cricket, they'll know you're there."

Meliu's eyebrows perked up. "The feline people?"

"Aye, dangerous as all the hells you spend your life trying to avoid."

They walked in silence for flickers as her thoughts turned over and over. "How much can we trust the Pigeonmaster of Yusdelên?"

"Before this? No fear. Now? They could send our message straight to their king, and how would we know?"

"We need to send word to Molikîn and Endelêun more than before. Can we trust Barkûsh pigeons?"

"I'd say so unless things have changed more than I know."

"Barkush, send pigeons, then into the Ilu lands. Solineus made friends with them; why not us?"

"Is Solineus this lucky or this good?"

Meliu pondered the question with a smirk. "Hard to say, but folks I'm scared of are scared of him."

"Either way, the Ilu don't eat humans but meet the wrong tribe, and they'll make us disappear right quick."

"I met an Ilu once named Nostrolum in Tek Hidrêng. Ivin befriended him, but he owes me."

Kurin laughed. "One Ilu of tens of thousands? Did he at least teach you his tongue?"

"No, but he made us remember two words, *gostelium finshol.*"

"Meaning what?"

It was Meliu's turn to laugh as the street once again turned crowded. She glanced around to see shops with barkers outside to entice buyers. "I don't know, but the way he said it while pointing south, I think he meant us to use the words to find him if we ever made it south to his homeland."

A groan followed by a disgusted grunt. "One cat with one name and two words isn't much to hang our hearts on."

"It isn't, but the Ironwing should know what happened today."

"He should."

"And we could die going either direction."

Kurin rubbed her forehead as she stopped to stare at a shingle painted with a wheelbarrow and pick. "We could. If your commander agrees, we'll head north for Klondihîk or Jumark. Haggle so well here, and we might not be broke before we die."

They entered the Pick and Barrow, which specialized in not only mining gear but cured meat and dried fruits for expeditions deep into mountainous caves, and walked out with an agreement in hand, but to speed delivery, they would pay enough to make her pray every day that Solineus would be in Mulshahar waiting for them. By evening, Commander Florinz agreed to her northern plan, like Kurin, so they were sure to get messages back home while holding not a drip of faith in her Ilu words. As the sun rose over the horizon the next day, Kingdomers loaded their pack animals, and they departed the city a candle after coins changed hands.

They were riding north with their full party when Meliu realized she hadn't managed to find a bath nor a bottle of wine, and her belly already complained about the measly baked potato and turkey that was her only meal in Yusdelên.

Thirty-Two

Begrudging Profits

Truth spoken by a man seeking power is most often demonstrable of a man who doesn't understand how power works unless spoken in confidence or to confuse his enemy.

—*Codex of Crowns*

A half dozen slaves laid on their backs like supplicant dogs hoping not to be kicked, the gems embedded in their faces glinting from the intense glow of Boborun lanterns. Glimdrem had heard rumors of their poor vision in the dark, and the bright of this cabin suggested it was true. Lord Captain Ushtrûôk sat behind a desk that would make a lesser being appear puny, the quilted skin of his head smooth and his attitude relaxed. The Edan words from his lips struck the ear as correct but clumsy. "Long time since I have seen a Trelelunin."

Glimdrem stood stone still, certain not to make a motion that might be interpreted as a bow or excess respect. "My last years out of the Mother Wood were spent on Sutan. My last dealings with your people were with Lord Captain Fardmorôk over a century ago."

"I served in his navy as a boy. He died some seventy years ago."

"I'm certain the Royal Navy felt his loss."

"So many claimed, but I never met him. Tell me, what brings you to Boborun waters?"

Glimdrem shook his head with a smirk. "Lultûhên waters."

"All waters bearing our flags are Boborun. All waters we claim are Boborun."

"Well, it's a matter of definition, I suppose. I have business in Lultûhol, business with no bearing on your current dispute."

"The might of Boboru doesn't ride the waves to allow passage. You are free to turn your ships and depart without levy."

"The Mother Wood pays no one to sail open waters."

"These waters are not open."

"Another matter of definition unworthy of an argument. I request passage to Lultûhol for one vessel. Your people will be allowed to search our cargo so you are satisfied we carry nothing that will assist the Lultûhên."

His lips curled, bearing the sharkish rows of teeth that reminded Glimdrem of Uvin. "The Boboru respect the Mother Wood, but this will not be allowed."

"Are the Boboru at war with Lultûhol?"

A huff before he answered. "No."

"Then I see no point to your barring our entry."

A rumbling chuckle, and several slaves cocked their heads before relaxing again. "Nothing disallows my letting you pass. Nothing you carry concerns me."

Glimdrem cocked a quizzical brow and played ignorant. "This blockade is more a prison then? I'm sorry, I haven't heard the *why* for all of this fuss. All I know is you trapped an associate of the Mother Wood within those walls who wasn't supposed to be there."

"Red Skull, Nozodrôk Belên?"

"The Korômonê pirate? No. The Mother Wood avoids business with thieves."

"This is good. He is why we are here."

"A blockade for a pirate? Seems extreme and expensive." A blank stare. "It matters not to me. A merchant from Mostul Ûbar is the man I seek. The Mother Wood contracted with him for some rare spices. We do not need the man, just the name of his contact in Umdûwor. Then we'll be on our way south."

The Lord Captain bore an uninspired gaze. "Such a simple thing."

"The spices in question are tricky, brought in once a year across the Deserts of Ul."

"The Edan value their cuisine so much to send you amid the humans?"

The vine said, *We share a dislike.*

Glimdrem's cheek twitched with the voice in his head, but he hadn't missed the cue. "Not all spices are used in food. The Edan didn't give me the particulars, as you might guess. Once I find the merchant's contact information, I will proceed to Umdûwor to negotiate the purchase. The trouble being I need to speak to this Mostulê cur. Now, if you don't mind our making a few trades, stealing a hefty profit from these humans during hard times, I will endeavor to do so."

The creature glared. "They can profit from nothing."

"What profit? Can they eat gold? You will know our supply list, and not a speck will disappear." Glimdrem arched his eyebrows over a devious smile. "You might consider letting a few smugglers through yourself to take advantage of bargains to strip their city."

The Lord Captain rubbed his textured scalp and licked his lips. "You say you won't take this human?"

"A human? He can rot in whatever hell his people prescribe to. I'm here for a name."

The Lord Captain laughed and then wiped his lips of spittle. "At least on one thing, we can agree."

"Like you, I seek a worthless human who somehow grew beyond less than pointless."

Ustrûôk's nose curled three times, and his stare didn't waiver before he raised his hands with a grunt. "The Lultûhên will think you a deception. Why should they welcome you?"

"The same reason you should let me pass: We Trelelunin are famous for our neutrality. Even if they turn us away, they won't dare murder us. Just like you. No risk, big reward."

"So confident are you that I won't kill you?"

"The sun will rise upon my eyes on the morrow, as it has for more than five centuries."

The Lord Captain sighed. "You're right. No risk, but no big reward either. I will not let you pass."

The vine said, *There is an old saying: a sigh has opened and ended a thousand negotiations.*

Glimdrem smiled. "Unless?"

"Big rewards bring big shares."

"I'm listening. But my Edan treasure is for other hands."

He waved a hand through the air as if shooing a fly. "No gold. You want a name. I want a location."

"Of this Red Skull?"

"The Notûlhên hide him, yes. I'd prefer his filthy, ugly head, but more, I want to know where the treasure he stole resides."

"Ahhh. You wonder if they will welcome me to their city but expect them to reveal what started this whole affair?"

An unnerving and toothy smile. "If you can talk your way through my blockade, stubborn and ridiculous humans might too succumb."

"I might have an idea." A temptation to mention the Contessa crossed his mind, but so too did her warning not to say her name. The vine said, *Don't.* "It will take time."

"A blockade is all about time. But we Boboru have a saying: Risk a tooth for the setting; risk a hand for the diamonds."

Glimdrem grimaced. "I suspect I lost something in the translation."

"The risk should be commensurate with the reward. Yes? I let you through, and you come back without my reward, all your ships go under without a witness for the Edan to blame us."

"That doesn't sound so fair to me."

My people have another saying about negotiations: He with the weight to tip the scales should. If you refuse the terms, raise your sails to the wind and depart as friends." He slapped the table and smiled.

"It's a fool's play. No." The vine whispered, *maybe.* "I should not entertain such insanity, but... If I bring you the location of either the man or the treasure, we sail free."

The Lord Captain's lips snarled open, his shark teeth sawing over one another back and forth as if considering what Trelelunin flesh might taste like. "Deal. One ship passes through, and the others stay here."

Glimdrem nodded with a smile. "Done." *And done,* hissed the vine. "You'll excuse me as I should depart for the *Flaming Wing* to prepare."

Ushtrûôk stood. "I will inform my people of my orders. Good luck, Trelelunin. The reward of killing you would pale before the reward of your success."

"Pleased to hear that." He turned and strode for the cabin door, stepping onto the deck to stand between his broad-shouldered escorts. *What have I agreed to?*

We will not fail. She will see to it.

Glimdrem turned his gaze to the *Flaming Wing*, and for a flicker, he questioned the vine's reasoning. But he didn't voice it even to himself. But still, the vine heard him and answered, *Who do you trust more, the woman or me?*

Which woman?

The vine didn't answer.

The Boboru made a cursory search of the *Flaming Wing*, but without a single human in the crew to draw suspicion, the Lord Captain and his thunderous party with two dozen slaves in tow departed candles before sundown without stepping no closer than five strides to the Contessa secreted away beneath the galley's tables. They sailed unmolested into Lultûhol's harbor with the Eleris' silver banner bearing a blue tree, and he felt the eyes before he could see them.

High walls constructed of massive laterite blocks made the city stand out as if colored by sunset, the orange hues welcoming them into a harbor filled with military vessels and merchants who hadn't left the port since the blockade began. What a sight they must be, a Trelelunin ship entering when anyone else would've been sunk beneath the waves. Would that instill fear, trust, loathing? He couldn't fathom how humans might react, but he figured only the desperate would see them as saviors.

He took the opportunity to practice his burgeoning grasp on the Tôlk language. "So tell me, Contessa, why doesn't Red Skull just flee by land? I'd assumed the Boboru sieged the walls as well, but see nothing."

"Your Tôlk is improving."

"I never imagined human languages would be so useful, I admit, but they aren't complicated. But apparently, neither is Edan for you."

"I'm glad you find it so simple." She turned her back to the rail to look at him. "I don't know for certain, but from Simêum to Rêonduhol, the plains beyond the city walls are ruled by the Hôvrumâ. Tribal nomads, best anyone knows, and they often watch the walls. The cities of Mostul and Ûbar managed to connect their walls into a single city, but at the cost of many lives. He might make it out alive, but where to go? Simêum? Mostul Ûbar? Hundreds of horizons through hostile lands. There isn't so much as a fishing village between."

"And no way to coordinate a pickup. These Hôvrumâ, human?"

"Yes, though I've never seen one."

"The Deserts of Ul have horsemen. I wonder if they're related."

She turned back to stare at the city and pointed at a ship sailing their way. "A greeting party."

"If we aren't allowed entry, my people are dead."

"My father is a *Kontzûl* of Mostul Ûbar, and you are from the Eleris; we'll be welcomed out of curiosity alone."

"I'm counting on this simple human logic."

"*We* are counting on it."

"And when we get inside, who do we speak to?"

A pause. "I don't know. I've never been to Lultûhol."

He coughed and twined his hands behind his back. "I should learn to ask more questions."

"Important people will find us."

It was easy to forget who he suspected her of being—of in part being?—when standing beside her and engaged in idle banter. If he *could* answer the how an archangel entered her body, he still wouldn't know the *why*. The Vale of Resting Winds sat nestled in a forest a thousand horizons from the city of Vitolêô. He found it easier to surrender on the question of how than he did the why, but nothing in this woman's life suggested itself important enough for an archangel,

one of the Twenty-Four who might have survived, to take over her life. Unless the answer hid in Lultûhol.

He turned to gaze upon her with a smile as she stared in silence at the oncoming city. *How dangerous is she?*

The vine said, *Should we kill her now to make sure we don't find out?*

Without a single ally aboard the *Flaming Wing*, it was the perfect time for murder. None of her people would ever know. *I don't think so.*

The other makes us nervous.

Glimdrem knew the vine to mean Solineus. *If the destruction in the Vale couldn't kill them, who says we could?*

And a third voice in his head said, *You are wiser than your other whispers.* The voice belonged to a dead archangel, the Twenty-Fifth, Uvîn Lô.

THIRTY-THREE

Guest in Chambers

And behold! Sol delivered the defeating blow, striking Restimfirîdêz in the primacy of his rule. His flaming paw stood atop the demon's shattered skull, and he spoke unto the masses. The followers who followed no more cheered; the followers who followed still withered as weeds in the desert and died, their souls stripped of their faith, their souls dropped into the fires of the bellows, their souls hammered into swords for a future war.

—*Codex of Crowns*

The days passed with Rinold sitting in her bed chamber, but she could only survive so many sleepless nights while sharing nap times with the twins. After four days of nothing, his visits turned into three nights a week, and then he slept in the adjoining room, and they relied upon Kinesee or the handmaiden Feneshu to luck into spotting the ghost and waking him.

Frustrating, infuriating, and boring were the kindest words she could muster to describe their lack of luck, if indeed it was luck and not ghosts avoiding them. So it was that she invited Izilfer to come and entertain her by instructing her in more Canonic Silone. Or, at least, that was the

excuse, but more often, they spent time sipping tea and talking about nothing in particular. The willubarm tea steamed fresh from the kettle this day, and they had extra guests. Though noon, Rinold snored from the reading room, and Izilfer had brought her young apprentice along, a girl named Hulerê. And they'd poured the tea when Puxele arrived to find out where her husband had gotten himself to.

Tea and biscuits for four as they closed the door to block the Squirrel's serenade.

Puxele puffed her tea and said, "Little Muldanu was happy as could be to have the twins to play with."

"Once they get a little older, they should play more often."

"Gak! How do you people drink this stuff?" Hulerê stared at her cup with twisted lips.

Kinesee said, "First, you let it cool, *then* you sweeten it." She pointed to a jar filled with cane sugar.

"Oh." She scooped four heaping spoonfuls and stirred. Sipped. "Too sweet, but still better."

"Shouldn't you two be at her studies? I don't want my boredom stopping your training."

Iziler snorted. "We just tell them I'm still instructing her—which now and again is true—but in truth? She only needs practice to surpass me and every healer I've ever known."

Hulere said, "I think she's just lazy."

Izilfer gasped. "Maybe we *should* go back to her studies. Her mouth wasn't as smart."

The women laughed, then laughed again when a snore resounded through the door. Puxele said, "Is that all he damned well does here?"

Kinesee said, "We heard a noise last night, so he sat awake until dawn, staring at that chair. Ghosts tend to appear there; must be comfortable or something."

"Or, it faces yer bed, and they're watching you."

"I made my peace with that some time ago. Kinda sorta." She giggled. "They seem harmless, and it's not like we could stop them anyhow. They're all over the city. We just don't see them most of the time."

"I've only seen a handful myself. I try to ignore 'em as much as they ignore me. It's all odder than the hells."

"I can't explain a thing about it."

Izilfer grinned. "We should open a bottle of wine some night and tell ghost stories around a fire. Maybe that will attract them."

Hulerê said, "Wine is worse than this stuff. No thanks."

Puxele grinned. "Or, we could use your prayers to scare him senseless."

Izilfer giggled. "You want Meliu for that. Elemental Life isn't all that frighten—"

The door rattled, gentle but undeniable, and all eyes turned—silence for flickers before it rattled again.

Hulerê eyed Izilfer. "You're doing that, aren't you?"

Izilfer shook her head, and Harlik opened the door with a quizzical look on his face. "Who's jiggling the door?"

A man stood beside Budoe out in the hall with a smile. With a long face and brown hair past his shoulders, complimented by a beard pointing to the middle of his chest, he felt unfamiliar in every way. The stranger smiled and spoke as he passed through the door, "Thank you, my good man," but neither Harlik nor Budoe acknowledged him or his words.

The color of his skin and the fact she couldn't see through him suggested he wasn't a ghost, but the manner in which the guards ignored him spoke otherwise. "Just a game, Harlik. You may close the door."

"Aye, Lady Choerkin."

The door clacked shut, and the stranger turned to her with his hands clasped at his waist. "Ladies! It is a pleasure."

Hulerê said, "Who is this man? He dresses funny."

The girl was right. He wore brown silk robes with a golden rope knotted around his waist. He also spoke Silone rather than the Canonic spoken by ghosts. The man strode to and took a seat in the chair ghosts seemed to prefer. "I am Lûdnarn of Olumiwâ, young lady."

"I don't know you."

"Nor should you."

Puxele stood and pushed her seat away. "I'm going to wake Rinold."

"We can all see him? Harlik and Budoe couldn't."

Izilfer nodded. "Who the hells is he? A ghost?"

Lûdnarn raised his hands in a plaintive gesture. "You could just ask me."

Kinesee said, "Fine. Answer then."

"Have you people grown so crass as to not say please? Or, for that matter, to not even ask me properly?"

"Please, would you tell us whether you're a ghost?"

"With less sass?" She glared, and he shrugged. Held up his index finger. "First, define ghosts."

Rinold slipped into the room with Puxele by his side. "Ya look enough of a man to turn into a ghost."

Lûdnarn's head bobbed. "Well, if killing a man made a ghost, the world would be filled with them, no? But I reckon that was more of a threat than a hypothesis on the origin of ghosts."

"A smart-mouth."

"I prefer antagonist."

Kinesee said, "A ghost is the soul of the dead who stayed in the mortal realm."

The stranger cupped his hand in his chin. "Mmmm. Supposing I died here, good luck to this man in killing me again. But am I a ghost? The definition seems too simple to fit me, but I will say no."

"Then define yourself."

"I'm afraid I can't. Not in some way that would satisfy both of us. And all these good people. I met your father once. That alone demanded I say hello the first chance I got. But, there is so much more to you."

"You met him here in Endelêun?"

He looked up and left to the ceiling, but when she followed his gaze, she saw nothing. "My memory is foggy. We met is the most I can say."

Kinesee studied his features, his clothes, and the words he spoke. "Your way of speaking is of Clan Emudar, but you, I'm not sure you even look Silone."

A wry wrinkle curled his grin. "Will you accuse me now of being a demon? Inhuman?"

"No. Just not Silone. Why are you here?"

He waved. "Hello!"

Rinold muttered, "Lemme shut his smart mouth."

"Ah! It is indeed true that size doesn't make a man's toughness. I don't know you, but I like your courage. Still, I'm here to speak to the Lady Choerkin."

Kinesee said, "There will be no fights unless this man starts one."

His face scrunched. "Oh, the fight has already begun, but I didn't start it. The fight began before you arrived. The fight began before you were born. The fight will continue long after you're all dead."

"What fight is that?"

"To survive! It's the war we all lose, all except the gods, anyhow. Your mother lost. Your father lost. You will lose. So, too, will your children, the only decision remaining being who loses first."

On the one hand, he spoke the truth, but after a flicker, her lips snarled. "Was that a threat?"

"Easy, mother lioness. No threat from me, just a warning every mother and father should hear and heed. I had children once, and they lost before me. If you think death is a nasty fate, face the destiny I did."

"I'm sorry for your pain." She rubbed her forehead and said, "The ghosts in the streets, did you die when they did?" There was something amiss about the man. Something different she couldn't put a finger on amid so many peculiarities.

"Oh, there we go, needing to define ghosts again." His lips curled to and fro. "No. I did not." The way he answered suggested a truth hiding something more.

"Who are they?"

"Your people, though I'm sure you figured that out."

"When did they die?"

He huffed and shrugged. "We all die in our time, and they died in theirs."

"No one event?"

A grimace. "I don't believe so, no."

"How's that possible?"

"How's it possible for tens of thousands to die in the same instant?"

Her elbows thudded the arms of her chair, and her fingers kneaded her forehead. She recalled Solineus telling her about a skeleton man who spoke in riddles and eyed the man. "You say you met my father. Are you The Touched?"

He blinked. "I'm forced to say I haven't a clue who you're talking about."

"Yeah, your words aren't riddle enough."

She licked her lips, and Rinold leaned into her ear. "Library."

She wanted to kick herself. "Do you know where there are hidden libraries in Endelêun? We're looking for books."

He studied her with a crooked smile. "Hidden libraries? Maybe. Hidden books? No. How humans be damned odd is it that there are libraries without books? What freakish hiccup of destiny could arrive at such a quixotic result? Perhaps it wasn't humans to be damned at all, but maybe the Edan? Scholars and collectors. Or maybe our damnation must be reserved for something we haven't yet a name?"

"I'll damn you if you don't tell me where these empty libraries are."

He chuckled. "Damnation would be a damnable redundancy for me, Lady Choerkin. Save your curses, if not for someone more worthy, for some damnable in the first place. But answer me this: Is every place that holds a book a library?"

"No."

"Then you realize now that what you search is, in fact, not a palace or a city, but an infinity, even if it's a smaller infinity than others."

She shook her head. "Even if a book could be anywhere inside the palace and city, it isn't infinity."

"Again, a matter of definitions."

"What the hells do you mean by that?"

"I'm not a dictionary, and I've already gone well beyond hello."

She groaned. "Again, why are you here? Did the ghosts I've seen in this room send you?"

He smirked and leaned in his seat with a cold stare. "No one sends me, but I send messages. Tell your father to stay away, or a lesson most bitter will be taught."

Her gut clenched at the grit in his voice, the threat in his tone, and the violence in his eyes. But she held his gaze. "A threat at last? Stay away from what? What the hells is that supposed to mean?"

He leaned back, then rocked forward to stand with a pleasant smile, and he raised his hand and waved. "Hello!" He strolled toward the door.

She jumped from her seat. "What the hells does that mean?"

He reached for the knob but disappeared before his fingers gripped.

The room stared at empty air, then stared at her.

Hulerê blurted, "That was amazing!"

Rinold's hard look for Kinesee wasn't so excited. "We need to get you and the twins out of here."

She chuckled, though not finding anything funny. "And go where? Where in the city wouldn't they find me?"

"Away from the city then."

"The jungle is far more dangerous."

"The Wiirê camp. The yellow-eyes would at least see the ghosts coming if even they could reach you. I doubt they can leave the city."

Kinesee shook her head, frustrated by the swirl of her thoughts without others helping to confuse her. "That wasn't no ghost."

The man gawked. "Oh, aye, and then what the hells was he?" He paused a flicker, then scowled. "A Face? You're saying that man was a Face?"

She froze. "My thoughts hadn't even got there yet."

Izilfer sighed before taking a drink of cooled tea. "Your guards didn't see him. Didn't hear him."

"Ivin spoke of guards ignoring the Face like it wasn't even there."

"Ignoring or not seeing? The difference is important."

Kinesee dredged her memories. "On the wall of Roemhiek, he... he said they ignored the Face. Yes, it surprised him because they looked right at him."

"I'm not saying it's impossible not to be seen, but from a foot away? While everyone else hears and sees you? That type of power on top of

changing his appearance? I doubt it." A nervous giggle. "And no way a Face could disappear like that. It had to be a ghost."

Hulerê stepped between them. "It wasn't a ghost."

All eyes turned to the girl. "What do you mean?"

"I've tried to connect to ghosts. When I do, it's like a tingle more than nothingness."

"You tried to link your souls? Gods, girl! What were you thinking?"

Hulere's head bowed at Izilfer's scream, and her words rang with humility. "I did what I did. It's almost a reflex. People, from newborn babes to high priests, feel more or less the same. This man was more. Human, maybe, but he wasn't all the way here."

"We'll talk about your foolishness later."

Kinesee said, "A man can't be here and not here. Can he? But how else to explain disappearing? I'm blessed confused."

Hulerê said, "You know how some fruits look delicious on the outside, but you bite to find them wormy and rotten? That's him. Only it's not him because he's not here."

Puxele said, "Like he was godsdamned Taken? A Shadow of Man?"

The girl shook her head with a blush, not daring to make eye contact with Izilfer. "There was nothing human feeling about the Taken. Just darkness. I can explain neither, but they were different."

Kinesee sighed, conjuring an image of the man in her mind. "His robes and that rope belt. They weren't Silone."

Rinold said, "Aye to that. You might be onto something. He wasn't Wiirê. Histê? Not like I've seen. And he was human, or at least looked it."

"He said he met my father. Only three peoples would make sense. One of the Tek Nations, Mulshahar, or Kingdomer."

Puxele said, "I'm doubtin' the Tek are worried about his return."

Rinold scratched his head. "My sweets is right, I'd wager. Mulshahar or one of them Eight Kingdoms. And if he's in Mulshahar, does that mean Kingdomer?"

Kinesee stood, arms folded across her chest. "I can't chance hiding in the mountains if that's true. I'm stuck here, which is where I want to be anyhow. My father wouldn't run, nor will I." In truth, she didn't know what Iku, her real father, would do, but as a fisherman who braved the weather and beasts of the Parapet Straits his whole life, she didn't think he'd tuck tail. She knew for damned sure Solineus wouldn't. "I can't march into battle, but I can wait to see if the fight comes to me."

Rinold muttered, "Maybe the Wiirê are right, and this place is cursed. But if the fight comes, I plan on being by your side."

Puxele said, "We all will be, and not just those of us in this room. Kinesee Choerkin will have the backing of all the clans."

Izilfer said, "And the Church. I'll speak with Sedut if you like."

Kinesee eyed her sister-in-law with a cocked head. It had been years since being held prisoner by High Priestess Sedut, and though she liked to think herself a forgiving soul, there remained a bitter grudge. "She and I have a history, but go ahead. I'll send a pigeon to Molikîn and see if the description strikes a chord with the Ironwing." She turned to face Puxele with a smile. "I don't know about you, but I could use some playtime with the children."

Thirty-Four

Red Skull Words

The Totokotwonu tore into the Kingdom of Meshhepetol with the fury of baying wolves and howled with bloodied muzzles to warn the world of their arrival a second time. Pity be for those who herald the Third Welcome.

—*The Oxeum Codex*

Nozodrôk Belên's pleasant smile wasn't the only thing that defied Glimdrem's expectations of how the murderous pirate should look. Black hair and a clean shave counted as the most striking, considering his reputation for unkempt red hair and shaggy beard, the origin of the name Red Skull long before his signature flag. But he was also short and scrawny, nothing approaching a lean, muscular fighter he'd expect men to speak of with fear.

The Contessa towered over him as she approached before taking a seat across from the pirate. Even when Glimdrem sat, the man remained standing, perhaps insecure over his height. Or judging by his pacing, he was a nervous man by nature who preferred to be on his feet.

Glimdrem leaned in his seat until the chair rested on two feet. "We're sure this is Red Skull?"

She replied in Tôlk. "He does seem a mite puny."

The man didn't stop his pacing nor look them in the eye. "I damned well am. Now tell me what the hell you want."

"You're aware there's a war brewing on the ocean all over you?"

"So an ignorant Mostulê bitch might say." He stopped pacing to lean on the table, staring hard at the woman. "Looksee here, lady, or contessa, or whatever they title you, this city crawls with Boborun spies and assassins. You drawing me out goes long strides to gettin' me killed and starting that there war."

The Contessa held her steady, emotionless gaze. "I came a long way and braved a Boborun blockade to ask you a simple question. A little respect and an honest answer is all I ask."

He stepped back and bowed with a mocking flourish. "Oh please, sweet lady, do ask."

"What makes you so valuable the Boboru and Lultûhên would go to war for you?"

His brows arched, and his hands clasped at his waist. "Good gracious, an intelligent question. You surprise me, princess."

"Surprise me with an answer."

A squint. "Tell me what the hell this slant-eared woodkin is doing here."

Glimdrem pondered his ears but didn't say a word.

"He's my writ of passage in and out of Lultûhol."

"I suppose so. Trelelunin?"

"I am. Did you think Woodkin would insult me?"

The pirate glanced back and forth before his eyes tilted to remain on the Contessa. "Is he serious?"

"I'm afraid he might be."

Glimdrem grinned. "Surely a man who'd be the runt of any human litter would refrain from insulting physical appearances, in particular with teeth so gnarled I'm uncertain how he eats without mangling his lips."

"Not bad, woodkin, but insults are best when kept pithy."

"Boys, please. There's a question that needs answering."

"You won't like the answer, princess."

"I'm better with any answer than I am with princess. It's Contessa."

"Bulessyu Contessa. The truth is, I don't know."

The woman stared, unreadable, but Glimdrem wagered the man played games. He squirmed in his seat as the two eyeballed one another. "You aren't lying, but you aren't speaking the whole truth."

"A quick wit, this woodkin."

The Contessa said, "Enlighten me further."

Nozodrôk hefted and spun a chair before slamming it to the ground, its back facing Poleen. He sat splay-legged and rested his arms on the chair's headrest. "I kinda came across a lil somethin'. More than a li'l. We all know of the Boborun treasure ships?"

"Rumors."

Glimdrem hadn't a clue what they spoke of but kept his mouth shut rather than appear ignorant.

"One or two pass through the Monsoon Straits during the Safe Season, and nobody touches 'em, righto? Right. No one dares touch one."

The Contessa leaned forward, hard eyes appraising the man. "But you did."

He raised his arms. "I don't wanna bear the mark of a brave man or a fool. The *Willibedoku*—"

"What the Saints is that?"

He chortled. "That there's the closest I can damned well come to the name of the ship, with that prattling gibberish tongue of theirs. They say the *Willibdeokumestowhatchamacallit* were sailing in from Sutân when she hit storms before reaching Toltûk and lost half her escort. The Lord Admiral sent her onward too late in the season, and after a fearsome storm struck, I followed from Holistên deep into the Strait. The *Willibujigger* took on water and, in the middle of another storm, started transferring treasure." He sucked his teeth and winked. "I took liberties with their wealth then and there."

"In the middle of a monsoon. Brave and foolish."

He snorted. "A blunder. Gold and gems, aye, but the whoresons came after me in a fury. Sank two of my ships before we split up. Word is they've torched more than a few whose captains merely *associated* with me."

"You stumbled on something more than treasure. What?"

He cupped his hands with a plaintive shake of his head. "As the Lamenting Father is my witness, I don't know."

Glimdrem asked, "You said from Sutân? A treasure ship?"

"I can't say for sure, now can I?"

"I spent ten years on Sutân and saw more things that'll kill a man than I did pieces of gold. The gems there are rough-cut by primitive peoples. Perhaps the ship came from Kûtu?" Stories spoke of more civilized regions on that nearby continent.

"Yer guess is good as mine, woodsy."

Glimdrem balled his fists until nails bit his palms. On the other hand, Uvin spoke of Oxeum somewhere in the region, a city more than capable of yielding priceless treasures. "Did rumors ever mention Oxeum?"

The pirate scratched his skull. "Never heard the word afore."

The Contessa said, "If you don't know what's so valuable, why hasn't the Lultûhên handed you and your cargo over?"

He clapped his hands with a whoop. "Ha ha! That's where it becomes a laugher. I'm a tellin' ya. It seems the Lultûhên, bless 'em, figured if the Boboru valued me and the treasure so much, they'd best not hand us to the bugger bastards, righto? Right. Stupid bastards, but it kept me alive so far."

"So nobody except the Boboru know why?"

He shrugged. "I find it amusing to imagine they know nothing as well."

Glimdrem looked at her, and she back at him before shrugging. "I imagine a pirate is a masterful liar."

Glimdrem rested his palms on the table and stared at the man. "More truths than lies, I'd suggest."

"I agree. Describe the treasure."

"Jewelry, golden statues." He shrugged.

Glimdrem asked, "Religious iconography?"

Nozodrôk raised his brow. "What's a what?"

"Objects that are religious symbols. They may hold more value than their materials alone." Or conceal a tome such as the *Oxeum Codex* as the monkey statue had.

"Ah hell, I've no idea about nothin' like that. But if'n so, what from Sutân would bear importance to the Boboru?"

"In my time on Sutân I saw nothing to suggest it so, but then, I know little of the Boborun faith."

"Exceptin' they take slaves."

The Contessa asked, "Would we be able to take a look?"

Nozodrôk laughed. "Oh, I'd be more'n happy to *give* it to you if it got me out of this damned city. Safely, that is. The Lultûhên took every scrap of the treasure I hadn't already sold the flicker after the first Boborun ships arrived and made threats. They tossed me in prison for a year until someone drugged me and tried to drag me out. After, they

razored my beard, dyed my hair, and secret me around the city like some favorite whore."

"Still a prisoner."

"Oh yes, more or less. I'm alive in case they need me to save their king."

"*Yostul.*"

"Whatever the hell they call him. If yer lookin' to see what I brought, you need permission from folks mightier than me, but I might lend a hand. I'm a guessin' you used up your favors just gettin' to see me."

"You might be surprised by the number of favors I keep in my pocket."

He stood and spun his chair away, and it clattered to the floor. "Looksee, m'lady. Princess. Contessa. Queen. Whatever the hell name you like best. When your favors come up short, drop my name."

"And at what cost does your favor come?"

"Get me the hell out of this city, and you'll have a pack full of favors owed by me and mine."

Glimdrem scoffed, but the Contessa took his words to heart. Or at least pretended to. "What use is a Korômonê pirate to me?"

"Ha! If you don't know that answer, yer more a fool than I imagine."

"Play it square with me, and I'll see what can be done."

He snorted with a nod and put his hands on his hips. "Good. I miss my beard."

Glimdrem suppressed a groan. "It's my ship that brought us here. I'm not risking a single life for this man."

Nozodrôk grunted. "Your friend is growin' on me. He's blunt. So, I'll be blunt. Without the will of your Saints or whatever god the Trelelunin pray to, there's no way you get me out of here while you're here. You're known, and they're watching. Always watching. They'll be ridin' me like a leech for a couple of months after this lil chat."

"So long as we all have this understanding."

"And understand this: so long as I'm in this here city, the Boboru will be here."

The Contessa stood. "I hope to speak with you again soon."

Glimdrem followed her from the room and kept silent until reaching Neoburo and the other Treleunin guards, and they stepped into the light of noon. He spoke in Edan as his eyes adjusted to the bright. "A murderer and pirate. You are serious about freeing him?"

"It depends on whether there's a pearl in the clam." A common saying in Edan, but this woman knowing it reinforced the notion of the impossible being real.

"What could be worth freeing such a man?"

"I do not know yet. But, people say things as bad and worse about me."

He shrugged. "They do, and I wager they are not all lies." Glimdrem sensed her smile even if it remained hidden.

"Best we aren't seen together too much. I'll work on getting to see the treasure. You do whatever you can."

"I will sit and wait. This is not my intrigue. It is yours." Something of a lie, seeing as artifacts from Sutân held an unquestionable curiosity for him.

She split from the group to walk alone, and Glimdrem watched until she turned away from the docks. Neoburo said, "We sit idle?"

"No. I want to see what the pirate brought from Sutân, and I do not trust this Contessa to get us in." He strode toward the docks with his men on his heels, but his mind turned to the nobles of this city and which might serve his needs best.

Thirty-Five

Two Women Running

Love plumbs the depths of the soul. Love gives heat to the cold. Love makes the whole heart broken. Love saves the fallen and forgotten. But what is so different when the lover becomes the sinner?

—*Book of Leds*

The *Fefemor* tied off at Pelican Dock three days after Murêshu's visit, and Solineus got to see his father for the first time since he sailed downriver from Endelêun and to sit down with Captain Edmordô for the first time since parting ways in the Monsoon Straits. It all felt like a lifetime ago.

Adinvan eyeballed Sîu the flicker they entered the captain's cabin and strode to lift her in a hug. "His mother is gonna be pleased as the heavens you two got together. No surprise, no surprise!"

Solineus didn't bother to ask the old man how he could tell before he too was crushed by a hug. "You're looking good for an aging lord."

"You'll be sproutin' gray hairs one of these moons, and I'm gonna laugh til I'm blue." He let go, stepped back, and must've caught sight

of Captain Intœñyô for the first time. "A Luxun captain? I'm surprised after all."

Solineus stepped to the side and gestured. "Father, Captain Edmordô, I'd like you to meet Captain Intœñyô of the Luxun Trade Fleet." The man bowed with a click of his heels as his plume fluffed. "Captain Intœñyô will be joining our partnership. I've no doubt we can all agree to the advantages."

Edmordô blinked twice before outrage set in. "You bring a partner without my consent?"

Solineus shook two fingers in the air with a smile. "I'm sure we can reach an agreement, considering the clout Captain Intœnyô will bring to the table. Please, let's all sit."

Edmordô took his seat last. "Our contract stands until I say otherwise."

"Understood. We—"

Adinvan said, "There are more important matters to attend."

Solineus sighed. "I guessed, so we'll try to make this quick." He eyed the two captains, but his gaze fell on Edmordô last. "Captain Intœñyô's joining us does not make our venture Luxun sanctioned; let's get that out of the way, right? That said, the veneer of Luxun presence will give the Boboru pause when demanding tribute or from boarding and searching any ship sailing with them. That's face value."

Edmordô nodded. "An imperfect ploy, but it could save us a hundred *smedên* per ship bypassed."

"More important is avoiding boarding parties or seizure, agreed?"

"Aye."

"His connections stretch from top to bottom of the Vandunêz continents. What value is that?" He caught the twitch in Edmordô's eye and spoke before the man's mouth could open. "We can't damned

well say, can we? But it's more than a hundred godsdamned smedên. What he brings to this table with a Luxun flag and his how many years trading these waters?"

Intœñyô said, "Forty-seven after my naval service."

"That's longer than either of us has been alive, Edmordô. That's why I'll cut my share to fifty-two percent of profits from seventy if both of you agree to an even split of the remainder." Both men's faces twitched. "Mighty fair, considering without me, there is no Helmveline. No Helelindin from the inner continent. And before you say more, yes, war will hit the coast, but under neutral sails, we should avoid most trouble. Consider also the expense I and my people will undertake in keeping the trade lanes open."

Edmordô sat back in his seat and flicked his fingers at his opposition. "Let the Luxun speak first."

"I had hoped for more of an even split, I admit. Your words, though honest, leave a great many details in question. Crew compensations, extenuating circumstances, damages, casualty and death wages, succession of partnership officers, and titles, just to name a few. But I accept the general parameters as offered."

"Edmordô?"

Fingers twisted an end of his mustache. "I concur on the missing details, and they aren't just whistles in the wind, but if you put so much faith in this Luxun to take a twenty percent cut, then I am agreed to an even cut on the remainder. Providing the books are kept in duplicate, one copy at a verifiable neutral party, such as the Mulshahar Exchange."

Solineus stood and slapped the table with a smile. "Excellent. I'll leave you two captains to hammer out the merchant details, and I'll look them over later before we consult the Exchange to seal the agreement. I recommend wine instead of whiskey."

He turned with a grin, offered Sîu his arm, and strode from the cabin with Adinvan on his heels. A glance revealed a deck with only a handful of sailors, so he strode to the rail near the gangplank and leaned on a post.

Adinvan said, "That was mighty godsdamned generous."

"Maybe, but I didn't want to waste time bickering. Those two might be three days in there before settling things. And right or wrong, I feel I owe Captain Intœñyô for helping us off Herald's Watch."

Sîu said, "He is a good man who will add to the profits."

Adinvan nodded. "Don't take me wrong, now. No matter how much I'd like to, I won't give you an argument. I don't know him, and you do." He shrugged.

Solineus said, "I assume we have bigger troubles in the south anyhow."

"Shittin' aye, we do. The five kings are all riled up, the best I can tell. Word of upriver shipyards, hard as the hells for us to reach, come from up and down the coast."

"Unless they're building better ships... Either way, it's a concern, but we knew they'd be comin'."

"I've got it on praisable word one of the southern kingdoms has hired Korômonê shipwrights. The crews will still be shit, but the ships will improve. That's all and good and not unexpected. My biggest fear in these waters is for the islander peoples. They aren't ready for this sort of war, and we don't have the ships to protect them. No, the bigger issue is the second rumor. Somethin' more is goin' on down south in Korômonê waters."

"Hiring Korô mercenaries?"

"Oh, aye, I've no doubt some ships are hired, but that's only so many. Way I see it, the Korô don't love them kingdoms much at the start. Dying for their gold will take a hard and desperate man, I

reckon. We'll see some Korô pirates turn to headhuntin' our ships, no doubt, but no serious threat to things that matter more. They're after something else."

Solineus turned to Sîu. "Any thoughts?"

"A few Korômonê traders dealt with Pôn. Rude and pompous but otherwise, nothing in common with the Histê. Most of what I know you can find on maps."

"Religion?"

"The Darôgotê, but I don't even know if it's a god or pantheon."

Adinvan nodded. "Aye, they bow to the sun and moon, but folks are mum or just don't know much. Names of cities, trade alliances, oh, and they've a wasteland to their south, deserts by a coupla different names. They've some grand king in the Rorismok Palace south of Narvhôdrên, and somethin' called Posdûonts lording over the cities who mostly fight each other."

"But not a clue as to what the Histê want from them?"

"Hells, it might be nothing, but I doubt it. When we arrived, the two had nothin' to do with one another, but since we took Mûulbon's Mouth and the bloodbath in Fulgumhîer I heard about, they've been talkin'. Never trust to coincidence, am I right?"

"Speaking of which," said Sîu, "you boys should be listening instead of yapping." She nodded toward two sailors at the end of the gangplank, one with a line of fresh fish thrown over his shoulder.

Solineus cocked his ear in their direction. "It's what I heard, aye. The old Holdimun Building is being bid on."

The other said, "A prince's mint, I'd wager. Notoholis Aprelêu looking to move in, maybe?"

Laughter. "Gods know, I hope not."

Sîu said, "I heard the name in the streets twice on the way here."

Solineus stepped down the plank, "Gentlemen! I heard you speaking of a building."

The fisherman said, "Aye, sir, you did. The old Holdimun Building. The Matron Holdimun died some years back, and her kin couldn't hold the business together."

"Whereabouts?"

"Straight across from the Osprey Dock, great pillars and a copper roof, you won't miss it."

Solineus reached into a pocket and flipped both men a *smedên.* "Thank you, gents."

The men smiled and walked their separate ways.

Sîu grinned. "Not so subtle."

"They probably grew tired of trying to get our attention."

Sîu giggled, and Adinvan said, "What the hells am I missing?"

"Let's take a walk."

"Your payments with the guard aren't due, are they?"

Solineus chuckled. "No. I think we're more untouchable than ever, for the time being, at least." As they walked, he talked, explaining their meeting with Murêshu, and a half candle's stroll later, they stood in front of a massive stone building, workers climbing scaffolding like ants to clean windows, polish copper, and tuckpoint the mortar of the stone. It wasn't a castle or a palace in function, but four-story towers and a crenelated wall with gargoyles served the illusion. The ridged copper roof gleamed in the sun, beautiful and complimenting the red-gold of the city's more famous buildings, and chiseled pillars two poles high held a roof over a ceramic tiled entry with ebony double doors.

Solineus strolled to a man who stood overseeing the work with hands on his hips. "This the Holdimun building I've been hearing about?"

"Right, you are. Narmun! Narmun! Careful of the leading on that window, you oaf!"

"One whale of a building. Prime ground?"

"You won't find a primer for sale without a king's mint for a buyout. Old Holdimun, she was a tyrant, but that's what it took to hold the trade together."

"What did they deal in?"

"Textiles from abroad, from what I understand, raw materials, and nothing I ever afforded." He chuckled.

"It's a building that makes a statement. What's the price?"

The man turned and looked him up and down with a smirk until his eyes flicked back and forth between the hilt above each shoulder, and his eyes fell back to the street. "Normal folks like me don't ask. Nice mule ears."

"Thank you."

He flipped the man a *smedên* and strode for the corner to head for the Exchange. "I told you these were respected boots."

Adinvan snorted. "I told you, my girl, he was born a smart ass. You don't want him."

"Too late. He's mine."

"Like a godsdamned stray ya keep kickin' into the river, and it comes back."

"He does, doesn't he?"

Solineus grinned at their banter and said, "Let's go see what this here building is going for."

Another advantage to the Holdimun building's location was that it was within a five wick's walk from the Exchange; that way, his father didn't have time to bring up more than a few childhood stories. Of course, he hadn't anticipated the man continuing his stories straight into the lobby.

"And when he was twelve, he walloped Lord Sodernine's boy upside the head in a spar and called him a pimple dick seein' as rumor spoke of the boy catching the itch from a local girl."

"I did not."

"Did!"

Solineus groaned as girls hustled his way with wine and bigger smiles than normal after hearing Adinvan's bellowed tale.

Adinvan nudged Sîu's shoulder. "His memory bein' gone is so much fun; he don't know what's horseshit and not."

"I heard that. Now, shut yer yap." He huffed and straightened as Sêeloru approached.

"Lords Mikjehemlut and lady Sîu! It's so wonderful to see you again so soon. How might I assist you today?" She gestured to the desk, and they took seats.

"I need a second chair, for starters, so I might regale my boy with his forgotten youth."

"He needs no such thing. We stumbled on the Holdimun Building today and noted it was for sale. Fortuitous as we've been considering a need for a warehouse and forming a trade company."

Sêeloru smiled. "Prudent. You'll need certified legal counsel who's a resident of Mulshahar to process such a deal in combination with the property."

"How about you?"

"Gracious, no. At my age? But I appreciate your faith in me."

"Too bad, I'll be looking to hire as a permanent position for all my dealings in Mulshahar, although, of course, my banking will remain here."

"Of course."

"I want someone who speaks Silone, Kingdomer, Gorô, Edan... anything else practical."

Sîu said, "Islander tongues."

Solineus nodded and watched as two young women stepped forward and two young men took prideful steps from farther away, but Murêshu stood still. His mistake took a flicker to sink in: she wasn't yet qualified in Trade Law.

Sêeloru waved her hand in the direction of the four who lined up at the side of the desk. "All of these fine people are qualified, in general, though I'm not certain of languages."

Solineus spoke in Edan, "If any of you speak the tongue of the Mother Wood, raise your right hand and nod at the same time." Only one woman complied with accuracy, while a man raised a hand but didn't nod. "If any of you speak the Goro tongue, raise your left hand and nod twice." All four complied. "If any of you speak Silone, raise both hands. None of you?"

Sîu said, "I would've thought someone would take it on themselves to learn the language of a new client."

Sêeloru clucked and shook her head. "I'm surprised no one took the initiative."

Solineus cast his eyes over the group and let his gaze linger on Murêshu. "You look like you have something to say." He pointed and spoke in Silone. "What do you wish to say?"

"I worked with Monzulor to study the language of Kaludor and took the opportunity to continue my studies."

Sêeloru rushed to stand beside the girl. "I fear she isn't yet qualified in Trade Law."

"No?"

Murêshu said, "No. But I've learned it all."

Sêeloru said, "What she knows does not matter. The law requires a certified practitioner."

"I see. What does certification require?"

The young woman who spoke Edan the best stepped forward. "I can learn Silone within two months if given a mentor. Best by learning from you and your people."

An unhappy wrinkle. "I'll be gone in a week, I hope. Is there any way to speed up this one's certification? I'm sorry. What is your name, girl?"

"Murêshu."

Sêeloru stuttered for a flicker, then recovered. "She, from what I hear, is a top student. A fee or donation might smooth things, seeing as she is so close. But I can't promise."

"If the donation is reasonable, I'll pay it. What would her contract cost?"

"Well, I... This is so sudden. Her contract extends another thirty-eight months, with the assumed Trade Law Certification, at least thirty-eight thousand Smedên. Nîsiminê here has only fourteen months remaining, so figure on fourteen thousand. No small savings for a guarantee."

Solineus gazed at the two women. He knew which he needed to hire but didn't want it to appear foolish. "This is tricky."

Nîsiminê said, "I have four years of legal experience beyond her training."

"An excellent point."

Murêshu said, "Master Yumûlm says I'm his finest student in twenty years."

"Despite my experience, I will extend my contract five years at my current pay."

Solineus laughed. "You ladies make my choice so difficult! Sîu, my dear. Which do you prefer?" He grinned at her, knowing how much she'd snarl at him later for tossing the battle her way.

But she didn't even flinch before a playful grin and an answer, "I like them both."

"Devilish." He turned, snagged a bottle from a third woman, and poured a glass. "Gods help me when my Sîu doesn't have an opinion. But at least now I know why you keep wine on hand. Father? Are you unhelpful as well?"

Adinvan grinned. "Afraid so."

Solineus sighed before taking a drink of wine, then a second sip. "You see, ladies, while Sîu finds you both appealing, I wonder not just who is most qualified but who is most trustworthy? You, Nîsiminê, are eager. A strong quality, but perhaps too eager to add five years. It makes me wonder who else you might work for. Yes? And you, Murêshu, were too timid to step forward when no one else spoke Silone."

"I am not timid."

"Not now that you've been challenged. Timid tigress." He slurped his wine and paced. "Here's what I'm going to do. I want a meeting set with the Holdimun Building's seller as soon as possible to discuss a price. If you, Murêshu, are certified by the time a deal is hammered, I will purchase your contract. If not, then Nîsiminê is the winner. I will hold you to the five years but not the pay."

Sîu said, "Have them join us at the negotiating table. Perhaps one will prove their worth. Perhaps they both will."

Solineus smiled and raised his glass. "Now I reckon you all see why she is my lady. So be it. Are we agreed?"

Murêshu smiled as she curtsied, all confidence. "Agreed."

Nîsiminê's curtsy came with the emotionless gaze of a predator, and he respected that. "Agreed."

Solineus freshened his wine and poured two glasses for Sîu and Adinvan before sitting. "About your business, ladies. Sêeloru, contact the buyer so I know when to expect a meeting."

A blushing smile from the woman. "I don't know who that is."

Solineus stared. "I'll find out."

"Excellent." She bustled from the desk, and Solineus waved at the remaining spectators. "Shoo now, away with you."

People scattered, and Adinvan leaned to whisper, "You put on a hells of a show."

Solineus grinned. "I'm sweating."

Sîu said, "What if she can't get certified?"

Solineus shook his head, convinced the Smiling Men would handle the timing, so long as the girl hadn't lied. "What I want to know is who Nîsiminê listens for."

"You're certain? Her aura was clean."

"Bet my life certain? No. We'll see them both again soon enough. Still, it doesn't matter. We're buying the building and hiring them both. Whoever Nîsiminê's ears belong to, it's a safe bet they aren't the Patrons of Mulshahar. We want her close and to know who's listenin'." He sipped his wine, wondering not what power outside of the Patrons of Mulshahar would be so curious as to send a spy, that could be anybody, but who could maneuver so fast.

THIRTY-SIX

The Ihomjo Mines

Noktoroku, the Boborun King of Efemorodu, sat atop his Throne of Flesh and watched the world bleed with a smile, content that if he was not to win this war, no one would.

—*The Oxeum Codex*

"A whole hells of a lot of my feeling good about this godsdamned plan is smoldering right godsdamn there." And in truth, he'd been feeling less and less good since stepping foot on Kaludor. The fire they'd been following since leaving Snow's Eye sat on a southern slope of Nerbendi Mountain, a location the Wolverine had long suspected being near Zjin's tribe of Colok, but this flat of rock overlooking sheer cliffs that only goats and Colok might call a trail didn't leave a clue as to who started the fire, why, and where they went. "I hope to hells your eyes see somethin' mine don't."

Rikis answered when the Edan remained silent. "We're bare-faced in the blizzard standing here."

"Aye, and our friends here don't give two pisses for the cold." He turned to Inslok. "I'll tell you now, I hunted Colok all over this mountain in the day and never did find wherever they call home."

Inslok rested his hand on the hilt of his scimitar as he scanned the area. "There are scuffs higher up the face of the cliff to the west, and prints I imagine human blurred by winds downhill."

"Humans. Taken, you mean." Pikarn was accustomed to Rinold the Squirrel seeing things he didn't. "Any dimples in the rocks from Shadows of Man?"

"Not that I notice from here."

"Aye, well, that's something good, at least. But we don't wanna follow anything in human boots unless it's our prints leading home. You think you can track the Colok?"

"Perhaps, but could you and the Trelelunin follow?"

He snorted with a chuckle; Trelelunin could bound up slopes he crawled as a young man. "If you're questioning your boys, this old man ain't goin' there."

Rikis said, "We could relight the fire and see if anyone comes."

"If Colok done lit the fire, I'd think they woulda stayed if able." He fidgeted, uncertain. "But might be they got away from whatever were after 'em. I'd say it's Inslok's call."

The fire blazed without striking flint, and for the first half-candle, Pikarn's nerves ate at his gut, but afterward, he grew bored and leaned against the nearby cliff. Then sat. Damned near nodded off before shaking the cobwebs and standing to pace for a time.

Rikis stepped in his path, nodding southwest. "What do you make of them clouds?"

"Rain. Won't make it to us til around sunset or after, but I don't want caught out in it if we can help it."

"If the Colok haven't arrived by now, they've a better chance at tracking us wherever we go than we do of finding them."

"Aye, that they do." He strolled to Inslok, who stood overlooking the cliff, where straight below, Trelelunin tended their horses.

"I'm thinkin' it's best if we make our way across the Omindi and into the mouth of the Ihomjo mines to shelter from the comin' storm."

Inslok gave a curt nod. "Indeed. A lightning storm could attract Daevu."

Pikarn snorted. "In that case, I insist we head for the Ihomjo."

They wound their way back down to the horses and departed within wicks, leaving the fire to smoke and burn for so long as it could. A couple of hours past midday, they dismounted and walked their horses down a switchback trail into Omindi Pass, and a candle later rode them up the opposite side. With no snow to block their way this time, they reached the abandoned miner's camp and the mouth of the cave before the sun settled on the western horizon and before sheets of cold rain swept the mountainside with peels of thunder rumbling above streaking bolts of lightning.

Pikarn gathered sticks from a pile of kindling and, to the amusement of the Trelelunin, started a fire the old-fashioned way with flint and tinder. Rikis joined him as a chilly wind howled into the adit of the mine, rubbing his hands over the flames as Pikarn heated water for tea with a kick of whiskey. "You're gettin' as bad as a Broldun with that whiskey."

"You want some?"

"Aye, just change my name."

"I tried to marry into the name but wasn't ugly enough."

"So you bedded her instead?"

"We all take what we can get in this life." He winked and poured the alcohol into two tin cups.

You'd make for a terrible Broldun, exceptin' the drinking part."

Inslok approached. "We made it this far without a serious threat from Shadows or Taken. It concerns me."

The Wolverine snorted as he topped off his whiskey with tea. "Oh aye, thanks to Daevu taking over the mountains. That *concerns* me, too."

"So long as it rains, this entry is safe from Shadows. I believe we should take this chance to explore this mine, as you theorized it was attached to the Chanting Caverns."

"Aye, and it was caved in if you recall."

A blink. "I said 'was attached'."

"You did at that, but what good you thinkin' it is to explore a collapsed tunnel?"

"It might be simple to clear."

"And I don't know the way one lick from here."

"If this is to be our base for forays into the Chanting Caverns, we should know its tunnels."

The damned Edan had him there, but he wasn't in the mood for walking horizons in the dark. "Aye, let's wait until dawn."

Rikis came to his rescue. "I'd say you should search the area for Colok now that you don't have us humans slowing you down."

Inslok cocked his head. "First, we should check these mines. If there is a group of Taken here, you shouldn't be left alone."

Rikis grinned. "Arm wrestle you for it."

Pikarn came so close to spitting his tea it dribbled from his lip. The two were of similar heights, but the Edan was of a more slender build. More like Solineus. More like a cougar compared to a bear, but bears surrendered their kills to cougars and wolverines alike sometimes. His first impression gave way to Inslok not being human. "You might think on that."

Inslok eyed them both. "What do you mean by arm wrestle?"

Rikis shrugged at Pikarn. "What's the worst that happens? He slams my hand to the table?" The Choerkin smiled at Inslok. "We sit

across the table from one another, lock hands like so, and try to take the other's arm down." He gestured, demonstrating his own victory with a grin.

"And you are saying, if you win, I search for Colok, but if you win, we search the mines as I suggest? This is agreeable."

Pikarn blurted, "No magic'n your way to a win!"

"Of course."

Rikis threw off his cloak and sat in a chair, its aging joints creaking under his weight. He rammed his elbow onto the table with a thud. The boy was a figurative monster with bulging arms, but some folks considered the Edan literal monsters, beings with powers outside the scope of human understanding. "Don't you go hurtin' this Edan; we need his sword arm."

Inslok sat across from Rikis, settled his elbow to the table, and took the Choerkin's hand. "Like this?"

"Aye, like that. On the count of three, you start." Pikarn eyeballed their grips, glanced between their eyes, and counted, "One. Two. Three!"

Inslok's arm fell back a fist before stopping, and Pikarn smiled. "You got the leverage, boy! Finish him. Take him down! Quit wastin' time." By now, the Wolverine's arm had been burning but still not in as poor a position. "Crush him!" But a glance showed Rikis' cheeks puffed and turning red.

Inslok said, "I am impressed by your strength." His face wasn't even flushed.

Pikarn sputtered, "I said no magic!"

Inslok's head bobbed and cocked as if independent of the effort his arm had to be exerting. "We all use Elemental Life to one extent or another. You, me, and Rikis. It is a healing force running through all living things, plants and animals alike."

"You know what the hell I mean!" Pikarn's eyes widened as he leaned into Rikis' face. "Now! Everything you got. Demolish this pompous woodkin."

"I am not *using* the Elements as you suggest."

Rikis grunted as his arm twitched, the back of his hand moving at the speed of a trebuchet's arm being winched—"No! No, no, no, no!"—the Wolverine protested until Rikis' knuckles tapped the table's top.

The Choerkin let go of Inslok and leaped to his feet, shaking his arm like a whip from hand to shoulder. "Godsdamned son of a bitch! Woah!" He leaned to the table, still shaking out his arm at his side.

The Wolverine sucked his teeth. "I hope yer still up for searching the mine."

"I'll be fine. Just give me a wick."

Inslok stood and said, "That was entertaining. You are a very strong man. We'll begin our search in a candle."

He wandered away, and Nevon stepped to the table with a smirk. "If your people don't have a saying for what happened, make one up."

Pikarn snorted. "Never bet an Edan?"

"It isn't funny, but excellent advice."

Rikis stood straight, rubbing his arm. "I've been slammed to the table before. Hells, I figured my father did me the worst, damn near breaking my knuckles. *That* was worse, even if it didn't make no noise. I might as well have been arm-wrestling a Colok."

Nevon nodded. "A Colok's hands are so big, their weight, they might challenge him."

Pikarn smirked. "Now I have another reason I wanna find the Colok. But first, thanks to this idiot Choerkin and his flabby arm, we gotta search this hole in the ground."

The miners who put their blood and sweat into what later became a tomb for many started their dig with a slope steep enough to feel in Pikarn's ankles as they descended, but at least there was nothing dark about the journey with three Edan in front. If their glowing forms hadn't sufficed to light the way, one of them ignited the tunnel forward and back with Elemental Light.

On the one hand, nothing would sneak up on them, and on the other, no way in hells anything other than a blind rat wouldn't know they were coming.

The entry shaft was maybe a hundred strides in length before leveling and reaching its first branches, two tunnels left and right at ninety-degree angles, precise and intended to explore the underground for veins of ore. Something about them lent the feel of these being original passages of a mine rediscovered. "You figure these are older tunnels?"

Inslok said, "I do. Did anyone mention where the collapse occurred?"

"Well, I seem to recall it being said to be deep, but what the hells does that mean? I can't say. I got the impression it was where they were workin'."

"There could be a shaft down anywhere, but we'll follow this tunnel first."

Their route remained more or less level as they passed a dozen more branches that appeared damned near identical with about fifteen strides between. Then, it ended in a divot chiseled from the wall, where three picks lay on the ground amid rubble. A handcart half-filled with chipped stones sat nearby.

Inslok glanced left and right down shadowless halls, then turned right without explaining his choice. "Do you know if your people had particular patterns when mining?"

Pikarn shrugged. "Can't say I spent much time underground, but from what little I did, I never noticed nothin' outside of the grid pattern to any tunnelin'."

"These remind me of tunnels beneath Ul-Matrothu."

"I'm afraid you lost me there, old man."

Inslok glanced his way. "Old man?"

"I'm old, meanin' it's good to point out you're older."

"I see. Ul-Matrothu is a series of mines in Mount Solmdrôk, one of the few diggings in the Mother Wood."

"I'll just assume there's a point."

"The miners there came upon a maze of caverns so chaotic they seemed dug by madmen, but there was no more point than to say these reminded me of those before reaching the maze."

Pikarn grimaced, afraid to ask. "And to what does that there maze lead to?"

"The best anyone knows, nowhere in particular."

"Fascinating. It looks like we have a shaft down up ahead."

"As suspected, the sound of the airflow suggested such."

Rikis thudded Pikarn's shoulder. "I can't believe you didn't hear that; it was so obvious."

"Oh, aye, I hear it now. Not so different than the sounds of m'boots dancin' on yer grave."

They descended a five-pole drop by ladder—passing four levels of tunnels—before reaching a slope that took them on a long, deep walk to a second series of squared turns. Pikarn snorted. "Well, leastwise, it ain't no maze. "

Inslok didn't say a word before striding ahead, turning left at the second turn. They moved onward, passing through a crossroads before entering a long stretch of tunnel. After a time, the Edan said, "There was a collapse ahead."

Nobody bothered to question him before the tunnel climbed and fell again, leading into a rubble-strewn chamber twenty paces around. Inslok held out his arms to stop their strides before entering. Bones, both shattered and whole, lay scattered, some still concealed in part by their burial in stone. A dozen picks joined the years-old carnage, looking as if dropped just yesterday.

"I damned well might know one of these men." He stepped forward, but Inslok's arm blocked him, and the Edan hissed.

Rikis said, "You hear something?"

Another hiss and Pikarn said, "I think that means shut the hells up."

Inslok lowered his arms and turned, gesturing to Neseldun and Limereu in a complex series of hand signals. Neseldun stepped to Pikarn's side and raised his arms, and The Wolverine felt beads of moisture forming on his skin. *Shits, they're expecting Shadows.*

A shimmering rainbow appeared in the Light the Edan projected into the room: red, orange, yellow, green, blue, indigo, and violet, a perfect arch hovering until sparkling beads wavered and danced into a display unimaginable and yet unimaginably real, *real* beyond the sense of sight, eliciting tinkling chimes as if water and light turned to crystal, and striking his nose with the smells of a thousand memories he couldn't name, and yet *unreal* in the uncountable variations of colors that dizzied his mind with wondrous possibilities, mesmerizing, tantalizing, and teasing until a shriek born from the Twelve Hells and the Bellows of the Forge shattered his trance, dropping him numb to his knees without a prayer.

Head lolling in a daze, he stared as an inconceivable form dropped from the ceiling, a mass without substance as colors sprayed and sparkled in and through the thing that shouldn't be. Shouldn't be alive, shouldn't be coming for him, shouldn't be in this world, shouldn't be

his end of days. His mind screamed, but if his voice made a sound, it was either a roar or a pathetic whimper, and it didn't matter which, for he understood the eternal damnation coming for his soul by way of his eyes. Closer, closer, narrowing tentacles tiny enough to penetrate his pupils and carry him away.

Splinters of infinite color fighting the singularity of Shadow exploded into shimmers of ruby red cast by Edan hands. Limereu's hands. And the scream of damnation fled his head, exiting his ears in reverse of how one should hear. And when he managed to blink again, all that remained was a perfect rainbow of red, orange, yellow, green, blue, indigo, and violet.

He wavered on his knees, leaning backward until his shoulders rested against someone's thighs. His mouth hung open, but he couldn't find the strength to close his lips. A creeping blink later, Inslok's hand approached his forehead, touched, and strength flowed into his muscles in euphoric spasms. Pikarn's teeth clacked in a seizing bite, eyes focusing as clear as in his youth, and he sprang to his feet. "Holy pissin' hells! What was that?"

"A flow of Elemental Life and Spirit combined. You are well?"

"Not even what I was talking about! That! That thing! The whole godsdamned blazing lights that about ate my shittin' itself soul!"

Inslok blinked. "It wasn't the Light about to eat your soul."

He turned to Limereu, hoping to find a more understanding and maybe sympathetic Edan. "The thing. What was it? Is it dead?"

"Dead? No. I couldn't banish it either if that was your next question."

"It wasn't, but it woulda been a good one. Now, what *was* it?"

"I don't know. Not a Shadow of Man."

"No shit?" He turned back to Inslok. "And you knew that damned thing was there?"

"No." He pointed, and Pikarn noticed a tunnel leading up for the first time. "But, I sensed the shaft above and yet could see nothing. It stood to reason that a being of Shadow or Elemental Dark hid the passage."

Rikis leaned past Pikarn's shoulder. "I'll be damned, look at that."

"You shut up. Next time, I hope that thing goes after you so we can share a decade of my nightmares to come. Little bastard Choerkin. So which was it, Dark or Shadow?"

The three Edan shared glances until Neseldun said, "There are implications in a section of the Oxeum Codex that speak of Shadow Demons who, for lack of a better understanding, ate or mated with *Mokotu-xe* of Elemental Dark. They bear the rather poetic name of Soul Scythes."

"Never did have an ear fer poetics. And you don't think you could've mentioned this?"

"Would it have helped?"

Pikarn stared for flickers. "No. I still woulda been too godsdamned terrified to shit m'self, but still... Hells with it. What's it mean? Where'd it come from?"

Inslok said, "We can only surmise it arrived from the Celestial Gate we seek to find."

Pikarn stepped into the room and looked up; a round shaft ran straight up, ignited by Light for a distance he couldn't guess. "That godsdamned gate was puny compared to Istinjoln. Like a year-old branch compared to a decades-old tree. Could something like that get through?"

Limereu huffed. "My memories remain fogged, but I'd say not if it is as you describe. However, a new Gate surges open. This beast may have been the first to arrive."

"And if the Queen of Shadow knows we're coming and sent this thing? One hells of a coincidence, don't you Edan think? First, these poor bastard miners dig right beneath this shaft, collapsing the ceiling on their heads, *then* that son of a bitch is waiting for us?"

"Your supposition bears merit."

Rikis snorted. "Godsdamned right it does."

Pikarn stared into the shaft, afraid to lower his eyes in case the thing came falling for him. Then, it struck him. "That there is round. We ain't seen a round hole in this damned place. I mean a perfect circle. And smooth. Your Edan eyes see a single pick mark?"

All three stepped forward and looked up, and Neseldun said, "Observant. Miners using Elemental Stone could achieve this."

"One godsdamned trouble, my people use iron."

"Yes, not even your priests would accomplish this."

Inslok said, "Fascinating, but we have a bigger problem." He cast his eyes on Limereu. "If we intend to rest in the entry above, can we ward its evil?"

She shook her head. "I don't believe so. Even if I could collect all the enchanted gem powder I used to ward Pikarn, this Soul Scythe is a force requiring forgotten expertise. Slowing its approach is the best we can hope for with runes alone. We should not underestimate its ability to harm any of us, even if it went after him first. I can put down an Elemental wall with crushed gems. I doubt it will stop the creature, but it will howl to cross it."

Pikarn didn't like the sound of anything that could kill an Edan but appreciated the notion of hurting it. "That's a whole lotta fancy chatter to me, and none of it sounds good, but what the hells does it mean? We get the hells out and go home?"

Inslok blinked. "No. It means we take more precautions and never travel alone in these caves or the Chanting Caverns when we get there. Until at least we understand this enemy or destroy it."

"I like the sound of that!" He clapped his hands, still burning with energy from Inslok's touch. "So, how about we start by getting away from this hole?"

THIRTY-SEVEN

Feline Grasses

I awoke in the tomb of the world without knowledge of my name or my past. I couldn't escape, trapped in a place I erred in thinking was timeless, until a man offered me a choice: Learn my name and return to the world, or live forever with parchment and pen instead of a name. Upon my decision, I discovered I made the same choice four times before.

—*Author Forgotten*

Kurin led them through Harberdên Pass five days after departing Yusdelên, and instead of riding for the capital of Klondihîk, they made for Jumark. In theory, anyone interested enough to guess their destination would assume they headed for Klondihîk, making the Pigeonmaster in Jumark less likely to be bought before they had a chance. The Kingdom of Barkûsh stood in pleasant contrast to Danlok, with the people warmer despite the chillier air, or maybe it was an overdue bath and bottle of wine in Jumark that mollified her impressions. Kurin carried their messages to the local Pigeonmaster alone to reduce suspicions and addressed them to a retired Wayfinder who would pass the notes along. Pigeons took flight, but there was no way to know if their flight paths were as promised. It was the best they could do, and she could only pray for the Pigeonmaster's integrity and the pigeons' health. Whether betrayed or not, she rode onto the Ilu-Stronô Plains in higher spirits and brimming with optimism.

An optimism others didn't share.

Commander Florinz and Edlmir flanked her every step of every horizon they crossed, and even with six outriders ahead who never left their line of sight, they found only signs of Ilu encampments, most several days old. The funny thing was that everyone but her was happy not to see the Ilu coming their way, and Meliu thought she might be crazy to wish for a meeting, but she couldn't help herself.

Without permanent cities or roads on the Ilu plains, the map in Meliu's head stood empty, but she figured they approached the halfway mark, and Kurin insisted they'd either run into a road, the sea, or both and find their way to Mulshahar with ease so long as nothing killed them. Ironic, considering that Meliu had yet to see a threat, anything other than poisonous snakes that preferred to slither out of their way instead of bite.

They reached a broad stream, or small river, heading toward sundown, and instead of crossing, they decided to take the opportunity to refill barrels and boil water for their canteens before moving on.

Meliu strolled to Kurin's fire and sat. "So, where are these terrible tigers out to kill us all? I haven't seen a one."

Kurin snorted and hung a pot of water for tea over the blaze. "They're watching us, and if the Hokandite is kind, they'll leave us be another couple of weeks so we can get to Mulshahar faster than expected."

"Watching? They've seen us pass?"

"No. Watching us, as in watching me boil water, and you make a fool of yourself."

Meliu didn't bother to look around; with tall grasses everywhere that weren't water and bank, there wasn't a point. "You're sure? How many?"

"Not enough to kill us all, four or five, I'd guess, but I wouldn't doubt there's a tribe or war party not far away. Rivers like this attract every man and beast that drinks." She grinned as she grabbed a tin cup from her pack. "Tea?"

"Got wine in there?"

"I'm sure you stocked a dozen bottles through Jumkar."

Meliu snorted. "Only two; a lady has to be practical in these lands." She gazed out the grasses blowing on the ridge. "You know where they are?"

"No. I caught signs throughout the day, and when we pitched camp grasses here and there drifted wrong. They could be anywhere, but they're here."

"Solineus got to meet them. Got to know them. One even licked his wound, so I'd wager they liked him."

"Liked the taste of him?"

"Well, it was a woman Ilu..."

Kurin chuckled. "Naughty priestess."

"My naughty thoughts are all I have these days." She stood. "They like Solineus, so I'll be like Solineus."

"What the devils are you talking about?"

"You'll see." She stepped to her packs on the ground and pulled out a bottle of wine. "Like Solineus with a touch of Meliu." She strode past Kurin, and Edlmir came running from behind.

"What the hells you doin'?"

"Shush and go away."

He stopped in his tracks. "Don't get yer ass eaten."

"I'm sure they'd pick a piece not so saddle-worn." The man didn't laugh, but she knew he wanted to. Her eyes scanned the rise of the hill, seeing nothing, and halfway up, she stopped and raised the bottle of wine. "*Gostelium finshol!* Solineus. Ivin." She tapped her chest. "Meliu. *Gostelium finshol.* Nostrolum."

The wind blew, and grass rustled, but she didn't see a thing. Then she heard Kurin from behind. "You wanted their attention. You got it."

"What the hells are you talking about? I see nothing? *Gostelium finshol!* Nostrolum." She tapped her chest. "Meliu. *Gostelium finshol.* Nostrolum."

A hulking shadow rose a mere ten paces in front of her, and she squeezed her bladder to keep from peeing herself, and a flicker later giggled without a good reason. The Ilu was close to seven feet tall with tawny golden fur and topaz eyes and wore little armor or protection from the weather. "*Gostelium finshol?*"

"*Gostelium finshol.* I know Nostrolum. Ivin and Solineus."

He pointed with the same predator's stare she recalled years ago on the Ar-Bdêin's boat. "Meliu?" He poked his chest. "Elummôer *sêtis vîsun ubul. Temû?*"

She smiled and spoke in Kingdomer. "I'm sorry, all I know is *gostelium finshol.* I met Nostrolum far to the north."

The Ilu looked left and right and said, "*Beveredesh nê mubolum?*" A hiss from twenty strides to her right shivered her spine, followed by another to her left. He looked back at her with a nod. "*Gostelium finshol.*" He turned and strode away up the hill, and seven more Ilu rose from the grasses all around to follow him.

"Wait!" She waved the bottle. "Wine? Damn it." The Ilu disappeared over the rise, and she strolled back to Kurin's fire to find the commander and Edlmir staring at her. Everyone stared. Meliu smiled at the Wayfinder. "For or five, my ass."

"I wasn't so far off."

Florinz frowned, no doubt squelching fiery words. "That was reckless. Forget yourself. You could've gotten us killed. You still might have."

She sighed with a shrug. "I don't think so. If they wanted us dead, they would've come at us by now." She looked to Kurin. "Am I right?"

"Ilu war parties have been known to gather by the hundreds fast. And the range of their bows? She is right. And she is wrong because she should not have gone."

Florinz nodded. "Done is done. What did he say?"

"I haven't a clue. If he spoke Kingdomer, he didn't let on, but I think I was right, *gostelium finshol* is a phrase they respect. Nostrolum probably told us this so we wouldn't die if ever we came to his homeland."

"But you don't know what the hells you said."

"Nope!"

"The next time madness strikes, give me fair warning."

"Agreed." She sat beside the fire and gave a flirty grin. "Drink on it?"

He shifted his weight. "After that, I could use a drink."

Edlmir pulled a flask from his jacket. "Don't bother wasting your wine on me. I'm good."

They drank, talked, and laughed until after the sun went down, and she looked into darkness now and again, expecting to see Ilu eyes gleaming in the fire's light, but the only glow was the streaking trails of light from lightning bugs dancing.

Meliu awoke as dawn's light lit her eyelids, and she prayed away a hint of hangover as she stood to stretch. Groggy men crawled from their bedrolls all around while others sat gnawing on dried foods, but her eyes went to the hills around them as soon as the fog faded from her thoughts. There was no sign of the Ilu, but then, she hadn't seen a sign the night before until one almost scared the piss right out of her.

They struck camp half a candle later and rode east, crossing the shallow river without catching sight of Ilu, and by the end of the day, Meliu's hopes of meeting them again deflated. They were a week out from their meeting with the Ilu when her mind turned back to reaching Mulshahar. The party was striking camp, and she was tying her bedroll to her saddle when she heard the shout.

"Runners to the east! Coming fast."

Commander Florinz bellowed, "How many?"

"Runnin' in a line. I'd guess a dozen."

Meliu swung into her saddle and trotted to within earshot of Florinz. "Fair warning, I'm going to go say hello."

"I don't suppose you'll wait for me to get saddled?"

"No." Meliu heeled her horse into a gallop and reined east until stopping atop the next rise. The Ilu weren't hiding this time, a train of jogging warriors with spear points glinting in the sun. She prayed for Elinwe's vision, and her heart jumped to escape through her smile. "Gods above! Nostrolum."

She leaned and squeezed her horse into a full run, struggling to believe her eyes even as she grew closer. Even as she reined to a stop just feet from his fanged grin. "Meliu!" He trotted to her side, looking up but not by so much as she'd expected. Somehow, she'd forgotten how massive Nostrolum was. "Elummôer said you speak Kingdomer?"

"I do."

He shook his head with a rumble-purr. "If I'd known, we could have spoken long ago."

She laughed, happier to see him than she'd ever imagined. "I learned their language after we met. By the gods! I'm so happy to see you made it home alive."

He nodded. "It wasn't an easy journey. And you made it, too! Though not home."

She shrugged, not even the reminder of Kaludor killing her smile. "Some things weren't meant to be."

He cocked his head, more serious in an instant. "Ivin Choerkin?"

It struck her, and the corners of her mouth fell a tick. "He made it home." Funny that she'd never quite thought of it that way. "For him, it was meant to be." He smiled, and her smile returned.

"I saw your face and hair in smoke visions, but never expected you here."

She recalled tales of Solineus' hallucinogenic journey, even if she suspected he left out details. "It's good to know some visions come true. You didn't run all this way for a few words. Come! Let's have breakfast. Meet my people."

He gave a curt nod. "Your fires, but our home, so we will feed you." He said something to his people, and eight of them trotted off down the ridgeline. She reined her horse and walked toward camp, and Nostrolum strode by her side.

"You are a leader of your people?"

He cocked his maned head for a flicker. "Like a king? No. I lead a hunting party and am what I think is called cousins with the *Ishûm*, which you might call king."

She nodded. "My people don't have a king either, and hopefully, we won't have one any time soon. Did you meet Solineus when he passed through this area?"

"I heard of Ivin's friend, but he traveled farther south and met the Pride of Mêolu. I was north, the Orstân Rift, when I heard of him. I heard word of your people reaching the mountains far to the east. What brings you to the Ilu-Stronô Plains?"

"We're heading for Mulshahar in hopes of finding Solineus."

He grunted. "The city we call Big Red for their domes. It is prettier than it is safe for my people anyhow."

She reined her horse near Kurin's fire, swung from the saddle, and dropped the reins when no one volunteered to take them. "Nostrolum, this is Kurin of Helmveline, a Wayfinder. Over there is Commander Florinz Ravinrin. The big bastard trying to hide behind shorter people is Edlmir."

Nostrolum nodded to each. "Welcome to the Ilu-Stronô Plains. A proper welcome."

Florinz bowed. "I thank you. Friends are a welcome sight wherever we travel."

Meliu said, "Let everyone know we're settling in for a second breakfast. I suspect a feast."

"Yes. There is a herd of bison not far away. Fresh meat."

Florinz turned to Edlmir. "Let everyone know we'll be here for a time." The Ravinrin stepped to stand before the great cat and offered his hand. "A proper welcome."

Nostrolum's paw swallowed the man's hand as they shook. "You have traveled far if I understand rumors of where your people settled. After demons drove you from your home?"

"The tell is sad but so. We were fortunate to meet the people of Helmveline on reaching the Dragonspans. The Foundations."

He smirked. "The Longtail Mountains."

"Let us sit and talk."

The group took a seat by the fire while the remaining Ilu kneeled, the longbows on their backs tickling the ground. Nostrolum turned to Kurin. "I have heard of Wayfinders. Great hunters."

The woman smiled. "We hunt, but our fame resides in waystones and a keen sense of direction."

"Yes. Wayfinders from Barkûsh and other kingdoms came to search the Rift over the years. Some we allowed, some we did not."

Kurin grunted, and her tone suggested she was more worried about what they were hunting for than whether they lived or died.

"That is news to me. I've only heard of the Orstân Rift. What did they seek?"

"They were less than forthcoming, which is why most never left."

Kurin grinned. "I hope none of those were from Hemveline."

Nostrolum shrugged and looked at Meliu. "I spoke often of the flame-haired woman with a prayer for Darkness who saved me. So much so that an Ilu I'd never met brought word of you to me."

"My hair is oddly famous."

A rumbling chuckle. "So, Mulshahar, to find the friend of Ivin. Why would he still be in Mulshahar?"

She shrugged with a roll of her eyes. "More apt he circled the continent than stayed there, but he has business dealings there."

Nostrolum grunted. "It is a striking city with a reputation for striking like a viper. Sometimes with vipers."

"The man has faced worse, I guarantee it."

"Let us hope. A journey so far suggests a great cause."

She ducked her head and sighed. "When we first passed south beyond the Foundations, Histê slavers took some of our people. We got word of where some of them are being held, on the coast near the Medrisên Sea, and hope to reach and free them with Solineus' help."

"A great and noble cause. I have heard of these Histê. Southern prides who roam the forests there speak of them with ill words."

"Ilu in the forest? We didn't see... Of course, we didn't see them."

"Where are your people?"

"A city called Ghustusvarênu, along the Arkudân River, wherever that is. From what we know, it's roughly fifty horizons inland."

Nostrolum nodded. "I know little about places so far to the south, but I've heard the river's name. I've kin in the forest Mulshahar calls Utumwu. If this Ghustusvarênu is close, they will know at least something about the area."

She smirked. "We don't have time to travel and ask."

"I will send word. If they are able to help, they will watch you and your people along the northern side of the Arkudân. If they can and are willing."

"We will appreciate all the help we can find."

"You saved me from slavery. The least I can do is help you save your people. With this Wayfinder, you make a straight line for Mulshahar, yes? Not always is the straight line the fastest."

Kurin said, "Any suggestions?"

"The route you take will lead straight into the Milobôs Badlands. It begins as innocent as the smile of a liar, but days later, the ruts and ravines twist your path, and if it floods? For my heroine of flaming hair, I have more than a suggestion. We will lead you as close to Mulshahar as we are able before saying farewell."

Commander Florinz said, "A generous offer—"

"That we can't accept," said Meliu, "unless you agree to teach me more of your language."

A joyful laugh thundered, revealing the size of his teeth and reminding her why she was happy they were friends. "Done."

Kurin said, "It makes me less useful, but learning new routes is what I love. Yet, something is sticking in my craw. These Wayfinders at the Rift, the ones you didn't kill—"

"I killed none."

"That your people killed. Even though they were killed, your people must have learned something from them. Why were they there? What were they looking for? It's not like the Rift is hard to find."

He shrugged. "Ruins of some city from the God Wars is what I heard."

"Your people must have questioned... wrestled more information from those killed."

"You mean torture?" He shrugged. "We Ilu ask with kindness and deal swift kills when we dislike the answer; that is the way of The Eternal Hunt. We are not your silly pussy cats who play with mice until they escape."

Kurin cleared her throat. "I didn't mean to imply—"

Meliu said, "He's joking. Trust me, this one has a peculiar sense of humor that goes so far as to play dress up."

"You ruint my fun!" Nostrolum grinned. "I was dashing in the dinner coat, don't lie."

"He was handsome despite the poor fit."

He grunted with a nod. "An honest human. But, no, my people didn't torture for answers. The deaths of these people were, to be raw, minor happenings. You have already given them more thought than those who killed them."

Kurin grimaced. "I see." She licked her lips and glanced at Meliu. "Does the name Hulumbor sound familiar? A city or ancient kingdom?"

Nostrolum scratched behind his ear. "Maybe?"

Meliu said, "What is Hulumbor?"

Kurin said, "A city, a kingdom, from the Forgotten past. There is a place in the Foundations called the Cliffs of Wisdom, where histories were carved so no Forgetting could steal them. There is a famous passage called *The Lie of the Raging Eye*, and one part reads: *And the priests prayed, and the Oracle of Menzên declared the Stone of Emf-hul found in the Temple of the Great Rift, and her visions would lead their way.* The Stone of Emf-hul is the coin Solineus recovered from Hîmr's shrine. Morik told me they believe that Pîlôstar the Skywind found the stone early in Remembered Time and placed it atop Hîmr's Shrine. Hidden in plain sight and damned near impossible to reach."

"If it was on the mountain, why search for it in the Rift?"

"Because few or none knew this truth." Her brow scrunched. "But some did know, the priestess who stole the coin among others. If they knew but still searched for the city, what were they looking for?"

Meliu said, "Then you think the Dark Waters might have been among them?"

Commander Florinz said, "I'm so lost, I need a Wayfinder. What is this coin? Stone?"

Kurin sucked her teeth and then whistled as her eyes rose to the sky. "Dark Waters, very likely. A long tale I'll save for later. Nostrolum, you're sure you heard nothing more?"

"No. But several died to not to give the answer."

Meliu groaned, then caught sight of Ilu in the distance, running in a line as before, but when she prayed for vision, she saw they carried the carcasses of two bison on poles. "Another mystery we haven't time to explore, but at least we'll have fresh meat soon."

Thirty-Eight

An Armor Too Far

In a time of unknowing, the enfeebled elder may be seen as a god. In a time of darkness, a woman on fire may be seen as a savior. In a time of war, a madman with violence in his heart may be seen as a hero.

—*Sememôto the Elder*

The lesson Loduma took from the meeting with Mîkêl wasn't that peace could be had for a price, but rather that he needed to get the Sword of Bdein from Sardôn Stôltmor before the son of a bitch found out he was in town. That was if he didn't already know. If Mîkêl wasn't in truth willing to trade the streets for peace, what might he have earned from the Stôltmors for a chance at Loduma's head? He doubted this. Mîkêl's sincerity won over even his skeptical heart enough not to expect betrayal, but reality forced him to consider it possible.

He'd already wasted too much time.

So, for the past two weeks, he and his men climbed their ladder into doom and explored the tunnels leading to the Palace of Bdein while Lundarn spread the rumor of Loduma being seen in several villages outside of Bdein and headed toward Gomjon. While Loduma knew one route, the tunnels branched dozens of times, and he needed to make sure none of them had been discovered. They Turned up nothing but dust, cobwebs, and the occasional skeleton of a rat, mouse, or bigger critter unknown. Nothing to pose a risk. This left him teaching his men of the palace and its passages the best he could recall. He drew a map and surprised the three men with how simple and relatively small the palace was.

Walking the defensive walls would put a horizon on a man's shoes, and the massive manor most folks considered "The Palace" stood as a horseshoe with hundreds of regal rooms and could house thousands. But having lived there, Loduma considered what many called the Manor of Ar-Bdein as The Palace proper, and it was four stories and only sixty rooms. An only that was a lot, but it was a hell of a lot easier than learning a number north of five hundred. Plus, he couldn't have drawn a map of the whole from memory.

The key, as Gimin pointed out every day, was where to find the Sword of Bdein.

They studied and explored and, on a drizzly, overcast day, doused their nerves and headed for his childhood home in the Palace of Bdein. Loduma flipped a latch after listening at the wall for half a candle, then shoved. Hinges opened on ancient grease with the slightest rub, and they stood inside a garderobe with a sink and toilet.

Gimin's eyes widened. "You shit into gold?"

Loduma grimaced, embarrassed by the excess after living his more recent years in common places, and whispered, "Pissed there too. It's not like we built this place."

Gimin shook his head in disgust, but Kworgin dropped his britches and sat. "Chilly as hell." He stood and tied himself back up with a grin. "Not every damned day I get to do that."

Loduma stifled a laugh and leaned on the door, opening it into an empty hall. This area of the palace was little used even when the household stood full of family and servants, something Stôltmor was unlikely to possess. He looked in both directions to see no one and exhaled, convincing himself he knew what he was doing. One of the great uncertainties was also a thing he expected he knew the answer to: Where did Sardôn Stôltmor live?

A wise man might choose to live in any of the sixty-two rooms, and a paranoid man might move around within the hundreds available to him. But Loduma considered Sardôn of middling intellect and confident to the point of arrogance. He was also a petty man who bore grudges against both the Ar-Bdeins for not showering his family with the influence they deserved and the Turlids for not crediting them with the plan to oust the Ar-Bdein family. No doubt, the Turlids feared the power-hungry Stôltmors, but they only dressed them down when they should have executed them. Just like his uncle Gier should've done. All this rationalizing pointed to Sardôn taking residence in one place, and one place only, the Chamber of the Ar, the lavish home to Geir Ar-Bdein, the last of his name to sleep there. And if Loduma's logic prevailed, the Sword of Bdein would rest in the Armory of the Ar alongside other family relics if they hadn't been plundered.

Gimin said, "I should go with you."

"No. You stay here. If I'm seen, I'll stand out less." He wore old clothes from his days in the palace, frilled silks that fit a little tighter than they used to, and he carried himself in the manner of nobility, something none of these three could say. "Remember. If you hear alarms, sit tight. Shouts and I don't come a runnin'? Sit tight, and you know where I'll be hidin' if alive. Don't come looking for me for at least four candles after the alarms end."

"And if we don't find you, get the hell out." Gimin nodded. "I still don't like it."

"I'm not in love with it either, but I'm married to it." He closed the door on them and strolled right and slipped into the stiff and dignified walk of an Ar-Bdein lord. He smiled as he passed through marble halls, not to fit in, but because of the memories this place regurgitated into his mind. Playing cat and mouse with his cousins and hiding from his uncles to avoid bruisings he may or may not have deserved. In his youth, he'd both hated and loved his kin, more the former than the latter, but looking back, he wondered how petty childhood vengeance brewed so hot that he managed to justify betraying them to the Turlids.

Not directly, no, but he'd know what Temûru Yûmin would do when he told her his uncle's plans. Doomed plans, a fool's plans, a dead man's plans, even without Loduma's betrayal, and he wagered the Turlids would let him live and won this bet. It took less than a year to realize his victory was a loss, as he and the sword were cast into the city to suffer the threats of both those loyal and disloyal to the Ar-Bdein. Another three months before he fled into the wilds and found himself in Thôn, hoping to die.

He turned into a hall and climbed stairs, taking him to the second floor, as only one staircase in the Manor of Ar-Bdein traveled all four floors, and the key had been in Gier's pocket when he died. He turned left, hearing voices down a hall, and instead of hiding, walked with slow arrogance and didn't bother to look at the voices who grew louder, and at least three people passed him a hall away. The cadence of his breaths didn't speed or slow, keeping steady as he'd been trained for negotiations and subterfuge. Flickers later, he climbed to the third floor, and moments later, all he had to do was take a victorious hop to land on the steps leading to his destination, but with no one in sight, he hesitated. Stood still, eyes passing back and forth.

More than ten years had passed since setting foot on these stone steps, and this time, he couldn't help but wonder if he walked into a trap. By all rights, whoever remained of the Stôltmor family should be enjoying lunch, leaving these upper halls empty of all but a few servants and perhaps a guard or two. Most servants should even be dining unless some task drew them here. Three deep breaths and he leaped as he'd promised, the way he'd done as a child, and climbed with silent, rolling strides until spotting legs draped in blue and green livery, the color of the Stôltmor's.

No hesitation now, and neither fear nor doubt, just a smile as he gripped daggers hidden in his sleeves. The guard carried a shortsword suitable for a fight in close quarters, a breastplate peaked from beneath the family colors, and mail links covered his arms, but he wore an open-faced helm. "Greetings! Is Sardôn in his chambers? I missed him at our noon meal."

The man's mouth opened, but Loduma leaped steps in strides, dagger rising to slash the right side of the man's throat before his sword was halfway from its sheath, and with a flick, his hand drove a dagger into his eye. He held the man as he died, easing him to the floor and taking two breaths before testing the door. Unlocked. Stôltmor arrogance on display, or a lack of faith in the lock. It was swung open on silent hinges, and he laid eyes on the immense room for the first time since the week the Ar-Bdeins were first driven from Bdein.

It wasn't what it used to be. The colors of the blankets and sheets had faded, and dust covered the walls and half-empty shelves where books had once been packed tight. He looked to the ceiling with a smile and breathed easier. A grandiose painting depicted the sky traveling from sunrise to sunset with Pulvûer in the middle. He held the Battle-ax of Novund in one hand and a cluster of grapes in the other, and upon the clouds floating across the room lounged his war maidens, beautiful priestesses he fantasized about as a youth. He snorted, disgusted that his time here was so short.

Doors sat to his left and right, sunrise and sunset, leading to the lord's and lady's dressing rooms, respectively. A temptation to look inside his aunt's chambers, forbidden to all men, tickled his fancy, but common sense won out. Without a soul in sight, he turned left and passed through the door, entering a closet big enough to stable six horses before reaching a second door. The space was barren compared to the past, but his goal was the Lord's Armory, better known as The Steel Room. Carved oak stood as the portal to his hopes and dreams, and as it whispered open, the pessimist inside expected to find nothing but guards.

His breath left him. He stifled a giddy laugh. The Sword of Bdein hung in the same place it had over a decade ago and where it had hung since before he was born until an ill wind carried it away. He stepped until his nose was within fingers of the blade, and his breath reflected back onto his lips with wet warmth. "You know me. I am Loduma Ar-Bdein, and I've come for you." The sword didn't care, and if it had, he imagined it might make light of him as an Ar-Bdein who should never have inherited such a treasure, a mere cousin of the bloodline. An Ar-Bdein who lost the sword to a witch and her northern barbarian. He lifted it from its hanger and slipped it into the sheath that lay beneath it, slung its belt over his shoulder, and then looked around.

The room was much like it had been on those rare times he'd been allowed inside, with many of the heirlooms still intact, with one glaring absence: Gier's breastplate and helmet likely sunk in the Mighty Fulgar after his murder. He ignored them and turned to leave but hesitated, glancing at the door to the master stair that would take him to the first floor faster than his previous route. He smacked his lips, then

strode straight to an alcove where an urn once sat, holding the ashes of Bîborn Ar-Bdein, the first to rule this city after the Great Forgetting. He didn't bother to ponder long on what they would've done with the man's remains or why and ran his finger along a crack in the mortar. The key rattled.

He smiled as he took the tip of a dagger and nudged the key into his waiting palm, and he dared consider that he might have missed his calling by not being a burglar. He strutted to an iron-banded door with a massive bolt for a lock, and the key slid home, turning with a click. He stepped into the stairwell, never intending to look back, but he did.

A panoply of armor with a helm hung not far away, covered by a blue and green tabard sewn with golden thread, but as he blinked, he swore the armor beneath might be Ar-Bdein. He swallowed his smarts after biting on temptation and reached the stand with swift strides, flipping the linen off and away. The armor didn't belong to his uncle but to some kin several generations removed. No breastplate, but it was double mail, so-called king's mail, because it was so expensive. He leaned to glance back through the closet and into the bedroom, then slung the sword from his shoulder, hefted the glinting mail over his head, and rattled it down his body with a grin like a child breaking into his parent's liquor cabinet.

A man hollered from outside, "Assassin!" and he heard swords being drawn, more than he wanted to fight. He grabbed the Sword of Bdein and sprinted for the stairwell, slamming the door, and only then remembering he left the key in its hole. He blinked and almost ran but instead blurted, "Shit!" as he cracked the door and reached his fingers outside. He nabbed the key, pulled, then pushed and turned and pushed before it slipped out, and he palmed it. He eased the door closed as feet and whispers entered the room with a rush and turned the key with a click he feared too loud. He held his breath a flicker, wondering if they'd heard before deciding he didn't care. He slinked down the first dozen steps as he righted the mail on his shoulders, then bound two and three steps at a time, passing floors without exits until reaching the bottom.

A deep breath and a listen before he slipped the key in the lock and turned, nudged the door open to glance into the hall. No one in sight, but running feet echoed and grew louder. He slipped the door closed, eased the lock back in place, and waited. The booted feet charged his way with the clamor of armored men, but they passed him by. He counted to twenty before opening the door a second time, then stepped into the hall and locked it from outside, then raised his leg to drop the key into his boot as a second prize. Confidence growing, he strutted toward the golden garderobe at the pace of a man who needed to use it.

He passed a hall and heard voices from its length too late, and instinct turned his eyes. Four guards froze as a chime rang out, a chime he'd heard only once in over twenty years of life in the palace: Intruder alarm. The high-pitched bells struck four times, and he knew they'd pause before repeating. The guards down the hall noticed him for the first time, a paused glance with quizzical stares, and he figured they would put him together with the chimes in a flicker. As soon as he was past the corner, he ran. If he could slip through the secret door without being seen, he'd be safe. Even if spotting him entering the garderobe, it would give him time enough for them to escape before Stôltmor's men found the latch.

Two soldiers with their hands on hilts turned a corner ahead, and he veered into a hall that led to the audience chamber—if he took to its natural end—and his jog turned into a sprint past four doors and two more halls until coming to an oval room where guests met to mingle in the past. Instead of continuing straight, he turned right,

slipping into the Chapel of Pulvûer's Peace—one of seven—from the backside. Prayer-Keepers would've been here every candle of the day in the past, but he was all alone today and thankful for it. He trotted into the vestibule, peeped into the hall, and jerked his head back. Several guards turned, walking his way with quick strides.

He backed into the deepest shadows he could find, an alcove, and crouched to catch his breath as much as hide. He stifled his breaths, forcing his lungs into a quieter pace and slowing his heart so its drumming didn't give him away. He took his daggers in hand and waited, comforted by the sword on his back and the armor that hastened his trouble. Sweat beaded and ran down his nose as footfalls arrived and paused. The rustle of robes nearby and a shadow stepped close then past him, but flickers later returned to the hall and moved on.

Loduma's eyes flicked back and forth like a nervous pendulum, waiting for footsteps to fade down the hall. Silence. But the hall passed the length of the vestibule and chapel. *How long until silence means gone?* He tried to count, but nerves got the best of him, so he ducked his head as if in prayer and waited until he could squat no more.

He crept to poke his head out and regretted it; the guards stood at the end of the hall expecting nothing but on watch. One appeared to look his way, and his feet propelled him into the hall on instinct, unwilling to assume that the man's eyesight might have failed. A two-hundred-foot lead on men in heavier armor, or so he promised himself, would keep him alive, but he forgot he wasn't so young anymore and spent the better part of his last couple of years sitting on his ass.

He turned and turned again with the sound of boots getting closer; he was where he needed to be, but there was no getting into the garderobe without being seen. "Gimin! Change of plans!"

He'd warned them to be ready if they heard the alarm, but the garderobe door didn't open. Did he run past the door and hope to make it back, or pray he could somehow bar the door? He hit the door, shoved it open, slammed it shut in a fury. "Gimin!" The door pounded, and his feet slid until they hit Kworgin's boots.

"I see ya brought friends."

"And if too many more come, we'll be dead before they can torture us."

Gimin stood with his sword ready in the tight space. "Let the bastards in."

Loduma eased off when the next blow came, and armored men stumbled and damned near tumbled as the door crushed him against the wall.

Gimin drove into the unsuspecting men, pommel smashing the back of a leaning head to ring his helm and send him to the floor. Loduma heard the fighting but couldn't see anymore until he squeezed from his trap and collapsed to the ground. Scrambled back to draw the Sword of Bdein and dipped the blade over Gimin's shoulder to strike a man in the face. Not a killing blow, but the man and others backed toward the hall for space to fight.

He lunged forward in chase and felt something strike up and under his mail and into his thigh. He snarled, looking down on the man Gimin had driven to the floor, and drove the sword to glance off his chin and into his throat. An ax sliced the air over his head as he went to a knee, and he drove low through a gap in combatants and ripped upward, the blade skating off armor until clipping the man's cheek as he leaned.

Kworgin bellowed as a slash ran bloody red down his arm, and a guard hooked his feet, dropping him to the ground to stomp on his head. Loduma leaped past Gimin with a powerful swing that crunched the bone of his face, starting beneath the nose and ending when the blade reached his ears. The man dropped like a lightning-struck bull, and Loduma stood over his friend, parrying an incoming strike and

another rattling his armor. Gimin struck another down, and in a flicker, they stood panting while surrounded by bodies.

Loduma rushed into the garderobe and opened the secret door. "Hurry! Get Kworgin inside."

Blood spattered Gimin enough he couldn't judge the man's wounds, but as Yovun dragged their friend, he stumbled, coughed, and blood leaked from his lips and down his chin.

Gimin said, "We should leave him."

"No! They will not have the pleasure of knowing they killed one of us. Pull!"

They hefted him into the tunnel and closed the door behind them, hoping the mess covered any blood trail. Loduma sheathed his sword and knelt beside Kworgin. "Awake, damn it." He ripped cloth and pressed it to the man's gash, but he could count the nails in the guard's boot by the marks left on Kworgin's forehead.

Gimin pointed to blood leaking into Loduma's boot. "You best be tending yourself. We can't drag him all the way back, and he'll be dead in wicks."

He didn't want to admit the Thônian was right, but he bowed his head. "We at least won't let him die alone."

Thirty-Nine

Treasure Haunt

In the Jungles of Sutan a storm brews without clouds, silent lightning, and floods without rain, a war without people and insanity without the sane. Bother you to look then bother you to find, bother you to forget and bother you to remind.

—Last Prophet of the Huntzillôn before departing for the Father Wood

Glimdrem found Narkar Imôm an affable enough fellow for a human. For a man of Nomnuvar, he appeared average in every way, with black hair and black eyes, and he stood a hand under six feet, but his girth stood out. Even with a Boborun blockade strangling the food supply, it seemed unlikely the man's belt had shrunk. And that, perhaps, pointed to the fact he wasn't average at all but a Lord Merchant. Or a Merchant Lord. Glimdrem's grasp of the Tôlk language made it difficult to determine in which order he should translate and think of them. Most human cities he'd visited had their share of lords and merchants, and no doubt there were merchants who were also lords, but in Lultûhol, they'd taken the extra step of formalizing the relationship

with the specific title of *nesfarmêum.* Glimdrem didn't care, but these people tended toward persnickety.

"*Nesfarmêum* Narkar, it's good to see you again." This stood as their sixth meeting, though most had been brief and informal. He wasn't the high-placed nobility that the Contessa no doubt courted, but he found most he'd spoken to boorish, stubborn, and petty anyhow. Narkar was different: Pleasant, open-minded, and ambitious. All these traits made him the finest target for manipulation that Glimdrem had found thus far.

"Likewise, my fine man." He sat at the table where a glass of brandy waited for him.

"I appreciate you taking this meeting with such little time in advance."

"Well, when a Trelelunin mentions a trade in the middle of a blockade, I'm forced to listen."

Glimdrem scrunched his face. "Oh. I do hope there wasn't too much of a mistranslation."

Narkar rocked back in his seat. "This isn't about a trade?"

"No, I fear not. Or at least, not in the sense it appears you were thinking."

He sipped his brandy with a salute. "This isn't easy to find these days. So, what do you have in mind?"

"I propose a means to end this blockade, and I hope you are the man to help me."

"End the blockade? You're serious?"

Glimdrem glanced around, feigning to make sure no one listened and waited for a serving wench to pass to build a sense of importance. "I know what they want."

Narkar glanced around the room in imitation. "The Boboru? They want Red Skull."

"No, they don't. They want what they think he has, but he doesn't have it. Don't get me wrong, they want the pirate as well, but they'd be content to separate the red from his skull at a later date if they get what they want."

He leaned close. "Which is what?"

"A map."

Narkar's eyes widened. "All this is over some son of a bitchin' map?"

"Not just any map. A map of Sutan." Glimdrem found it the easiest lie, seeing as it was close to what he dreamed of. "A hidden map leading to a lost city of gold, if you believe such tales." The best lie because humans wanted to believe it was real. "How do you think I got past the blockade? They sent me to find it. The Contessa doesn't even know."

He sipped and then licked his lips. "And where is this map supposed to be?"

"Wherever they took Red Skull's treasures, don't you think?"

"If there was such a map, wouldn't the lords of Lultûhol have found it?"

Glimdrem scoffed. "Unless you were looking for a map, you wouldn't see this one. And even if looking, if you don't know what you're looking for, you won't find it."

"But you know. Still, why hand them such a map?"

Glimdrem scoffed. "I have my doubts the map is real. I have watched humans seek the lost city of Galbareth for four hundred years or more, and the quest has piled up more bones than gold. If it brings peace? Let them have their fun in an impossible search. But you, you would be the one who broke the blockade."

Narkar swirled his drink and rapped his fingers on the table. "I'd rather be the man who found a city of gold."

"Would you rather be alive or dead?"

"And what if the map isn't there?"

Glimdrem shrugged. "Nothing risked, and nothing lost. Just get me inside to look."

The man stroked his chin. "What's in it for you?"

"They hold the ships of an associate of mine and their cargo. Human associates, so I can hardly bring down the wrath of the Mother Wood. Let me know if you can't help, or point me to someone who can."

"I am *Nesfarmêum.* I know where to look even if I don't know where they hold Red Skulls cargo." He stood and drained his drink. "I'll contact you when I find it."

Glimdrem smiled as he watched the man exit the tavern, knowing Narkar would search for the treasure first but also knowing there was nothing to find.

It took two weeks for Narkar to meet with him again, and he arrived all pride and bluster, but Glimdrem understood that the depths of his heart burned with angst over having failed to find the promised map. His smiles would fade every time he thought Glimdrem wasn't paying attention and blossom every time he made eye contact as they traveled to a mysterious location in a carriage with its blinds drawn closed. When the clop of hooves echoed, he knew they'd entered a tunnel without stopping, and flickers later, his seat shifted to prove they descended.

"The treasure's location wasn't so hard to find, but access proved difficult."

"Did it indeed?"

"I knew a woman who knew a man, and they're both greedy. I promised a bigger reward if you found what you're looking for."

"You're a gambler, *Nesfarmêum* Narkar?"

A chuckle. "Not often, but it's a matter of risk to reward."

"As it ever is."

The carriage cornered and stopped, and a woman in a white-faced ceramic mask depicting some sort of devil with three horns opened the door for them. They stepped onto a floor of natural stone in an empty halo of lantern light, soft echoes traveling far in both directions. He grinned, wanting nothing more than to make a quip about the woman's looks and a mask, but instead said, "Goodness. Mighty fearsome, but how will I know who to pay?"

She didn't say a word, instead leading them to an arched entry. She gestured, and Narkar led the way with the woman remaining behind.

"Jokes might be best avoided."

"I'd say she needs a good laugh and a bottle of wine to smooth her mood."

"I won't claim she don't, but just the same?"

"No jokes."

They wandered a winding but brief path to another door where a man wearing a similar mask, only in black with a white streak from brow to chin, stood beside a door with the locks already removed. Narkar nodded without a word, and the man opened the entry to a bright glow.

Glimdrem had high expectations for the room and its treasures, but his hopes dwindled as his eyes adjusted and the door clanged shut behind them. "This is it?" No doubt it was worth a fortune; the corner stacked with rolled tapestries or carpets might well keep a family in luxury for generations, but the lack of anything religious in nature brought a nibble to his confidence.

"There are three more rooms."

"Ah! Well. How long do I have?"

"As long as you like... so long as I'm not starving. No one will arrive without our hosts knowing about it."

Glimdrem snorted as he glanced around the room. "If there are three more rooms, you're going to get hungry unless I get lucky."

"I packed some jerky and water."

"Good man!" He strolled three steps with Narkar on his heels. "This will go better without you hovering. Be useful and look for anything with indistinct scribbles. Imperfections. Anything out of the ordinary." He strode onward by himself, glancing down rows of tables with scattered items. Plates, bowls, and chalices ranged from exquisite ceramics to silver and gold, and the amount of pottery staggered his mind. But he learned one thing already: Their origin was the continent of Sutân. If the craftsmanship didn't prove it, the styling did with the waved edges of the plates and triple-roped urns.

Glimdrem huffed as he stopped and turned a circle. "Is there space to unroll carpets over there?"

"In the room beside it, yes."

Glimdrem smirked as the man gave away his having been here before. "Unroll and stack them. We'll want to check the weave on both sides."

A flicker's pause. "All of them?"

"Come now, they are countable with fingers and toes... more or less."

"More."

"Do you want to be useful or not?"

The man lumbered toward the corner and hefted a roll over his shoulder, and Glimdrem turned his back to the rows. Enough rows that he could toil for a day in this one room if he chose to examine everything. Impractical and unnecessary. The object of his desire was either a book or a map, along with something to pass off as the Bobrorun's great desire for Narkar.

He wandered up and down several rows in frustration before glancing into the next room, and it was here that his eyes widened. Rows upon rows of statues ranged from ugly to beautiful and mundane to bewildering, and with at least two dozen, he could name the depicted god without hesitation. His heart at once leaped with hope and chugged with anguish. If hidden in a statue, in particular, a large statue, he would need to get it out. He'd need a key as he did with the monkey statue, and that small necessity might lay hidden amid a thousand odd trinkets. This detail wasn't about to stop him.

He stepped to the closest statue with hastened steps, a bronze depiction of the god Jumbalêyô-tômor-o, a man with an elephant's head, tusks and all. The monstrosity weighed at least three hundred stones, and while the base could hold half a dozen codices, he shook his head. The next statue was of a god he couldn't name and was too small to hold the Oxeum Codex, but were all the codices the same size? It was a time saver with flaws to accept they would be, so he moved to the next statue and the next with a growing impatience. He lifted a jade statue similar in size to the blind monkey, a carving of Tênsû-illîuô, and despite not finding a seam or location for a key, he couldn't quite put it down.

I like you. I'm not sure about your six breasts, but your maker was a master.

The vine said, *She is lovely for a murderous whore, and such a handsome man two steps away, her even more vile husband.*

Glimdrem glanced, and indeed, Suqwûtu-mokok stood naked with a bow in one hand and a boar's head in the other. The statues and the gods depicted were of similar sizes and were from the Gôlkumurâng pantheon. *But are they related to the Blind Monkey?* He blinked, perhaps not having thought of it before since he wasn't sure if the monkey was from a pantheon at all. He needed the answer. It was another way to trim the count of statues. He stepped down the row and froze. *Why did*

someone hide a book in a statue in the first place? He moved slower down the row with his mind distracted.

You hide books to preserve them. To protect them from what? Rats were always a huge concern, but it felt impractical unless the rats were a sieging army. *Oxeum was at war with the Totokotwonu and was destroyed. If I were a scholar watching an enemy descend on my home, I would also want to preserve our history.*

He knocked on a statue's base, a jackal with the head of a human wielding a spear, and shoved it aside.

He mumbled aloud, "They would have needed to see the end coming long in advance to craft enough statues."

The vine hushed him. *There are ears.*

Glimdrem glanced around the room but saw no one. *You are paranoid.*

Then so are you.

He chuckled and turned his eye to another statue, a jade woman nude but for her hair wrapping her body as she rode a horse carved of onyx. He lifted the statue by grasping the woman's back and expected it to be two pieces, but he was wrong. He held it up, curious, and couldn't see a seam where the two stones came together. *God Wars, no doubt, fusing stones. A third suspicious statue.* He sighed as he put the three side by side, wondering if he didn't look upon a vast fortune in hidden lore. *Hidden, but hidden, why?*

The question plagued him still, and his head cocked in thought. *Legends from the Age of God Wars speak of massive libraries, yet the Edan have not found even one. Their library is a collection of books found scattered around the world. Libraries are found empty. Destroyed. Gone. Did the Oxeum scholars know what was coming? Did they hide the books from the First Forgetting?* The notion sounded like the jibbering of a madman.

The vine said, *How could they anticipate an impossibility?*

It wasn't impossible, now was it? The Eight Kingdoms claim their gods brought on the Forgettings. What if this was less farce than he ever imagined? How best to protect their histories, then? Books burned, got wet, or were eaten by rats and bugs, among other destructions. Books held timeless knowledge but didn't withstand time's passage. The Kingdomers, after the First Forgetting, carved history into the face of a cliff. What if the scholars covered theirs in stone and scattered them around a city or even an entire country? Maybe the world.

The notion boosted his confidence in the possibility of these statues holding more codices, but it didn't help his myriad of troubles. How to open them? How to smuggle them out? It would be even worse if he needed to take the statues whole.

"There you are." Narkar strode into the room. "I see the statues caught your eye."

"They did, but my imaginings could drive me to madness while looking for patterns that might form a map or give me a clue."

"If stone is maddening, wait until you stare at a dozen tapestries. I've got them rolled out, as you said."

"Good man." Glimdrem walked his way despite the aggravation of being interrupted. "Let us see what you have revealed."

Battle scenes, hunting scenes, family lineage, and even orgies with man-like beasts involved, but the most frustrating were those without such obvious stories to tell. Tapestries woven in wild circular patterns or eternal knots that might mean a thousand things if he drank enough wine and crossed his eyes right. But as they rolled and hefted their fourteenth tapestry, with Glimdrem helping the man carry it away more to save time than to be polite, his bored and blurring eyes refocused, and he fought a chill: A monkey with rubies for eyes stared at him. A blind monkey no more, even if the ruby was red dye and silk.

"You see something?"

"Maybe." The monkey sat in the left corner amid a floral motif that ran in patterns throughout—except for the border, which was a hand wide, dyed blue, and draping golden tassels. For its craftsmanship and beauty alone, it would be worth a fortune, but there stared the monkey straight at him. He rubbed his eyes to blacken his vision and collect his thoughts, then opened them again.

A woman stood with her hands clasped over her head, but her chest revealed six breasts. *Tênsû-illîuô, but a different pose.* It didn't take long to find her husband, and though he carried a buck's head instead of a boar, the pose was similar. *The Blind Monkey is somehow related,* and as his eyes passed over the monstrous tapestry, he calculated there were no less than eighty-four iconographic figures that might be turned into statues. Glimdrem fought the smile that wanted to spread across his face.

"You see this monkey here?"

"Yes, I sure do. Ugly little bugger with devilish red eyes."

He chuckled. "I suspect his red eyes are meant to portray rubies."

"Rubies? I like the sound of rubies."

"I spent years on the continent of Sutan and saw a statue of this monkey."

"And you took its eyes?"

"No, someone beat us to that, but will you allow me to continue?"

"Of course."

"The monkey statue was in the southwest, matching the lower left corner here." He pointed, ready to throw down a thick layer of manure. "That monstrosity there, with teeth and eight legs? That's a carving on the side of a pyramid. That man there depicts a god I can't name, but the statue stands covered in vines in a ruined temple or city. But what does it mean, you ask? They all match about where they'd be on the continent relative to one another."

The man leaned and stared. "All of them?"

"No, I doubt it. You'd need to know which ones matter. Hence, the map is a puzzle even after finding it. I have no way of knowing which one the Boboru believe is a city of gold, but this is a map, even if an unconventional one."

"You're certain?"

"I need this tapestry."

The man groaned and leaned back with a broadening smile. "We could take it and sail to Sutan."

Glimdrem's eyes widened as he laughed. "Ho ho! As I said, I have been there. You would want to be eight feet tall and weigh a hundred and a half stones to go there and do it with an army. The mannish beasts of Sutan are the least of your worries. That thing with fanged, gaping jaws and eight legs isn't some religious fantasy. It's real, it's poisonous, and it swings through the trees to drop on you without warning. It killed half a dozen of our party and almost me."

The man sucked his teeth with a frown. "Better to let the Boboru die in their folly, is what you're saying." The fact Glimdrem spoke the truth and not a lie, no doubt, sold the man on the dangers with little argument.

"No sane man goes to Sutan. Can you get this to my ship?"

The man rubbed his forehead and pulled his hair taut. "It's big. Damned big, but yes. I'll get it to your ship if the price is right."

Glimdrem's thoughts groaned, but he smiled. "What's the price, considering the stature you're bound to gain?"

"Mmmm, we're in this together, you remember?"

"I do. But you won't want to be the one delivering the tapestry. The Boboru are true to their word, but their word is also to burn any human ship that gets close. I will take the tapestry to them and make sure it's what they want. If you don't want to deliver it, you sure don't want to deliver the wrong treasure."

Narkar laughed. "I've seen a Boborun ship with rows of gallows, an entire crew strung up."

"I will make the delivery. If I'm wrong, they will send me back. If right, I will have the Lord Captain send a special request for you to join him in negotiating an end to the blockade."

He licked his lips with a scrunched brow. "That simple?"

"The Boboru are never *that* simple. Lord Captain Ushtrûôk might make some symbolic demands. Restitutions. A new treaty. But he will have what he wants, and from there, an able negotiator such as yourself should have no problem."

"Dandy. Now, here's what I say. I'll pay half of whatever these leech bastards want, but you have to pick up the rest of the cost of lading."

"Done." With the Contessa's gold onboard his ship, how much could she argue? "You go find out the price; I want to look over those statues."

He nodded and took three strides away before turning. "Don't try to filch nothing."

He smiled because he couldn't take what he wanted. "I won't."

Narkar strode away with a spring in his step, and Glimdrem sauntered, both pleased and aggravated. He needed these statues, maybe even more than three, even if he had to take a hammer to them to find what rested inside, but it was an impossibility.

The vine said, *Impossible,* in the middle of a chuckle.

"I no longer believe in the impossible."

Nor should you.

"Then tell me how the scholars knew of the First Forgetting and the destruction of knowledge before it happened."

Silence for flickers, and then a voice came from behind him. "Did they?" Uvin's voice sent a chill down his spine.

He turned, and for a flicker, he saw a spectral image of the archangel, the twenty-fifth, so brilliant and so unlucky with his toothy smile. Glimdrem spoke aloud, "They did."

"They knew." Glimdrem could almost smell his breath.

The dead man faded into nothing as Glimdrem asked, "How?"

The vine said, *Are you even asking the right question?*

Glimdrem snorted as he reached the row of statues. In this desperate search, he didn't find the answer but found seven statues he suspected held lore the Edan would murder and go to war for. The notion thrilled him despite not knowing how to reach the treasure. Still, knowing where to dig was half the battle.

FORTY

Memories Lasting

I have slept in the belly of the Dontupûor, lived the stench of their bowels, and understand the feces they leave behind better than any living being, and thus I can speak these words to you in certitude: Be you king or be you peasant, be you warrior or be you priest, be you innocent or be you guilty, in the eyes of the Dontupûor you are but a slave.

—Selufduwênu of Ôxêum to King Jesupilêtô the Third

Pikarn spent the next week holed up at the entrance of the Ihomjo Mines with Neseldun and Limereu never far away while Inslok and a handful of Trelelunin searched the mountainsides for signs of Colok. They found remnants of camps in the region, but nothing recent; the notion of more Daevu than Colok still haunted the Wolverine's imaginings. However, after his most recent run-in, he had more immediate worries for his nightmares to take shape. The good news, if it could be called such, was that the Edan, after much debate, figured the Soul Scythe was unlikely to attack through Elemental Light and that their display of Water and Light provoked a desperate attack instead of its flight.

When ten days had come and gone, they took off on foot for the Chanting Caverns, leaving a dozen Trelelunin and all their horses behind in the Ihomjo with a trail of glimmering ruby powder to keep the Soul Scythe away. Pikarn wasn't sure who was safer, but if they lost the horses, he knew the walk back to Berul Island would be through one or two hells.

The Omindi Pass stood clear of snow this time of year and at these altitudes, a blessing from Burdenis if there ever was one, as his bones felt they aged more than they ought to in the years between his trips to this region. They scaled the slope and walked the narrow path leading to the cavern entrance without the worry of ice under a bright sun, and when they arrived at the Cat's Eye entrance to the cave, it was almost as if the horrors of the past were no longer real. Flowering brush grew around the stone once soot-marked and fire-scarred as time cleansed the entrance of everything but his memories. A nest of songbirds trilled at their approach.

He paused to stare and remember.

Limereu stepped to his side and matched his gaze. "You have the look of a man paying homage to those lost."

"Aye. Suvarn was our first soul lost to these godsdamned demons, right here in these caves, but he wasn't the last nor most painful. Modan Hiklar, the gods praise his strength, died at Snow's Eye from a Shadow's wound."

"You didn't speak of him when we were there."

"Maybe not that you heard, but I thought of him every wick. Truth be told, we were lucky not to lose more good people. Friends." He turned to face her. "You're more perceptive than your kin. Sometimes, I wonder if you play-act your ignorance of us human folk to fit in with your people."

An emotionless, very Edan face gazed upon him. "My emotions and understanding of them has faded since my return from the Father Wood. Even being away from the Mother Wood hones a certain empathy, so I grasp your feelings more than Inslok and Neseldun."

He chortled and strode toward the cave's entrance, the slit in the world already surrounded by Trelelunin. "That, lady, is an understatement for the ages."

Pikarn marched into the mouth of the cave to join Rikis by Inslok's side. Rikis smirked and said, "We made it with no Shadows or Taken, but no Colok either."

Pikarn grunted. "I know it should make me feel better than not, but it pricks at my nerves. We should've found something or somebody other than a Soul Scythe nobody expected." He added the last bit so Inslok wouldn't correct him, but his attempt stood as insufficient.

"You forget the Daevu."

The Wolverine ignored the Edan's words and strode deeper into the cave lit by steady and brilliant Light instead of the guttering torches of his previous journey. They found the guard post with its small stable unchanged from the last time he was here. A leather harness still hung from the wall, no doubt brittle and its brass tarnished, but there wasn't a soul in the mountains to steal it.

Inslok said, "They kept horses?"

"A couple of mountain ponies at most for carrying messages to Istinjoln, from what I understand. We were, in part anyhow, comin' up to investigate a messenger's death. We didn't know he came from here, or for that matter, that this here hole in the mountain existed."

They angled right with a gentle descent, a part of the journey he remembered without question, and soon the slope grew steeper. He grinned. "Right about here is where Ivin Choerkin stepped on a blind cave rat and earned the nickname Ratsmasher."

Rikis chuckled, "I can just imagine that."

"Oh yea, broke the damned things back then stomped the life out of its misery while pissin' this or that with the Squirrel."

Limereu said, "I've seen a few of the critters scuttling out of our way."

"Aye, I'm guessin' they learned their lesson." A brief giggle from the woman that might have been more polite than real before Pikarn spoke his thoughts aloud. "Way I remember it, we'll level out a bit and turn right into the Hall of Faces. Hard to get lost before then."

"Faces, as in the shapeshifter legend?"

"No. Hells no. You'll see."

Without shadows, the imposing figure of the carved stalagmite wasn't so much as worth a startle when it appeared, but he did mark the fact they were on the right trail. They turned right as he expected, and a multitude of carvings appeared in the Light, more than he'd imagined.

Rikis hissed beside him. "Those are godsdamned ugly; what are they supposed to be?"

Pikarn grunted as the hollowed-out stone eyes of a winged snake with two heads seemed to follow his steps with its lifeless gaze. "Meliu didn't know, so I sure the hells don't."

Inslok said, "This is a *Râmêdjun* hall, dedicated to the gods and other beings belonging to the Gôlkumurâng Pantheon. I know very little, but the guardian statue at the entrance is known as Derumîju, the Protector of Sins."

Rikis said, "Protector of Sins? What's that even mean?"

"It is vital in the *Râmêdjun* that the devout avoid sinning to achieve ascendance to their paradise. The devout could not simply be without sin; they needed to face sin throughout their lives and overcome their temptations. Derumîju, it is said, made certain that the world

presented adequate temptations for every deserving soul to reach paradise and for those unworthy to fail."

Rikis chuckled. "The son of a bitch must do a fine job. I have never seen a lack of temptations!"

"Their sins might not be the same as those of the Pantheon of Sol."

Pikarn grunted at a three-headed cat carving with a scorpion's stinger on its tail. "Meliu said some folks figured these Vanquished Gods. Is that so?"

Inslok walked in silence for several strides. "The definition of Vanquished makes the answer tricky. We know little of the religion with few surviving books in our libraries, and to our knowledge, no one worships the Gôlkumurâng Pantheon today, but there are great swaths of land with unknown peoples."

"That's s'posed to answer my question?"

"If no one worships them, then you might consider them Vanquished Gods. However, if by Vanquished Gods you mean their religion was defeated and their gods driven from the mortal realms during the Age of God Wars, then the answer is likely no."

"Fine and dandy, that is, but when I say Vanquished, I mean gods banished but trying to find their way back to our world? That there is how the Church in Istinjoln considered 'em, and the Defiled were their tools to return to this here world."

Rikis nodded. "Aye, that's more or less what we were taught."

Inslok said, "I think this is unanswerable."

But Limereu said, "Perhaps it is, but allow me to conjecture with human logic."

"By all means."

"Thank you. By the simplistic definition of Vanquished, meaning banished and unable to reach the mortal realms, the Pantheon of Sol

could be called Vanquished along with all the pantheons worshipped during the Age of God Wars."

Rikis blurted, "Whoa, whoa! I don't think you're following this straight."

She shrugged. "I am attempting to correct you if you'd bother to listen."

Pikarn jabbed the boy's ribs with an elbow. "Shut yer yap and pay attention." He snickered at the Choerkin's glare.

"If, indeed, the Pantheon of Sol is not Vanquished, then what Vanquished must come to mean is both banished and unworshipped. During the Age of God Wars, wars were fought to kill the enemy, as you would imagine, but they were also fought to seize the followers of enemy religions. A dead adherent hurt a religion and its gods, but an adherent converted to the conquering religion was more valuable still."

Pikarn thought on it a flicker. "So, you're sayin' that scroll Ivin read, the one that tried to Sunder folks from the pantheon, was used to vanquish gods? By stealing their worshippers?"

"Yes. Or at least such a powerful magic contributed to the weakening of the tether other gods had with the Mortal Realm. There are many aspects to the God Wars and dynamic we don't understand."

"I done got the gist. Damned things are still ugly as a Broldun after a shave."

Rikis punched his shoulder. "Says the man beddin' one."

"That one don't shave, and that's rare for their women folks." He pointed. "There, I think that hairy buffalo there is Polus' cousin." He and Rikis chuckled while the Edan walked on with flat faces bordering on a frown. "Come on, Limereu, you met that Broldun, tell me it ain't so."

She stopped to gaze at the stone beast, which, despite standing thirty feet away, was huge enough to see details. "Something around the eyes, perhaps."

"I knew you were my favorite Edan for a reason."

They rounded a corner left and soon after found themselves standing at a crossroads with passages more or less heading toward the four points of a compass. He remembered the hall as he eyed the three passages open to him.

Rikis shot him a grin that reminded Pikarn of Kotin as a young man. "Wolverine versus Squirrel, which, oh which, is better?"

"Watch it, boy, it's been damned near five years. Funny, ain't it? I remember Meliu questioning our path right here, but I don't recall which way we took right off. We didn't go straight." He looked left and right, directions he figured close to north and south. "North." He took half a step and stopped with a smile. "No. She said that tunnel led to something called the Tears of the Gods. She hid from the Shadows there, some sorta glowing stalactites or some such."

The Edan shared a look even as he spun to head south. Limereu said, "Glowing?"

"Aye. She said some mineral in the rock glows. She figured some magic or another in the Tears mighta blocked the Shadows from finding her."

Inslok addressed Limereu, "Luminescence isn't so unusual."

"But if it hid her, it could be Elemental in nature. Spirit? A quartz formation, perhaps."

"Likelihood?"

"From the description of the Shrine of Burdenis, I've heard, it's likely beneath an old caldera. The force of age-old volcanic activity is conducive to both hot springs and Elementally infused minerals. Variants of quartz are also prone to Spirit infusion, which might account for her ability to hide."

Inslok stared at the woman for flickers, unreadable. "Of immediate use?"

"Less likely but possible. We should inspect the formation now or on our way out. If infused with Spirit, I might be able to manipulate enough to block the Soul Scythe or keep Shadows of Man at bay."

Pikarn cleared his throat. "We haven't seen a damned thing down here, but I can't believe it'll last. If there's somethin' there to help us, I'd say we find out now."

Inslok eyed him. "You're sure it's there?"

"I never saw it. It's what the lil priestess said."

Neseldun said, "We can assume the Soul Scythe can reach the Shrine of Burdenis and, therefore, us. It attacked through Light and Water, which speaks to our not understanding the creature. Our not understanding what we walked into."

Rikis jumped in. "In other words—"

Inslok said, "I don't like changes without a plan. Do we know how far?"

The Wolverine grunted. "She didn't say a thing."

"The number of turns?"

"No."

"So we know nothing." Inslok stood like a terrifying statue, only perfect in his symmetry, unlike everything the carvings in the Hall of Faces stood for. Emotionless and unwavering, stern like an angry father. "We will inspect these Tears of the Gods."

Pikarn opened his mouth to argue before the words sank in, then clapped his teeth shut and followed the Edan as the trio strode north. They traveled thirty strides before they halted to stare at two crack-wide branches on their left and right, and ahead, a stalagmite broad enough to be a column narrowed their path. Inslok proved himself a hard man to read, but Pikarn was at least certain the Edan wasn't pleased. Whatever could be said about the narrowing way forward, it was the only practical route, and after a few flickers, they moved onward.

A hundred then two hundred strides before reaching the tunnel's end, a low ceilinged chamber with stalactites hanging from high, but nothing out of the ordinary. A closer look suggested it didn't really end, but instead, a curved slope led up like nature's spiral stair. Even as Inslok walked toward the climb, Pikarn glanced around the room, looking for a spot that a short priestess could reach to climb. A drip echoed, and he pointed west where a stalactite reached low enough it almost kissed a stalagmite. "There. She could've climbed there. Dowse your Light."

Inslok turned with a nod, and the room went pitch black, or at least for a flicker it did, before his eyes adjusted to a dim glow. Rikis said, "Where the hells is that coming from?"

Pikarn heard Limereu's voice but couldn't see her. "The Tears of the Gods."

He strolled for a different view, rounding a corner to see a stalactite aglow with trailing trickles of light that went dark when the water fell from the formation's tip. "Tears. Flowing Elemental magic?"

Limereu said, "No. Water running over exposed crystal, quartz, I'd guess." Her shadowy face looked to the floor of the room, a swale in the stone. "At some point, where we stand was a hot spring."

"All I need to know is if the stuff is useful."

She stepped close to the stalactite and touched its glow with outstretched hands. The light of the crystals surged, and she pulled back. "The crystal shouldn't have done that. Unless..." She pulled a dagger, flipping it and pulling back her arm to strike with the pommel.

"You sure that's a good idea?"

She hesitated. "It's infused with Spirit, harmless." She rapped the crystal, and it pulsed.

Brilliant Light surged.

Pikarn covered his eyes and could hear Rikis grunt beside him. "Shits!" He blinked in a flurry, spots of dancing colors scattering across his vision. "Godsdamnit! I'm blind."

Limereu's voice came soothing. "Your vision should return in flickers."

He rubbed his eyes, and Rikis cursed beside him. "Whoreson! That was bright as the godsdamned sun. Where are you?"

"I'm here."

Inslok's voice, "We're all here."

Pikarn's blinks slowed, tears warming his face before he wiped them, and the bright white faded into black. His pulse slowed. "I think I can see again. Give me some light."

"There is Light."

Pikarn shook his head and rubbed his eyes again, and this time, there was a faint glow. The Tears of the Gods. A dozen stalactites glowing brighter than he remembered with drizzling trails of illumination. "Don't be shittin' with me...." He glanced at Rikis, the man still with hands rubbing his face, then spun. No one else. Disappeared. Three Edan and two dozen Trelelunin, gone. He screamed, "Limereu!"

A voice came from straight in front of his face. "I'm here. Where are you?"

"What the hells you talking about, here?" He waved his arms in front of him, finding naught but empty air. "Inslok!"

"I'm here." But the voice faded as if a dying echo.

"Don't you godsdamned be tellin' me you're here when I can't see you!"

A shriek born from the hells, and Pikarn knew the Soul Scythe haunted them, even if he couldn't see the pitch in the darkness. Silence ensued.

Rikis stared at him with sword and shield in hand. "Where the hells did they go?"

Indistinct murmurs replaced voices, compounding the sense of abandonment, and Pikarn licked his lips as his eyes flicked back and forth from darkness to darkness, from the climb at one of the end rooms to the hall they entered from. "I'm thinkin' we don't have time to figure it out." He sped to the stalactite hanging lowest, the one he figured Meliu climbed and looked up. "Now, where the hells do you think that girl hid?"

Rikis grimaced as his head tilted back. "The priestess weighed maybe thirty stones and could squeeze into a crack."

"I don't even see where her tiny butt could hide." A second shriek echoed closer, and as its horror faded, other indistinct noises in the distance raised the hairs of his neck. "We got company a comin'. Boost my ass up."

Rikis dropped his weapons with a clatter and stirruped his hands, lifting the Wolverine without so much as a grunt, and Pikarn raised his arms, fumbling around for a grip.

"Hurry it up, old man, I think we've got Taken on the way."

"If that priestess could reach something, so should..." His fingers snagged a grip. "Lift!" And a flicker later, he pulled his chin atop a ledge, swung his feet, and shoved with a breathy grunt. "Godsdamned weren't so big!" He lifted his legs, pushing against a glowing stalactite, and scooted deeper. Glowing trails of crystals lit the ledge, and it took a flicker to recognize they'd been carved into Canonic Silone letters and words.

He grunted, groaned, and fought his size to spin back around to lean over the ledge with arms draping. "Grab hold!"

Rikis's huge hands snagged his forearms, and Pikarn raised his feet to wedge against the low ceiling and keep from being yanked out by the Choerkin. Rikis heaved and swung his feet high, spreading his legs to catch between two stalactites.

A flicker later, a shuffling figure skulked beneath them. "Shhh."

Rikis froze, and the Wolverine's shoulders and elbows strained under the weight.

The first Taken moved on, but a second and third arrived to stand straight beneath them, twisted bodies clad in priestly robes, but the way they hung limp, he guessed one was missing most of its right arm, and as the third shifted its weight, the glow showed missing skull.

A shriek, and the Taken crouched before trotting away, but two flickers into pulling Rikis higher a darkness passed beneath them: A Shadow of Man, and he sucked his breath wide-eyed. Taken, they could at least fight. He fought back a groan even after the thing moved on and whispered, "All I got on three."

He mouthed the count and heaved with the big Choerkin kicking and pulling. Boots grated on stone, and a Shadow of Man howled. "Up, up, up!" Pikarn roared and dragged the man back and up to see Taken darting and leaping the Choerkin's disappearing legs.

He squirmed his shield from over his shoulder and handed it to Rikis as soon as the man got turned. "So much for hiding out unseen!" Pikarn unslung a water-filled skin and pulled an ax from his belt as a Taken sprung high enough to collide with the shield.

Rikis rocked upward with a second collision from below. "Shittin' things hit hard!"

"That's why yer on the shield. Didn't know the arm wrestlin' would win you that, eh?"

Bang. Bang. The man bounced with each hit. "Shut up and take some arms off."

"Just be happy I quit carryin' the wooden shield." He swung once and twice at a reaching hand, but the angle was awkward as the hells. "It puts an ache in my shoulders, but it'll take a beatin'!" Fingers flew as his ax struck with as much luck in its timing as skill.

"Edan steel is almost as helpful as an Edan at this point. Almost!" A Taken hit square, driving so hard Rikis banged his helm on the roof above.

Pikarn dared a leaning look to see a Taken jump from another's back, swung, and cleaved bone from the thing's forehead. "Sons of bitches are getting smart." A Shadow streaked into view and climbed, shadowy fingers digging into a stalactite, and the Wolverine gave his water bottle a squeeze even as Rikis deflected another Taken. The creature screamed and disappeared.

"Unless you gotta piss real bad, it's a matter of time before we're dead." Two more slams rang from the shield's face.

Pikarn saved his breath for swinging, taking a hand at the wrist and cleaving flesh from forearms with a score of blows. A Shadow blackened a stalactite's glow across from them and leaped, a stretching arm fingers from Rikis' face before a stream of water sent the thing screaming to the ground.

Bang, bang, bang, bang, bang, the shield rattled at what seemed an impossible pace, like drummers striking the rim in a fury, and Pikarn saw fatigue setting in and beads of sweat glistening in the light from Tears of the Gods. He fell to his chest, gripping the shield to help, still flailing with his ax until eyes appeared; the bladed beard struck its skull, dropping the creature, but the grip of bone pulled the haft from his hand.

He fumbled for his other ax and pulled it free from its hanger in time to strike a face. "You good?"

"Still alive!"

"Hold tight!" Pikarn let go of the shield, reached a hand high to prop himself over the opening, and hewed at a leaping Taken. Once, twice, three times, he struck before one fell without getting up. He bellowed and swung at a Taken as a Shadow scaled the wall, and he fell back, throat ripping with a scream as he streamed water over Rikis' head until the skin flagged empty. The shriek of the Soul Scythe rang in the distance.

But the Shadow never appeared, and the banging stopped.

Forty-One

Memories Concluded

In Zigmorund did a warrior live who never won nor lost a fight so great was his reputation. Consider you this a truth or a fable? A possibility or impossibility? In Zigmorund did a beauty live who never danced or loved, so beautiful that once set eyes upon her, to look away was to die of sorrow. An unseen queen with handmaidens blind, lonely in her perfection.

—The Codex of Sol

Pikarn breathed hard and stared before flinging himself forward, propping his left arm stiff with his ax cocked in his right. Blinked into the brilliance of Light as he looked into Limereu's eyes, gazing up at him with confusion stretching her Edan calm. "How did you two get up there? Why?"

"Climbed! And why? Look around you!" But when his words focused his attention, he realized the floor below was empty of body parts and a dead Taken or two.

Rikis lowered the shield and blurted, "Hells! Where've you bastards been? We damned near died."

The woman blinked. "I don't understand."

"Taken! Shadows of Man!"

She nodded. "Yes, but they never reached this hall."

Pikarn squirmed past Rikis and lowered himself to the ground while the younger man followed with a jump. "You people disappeared, and they came for us. We heard the shrieks of the Scythe in the distance. The Taken jumped at us, a Shadow coming, and they disappeared like you did."

"The scythe is indeed close, but we have not seen it. As for Taken and Shadows, Inslok, Neseldun, and the Trelelunin dispatched their salvo." She held up a chunk of glowing crystal. "The quartz here, or some of it, is infused with Spirit. We collected some while trying to find you, and it might prove useful down the road."

He gawked. "That's damned wonderful, don't let my tone make you think it ain't, but tell me what godsdamned happened here! How the hells were we fighting Taken and Shadows, you didn't see?"

Her head cocked. "Some sort of delusion invoked by hysterical fear, I suspect."

Never before had he wanted to strangle a woman. "You think we both were fighting our imaginations?" He squinted. "You're joking."

"Was it funny?"

"You picked one hells of a time to practice your humor."

"From what I understand, the tense situation should render my words more funny."

He snort-chuckled. "Tomorrow it might. Now tell me what the hells happened."

"I lack an answer. When I struck the Tears of the Gods, it triggered a release of Spirit that the Shadows of Man felt. If I ever knew of such a phenomenon, it was in a different life. You disappeared, and the fight came fast."

"Came fast, damned right."

Inslok strolled close. "We should leave this place. With the Scythe and Shadows knowing we are here, we'll need to get to the shrine and establish a perimeter before they find a way to thwart us." He turned and walked south; Pikarn followed and Rikis jogged to catch up after picking up the shield and sword he dropped earlier.

Pikarn reached into his pack and ripped a strip of jerky. "Did we lose anyone?"

"We lost you for a couple of wicks."

Pikarn shook his head with a grimace, biting meat and chewing before saying, "More godsdamned humor? Answer the question."

"No. Minor wounds from Taken while killing forty-three and sending at least a dozen Shadows back to their queen."

Rikis snorted. "That's better'n we did."

"I see no bodies."

Rikis grumbled and shook his head, leaving Pikarn to respond. "Think I killed two no matter what you say."

They walked in silence until they reached the crossroads and continued south. "Something unexplainable happened, and it isn't worth quibbling over until we have time to sit and consider."

The Wolverine sighed. "Aye. Right." They reached another chamber with multiple exits, and they stopped with all eyes on him. "Gimme a wick." But it took only flickers. "Left tunnel. If it's the correct one, we'll narrow for a while before coming to a column in the middle we'll need to squeeze our asses around. After? We need to find a climb on the left wall."

The party slowed on reaching the expected point as they passed around the column, and the toeholds for their climb stood out like the rungs of a ladder in the Light of the Edan, but as he climbed, a Trelelunin shouted from the rear. Pikarn looked up at Inslok, who stood on the ledge above him in wait.

"What the hells did he say?"

"We have Shadows of Man following us."

He approached the top, stretching one last time before the remaining holds fit his stature better. "How many?"

"Many. It is difficult to count when they blend together in darkness."

Pikarn hefted himself over the top and got out of Rikis's way. "A guess, Edan."

There was a pause as Inslok turned to lead them down the hall. "By many, Nevon meant over a hundred, but your language just uses 'many,' which is a weakness of your tongue."

"It's not a godsdamned weakness, we just... never mind." Annoyance with the Edan made the count take flickers to settle in. "One hundred or more. If ever we thought to surprise these creatures, that's dead and buried."

Rikis snorted. "Has been since we erred in exploring the Ihomjo."

Inslok said, "We lost surprise, but so did the Queen of Shadows. The Soul Scythe is a known, now."

They followed the curving tunnel. "Still, a hundred Shadows puts me on edge."

"The number is irrelevant."

Pikarn snorted. "Aye! So long as you don't disappear again."

"The tears of the Gods are unique enough I've never seen their like; I doubt we will experience such a thing again."

The arch of the narrow tunnel ended as it opened into an expansive cavern. "The Crack of Burdenis isn't far." The cavern stood as he remembered, forty strides wide and rising into a high ceiling, but dark lines ran the walls now where there was once fire. "Troughs carved into the walls burned oil to light the place, but I'm guessing they burnt out years ago." He pointed at the ceiling and its golden sparkles and grinned. "They called this place The Fool's Haul."

"For the pyrite in the ceiling?"

His grin faded along with his hope an Edan might be fooled like he had been. "Yeah. That. The Crack is just ahead. That's where the ceiling shows its glory."

Neseldun approached. "I fanned a mist at the climb behind us. It should stop the Shadows for a time. A fist of warriors watches to see if Taken advance." Pikarn learned on this journey that what the Edan called a fist was five Trelelunin. Here in the Chanting Caverns, standard procedure was two standing with shield and spear, two with bows behind them, and the fifth the commander with shield and sword at the ready.

Inslok gave a curt nod. "We descend into the Crack. This is true?"

"Aye, that we will."

"Stay with us for a time, Neseldun."

Rikis walked with his eyes up, and as their path curved into the greater hall, he gasped. Pikarn followed his gaze, and his vision alighted on a wonder he'd never thought to see a second time; the massive circle of gold with a silver snowflake in its middle rested in the ceiling above the Crack of Burdenis, unchanged and uncaring for the time passed and lives lost since his last visit.

The sight's grandeur even impressed the Edan as their Light focused high above, the silver and gold glowing with an awe-inspiring brilliance that stopped the Wolverine's strides so he could stare. "Gods above, it's even more beautiful."

Rikis muttered, "That isn't no pyrite."

Silence as everyone stopped, and Neseldun said, "Neither are the ores mere gold and silver. The snowflake is *ofdolus,* infused silver, and the ring is *timôu,* infused gold. God Wars craftsmanship."

Pikarn didn't bother to tear his eyes from the view, marveling at the perfection of the snowflake's angles. "This has been here so long? I reckoned the priests built it."

"It might've been priests of the Pantheon of Sol, but not in recent times. Your people might be able to work the metals, but this? No. Age of Warlords is possible, but I doubt it. It might be more than decoration, but without knowing its history...."

Inslok strode onward, stopping where the pulley once stood. "It is spectacular and worthy of research and study, but we have more important objectives."

Pikarn lowered his eyes and walked but couldn't resist glances at the ceiling. "Damned right you are. The switchback stairs are yonder. Now you mentioned it, the priestess said the stairs were here too when they found this place after the Great Forgetting."

On arrival at its edge, Limereu gestured at the dark hole in the world, and Light flooded the depths. A glance and Pikarn's gut fell even as his breath escaped his lips. He swallowed with a queasy splat in his gut. "I were better off not seein' the bottom." But at the least, the Crack's floor was barren stone devoid of demons and the possessed.

Rikis stood by his ear. "You ran up that?"

"Remember that the next time ya think of givin' this old man guff."

Inslok stepped to the edge of the stairs. "Neseldun, make it rain."

The other Edan stepped up and raised his arms, and without a word or another gesture, droplets formed in the air, hovering a flicker to form immaculate rainbows before falling in a soft whoosh. Pikarn peeked over the edge, a soft echoing rush in his ears and a plummeting rainbow in his eyes, waiting, waiting, until the inevitable crashing splash... and even more satisfying wails of what he figured the death cry of two or three Shadows of Man.

Pikarn elbowed Rikis. "Helluva lot better than pissin' on 'em."

Inslok gestured, and a fist of Trelelunin stepped onto the stairs in the lead before they followed, and by the time he'd zig-zagged down to the bottom, Pikarn was impressed with himself anew for surviving the jaunt out of the place back in the day.

Puddles stood in sinks across the chasm's floor where maybe it had never rained before, and he hefted a skin to take a drink. Water splashed in his yawning mouth as he stared up at the snowflake, no less beautiful from so deep in the ground, when a blackness appeared along the ledge above. A Shadow of Man was followed by more, but he gave thanks it wasn't the Soul Scythe. He swallowed and looked to Neseldun.

"What the hells does a Soul Scythe look like anyhow? Might it look like a Shadow of Man?" He'd kind of assumed it was a blob of Shadow since it blocked the shaft, but he hadn't thought on it long.

"What references I saw were nonspecific. Ah! You wonder if it can appear as a Shadow of Man."

"A Shadow of Man enters the room, you throw Water at it, and it kills you. Tell me you don't wanna know."

"A salient point."

Pikarn chuckled. "If you slept, it would keep you up at night."

"Edan do sleep. It's just not... A reference to my worrying if your supposition is correct."

Inslok raised an arm as the last of the Trelelunin set foot on the wet floor, beckoning him to his side. "Human humor, what can I say?"

Rikis reached Inslok at the same time Pikarn did and said, "That's a helluva lot of Shadows looking down on us. If they fell like rain, we'd be screaming as their brothers did."

Inslok nodded with a glance to the row of darkness above. "A good reason to be moving on. I sense multiple exits."

Pikarn nodded toward the length of the Crack and started walking. "Northeastish, is it? I don't know no other passages, just the one at the end up here."

They stepped into a tunnel that narrowed, and could no longer see the snowflake above when the shriek of the scythe sent a chill from his ears to the tips of his toes. "You think that thing leads the Shadows of Man and Taken?"

"I do."

"So, we aren't dealing with a mud-headed enemy no more."

"I can't be certain of any degree of intellect, let alone tactical abilities, but while I suspect they are limited, assume the worst."

They walked twenty strides into a turn, and Pikarn scratched a sudden itch beneath his beard. "Worst case is we're whistling our way into a trap."

"Not all traps are successful. Strings of traps laid in the forest and streams may go empty for days or weeks and miss their prey."

The tunnel bent again before Pikarn spoke, his thoughts on the chamber ahead where so many holies had met their end. More disturbing was the lack of emotion. Was Inslok just being an Edan, or had he expected a trap all along? Was this a trap within a trap, the Edan using them for bait to draw out the enemy? He wasn't even sure if the latter was optimism or pessimism. "I don't like it either way."

Inslok didn't bother to answer, and within a dozen strides, they entered the guard room where Taken had mutilated holies. An overturned table with a blood-stained leg still lay in the corner, and splashes of black that might be blood still marked the walls and floor, but the remains of the dead were gone. Not even a fragment of shattered bone remained as the fist of Trelelunin entering first spread out in front of him.

Limereu said, "I sense a lot of death in this place."

"Oh, aye. We couldn't even tell how many." Inslok stepped in front of him, nose upturned as if sniffing the air. "What the hells are your doin'?"

"Something in the air feels wrong."

"And that's our cue to be movin' on. Straight."

"You're certain?"

"Aye, certain as the Twelve Hells, and the Forge is in front of us. If there's a trap a waitin' before the Shrine, it's just ahead. We've a stretch of tunnel so tight it'll give you a shave." When the first Trelelunin slithered from view, the Wolverine's fingers twitched on the hafts of his axes, his gut telling him they'd be attacked on one side or the other, and even after they whistled that the path lay clear and he reached the other side, his chest was as tight with worry then as in the middle of the squeeze through. Only when the last of the Trelelunin emerged did he admit to himself that his innards were wrong.

They strode the tunnel, reaching a switchback climb that forced Pikarn to congratulate himself on remembering the path so well, and in short order, they stood in what Meliu had named the Chamber of the Lost.

"This here's the place Meliu expected to find the *Codex of Sol.*"

Rikis snorted, but Inslok was curious. "But it was found at the Shrine."

"Aye. She expected more books to be here, but that was the one she wanted most. From here, there's no getting lost. My godsdamned nightmares remembered this hole in the ground better than I thought."

They passed through the Chamber of the Lost without a further word, and wicks later, as the passage widened in a familiar straight-away, he heard an Edan call from behind, and this time he didn't need a translation. "Many Shadows behind us."

Inslok said, "An unknown number."

Rikis grunted and spat. "I'm beginning to see these caves will be my tomb."

Pikarn ripped jerky and chewed. "Aye, well, if yer Taken, I promise I won't drop yer Choerkin ass until yer good and outside."

"That's mighty generous of you."

The slope rose, and Pikarn couldn't resist looking over his shoulder. Light illuminated the helmeted heads of every Trelelunin behind them and reached the ceiling of their last turn, but beneath the Light, a blackened mass followed them, so dense it showed no individuals. He grunted and turned his eyes forward. "And that there's why they tell ya to never look over your shoulder."

Inslok said, "A thousand Shadows of Man couldn't reach you."

"Aye, exactly right. Why the hells no Taken? A thousand Shadows would scream and die, but a thousand Taken could overrun us."

Rikis said, "Because they don't have the numbers here."

"Maybe so." But the notion bugged the hells out of him. "A hundred, two hundred, at least they'd have a chance. The bastards are up to something."

The passage widened, and they strode onto the crenelated balcony overlooking the Shrine of Burdenis. The massive cavern ignited with Light as they entered, and he saw nothing different than he'd left behind. Overturned braziers and scattered robes where a holy had fallen, and diamond powder still glowing with Elemental energies. Pikarn stepped to the railing to stare.

"It sure the hells don't look like no trap, but the best traps never do."

Rikis sighed beside him. "Way I see it, if this here's a trap, we've been in it since a hundred strides after stepping foot through the entrance."

Pikarn spat over the railing, half expecting to hear a Shadow scream. "If it's a trap, damn me, but we might as well spring it."

Inslok nodded and pointed toward both stairs leading to the floor below. A fist descended in each direction, and they followed to the left, taking the same stair he had taken years before. He clutched his face and rubbed his beard as he stared at the diamond-covered Shrine of

Burdenis, his strides slow in their approach, and when he glanced back up the stairs, he saw a roiling mass of Shadows enter and hover to the railing and top of both stairs. They stopped, and his gut drew tight as a bowstring.

"They're just watching us." Pikarn exhaled then puffed his chest, returning his eyes to their goal, the Shrine of Burdenis and the invisible Celestial Gate they assumed was still there.

The Light was so brilliant and the Shrine so aglow that when a man sat up from the altar, Pikarn recognized something foul afoot before understanding why.

No human should be here alone.

No one should cast a shadow.

But he was, and he did.

While a dozen Trelelunin guarded the bases of the stairs, the rest fanned out with arrows nocked taut against strings. Inslok and the other Edan paused before striding forward; Rikis glanced at Pikarn, and Pikarn shrugged, knowing the trap sprung and the only question left to answer was whether it caught them by the foot, the hand, or the head. They followed Inslok but with hesitant, none-too-eager steps, and the Wolverine, for one, was happy when Inslok brought them to a halt a dozen strides from the mysterious figure.

Despite the Light that revealed details in people's faces beyond the bright of day, this man's visage was either a blotch or a blur or perhaps the result of a disfiguring scar. Pikarn thought him Taken for a flicker, but a crooked, toothy smile that glowed in the Light wiped that notion away. He raised his arms wide in a sweeping gesture. "Welcome, children of the Eleris. Welcome."

Inslok's head turned to Pikarn, and he spoke in his typical dry tones, "I was wrong. The Soul Scythe does not lead here."

Forty-Two

Memories Renewed

Smoke Breathers and Dirt Eaters,
founders with polluted souls tainted
into indignation and meaningless words.
The Four-Eyed Witch my lover and your thief,
looking so good lying in your bed,
rolling in your head,
laughing fumes a bloodless bleed from your nostrils
and suckling your babe on breasts feeding doom,
as you strum the loom to a noiseless tune
you'll wear as you walk to your grave.

—*Tomes of the Touched*

"Who or what the hells is that?" Pikarn appreciated, despite the domineering Edan confidence that implied always knowing everything and never being wrong, how Inslok admitted to being wrong in a manner as matter of fact as he stated his opinions as truth, but right now, he wished the man had been wrong about something less important.

The three Edan shared glances, the kind that made the Wolverine wonder if they needed words to speak, before Limereu answered. "I won't know until we ask."

The man leaped from the altar, his fall a shave slower than nature demanded, his landing making not a sound, and his shadow trailing his motions by a flicker in time. "Limereu Lesedreden, is that you? I recognize your face, but you don't recognize me?" He gestured with a flourish of fingers at the mass of scars from what must've been burns to his face. "I'm hurt you don't remember the good looks you and your lover destroyed."

"Was it the First or the Great Forgetting? If I've forgotten, reintroduce yourself."

"Which would you rather have answered, when you forgot or why I have not? Me, a mere mortal, no more than a human, while the mighty Edan forgot it all?" He winked in Inslok's direction. "Inslok remembers, don't you? How could you forget the man you maimed?"

"I do not, though I met a demon in Istinjoln who also claimed to know me."

The man strode to stand mere paces away from them with a frightening scowl on lips twisted by burns. "Demon? Demon! What a powerful name for a thing you created and don't understand."

Limereu said, "Tell me how you didn't forget."

He smirked at her. "The Great Forgetting is when you forgot me." The gnarled face turned to Rikis first, then Pikarn, studying them. "How does it feel to ally yourselves with enemies?"

The Wolverine puffed his chest and glared with fingers resting on the hafts of his axes. "These people are friends helpin' to destroy the murderous Shadows."

"Ahhhh. Murderous by creation. Murderous by nature. Murderous by intent. Who is more to blame, the assassin hired or the voice behind their orders?" He gestured to the throng of Shadows overlooking their conversation from the balcony rails. "Who are you to disparage your twisted brothers and your twisted sisters? For how long will they take it before turning their backs on you?"

"Turn their backs! They slaughtered my people and drove us from our homes."

Eyes rolled in flame-scarred sockets, and he shifted to face Rikis. "And you, Choerkin by blood but not title, it's a shame you are too blind to see more foes than you know."

"You'd dare claim yourself a friend of the Choerkin?"

"Once a friend of a Choerkin, but never a friend of the Choerkin."

"Choerkin will never befriend a servant of the Queen of Shadows."

"A melodramatic title for a tragic and dramatic soul, but I could never befriend an ally of the Edan. Could we be friends? Should we be friends? Would I like us to be friends? Yes. But we never will be. War is now, and war is coming. Are you ready without your Warlord Choerkin? Do you possess prayer for the possessed?" He turned back to Pikarn. "You are a man who eats his fear. We could be friends."

Pikarn snorted. "What's yer game, demon."

"My goodness, I'm a demon, too?"

Inslok said, "You are."

"Ohhh, coming from the mouth of the most vile entity I've ever met, that is most precious. But are you sure?"

"Look around you, the only thing who casts a shadow, a trickster shadow displaced in Time. What other than a demon would you call yourself?"

The man's voice changed, deep and thunderous, and though his mouth moved, the sound came from all around and died in the hall without an echo. "A god." He smiled, and when he spoke again, it was with his normal voice. "But I am no more a god than I am a demon."

"Share with us your name."

"Is this the silly superstition of the Ilu and others that to know a demon's name is to control it? No, an Edan wouldn't be so foolish, but this one is foolish enough to forget that he knows my name already."

"Then why hesitate to speak it to me?"

Despite all the scar tissue, a smirk stretched the man's face beyond natural proportions. "Pure amusement. But, now, I wish to speak to the Silone."

Pikarn blinked with a scowl, and when his eyes opened, he and Rikis stood alone with the man: no Edan, no Trelelunin, not even the Shadows of Man lurking behind them.

Rikis murmured, "A bit like the fight at the Tears of the Gods."

The being raised a finger. "Not at all like that unfortunate incident, outside of the superficial."

Pikarn pulled his axes. "If this's a fight, let's get it done with."

The man's eyes rolled, and he waved his hand in a conciliatory gesture. "If this were a fight, you'd be dead. The enemies you call friends, too."

"The Edan wouldn't fall so easy."

"You may call me Emuk if you like, but you won't recall the name when I return you to your enemies."

"Why give a pointless name?"

"Courtesy." He turned and strode toward the altar glowing with a patina of enchanted and powdered diamond, a finger over his shoulder beckoning them to follow. Pikarn hesitated before taking strides but kept his axes in hand, and Rikis walked close by his side. "There was a day I feared Inslok, but that day lies a millennium in the past."

"You say you aren't a demon, yet you claim to have lived a thousand years. Why wear a human facade?"

Emuk hopped and spun to sit on the Altar of Burdenis, the motion so smooth he appeared to float in subtle defiance of nature. "Not all immortals are born that way. Humans, both mighty and poor, have sought immortality, but only the unfortunate succeed."

"Human in truth? If true, I'll agree with you on one thing: it's unfortunate you're immortal instead of dead."

"It's a problem I wish to someday remedy; we're immortal one and all until the moment we die, in a manner of speaking. But of all the damned people they could've sent to help me, they sent you two."

"We weren't sent."

"No? I applaud the both of you for your bravery, then, but there are others who would've been more useful."

Rikis snorted. "Lay your head on that there altar and I'll be happy to take it off."

A chuckle. "You would've made a fine Warlord Choerkin, but it went to the youngest brother instead." His head cocked. "It's almost like the old ways when the most worthy took the name instead of being born to it. But I am sorry to disappoint, in that my head is not for the taking."

"Demon, or how the hells do you know about my brother?"

"What I am lacks a suitable definition, but I was born human, and what you see before you is the gift of my mother's sacrifice."

"You blamed Limereu and Inslok."

"Lovers most foul, though they remember nothing of each other's arms. They are to blame for mother's need to sacrifice. To save me."

The soft cry of a baby echoed in the distance, and Pikarn crouched wide-eyed, his ears unable to discern the direction of its whimper. "What sick hell is this?"

The man raised a brow. "Of what do you speak?"

"A baby, you bastard. I hear it crying."

Rikis shook his head. "I hear nothing."

"Your godsdamned ears are plugged, or this bastard messes with me. Us." The child's cry carried a gurgle, and it took determination not to run and search in all directions.

"I promise, there is no baby here."

Pikarn stood straight with a glare. Shook his head. A living child on Kaludor defied reason. "That's the first thing you've said that I figure I should believe. So, tell me, Emuk, what the hells are you doing here? We came to destroy your Celestial Gate."

The man ducked his head with a chuckle, and when his face rose again, he smiled. "A happy coincidence. I came to close it as well. And I came to send you home."

Darkness.

Abject.

Without a fear. Instead, calm.

His breaths warmed his face, and he realized he breathed beneath a heavy blanket with his eyes closed. Eyelids fluttered, and a shaky hand pulled away the covers. Sun shone through a window, and muttering voices spoke from beyond a door. He lay on a tick and pillow stuffed with down. A small table sat nearby with a lantern whose bowl was blown from familiar green glass. The wick sat without a flame, but he'd watched it burn countless hours during his life. A hand strayed to his chin to find bare skin instead of a thick beard.

Pikarn cast the wool blanket aside and swung his feet over the edge, finding boots he'd worn holes through decades ago and thrown away. *Home.* The walled village of Isterum, with its stone manor held by his family for the past three decades, and the short tower locals exaggerated into a keep. He glanced out the frosted window as wind whistled through its cracks, and in its sunny glow, he saw people passing by. A big man with a long nose laughed as he passed, his girth swollen by a heavy coat, and he'd swear it was Nujint, the local miller. Why did the notion of being home feel so familiar? Why wouldn't being home be familiar?

His toes slipped into fluffy sheepskin, hugging his feet as if they'd never left. He still remembered the day his father and uncle packed the curlhorn down from the mountainside, dinner, and after tanning, new boots come spring.

Muffled chuckles through the door, and he threw on a vest as he strode to the frame to give a listen. Silence until he gripped the handle and twisted. The hinges creaked with a squeal to match his memories. The fireplace's hearth blazed to his right, and a dining table sat in the middle of the room, surrounded by chairs polished a thousand times by his own ass. A crib sat in the corner filled with blankets and pillows instead of a baby, and mother's three brass deer still sat on the mantle. His breath fled when his father turned to face him with a smile from beneath his bushy brown beard.

Pillum said, "Good gods, boy, I thought you were gonna sleep the day away."

Uncle Graem chortled and said, "I bet he done snuck into yer whiskey last night."

"Check his chest for hairs and his tongue for burns to find out."

Both men chuckled, but Pikarn stumbled and lunged into Pillum, arms stretching around his broad chest for a hug. His thoughts scrambled into numbness, and words wouldn't come from his mouth.

A powerful hand rubbed his head. "Ain't had a hug like that since you were six."

How old am I? The idea of the question jittered his brain, but he was so thrilled to be home that he ignored the worry. "It's so good to see you both." Images of priests speaking at a snow-blown funeral before two pyres were set ablaze flashed through his mind but were blinked away.

The front door to the cabin blew open, or so he thought, until a man bearing a load of firewood in his arms stepped inside. Pikarn

squinted, not recognizing his narrow, shaved face with two vertical white scars streaking beneath his eyes, but Pillum stepped to take kindling from his arm. "Good of you to lend a hand."

The man smiled, and Pikarn knew his name. "Uncle Emuk. I didn't know you were here."

"I arrived from Choerkin Fost when you were sleeping, well after midnight. It's a wonder I'm alive after knocking on your mother's door at such an hour. I should have slept with the guards."

"Where is mo—" He killed his words with a smile as a stout woman meandered from the kitchen with graying sprigs over her ears, swatting flour from her hands. He didn't even run for Teru, the aching desire for normality shunting away prickles of nerves challenging his acceptance of this reality.

His mother said, "Gonna be right like a holiday with so much family here."

Emuk said, "And I have good news, but I was waiting for the boy here to awake! After last summer at the Fost, he's been invited back to train with the Choerkin boys." Lovar and Kotin were five years apart, with Pikarn born between, but there was an undeniable camaraderie between the three despite their age differences. Lovar would head the clan one day while the other sailed to rule Herald's Watch, but the rivalry was more playful than grudging. The three of them had wrestled and sparred for two months while dreaming of the battles they'd fight.

His father whooped, clapped, and slapped him on the shoulder while his mother laughed and smiled.

He'd lived this before; Pikarn remembered being excited, but when he looked at his mom, he knew now that her joy covered her fear for him and a desire for him to stay. Only after she died did he find out she suspected her illness even now. She didn't want him to

go but wouldn't dare stop him. He turned to Pillum; he and Uncle Graem would die in a blizzard in the mountains after a Colok attack in seven years.

His head cocked as a memory emerged of choosing two axes to carry in honor of their loss. A flicker of his past forgotten over the decades. "I don't wanna go to the Fost."

All eyes turned to him, and his father said, "What're you spoutin' on about, boy? You've been waiting on the invite damned near a year."

If he stayed, could he save their lives? He stared at his mother. He might not be able to save her, but could he give some extra comfort? "I don't feel like I should go." Her eyes glanced at the crib with its pillows and blankets. "Where is little Shures?" Uncle Graem's daughter had lived with them since birth, with Graem and his wife Ednu moving back from the mountains when she was four months pregnant.

Pillum said, "She's upstairs with the wet nurse."

Pikarn wandered to the crib and rubbed the rail to find dust caking his fingers. "None of our kin ever had a wet nurse."

Teru said, "Ednu went for a stroll with her."

A frosted window and the miller bundled in a heavy coat flicked through his mind. "It's no summer day out there, and Ednu wouldn't chill that child for nothin'."

Graem said, "Ednu took ill and is upstairs with Shures."

Three reasons before finding one that made sense, except it was wrong. *I lived this before.* Determined strides took him to the foot and carried him up the stairs with echoes, and a short walk down the hall took him to his aunt and uncle's door. He raised knuckles to knock, but his hand dropped to the brass knob and turned. Hinges creaked, an eerie echo of his bedroom door as it opened.

Ednu lay in bed beneath covers, chest rising and falling, but her head tilted with mouth draped open. "Auntie?" Wool blankets rose and fell, rose and fell too much for mere breaths, and faint pink drips soaked through the fabric, growing into red splotches. "Auntie!"

He strode and reached, yanking the blanket from the bed, revealing a puddle of blood in the middle of which Ednu's arms still hugged a baby to her chest—suckling and feeding on flesh instead of milk.

"No!" and the blood-faced child turned on him, its tiny fingernails claws and its once doe-brown eyes blackened by wriggling tendrils of Shadow. His stomach queased in an instant, and he fought back bile as the thing smiled with a single bloody tooth. Loped on all fours to leap.

Pikarn stumbled backward, catching the creature in midair and slamming it to the floor, but he fell over his own feet and into the hall as the scrambling Taken slicked the wooden floor with its mother's blood and came again. He scrambled, kicked her away, and made it to his feet in time to catch Shures only a flicker before tearing into his face. She weighed no more than a few bricks but fought with inhuman ferocity; his grip slipped, and he caught her by the legs even as claws ripped his vest and streaked blood. He spun, slamming her head into the door's frame with a sickening crunch that spattered black blood, and the trail of gore seeping down the wood slithered with Shadow.

He dropped the child, who should have been dead but wasn't, and ran for the stairs. "Shadows of Man! They're here!" He stumbled and slid down the stairs with the rails the only thing keeping him from a bone-cracking fall, but when he reached the main room, his kin stared as if they'd heard nothing. The rhythmic beat of a loping predator on all fours came from behind. "It's coming for us! Run."

Instead, his mother sprung toward him, mouth agape with an ear-shattering scream. He raised his hand to fend her off, and an ax plunged into her skull. A blink as she stumbled back, the steel beard grinding from her forehead as she leaned to fall dead with worms of

Shadow creeping from the wound. The ax was his, but he didn't even know where it came from.

Through three blinks, he stared as his mother's final breaths left her, and he turned to see Pillum and Uncle Graem charging. In the fleeting flickers between living and dying, he vowed to let them end him, then vowed to run, but his arms swung in unison to plant curving edges into throats that sprayed black blood to drench his beard and vest. His father's and uncle's bodies drove to either side of his legs with fingers clawing and grasping, even when dying, trying to kill.

A scream of horror erupted from his lungs as tears streamed his face, but it ended as a blow from behind took his breath. Tiny arms with clawed fingers wrapped around his head and scratched dripping streaks into his cheeks. The child, less than a year old, climbed from the back of his head to block his view of the ceiling as he fell, a maniacal smile spreading bloodied lips that came to kiss him with a tongue of Shadow—choking his desperate breath.

The tongue wriggled in his throat, and in the baby's eyes, he saw a great sadness. A sorrow full of anguish, full of a pain he knew he'd come to know well as evil burrowed through the back of his throat and into his skull to find his spine on the way to his soul.

Uncle Emuk stood over him with hands twined behind his back, stern as if gazing upon a misbehaving child sent to the corner of the room. "What the hells have you done, Pikarn?"

But he couldn't answer. Couldn't breathe air as Shadow drifted into his lungs with every attempted breath.

"What the hells have you done, Pikarn?"

His body convulsed and seized, and still no air came.

Something rammed past the Shadow and into his throat, and he awoke prone with Rikis' fingers shoved down his throat. "What the hells have you done? Pikarn! Breathe."

And he did, throwing the man's arms aside in a gasping heave as he sat up. Desperate breaths as he clutched his face and the back of his head; no blood, no demon niece feeding him Shadow.

The stranger appeared at his side, and he turned his head to stare. He wanted to curse the bastard, but his voice refused to come.

"Whatever is the matter, friend?"

A gasping breath filled his lungs with a raspy rush. "Whoreson!" He stared at the man's fiery scars, and a name came to mind: Emuk. He blinked and shook his head as he sputtered and coughed phlegm. Spat, and found himself relieved it was frothy white instead of black as shadow. "Whoreson!" Emuk was his uncle's name, not this man's, but his real uncle hadn't born scars down his face like in the dream. "I'm gonna kill you, sure as shit."

The stranger crouched with a smile. "You are welcome to try, and I'd welcome my end, but haven't you killed enough kin?"

"A dream. A nightmare, you cud-chewing bastard."

Emuk gestured to a wall of Shadows standing along the rail above them like a theater audience enthralled by the spectacle below. He pointed to Rikis sitting nearby and breathing hard. "They are your kin." He pointed to the Edan, all three of whom appeared frozen in time. "These putrid creatures aren't your blood. They don't care for you. If you live, they'll piss on you as you walk toward your mortal end, or they'll murder you without a twinge of emotion. But your kin! Your family watching from above? They will cry when they infest your body, weep as they desecrate your soul, and wail as a mother losing her child when you finally die. Kin. Family."

He remembered the sadness in the eyes of the baby killing him with Shadow and the tears he felt the thing was about to shed. "Demons! Murderous demons, you and them alike. Stay out of my mind, whoreson."

The stranger huffed as he stood, but the rolling ripples of his scarred face remained placid with a gleaming white smile. "You will see." He turned and strode toward the altar, and this time when he leaped, a split in reality formed, a dark crease of nothing that sucked the stranger between its lips as he turned to gray vapor and then disappeared.

Pikarn coughed and spat again, turning his watering eyes on Rikis. "What the hells did you see?"

"Nothing much. He said he was going to send you home, and the next thing I knew, you fell and were trying to swallow your tongue."

A groan as he stood with aching muscles in his shoulders. Inslok and the others moved as if never frozen, and Limereu said, "Something happened."

"Sure as shits it did, but I don't understand what or why."

Inslok nodded. "I think I witnessed something similar with The Touched. Tell us everything you experienced."

The Wolverine wasn't sure he was in the mood to share. "He gave me a name, but as promised, I forgot it. For some reason, I remember the bastard calling himself Emuk, but that was my uncle's name." Or was it? He stared at his toes, uncertain of his wits. "My uncle's name, yes. If he'd said Emuk at the start, I would've known it for my uncle's." He wished he was as certain as his words.

"Tell us everything."

Pikarn sighed and started his tale, but with every word, he felt a Shadowy tongue in his mouth.

FORTY-THREE

Seventh Surprise Red

Fear weakens the warrior but makes wiser most.

—*Oxeum Proverb*

Glimdrem strolled to the Contessa's room at the Sailing Fish in need of what he figured was an astonishing sum of wealth, twenty-thousand *mogdul.* He doubted the tapestry was worth so much on the open market, but considering it resided somewhere hidden and guarded, the price might not be so bad.

The Contessa sat in a luxurious room with a bed decorated with silks and feathers and a candelabra of gold hanging from above. However, despite her wealth and stature, she still dined on eggs and bread as all foreigners suffered rationing. Her silver fork dinged on her silver plate.

"Twenty thousand for what?"

"A tapestry among Red Skull's seized goods. I don't think it's what the Boboru seeks, but I want it. I believe it dates from the Age of God Wars."

"Is it beautiful?"

He grinned with its memory in his mind. "The craftsmanship is impeccable, but pretty is not a word I'd use. I think it holds a sort of map locating temples on the continent of Sutan."

She blinked before a blank stare. "The place you almost died?"

"Yes."

She picked up the fork, stabbed a bite of egg, then eyed him with it dangling. "Happy birthday."

His head cocked. "I don't know my birthday." He chuckled at himself for being slow. "Thank you for the gift." He grew suspicious in an instant at the ease with which she parted ways with her treasure and vowed to keep a close eye on the woman.

She chewed the egg and swallowed, washing it down with water. "You realize, of course, this will cost much more than twenty-thousand."

"How do you mean?"

"If you sail back to the Boboru with a single tapestry that wasn't there before, what will they think? And if it's recognized as stolen?"

"I take your point."

"Good. But don't worry, I'll make some purchases throughout the city and, with luck, break even when trading it later."

Glimdrem's tapestry was paid for by the end of the day and was carried aboard the *Flaming Wing* the next morning, and when she promised to load the ship with goods, he'd underestimated her ability to spend *mogdul*. He watched as at least three dozen rolled carpets were brought aboard, followed by stacks of hand-carved furniture. He suspected she wouldn't break even but make a profit, considering that a city under blockade would offer bargains.

Three days later, she touched his shoulder and said, "A Lultûhol inspector will be visiting your ship today. Show him everything. He fills one side of his coffers with Boborun gold."

He didn't ask how she knew, nor did he argue with her advice; he welcomed the trade inspector and his people aboard, then directed them to everything in their hull. Two days later, the ship had suffered a more thorough search than given by the Boboru on entry, and by afternoon, the Contessa lay secreted away. They raised sail for the blockade soon after, and upon arrival, Lord Captain Ushtrûôk greeted him in person after Glimdrem climbed a rope ladder to reach the higher ship.

The Lord Captain was ugly as ever with a fanged sneer that might be a smile as half a dozen Boboru descended ropes to the *Flaming Wing* below. "I hear you traded well. You will see a profit on the venture, I suggest."

"If I didn't, it would be suspicious."

A grunt-growl from the man as he nodded. "We Boboru never begrudge a profit, so long as the job is done."

"Shall we speak in private?"

"This is as private as need be."

Glimdrem glanced up at five officers surrounding them and struck his gambit. "I met with Red Skull, and he confessed to his pirating, but they move him around. There is no way for me to tell you where he is now or will be tomorrow."

"You failed."

"Did you expect me to steal him for you? I didn't fail. I saw where the treasure is held but don't know where it is."

"You failed."

"Your impatience is a failing. A man named *Nesfarmêum* Narkar Imôm took me to the treasure. I led him to believe that a tapestry was what you and the Boborun Nation wanted. I bought it, and it sits in my hull as we speak."

The man's shoulders bunched with thick muscle, and he hissed, "We do not want a tapestry."

Glimdrem raised a hand. "All a ruse. I told him *a* truth that giving you what you want will end the blockade, but I lied about what it is. He is waiting for word from you now at the docks and expects to speak with you and make peace. To be a hero. I don't think you'll have trouble getting him to tell you where the treasure is."

Ushtrûôk's anger eased with a smile more sinister than normal. "And Red Skull?"

"Any man able to find the treasure can find the man. And even if not, which matters more? Treasure or the man?"

"Both."

"Kill the man, and are you closer to the treasure? No, the Lultûhol hold and hide it. Take the treasure and make peace; someday soon, the rabbit will soon crawl from its hole to die."

"I will ram a spike through his spine until it comes out his Red Skull even as he is skinned and torn limb from limb. Then I will feast on his blood and soul."

Glimdrem blinked, and his gut squirmed. "I didn't need the details, but send whatever message you need to these fool humans."

The Lord Captain shrugged with his head bobbing. "I do not know about peace; there may be no peace without Red Skull, but after your ship is searched and I have this *Nesfarmêum* Narkar, you may set sail."

"Fair enough. And if I can be so bold, might I keep the tapestry? My esteem in the eyes of the Edan will grow with such a historical piece." It was a bold play, one he figured might turn against him, but if the Lord Captain thought he was attempting to steal it, things would go worse.

The monstrous man snarled. "As I spoke, we do not begrudge a profit. It is yours so long as you do not deceive us."

"I didn't want you to think I was stealing if I departed with it."

He softened. "Understood. What does this tapestry depict?"

Glimdrem hid a grimace beneath a smirk, fearing the Boboru knew more than he said. "Religious figures in a field woven in a jungle motif."

His stare could be best described as confused. "I liked the one with monsters and gods killing each other. Your Edan, they have poor taste?"

He chuckled, "No, no. Well, maybe. They see it as history. To study cultures from the past."

The Lord Captain grunted and waved his hand in the air. "It is yours."

They stood on the deck for two candles, waiting for the search team to finish, and Glimdrem struggled not to ask the questions he wanted to ask. What about Oxeum? Did he know what was hidden in Sutan's impenetrable mountains? How far did the Boboru make it before turning back? But he remained silent until the Boboru finished their search, less thorough than the one while docked, which suggested the Contessa was right: They owned the trade master in Lultûhol.

Glimdrem bowed to Ushtrûôk and returned to his ship well before sunset, in time for the *Flaming Wing* to maneuver around the lead Boborun vessel and wait for *Nesfarmêum* Narkar to arrive to an ugly surprise.

Once the ship bobbed in the waters waiting, Glimdrem made his way to the galley and pried open what might have become the Contessa's tomb. The lady smiled up at him, and he offered his hand, surprising even himself with the gesture.

She pulled herself to her feet. "Thank you. I assume it went well? I heard giant feet above me, but nothing more."

"We have a short wait, but yes. You understood the situation and used it to our advantage."

She smirked. "I did at that. Did you find what you sought in Red Skull's loot?"

"Did I... Why yes, I think I did."

"The tapestry?

"Indeed." A lie, or perhaps a fib. It was part of what he needed, but the statues remained behind. He fidgeted, uncertain of how much to say. "I may have figured out what the Boboru want, but I'm unsure."

She leaped to her feet, grabbed a silver mug, and poured herself water. "It was getting a bit dry in my coffin." She drank and cast him a grin worthy of a dragon. "I know what the Boboru want, and I have it."

"You do? Tell me."

She shook her head. "I'll do one better; I'll show it to you, but only after we're clear of this blockade."

"In that case, we deserve better than water." He strolled to a cabinet and pulled down a bottle of wine. Flickers later, he pulled the cork and poured.

"I don't drink often, but you're right. We deserve it."

"You will end the blockade soon, then? Turning over whatever this thing is?"

She smirked and mumbled gibberish to herself. "Not yet."

The answer struck him as peculiar. "You will let the people go hungry?"

"Not for so long as that, I hope. Lultûhol is still well-provisioned."

He studied her, uncertain of what to think. If the Boboru found the treasure hall but not what they wanted, it might bode ill for his future in these waters. And he needed a future if he was going to retrieve those statues. His tongue couldn't resist asking, "How big is this thing?"

She smiled and raised her glass but didn't say a word. They sat, sipped, and poured until the crew's shouts rang out and sails unfurled above. Within wicks, the *Flaming Wing* leaned into a turn, and they sailed north. Glimdrem stood with a smile. "I assume your mysterious treasure resides in the hull with all the furniture you bought? It wouldn't have been a chair. They're nice chairs, but...."

She giggled as she led him from the room. "No." They made their way below deck until they came to the door to the cargo room, where they stashed everything, two sailors stepping aside. "We'll need your men."

Glimdrem nodded to the Trelelunin, and they followed. He gazed around the room, unable to pick out anything that didn't blend with the more modern work. "I admit, I'm at a loss."

The Contessa strolled to the rolls of carpets, leaned, and tapped one near the back. "You men, pull this one out."

The sailors grabbed ahold and pulled as Glimdrem's brow scrunched. "This is some sort of game. That's the tapestry I brought aboard." He blinked at how it slipped from beneath the others without being forced; by all rights, it should've been crushed.

"We all play games, don't we?"

"I suppose we do." And he saw hers when the middle of the tapestry bulged like a python that had eaten a gator. "A bold strategy, Contessa."

"Oh, you've no idea yet." She nodded to the sailors. "Unroll it."

Both men put a foot to the ends and gave a shove, the mysterious thing clunking across the floor until the final wrap loosened and flopped open of its own accord.

Nozodrôk Belên, better known as Red Skull, stood with a groan and a smile. "Heavens be praised! It's damned good to see you two again."

Glimdrem's gut cinched. "How? The Captain. My men."

The Contessa strolled close to slap his shoulder. "Not a one of them knew, I promise."

"How?"

"A girl must have her secrets."

He turned his gaze from the smirking pirate, happy enough he might break into a jig, to her twinkling, playful eyes. "I guess they must." He'd always assumed that being part human made her something less than Xanesu, but now he knew the Contessa was *more* than just Xanesu. He vowed to figure out how she achieved this miracle and swore never to underestimate her again.

Forty-Four

Plans Struck

Why do you run from me? Why do you fear me?
Where do you go when you dream of me?
Where do you go when I dream of you?
Are you still or are you not?
Shave your tongue of the hair of the dog,
take my hand and run the slogging bog
of liquid possession in the dragon's laughter,
Little Mouse Man of the Gods,
why didn't you run from me? Why didn't you fear me?
Paint the dragon's scales on your tongue;
die the truth of anguish.

—*Tomes of the Touched*

The red-gold towers of Mulshahar shown beneath a noontime sun when, at last, they arrived. With Nostrolum and his people leading the way, they crossed a road leading south to the coast that would then take them to Mulshahar, choosing to avoid people and any risk to the Ilu in order to continue in their company. Meliu's excuse was simple: to learn more of their language, but the truth was she enjoyed the great cat's company maybe more than she should have. Being with him reminded her of Ivin. Reminded her of a time maybe more

dangerous, of a time maybe even more complicated, but also a time when ignorance concealed the threats ahead of them and a time when attraction could turn to love. Nostrolum was her waystone, leading to memories she often left forgotten.

But time and horizons passed, leading to the beauty of a gleaming city and the pain of leaving her waystone behind.

"We will meet again, *Reshodunûes*." He grinned, far too proud of his new nickname for her, which meant Flaming Dark.

Only now, as they said goodbye, did the name grow on her. "If I had an extra dress, I'd give it to you. A disguise, so you might sneak up on me the next time we meet."

A rumbling laugh erupted as he lifted her in a hug. "If ever you see Ivin—"

"Tell him to come find you. I will." In their time together, she never had the words or will to explain to him why she never expected to see the Choerkin again. Then again, expectations had a way of changing.

"You are forever welcome among my people." He eased her feet back to the ground and gave her a toothy smile that might look goofy if it didn't look so dangerous. "May the Eternal Hunt bring us together again soon." He leaned until bumping her forehead with his.

"Farewell, Nostrolum."

He turned and jogged northeast with his people, and she found it difficult to tear her eyes from their languid tails swooshing until Edlmir stepped to her side. "Thunder sticks, ghosts, giant invisible man-eating worms, and now giant cats who could chew my face off as they chat. I'm not sure I wanna know what comes next."

"Well, at least you missed the horde of Wakened monkeys."

"Aye, well, only 'cause I was captured into slavery by bastards with glowing yellow eyes." Lucky and Grunt appeared as if from nowhere with the departure of the Ilu warriors. "No offense to you two and yer eyes."

The Wiirê men ignored the comments, while Meliu was reminded of the White Lion at Tomarok and said, "Well, these two have seen me talking to a transparent White Lion and now Ilu, so they might be wondering what they've gotten themselves into as well." She turned to gaze over shining domes to the shimmering waters of Kônu Bay and wondered what she had gotten the yellow-eyed duo into. There was no way to know how the people of Mulshahar would react to their eyes even if they covered their bodies in local garb. "It's beautiful, but...."

"So are you, but...."

She turned to his smirk, deciding not to pursue his line of thinking. "Don't feel bad; you're a special kind of ugly."

He chuckled, and even Lucky and Grunt grinned to prove their Silone improved.

They traveled down a winding road to the coast and sloshing white-capped waves on a rocky beach to join Reshmuhar Road, which took them to the gates of Mulshahar. Once inside, its beauty thinned, the crowded streets and the fish market smell turning it into just another city. With gates wide enough for four wagons to pass side by side, they entered with only cursory glances from a dozen guards to either side and the archers above. No one did more than glance at the Wiirê men and their yellow eyes, which struck her as peculiar. Did they see so many Wiirê, or were they used to unusual foreigners in general? Or maybe they were too captivated by her enchanted red hair. She giggled to herself as they passed through thirty feet of wall, feeling blessed not to have to answer questions.

But by the time they stood a hundred strides into the city with no idea where to go next, she almost wished the guards had said something so she could question them in kind. But she didn't wish it enough to turn around and draw attention to themselves, so she stared and said, "Now what?"

Kurin shrugged. "It's a big place. I knew how to find it, but I've never been here."

Commander Florinz grunted as his horse stomped the pavers. "Did Solineus give any clues where he might be found?"

"The stories I heard spoke of a bank or currency exchange."

"Dozens of banks or more in a city this size?" He spat.

"An exchange might be more rare." She dismounted and led the animal to a merchant's stall where a woman held fruits aloft. Meliu didn't recognize the language but figured it wouldn't hurt to try Kingdomer. "Excuse me, miss? Where might I find a currency exchange?"

The young lady stared and said something so fast that Meliu couldn't pick out a word in the string, and then she stared straight past her. Then a finger tapped her shoulder, and she turned to find a gray-haired woman with a wrinkled face. "Your accent is funny; from what Kingdom do you hail?"

Meliu smiled and curtsied. "None of the eight, but I figured it was my best chance for a shared tongue."

The woman giggled with a nod. "Mulshahar is full of languages. What directions did you seek?"

"A currency exchange."

The woman nodded. "Most caravansaries and some shops will swap coins. How much value?"

Meliu went from admiring the woman's friendliness to wondering if she was a thief sizing up a target. "I'm more looking for a man, a wealthy man."

"Aren't we all, honey?"

She gave the woman a grin. "Where would a wealthy foreigner exchange his coins on arriving?"

She cocked her head. "Who are you looking for?"

"Solineus Mikjehemlut, a foreigner from the far north."

"Ah! A name I've heard whispered. The Mulshahar Exchange, no doubt."

Meliu squinted, wondering if the woman was yanking her hair or if the man was already so famous in a city so large. "You know where he is, by chance?"

A laugh. "I don't travel in such circles. Looking for him, they say to stay away from his islander girl. But I can give you directions to the Mulshahar Exchange."

She giggled to herself: *The man and Sîu are so famous.* "Just a flicker, please. My friend is better with directions." She waved her arm at Kurin, and a wick later, Meliu was back in her saddle with the Wayfinder guiding them through the streets. With busy streets and the size of their party, it was maybe a candle later that she, Kurin, Florinz, and Edlmir walked through the magnificent doors of the Mulshahar Exchange.

The hall was a garish display of wealth to rival or surpass the nobles in the city of Bdein, and the people working here carried themselves with noses held just as high. Men and women strode across the plush carpet from office to office and desk to desk with negligible glances their way. Except one young man winked her way. She whispered to Kurin, "Gods, the men are as beautiful as the women. I could get used to this place."

"I feel like a crab without a shell."

Meliu smiled, as even the winker didn't take a step their way. These people surmised they had no money or caught a whiff of their road stink. Then she noticed a woman sauntering their way, a beauty like the rest, with fine silks draping her body in a rainbow of colors and golden jewelry. She stopped three strides away and spoke in the local tongue. "*Modilu mohosh?*"

"Do you speak Kingdomer?"

Her disinterest faded. "I do. Welcome to the Mulshahar Exchange. What service might we offer today?"

"Well, we have some bullion to exchange, but it's more that I'm looking for a man who may have business here. Solineus Mikjehemlut."

The woman's brows arched over a genuine smile. "You must be Meliu. My name is Nîsiminê." It was difficult to decide which was the most surprising: the woman knowing her name or her speaking in perfect Silone, but her next words caught her the most off guard. "Anything important you have to say should be spoken in Silone and to me."

Solineus stood with hands on his hips inside the main hall of the Holdimun Building, feeling useless and yet, somehow, in charge of it all. Workers went about their jobs dusting the heights of the ceiling while painters followed behind, touching up the colors after filling cracks so tiny Solineus couldn't see them from where he stood. The sky full of angels and birds was a bit like watching the dawn, the fresh paint where the full sun shone, the rest in the predawn.

With the attached warehouses cleaned of all debris left behind by the Holdimun Trading Company, work progressed faster than expected. In normal times, this would've been a boon, but with his itch to sail south, even fast wasn't fast enough.

"Do all merchant lords in these parts oversee their crews with swords?" The woman's voice echoed from the front doors behind him, and he knew her name before he blinked twice.

"You never know when you'll be snuck up on." He turned with a smirking smile. "When I got word of you coming so far west, I thought it a joke."

Meliu stared at the ceiling as she strode his way. "Did you seriously buy this place?"

"The price of doing business in Mulshahar."

She whistled. "I don't wanna know the price." She stopped and offered her hand. "I might hug you, but I've been warned about a certain islander girl. Twice."

Solineus clasped her hand and pulled her in for a quick hug. "She likes you because she knows you're still pining for a Choerkin."

She pulled back. "Am not." She huffed. "Where can we speak alone?"

He led her to the main office, the room furnished so far with only a few chairs, a desk, and a chandelier glowing with perpetual Light that came with the building and yet, somehow, cost more than all the work done so far. He closed the door behind them. "How'd you find me?"

Meliu stared at the chandelier overhead, mouth agape, and he couldn't blame her. "Nîsiminê, at the Mulshahar Exchange. You don't hide very well. Gods, I've never seen... the crystal swans! The rainbows. It's stunning."

"Please, sit. I spent enough on these chairs that someone should use them. The chandelier, well, I never did learn how much I paid for it." He sat in a chair and gestured to another in front of the desk.

"You don't sit behind the desk?"

Solineus licked his smiling lips as he glanced at the supple leather of the seat. "I don't feel like a behind-the-desk person."

She grinned, an enticing grin that no doubt was part of how she seduced Ivin. Though he must admit, he doubted it had been a challenge. "That's good."

"Is it? So what brings you a thousand horizons to find me that doesn't involve my sitting behind a desk?"

She reached into her pack, pulled out a bottle of wine, and yanked the knobbed cork. As soon as the bottle rested on the desk, she pulled out two cups. "Unless you have better glasses?"

He chuckled. "Not here."

"These have sufficed for a long distance now." She poured and handed him a drink, but he didn't sip. Meliu, on the other hand, wasn't shy about slurping. "I've been saving this one, but I can find better now that I'm here." Her legs stretched, and she kicked off one worn leather boot, then the other with a sigh. "Oh, gods, how can heaven be the lack of shoes?"

He stomped his feet, the mule ears on his boots flapping. "I'll get you a pair of these, custom crafted and fit berôt skin. I godsdamned guarantee you won't wear them out, and they hug your feet like a mother hugging her newborn."

The priestess stared and sipped wine. "Can I tuck in the flaps?"

"Mule ears. And yes, some folks do, but *not* when you're around my father."

She grinned. "That's a peculiar price to pay."

"It's the price for the most comfortable boots you'll slip on your feet in this or any other lifetime."

"Does Sîu have a pair?"

"I can barely get her to wear a blouse."

She giggled. "It's the strangest price I ever paid for anything, but I accept."

"If you tell him these chairs are overpriced and uncomfortable, I'll buy you two pairs."

"Let's see how comfortable they are before I pay a price too high."

"Fair enough!" He leaned in his seat and sipped the wine; notes of berry struck his tongue, but he couldn't name the fruit. "Now that the important matters are behind us, why the hells are you here?"

"I've business in Ghustusvarênu, a Histê city along the Arkudân River."

Solineus took a bigger drink of wine. "I'm guessing you aren't trading in booze."

"Word arrived that some of those taken prisoner by the Wiirê Breath Stealer and her slavers are held there."

"That right? Gonna step on in and buy their freedom?"

"I was hoping for your help, and Adinvan's, to go in and cut them free."

Every muscle in his body wanted to jump at the chance, but he calmed his tongue with a drink. By the time he swallowed, he controlled his vigor. "Does Ghustusvarênu have a shipyard, do you know?"

"I don't. Why?"

"Adinvan has heard word of the Histê building better ships with foreign help, but the rumors put the shipyards everywhere like they're pouring shit into the rumor mill. We're having a hells of a time finding where the truth lies."

She shook her head and then grinned. "The only way we'll know is to take a look."

Solineus stared into his cup. "As much as I'd like to go with you, there are other important matters in the south, on top of the shipyards."

"In fact, there are important matters to the east. A mutual friend of ours stirred up trouble in Yusdelên."

"Yusdelên? In the Kingdom of Danlok? I don't even know anyone there. The once I saw the place we stopped long enough to sleep."

"The Ironwing can stir trouble from long distances. Histê bought contracts for steel arms and armor, but the Ironwing killed their deal. The Danlok produced the weapons and armor but refused to deliver and kept the gold."

"I doubt it will dent the Histê treasuries. Favored slaves wear gold and jewels."

"And they slaughtered the Histê in the street for everyone to see when they complained."

Solineus' head lolled back, and he stared at the ceiling. "What the hells were the Danlokians thinking?"

"If you can trust their word, the Ironwing wanted to rile them up."

"A distraction? A threat? Why?"

"I hoped you might know."

He scratched his head and gulped the wine before refilling. If he were dreaming, he'd say the Ironwing was pulling them into a war that would have to be fought from multiple fronts, but despite how the world seemed in Mulshahar with his wealth, life still wasn't a fantasy. The man had his reasons. "I don't see him acting on a whim. We're missing a piece."

"The Dark Waters Cult is active too; I saw hundreds of them in the streets there. Could it be related?"

His face stretched into a grimace as he shrugged. "I'm at a loss. The southern Histê Kingdoms have been plying the Korômonê with gold, maybe for ships, maybe for steel, maybe for mercenaries. I plan on heading that way."

Meliu sighed and refilled her wine. "The slaves are in Ghustusvarênu, which is also south. If not your help, I'll need that of the Emudar."

"Adinvan will, no doubt, be eager to bash some heads."

"Good. I lucked into meeting Nostrolum—"

"The Ilu?"

"Yes. He has kin who might know about the city and the region. If so, and we get lucky, they'll be looking for us on the northern side of the Arkudân River."

"The Arkudân is the southern border of the Utumwu Forest, I think. It's not so far away from here; all things are relative. How many men did you bring?"

"Fifty warriors of the clans, along with Lucky and Grunt, plus Commander Florinz Ravinrin and Edlmir."

Solineus laughed. "Complaining, no doubt."

"Oh, he does. I managed six priests and a dozen monks as well. We didn't lose a soul on the way here."

"Well! The gods favored your journey so far. Sîu hasn't even made it back to Pôn." He sighed.

She mocked his exasperation with a grin. "You look too young to be a grandfather."

He laughed, tension easing from his soul with the swift change of subject. "Cut me to the marrow, why don't you?"

"I'll regale you with everything I know of your grandchildren, Kinesee and Alu, too, if you sail with me."

He sipped his drink, finding flavors of plum and cinnamon strengthening as the wine took on air. "You're determined."

She wiggled her eyebrows. "I am."

"No promises, but... Ah hells, I can't say no." A knock on the door. "Enter."

Murêshu's head slipped inside with dangling blond locks as the carved oak swung on silent hinges. "Vondilelê, the merchant from the Notoholis Aprelêu, is here, but I see you have company."

"Murêshu, this is Meliu, a High Priestess of the Pantheon of Sol. And a friend."

The woman's eyes widened. "Oh! A pleasure. I hope my Silone is acceptable?"

Meliu nodded while fighting a smile. "It's exquisite."

Solineus said, "You go ahead and handle the Notoholis man; you know the Gorotan better than I do, anyhow. And if you can send someone for a bottle of wine, I think we're going to need it."

"I'll see to it."

She closed the door, and he turned back to meet Meliu's smirking stare as she sucked wine through her teeth. "What?"

"Oh, Sîu has gotta *love* her."

He laughed with wine in his mouth and wiped his lips. "You might be surprised. Sîu has taken a shine to her."

"What's with you and pretty girls anyhow?"

Solineus kicked back with a smile. "You tell me, a beautiful woman sitting in my office drinking wine with her boots off."

She coughed, blushed, and, he suspected, wanted to kick herself. "Yeah."

It was rare to see her uncomfortable, and part of him wanted to revel in her squirm, but instead, he drank and said, "Tell me what trouble the twins are giving my daughters."

Forty-Five

Plans in Shadow

Make your deaths worth having lived for.

—Warlord Kîpôk,
at the Battle of Himdeulêun

Lôdumâ stretched fresh linen over the gash in his thigh, close enough to his groin to add insult to injury while wondering if he'd walk with a limp the rest of his life if he didn't find a priest soon. Bouncing in the back of a wagon to pound the pain of every cut, bruise, and ache was what he deserved. With Kworgin dead and Yorvun spittling blood onto his lips and face with a cough every three or four breaths, he didn't doubt his faithful friend would be next.

Gimin spurred his horse to ride beside the wagon's wheel. "We may yet save him."

Sometimes, Lôdumâ feared the Thônian read his mind. "We kept him from a river ride out of Bdein. Much more, I can't say."

"You should be thankful you weren't castrated and have the Sword of Bdein."

Lôdumâ cast a dubious eye upon the blade's steel. The quality of its metal and flesh-hewing edges was undeniable, but after dreaming for years of recovering this inanimate thing, he, at last, wondered about its true value. "Was it worth Kworgin's life? Yorvun, here?"

Gimin didn't look at the ailing man, instead staring into the road's distance. "A man's life can't be valued against an ideal or a belief. Tens of thousands have died in wars for ideas; is it worse for two men to die for a sword that carries with it the promise of an idea?"

"History has a way of making things appear worth the sacrifices. I knew these men. I loved these men. They had names and died for me."

"Every warlord of the past suffered through victories. You didn't know the names of their soldiers. You've lost men before."

"Most when I was drunk and wanted to die myself."

They rode in silence for a spell. "What now, then? We quit?"

Lôdumâ turned his gaze to Yorvun, his coughs ending as his breaths grew more shallow. He considered whether it would be a kindness to end his suffering. "And throw the thing into the river."

"And let them die for nothing?"

"Shall I have thousands more die to make their deaths meaningful?"

"If you want to make them meaningless, go! Go kneel on the banks of the Mighty Fulgar and plunge the blade through your heart. Let the currents carry you both away."

"Don't tempt me."

"I say again, what now? You know what must be done."

"Do I?" He picked up the Sword of Bdein. Taking this family treasure from the Stôltmor had seemed his ultimate goal, a culmination of reclamation and revenge, but it wasn't. Gimin was right: Lôdumâ did know the answer; he just wanted not to say it, not to take responsibility for the havoc the words would wreck in pursuit of the goal he chased. "We will topple Stôltmor and take Bdein."

"This is wrong."

Gimin was right again, but again, Lôdumâ didn't wish to say it aloud. "We must kill the Bishop and return rule to the rightful king. We'll need allies."

Gimin patted his horse with a grin. "Who?"

"Gomjon, for a start."

Gimin sucked his teeth and whistled, a sure sign of disagreeing. "We should start smaller."

He lifted the Sword of Bdein to point at the sky, gazing at the faint reflection of himself in its dull gray mirror. "I never slouched my training with a sword, but never could I compare myself to my Uncle Eremô. Gîer possessed a devil in his wits, but Eremô put us all to shame. Eremô held to a theory of combat: If you start the fight too slow, you'll be quick to lose. If we're to win this war or start a war at all, we need the first blow to be swift and decisive."

"I'm listnin'."

"Gomjon sits on the coast, a vital trade port. I wager it hasn't fallen into ruin like Bdein. The Ar-Gomjon never liked the heavy hand of the Bishop. They'll listen."

"And if they don't still rule?"

He shrugged and lay the sword down beside him. "We find another way. Make friends of Gomjon. Bring the people of Bdein together. When the Bishop comes for us, we kick her teeth in."

"The king?"

Lôdumâ blinked. "Yes, we need to know more of the king. If he's even alive."

"And if your old friend is a willing puppet?"

He snorted. "Then he'll step aside or die."

They found an herbalist for his leg the next day, and the pain subsided, but Lôdumâ refused to return to the saddle until two days after Yorvun died. They buried him on a hill overlooking the Mighty Fulgar River, better than Kworgin received but not what he deserved. A week out, they encountered and slaughtered one of the Bishop's Patrols, but not before the fools demanded a tithe and a surrender of their arms. He was pissy enough to have killed them anyhow, but he appreciated the gift of an excuse.

It was the first blow in a war the Bishop didn't yet know she was fighting, and it was this thought that soothed his anger more than the killing itself.

Twenty-four days later, they gazed upon the walls of Gomjon. Even from a distance, he recognized that the city had faired better than Bdein. Guards walked the walls, and a line of people stood waiting to enter the gates, but what interested Lôdumâ was the ships sitting in the harbor and anchored out from shore. Sailors carried news and liked to talk.

He led Gimin and five men of his retinue to the beach, bought five kegs of ale from one crew, and let his people drink their fill before inviting any and all from up and down the beach. In no time, men sawed at fiddles and banged on drums, and a hundred or more souls joined the party. Bonfires burned as the sun set, and he bought more kegs before finding Captain Kizimor of the *Middle Fin*, a man born and raised in Gomjon. He plied the man with ale, then pulled a bottle of whiskey from his jacket. He saluted, sipped, and handed him the drink.

"So, tell me, friend, what's the state of the Ar-Gomjon?"

The man took liberties with the bottle before wiping his mouth with a shrug. "Way I hear, Mrîgus Ar-Gomjon still rules, but he lost half his family to Rot. The city was hit right hard, but not so bad as others, aye? Ten to twenty-thousand dead before the dyin' slowed."

"I'd just left Bdein when Rot struck. Did they bar the gates?"

"You betcha! For a month and a half, there weren't much in the way of people in and out."

Lôdumâ smiled to squelch the fire in his gut. Twenty thousand when low estimates in Bdein hit a hundred thousand; had the quarantine doomed more to die? "No. Impossible. The Bishop still watches the roads and bans travel."

The man took a slug of liquor and glanced around. "You see the Bishop's soldiers here? Nah. I can't speak to you inland folks, but we've been trading and carrying supplies to Bdein and other cities and villages. More woulda died if we didn't keep the food movin', am I right?"

His teeth clenched. "More. Yes."

A cry rang out, "Longship!"

Lôdumâ leaped to his feet, eyes turning for the sea. Stars sprinkled across the northern horizon, and several ships sat bobbing, but a single square sail blocked a patch of sky. "A Silone ship?" In the old days, they'd be grabbing their bows and swords in anticipation of a raid, but now, most folks just stared.

"Looks like it is, it sure does."

Lôdumâ snagged his whiskey from the man, took a drink, and handed it back. "We'll speak more." The man raised the bottle as Lôdumâ turned, spotting Gimin standing atop a rise tufted by knee-high grasses. He reached the Thônian as a cloud passed from in front of the moon, and its light blinked on the waves and put a soft glow on the vessel. Sailors stood at the prow, but the ship remained at full sail. "What do your blackened eyes see?"

"A Silone longboat. A dozen men I can see." He blinked and shook his head. "I sense no one watching us. No one watching at all."

Lôdumâ shrugged. "Good! No reason to be watching us."

"Not good."

He turned his gaze back to the ship with a snort—full sail, still, and coming fast. Longboats ran ashore often enough, unlike a cog or caravel, but the boat's speed... He licked his lips and opened his mouth to shout when the men at the prow disappeared. Fell? Dropped to their knees? "Arms! To arms! Arms! Attack and blood!" He drew the Sword of Bdein and took a half step before Gimin grabbed his shoulder.

"They should run."

He turned to snarl at the man, for a flicker, imagining Ivin Choerkin coming for his sword a second time. "We don't run from godsdamned Silone raiders!" He slapped Gimin's arm away and ran down the hill, eyes locked on the boat as its keel struck the sandy shore with a grinding thud. Figures rose and flung themselves over the rail, leaping so high he questioned his senses, forcing his rational mind to accept it as a trick of his perception at night and after whiskey. Sailors charged into the Silone, weapons chopping and hewing with grunts and screams. A Silone raider launched over the edge of the ship, striking the beach and leaping again, landing atop the shoulders of a sailor, like some giant bird come to carry the man away, and this time, his rational mind forced him to accept what shouldn't be. The sailor shuddered and began to collapse under the weight, but the Silone stood with a lurch atop his shoulders and raised the man's head high in a spray of night-blackened blood.

A shriek from the ship and a dozen more men rushed over the rail, except they didn't run, they didn't leap; they sailed like autumn leaves falling from trees to settle on the ground, weaponless hands striking the men who made it to the front lines. Screams. Bellows. Terrified anguish.

Lôdumâ slid to a stop, burying himself up to his ankles in the sand. He watched darkness dance past a fire, a darkness darker than Gimin's eyes. *Demons of shadow. Ivin and his priestess didn't lie.* A body flew through the air, spun and hefted by a Taken, and Lôdumâ screamed, dragging his feet from the sand to run, to fight, and to kill. Twenty desperate strides later, the Sword of Bdein bit into the back of a woman feeding on the face of a man. She stood straight and turned, smiling at him with blood dripping from lipless teeth, and he swung with every bit of power he could muster, sending her head flipping to the sand with a thud followed by her body. He stood panting, and a Shadow shrieked a painful ringing into his ears. The creature lifted a man, and Lôdumâ charged, but the Sword of Bdein passed through its form as it would air.

He stood staring with mouth agape as the thing threw the man to the ground and plunged headfirst into his screaming, quaking body. "Grace of the gods."

A hand grabbed his shoulder and tugged, then jerked him away. Gimin said, "We need to run."

He peddled five steps backward, eyes unable to leave the darkness disappearing into the writhing man, and he tripped. Hand hitting the sand for balance and failing. Fell. Banged his shoulder on a log. By his feet, a body with a face split in twain, and he muttered to himself, "Run. Run, you dumb bastard."

Gimin offered a hand, but Lôdumâ scrambled to his feet and into a stumbling gait.

A hundred strides. Two hundred strides. Three hundred strides at a dead sprint before they turned to look back, fighting for breath as people below fought or fled for their lives. "We were warned. I didn't listen."

Forty-Six

Plans Unknown

Immortal Ice rests in a field of Fire
never melting and forever growing higher.
How, you ask? How indeed. How in need.
How to whistle through splits in the reed.
Proven wise, to see through lies,
to make it this far, you have.
Answer the how and laugh the why
to understand how even the immortal must die.

—*Tomes of the Touched*

Ivin reached for the door to Skywatch with a hesitation he couldn't fathom, his hand paused mere hairs from gripping the ikoruv handle. He'd been in the stars several times since his first journey, and though what he saw often confused him, the visions didn't invade his dreams with terror. *The only truth the priests ever spoke to me was that forward is the path to everywhere, but no bones will show the path to you.* Kotin's voice echoed from the day Meris last broke bones for Ivin, and they brought a shiver.

But Meris no longer resided in the stars. He wasn't here to see a true priest or to have his future told to him. He was here to see Eliles.

No. He was here to see his friends scattered around the world, to see what challenges they faced, and to reassure himself all was as well as could be hoped.

He opened the door with a deep breath and strode for the stairs as if he'd jumped into drowning waters, and didn't breathe easy until climbing glowing stairs and poking his head above the floor.

Eliles smiled. "You're late."

He grimaced, then smirked. "How the hells can you tell?"

"I can't." She led him a few feet and sat with the music of the stars reverberating around them.

He eased onto the floor beside her, uncomfortable with the comfort he felt by her side but unable to deny the sensation. He clapped his hands together. "No dancing around today. Show me Kinesee."

"Elinwe, show me the way to Kinesee Choerkin."

The world the stars showed blurred as always and streaked south, but he grew accustomed to the travel by now. They sped into the city of Endelêun, into its palace, slowing as their vision entered their bedroom. He coughed, at first uncomfortable for Eliles to see his wife in bed, but the way she lay curled twisted his gut. "She's crying. Something's wrong."

He stood and strode forward as if he could walk to her but stopped to wobble as the vision blurred and his balance failed. He sat again, shaking his head before reopening his eyes. Kinesee clutched a young child in her arms, holding tight. "My daughter?"

"Yes, I think so."

"What's wrong? Is my daughter sick?" They sat so close she could see the girl breathin, quiet and easy despite her mother's swollen red eyes. "No. My son. Where the hells is my boy?" His heart chugged.

"I don't know. It could be nothing."

"Nothing?" He spat the word, but smothered his emotions. "It could be." They sat staring in silence for flickers, then he sighed with a drooping head. "This is wrong. We shouldn't be here. Take me to Solineus."

"Elinwe, show me Solineus Mikjehemlut."

Their vision as it swung west until they arrived focused on a dense forest. He saw nothing of the man through the canopy. Nothing of anyone, until a dozen people burst into a clearing, running hard with the vision following like a soaring vulture. Red hair and black flowed in the wake of two women running beside the figure he assumed was Solineus. "Son of a bitch. Meliu?"

They disappeared into the trees, and less than a wick later, Histê warriors surged into the clearing, and he watched as at least fifty gave chase into the forest.

He rose to his knees and swiped his brow. "Godsdamnit. Godsdamn. Rikis. Show me Rikis."

"Elinwe, take me to Rikis Choerkin."

Ivin wavered on his knees like a faithful reaching rapture in prayer as the world spun him into abject darkness, and he roared in horror before his eyes adjusted, but what he saw brought no comfort. A vertical glow struck from a diamond-encrusted dais, and two men lay nearby, surrounded by Trelelunin and three Edan. He knew the place.

"The Chanting Caverns."

"They're alive. Asleep."

"They went to the Gate there. To close it?"

"Maybe. But they haven't yet."

"But they went with hope." He breathed easier until he realized the darkness outside the circle of Trelelunin slithered with wavering forms. "Shadows of Man. Hundreds of them." He fell back to his ass, planting his hands on the cool latcu. "I can't save them."

"We could try—"

"No. Even if I could leave, they'd be dead by the time I got there, or Inslok would have them out."

She slipped to his and took his face in her hands. "It might be possible."

He brushed her hands in a halfhearted gesture. Breathed deep. "We can't trust the visions. These are Elinwe's stars. That means Sol's stars. If he needs me off this island, what lies wouldn't he tell?"

A glow in the corner of his eye, and they both turned as the gate swelled, its faint glow spreading with a green tint. A massive eye turned to look at them, and clawed fingers split the universe's wound. A hand so huge it could crush five men.

He leaped to his feet. "They don't see it. How don't they see it?"

The arm stretched, reaching higher. "Because it's not coming for them. Elinwe, show me now!"

Ivin careened to his knees as they lurched to a sky of stars, and he bent as if in prayer. "Give me strength. How the hells did the Queen of Shadow know we were watching."

"I don't know."

His breaths fogged the latcu floor. "Kill me before you let me leave this island."

Ieru spun and danced in the expanse of stars beneath the length of the Spear of Bontore before it was bent or broken while waiting for the Shower of Stars in order to escape into the real world. She hummed an imagined tune with the lack of the floor's song and wondered what fun she might find on the island today. Grapes were good every time, but she also had a hankering for mashed potatoes.

A hankering for mashed potatoes.

Grapes are good every day.

Hankering for mashed potatoes.

Her spin on the ball of her foot stuttered with the words in her head, and she dropped to hands and knees. Despite realizing the repetition, her voice echoed in her head:

Hankering for mashed potatoes.

Her searching eyes found nothing out of the ordinary until she slipped to the side and looked back to see her ghostly self in a spin on her toe. This other Ieru didn't drop to a knee; she smiled and leaped before disappearing, leaving her wide-eyed and fearful.

She froze as her muscles bunched. *Watching me.* She glanced up; tiny eyes perfect in shape but too small to know the color. Or were they humongous but shrunk by perspective and distance? A warm breeze caressed her skin. She swallowed hard as her heart skipped and stalled. *Winds don't come to Skywatch.* A second puff, damp and acrid in her nose. *A breath.*

She bolted, shoes slipping and sliding until she reached a dead sprint. Navigating the stars proved tricky sometimes, with distances and directions so vast, but traveling from the Shower of Stars to camp was instinct without the need for stars as a guide. Her pace slowed during the wicks leading home, but her breaths still came labored as she headed straight for a group sitting around a Fire.

Auntie Niseem smirked. "Well, look who bothered to return."

Ieru's hands fell to her knees. "Eyes. Watching me."

Other priests stared, but Auntie stood, wrenched her arm, and dragged her away. "What foolishness is this?"

She stripped her arm free. "Eyes in the stars!"

"Eyes of what?"

"Nothing! Just eyes."

Niseem's head drooped. "People see things in the stars all the time. There's nothing there."

"Nothing doesn't breathe on me."

She grunted at her. "You've spent too much time alone in the stars. Too much time with your *friends.*"

"I have no friends!"

"Eliles and the Choerkin?"

Ieru scrunched her lips into a snarl. "I—"

"Did you think I wouldn't know?"

"I don't care! There were eyes staring at me." Sol's star streaked across the sky above Niseem's head.

"Time in the stars will—"

"Eliles would believe me!" She shoved past Auntie and ran in the only direction she could run, back toward the eyes, back to the passage that would appear in the Shower of Stars, back to the Evil Queen who would listen.

She looked over her shoulder and slowed with the lack of chase, gauged the time until the Shower would begin, and eased into a trot, a pace she could maintain for a candle or more.

Breaths came easier as she stared into the eyeless distance. "I'm never coming back. Never ever." A steady jog into eternity, but with a finite destination. The first streaking stars of the Showers appeared above and she sped into a loping run, and when she looked down again, the eyes stared straight at her.

She screamed but didn't so much as veer. *Straight. Run straight. There's nothing in the stars.* Every adult she'd met promised her this truth, except Eliles. The only person she trusted spoke of dragons and skeletons. She stifled her terror into a tremble that chilled her shoulders, a shiver that died in the heat of her heart running.

I am the Evil Queen's friend. You will not eat me.

Unblinking and growing closer, an emotionless disembodied threat streaked her way as if sliding down a cable instead of rising and falling as a running animal. From the size of a child to an adult to larger than a bull's head, the eyes grew without an indication of when they'd be on top of her.

Until a rush of hot and humid washed over her in a putrid gust. She screamed and burst into a final sprint that would carry her to her end or her salvation. The eyes swelled into three dimensions, the colors of the iris a blurred swirl of blue, green, black, brown, violet, and red, and she dropped to hip in a slide beneath, and the putrescence of breath disappeared in a gust of fresh air.

She smiled a flicker before claws dug at her ribs, the fabric of robes tearing, and a shriek ripped from her lungs as she beat at the thing's grip. Shoved and kicked and pushed herself away and across the floor, panting, and the chimes of the floor mingling with the squeak of bloodied hands pushing and streaking the latcu floor.

Spectral hands disappeared and she didn't wait to see if the eyes followed. She spun and closed her eyes to pray:

"Elinwe, show me the way to now."

The stars didn't budge and a breath warmed her neck.

"Elinwe! Show the way to now!"

Fetid stench washed over her, burning her nostrils.

"Elinwe! Show me the way!"

A bite to her shoulder, but the teeth didn't penetrate her robes.

"Show me the way! Show me the way!"

Eliles crawled to Ivin's side and leaned over him with comforting hands on his shoulders. "You're right. Lies. All lies. We're safe here."

"Show me the way!"

The scream repeated, and she lurched to her feet and into a run with Ivin by her side. Her eyes revealed nothing, and she focused. In the stars there wasn't a sense of distance, but her sense of direction was unerring. "This way."

They ran until seeing Ieru still screaming in the distance, and she sped at unnatural speeds until sliding to the girl's side with instinctual Fire billowing into a wall around them all. Blood streaked the floor, and stickied her hands.

"It's all right. I have you. I have you."

The girl's eyes fluttered open with tears streaming down her cheeks as Ivin reached them with his sword in hand. "The eyes. They came for me."

Ivin kneeled. "What the hells do you mean?"

"I, I ran to Auntie. She didn't believe me. I was running to reach you. The Shower of Stars. It attacked me, ripped at me. It had me."

Eliles hugged her tight. "I've got you. You're safe."

A violent shake of the girl's head. "No, no. Not safe. It came with me through the Shower of Stars."

Eliles stiffened. "It did what?"

"It bit me when I was trying to get to now."

Eliles met Ivin's gaze, then whispered to the child, "Did it try to kill you, or just hold on?"

"Kill me! Look!" She elbowed Eliles back and raised bloodied palms. Snuffled. "It held me. I escaped. I... You think it wanted me to take it with me?" The girl pulled her robes from her shoulders, toothy bruises blossoming.

Eliles touched the wounds, feeling for the damage with Life. "When it bit you? Was it biting you when Elinwe brought you to now?"

"I don't think so."

Eliles kissed her forehead and stood. "Get her out of the stars. Get her safe."

Ivin's lips twisted into a snarl. "No, I won't leave you."

"Neither of you can be here, and we must know. Don't argue. Go. Wait for me." With a thought Fire subsided, and a white beam of Light appeared in the distance. "Don't be fools."

"You think it's the Queen of Shadows?"

"I don't know what to think."

The Choerkin sheathed his sword and lifted the girl. "I'll be here waiting by the time you come back."

He ended the temptation to kiss him when he turned and loped toward the Light. She planted her feet, sat, and by the time Ivin's song disappeared from the stars she laid flat on her belly in wait for the time shift, and she whispered, "Elinwe, show me the way to twenty-five ninety-four, two thousand five hundred and ninety-four years after Luxukoni time began, the nineteenth candle of the fifth of Kelevra."

The universe blurred until it stopped with the constellations as expected, and she crept to a knee to look up and all around.

Nothing but stars. *The time isn't right.* She stood and waited for the first shooting star, then breathed deep to gather her wits and energies. Spirit flooded her being from the cosmos around her, and she sent it in search of anything alive, finding nothing.

Until the Shower of Stars began.

When she touched people with Spirit she got a sense of who they were, loose patterns of emotion amid the tight weave of energy within the body that seemed a unique identifier. Or at least unique enough to put a name to a person she'd felt before. Animals, from birds to horses, the same. The *something* warbling on the edge of her perception wasn't trapped in a weave, the whole being more similar to emotion, flowing and free, but there was a total lack of feelings. No hate, fear, love, or sorrow. An emptiness. A void. What she was tempted to call lifelessness, and yet, she knew this would be a lie.

She closed her eyes to locate the vague sense of being, and no surprise it emanated from beneath the Shower of Stars. "King Priest Esreriun?" Nervous words in humor, but if he'd answered, she might not have been surprised. But he didn't.

She swallowed to wet her drying throat and strode forward with slow, cautious, sliding steps to bring as little music to the stars as she could. *Don't be dumb and walk into the Shower.* But how not to except to stay away? There wasn't a line in the universe to say where one reality shifted to another.

She strengthened her prayer. Pushed energy.

Life.

Hate.

And her body lifted in the air to a screech that echoed the universe. Her breath left her in a rush, and a talon dug at her calf, thigh, lower back, and shoulders, its grip massive and threatening to crush her like a mouse in some great cat's paw.

She reached out for the Sliver in desperation, but her flailing arms and lack of breath fought against her. She felt its energy, felt its tug, but the agony was too great. For a flicker, she wondered if she shouldn't taken the Maimer's Lash more often to prepare her for this moment, but then the grip eased, flipping her upside down for the blood to rush to her head in a wave of dizzy.

A thunderous voice, even if it was only in her head. "Let me in."

She grunted in defiance, unable to say no, and the beast squeezed harder.

"Let me in." The invisible hand flipped her upright and shook her until she reeled on the verge of blacking out as bones cracked and blood flowed. "Let me in."

Blurry eyes stared at the stars as her head lolled. Some said the sun and stars were all the Fire of Sol. An aching breath as she closed

her eyes, and she felt the warmth of her little friend, almost forgotten after all these years. Through parched lips, she spoke. "Save me." A tiny orange glow appeared on the tip of her nose, and she would've laughed at her foolishness for such a request from such a tiny thing.

Her cold nose warmed as the tiny being spun, growing bigger, throwing sparks, and then the sky went black, the only light sitting on her nose. She assumed it was death coming for her until tens of thousands Fires streamed into the invisible force holding her, and the thing screamed, dropping her.

She hit the floor with the sound of a broken drum echoing across the universe and she crawled fighting for breath. Hand, knee, hand, knee, breathe. "Elinwe, give me Life, and the Elements flooded her being the holes sealing, bones mending, and energy returning. She reached for the Sliver of Star and found its power as she stood, and in flickers, she rose above the surface of the stars, turning and ready to unleash the tempest.

But the Shower of Stars was gone. So too the being of Spirit. Only a tiny Fire remained, hovering to return to her side. The stars shined above as they always did, and as she released her hold on the Sliver she settled back to the floor with gentle rings of the xylophone.

She didn't bother to sit. "Elinwe, show me now."

The universe shifted until she stood beside Ivin with the tiny Fire between them.

He jumped at the sight of her, leaning to look around her little friend. "Well?"

"It's not the Queen of Shadows. I think it's male. And I think it's trapped in the Shower of Stars."

"Trapped? You can kill it?"

She held up a finger for her friend to sit on, then walked for the stairs. "I don't think so. But, there's good news. I don't think you need to leave the island to find a war."

Forty-Seven

Plans Taken

A lantern unlit casts as much light as one burning but covered. It does a soul no good to be wise if it never shows its wisdom.

—*The Oxeum Codex*

Ghosts, it turned out, were a bit like rain: when you wanted them most, they proved scarce. Or perhaps they didn't like the guest who had been showing up daily for a month. Neesebelu warmed up to Rinold by the end of the first morning, but after two weeks, Kovin still eyed him like some sort of intruder, and after a while, Kinesee could only giggle as the boy slapped at the man with a tiny play sword. Bonding by playing dead worked, and it came like a flash flood. One moment, he ran the Squirrel through, and the next, he laughed with him and toddled around the room being chased.

But this was yet another morning, and she awoke with the curtains wide open to ensure dawn's first light broke her eyelids open. She blinked and sat up, dressed in a hurry, knowing Rinold waited outside the door—the man claimed the prison that was Endelêun didn't allow him to sleep past the break of day—and slipped past the dozing twins

to welcome Rinold and her handmaiden Feneshu, and said, "Good morning."

Feneshu smiled and ducked her head in a bow as always. "Good morn, m'lady."

And Rinold whispered, "Puxele says mornin' to ya," as always.

And as always, they took seats to stare at an empty chair.

The first day felt dramatic, the second day felt overdue, the twentieth boring, and today, it felt ridiculous. She rubbed her head as a candle passed, and the twins awoke to eat and romp around the room, probably wondering why the adults sat around so much.

She sighed and slapped her hands on the arms of her chair. "I'm sorry, Rinold! I've drug you into a fool's run."

"Don't fret it; you feed me good."

She glanced at the table to realize breakfast hadn't arrived, and she sighed, a pang in her gut suggesting she starved, but only after being reminded they hadn't eaten. She strode to the door, leaving Feneshu sitting on the floor playing with the twins, and opened it to find Harlik and Budoe. "Breakfast is late. Would one of you see why?"

The guards glanced at one another, and she wasn't sure if they'd fight over standing still or getting a chance to stretch their legs. Harlik said, "I'll see to it, Lady Choerkin."

"Thank you."

She clicked the door shut and made it to her seat when the knob of the door rattled. Rinold and her stared, expecting someone to enter. No one. Just the rattle and shake. And it didn't stop.

The last time the door rattled, Lûdnarn's ghost entered, but then it had been like someone turning the knob. Now, something tried to force the door, and it brought terror.

"Harlik! What're you doing?"

"Nothin' m'lady."

Rinold blurted, "Then who the hells is shaking the shit outa the door?"

Silence from the man, even though the knob twisted without opening the door. Feneshu grabbed the children in her arms. "What's happening?"

Kinesee eased toward the door, shouting, "No one is shaking the door?"

"M'Lady, it isn't shaking."

Rinold stepped in front of her and grabbed the handle, and all went silent. He twisted, and the door opened on a hinge in need of oil. Harlik stood alone. "You didn't hear or see that?"

The warrior shook his head. "What're you talking about?"

Rinold shut the door, holding onto the knob. He stared. Waited. A candle passed before he let go, and the knob rattled and shook in an instant. "You don't see no ghosts?"

"Not a one."

"Well, they're here." He grabbed the knob, and all went silent. He let go, and it rattled with a ferocity that made Kinesee want to scream. He clutched it again, and the door thrust open as if driven by a bull, throwing Rinold from his feet and into the wall. Kinesee screamed as her friend crumpled against the wall, "Harlik!" But the man stood guard in the hall, oblivious and unmoving. No. Not frozen. He shifted his feet but didn't so much as turn his head. *We are hidden from him.*

A shrill scream pained her ears, and she spun to Feneshu. The handmaid's arms reached into the air, holding nothing. Tugging. Fighting. Something tugged at her leg, and she looked down to find Neesebelu staring up at her. *Kovin!*

Looking at Feneshu again, she saw little hands sticking from her grip. This meant his feet faced the door despite her inability to see any more of him. She screamed and dove, wrapping her arms around

the woman's waist and heaving with all her strength. Looking over the woman's shoulder, Kovin's little face appeared in the air. From nothingness. "Mommy!"

"Baby! We won't let you go! Rinold!"

The man stumbled to his feet with his sword in hand and swung where legs would be if a person pulled on the boy. Nothing. Again and again, nothing, and Kovin's face faded. "Rinold!"

The Squirrel tossed his sword and came to her, slipping between Feneshu's arms and taking hold of her hands and Kovin's forearms. "I won't let go, pull!"

She feared her son would be torn apart, feared he'd disappear, feared being pulled into the netherworld, but her arms pulled with desperate strength. Muscles bunched and burned, a grimace spreading her face as her feet pressed against stone, and her head turned with squinting, tear-filled eyes to see Neesebelu's sweet smile. Passing her. "Flying, mommy."

"No!" She shrieked, and in an instant of instinct, she let go of Feneshu and lunged, arms outstretched as she dove through the air. Hair floating in the air as she fell, fingers splayed so wide they hurt, and passing right through the girl's chest and legs.

Kinesee hit the floor, driving air from her lungs and coughing. She spun to her back to see Feneshu fall backward with a cry and Rinold's failing grip as he slipped forward, his hands disappearing in the air with Kovin's. She scrambled on all fours, clutched Rinold's waist, and wished she wasn't some forty-five-stone girl but one of those men who lifted half a boulder above their head. She screamed with a vision of her muscles bulging, but though tall for a woman, she wasn't the giant of her imaginings, and she slid with Rinold, grunting and heaving.

"What the hells?" Izilfer appeared in the doorway, Harlik behind her and still unmoving as if the scene behind him didn't exist.

Feneshu's arms wrapped Kinesee's waist as they both screamed, "Help us!"

The priestess in white didn't run for them and take hold to pull; she stared before her eyes closed, and a flicker later, the world of color turned black, white, and gray. Kovin hung in the air, mouth agape, and a mass of writhing gray had hold of him, whether with its hands or mouth, she couldn't say. All she knew was that the thing had her baby and wasn't alone. Creatures danced all around, but not ghosts. Her first thoughts spun to Shadows of Man, but not one could she call humanoid. Monsters. Wraiths. Demons. Even as she hauled on Rinold's waist, she wanted to put a name to things to help make sense of it all, but there was no name.

Kinesee's grip slipped, and Rinold lifted from his feet with a bellow, his arms matching the gray of Kovin's cheeks until the boy jerked free and the man fell to his face.

Kovin's cry echoed as if from everywhere at once, but the entity of gray wisps swallowed him and fled through the door.

Straight past Izilfer's stunned stare.

Kinesee lurched to her feet. "My son! Get my son!" She swiped swirling arms gray from her path; no sensation. Nothing was there, and she sprinted through the door with Rinold and Izilfer on her heels.

Izilfer said, "What the hells are these things?"

Kinesee didn't answer, her eyes panic-wide and her face chilled by tears leaving freezing streaks down her face. *Cold. Follow the cold.*

They ran down halls, passing servants, guards, and clan-blood, none of whom seemed to see them. Kineese's fid slid rounding a corner, and she slammed into the wall, crumpling to a knee, and by the time she stood in the hall, the cold had disappeared.

"No! No!" She stood at a 'trident' crossing where one hall went straight ahead and two more angled left and right, but she knew all

three led to rooms. Seventy-two rooms, eighteen to both sides of the central hall and eighteen more on the exterior side of the other two. She wished she didn't live in a palace in the tropics. She wished she lived in a one-room house on a frozen shore where evil couldn't hide her baby.

Rinold stopped behind her, but Izilfer raced past her. "Come on!"

Kinesee ran past thirteen doors before Izilfer stopped to grab a knob. Struggled. "Locked!"

Rinold shoved her and kicked; the ancient door shattered at the latch with his second kick, and they stormed inside. A man and a woman sat on a bed, kissing, half-naked. Kinesee gasped, but neither of the pair noticed them.

"Alive or ghosts?"

Izilfer's eyes didn't linger on the pair, but she said, "To be honest, I don't care at this point." She ran to a wall, her hands slapping tapestry-covered stones. "Damn it! It went through here, I swear it."

Kinese scanned the room. "A secret door. Find it."

Izilfer closed her eyes and walked the room, waving her arms, even as Kinesee ripped the tapestry from the wall, its woven forested hunting scene rumbling to the floor in fabric waves. She beat on the wall with her fists and looked for cracks. "There's a seam!"

And in that moment, a grinding screech echoed. "Found it!"

The wall pivoted for what seemed an eternity before the three squeezed into a gray space of unnatural light, a space so narrow that it rubbed her shoulder blades and breasts at the same time before coming to a free fall into blackness. She stood, panting, glancing at the pit and the tight hall beyond. "Which way did it take him?"

Izilfer said, "Down."

The back of Kinesee's head knocked the wall. "Of course it did. Light?"

The hole blazed into shadowless Light but carried with it a peculiar orange tint. "Thank the gods, a ladder." She jumped in and climbed. Down. Down. Down. What seemed an eternity of down, even if it turned out to be three or poles deep before she set foot in a small pentagonal chamber with passages striking from each wall. "Which way?"

Izilfer leaped from the ladder to land beside her and pointed, and they ran into shadowless Light. Ran until they collided with an oaken door that refused to budge. They pounded and kicked. Izilfer prayed. Rinold struck his dagger into the lock, twisting and prying. Nothing.

They stood and stared. Defeated in the hunt for a creature they couldn't name, defeated in a search for her one-year-old son, defeated by a simple locked door. Tears streamed her cheeks, kicks weakened by exhaustion landing with dull and pointless thuds until she collapsed to the floor to sit and cry.

Until the door clicked and creaked open.

Kinesee stood, tears dried as if blown away by a desert wind, and she stepped into the dim room with Rinold and Izilfer by her side with hope rising. Until Light ignited the room into reality. Chains and shackles hung from the walls, an iron cage sized for a man dangling from the ceiling, a chair with a spike where a person would sit, a giant wooden wheel with chains drooping from its sides, and a dozen other rusty contraptions. The rack intended to stretch its victims, she recalled from stories she preferred not to remember, even if they were exciting tales of adventure at the time.

Izilfer stopped by her side, eyes plying the room where the only exit was the one they came through. "The cold. The trail ends here."

She swallowed the growing lump in her throat. "A torture chamber, just like in the old stories. What does it mean?" Tears ran anew

down her cheeks, and she crumpled to the floor, this time planning never to rise again.

Rinold's hand touched her shoulder with a gentle squeeze. "We'll find him. I swear it on my life."

She nodded in hopeless agreement and, at the same time, screamed, "How can you find someone who is gone from our world?"

Izilfer kneeled and muttered, "We pray. The Pantheon of Sol will show us the way."

Tremors turned to shaking fury. "The gods? The gods who drove our people from our lands? Who brought those demons who murdered my family? Who did nothing as people starved? Who wanted my husband and me dead?"

She shook until the agony and anger faded, until panting and staring at the floor, waiting for comforting words that would fail, waiting for an argument to bolster her faith in the gods.

Something brushed her face, both prickly and soft, but when she looked, she saw nothing except Rinold and Izilfer standing frozen in time. Not just in time; their breaths cast a fog, and when she shivered, Kinesee realized for the first time that the room had grown chill.

A sonorous voice with power in its reverberations said, "Long have I sought you, only to find you in the darkest of places."

She glanced around the room. "Who are you? Where are you?"

"I am he who will help you." Reality fluttered in white waves of a mirage, forming into a massive white lion, his mane shimmering with sparkles of ice, and she realized the brush on her cheek had been his whiskers and fur.

She bowed her head. "Save my boy."

"Speak these words after me, and your will is my will. Your dreams are my dreams. Your pain is my pain. Your victory is my victory. Now we have found one another, never again will we need to search."

The power of his voice flowed over her in rippling waves, both cool and soothing. She nodded and licked tears from her lips.

"You will find your sun."

"I will find my son."

"You will get your sun back."

"I will get my son back."

"You will free the ice of his cold."

"I will free the ice of his cold."

"Praise Rin."

"Praise Rin."

The Morass

The End is a peculiar place, a fable if you will, believed in by so many. All things end and all things begin, except those that don't. I once ended a king, but it was his beginning. I ended once, died if you prefer, and it changed the moment of my birth, if ever it was a moment, and my death stretched into eternity—if indeed not ending is a possibility—which, of course, you might surmise is the point of this argument. Is it really?

Can my death run beside and parallel to my birthing before even entering the womb? Mortals prefer all things in decisive terms: Sun, moon, star; gold, silver, pyrite; beginning, middle, end. Ah! you recognized my game, an intended shame.

The great playwright Shezbul em-Tûlo once spoke of the morass in the middle, act two, in crude terms of theater and its certainty, a place of uncertainty where even the greatest mind could wander forever lost, if a mind is capable of losing itself—I suggest it more likely it was never able to be found to begin—which begins us back to the start. A beginning an awful lot like an ending. A fable of a playwright who ended before my ending

that didn't end a thing, except the opportunity to tell the great man a truth: There is no beginning, no ending, only the morass in the middle, but therein lies the paradox, for the morass could only be in the middle if there is a beginning and an ending. Do you understand? The great man would or will, depending on the infinity of his ending.

—Tomes of the Touched

Books by L. James Rice

Sundering the Gods

Eve of Snows

Trail of Pyres

Whispers of Ghosts

Sundering the Crowns

Shadows of Man

Silhouettes in Doom
12/12/2024

The Monsoon Straits Trilogy

The Contessa of Mostul Ûbar

Best Painted in Blood
Coming 2024

Prequel to Eve of Snows

The War of Seven Lies
06/01/2024

If you enjoyed this book, or hate it so much you want to read more, follow me on Facebook at

https://www.facebook.com/SunderingTheGods/:

or Join my Mailing List at:

http://sunderingthegods.com/newsletter-signup/

Fan mail, hate mail, and requests to send me millions of dollars from Nigeria, may be directed to:

LJRice@SunderingTheGods.com

Additional Maps and information on the World of the Sister Continents may be found at:

LJamesRice.Com

www.ingramcontent.com/pod-product-compliance
Lightning Source LLC
Chambersburg PA
CBHW031957040826
48979CB00043B/1508/J